Please return or renew by
latest date below

LOANS MAY BE RENEWED BY PHONE
648-5710

PRISONERS OF ARIONN

OTHER BOOKS BY BRIAN HERBERT

Man of Two Worlds, with Frank Herbert
Sudanna, Sudanna
The Garbage Chronicles
Sidney's Comet
Incredible Insurance Claims
Classic Comebacks

PRISONERS
OF
ARIONN

BRIAN HERBERT

ARBOR HOUSE
New York

Manufactured in the United States of America

10 9 8 7 6 5 4 3 2 1

Library of Congress Cataloging in Publication Data

Herbert, Brian
Prisoners of Arionn.

I. Title.
PS3558.E617P7   1987   813'.54   86-28882
ISBN: 0-87795-886-6

For my mother and father,
with gratitude for their
patience and love.

Soar heart, soar
To the reach,
To the reach and beyond.
Far beyond,
Through the bounds
Of Illusion.

—RACHEL FOUQUET

PRISONERS OF ARIONN

ONE

PHASE 3.01: Using Qalbeams we sliced the planetary crust horizontally without disturbing any of the inhabitants living above, risdo-bracing the narrow gap as it formed. This slice extended beneath a portion of the Pacific Ocean along the continental shelf. When we had an adequate cut, pleosaturate (formed with native materials) was forced in, forming a perfectly round base for the eventual space habitat.

PHASE 3.02: We bathed the surface of the affected region in dense, signal-obstructing fog of the Opommi variety.

PHASE 3.03: Following the perimeter of this subsurface base, vertical crust cuts were thrust upward (with bracing and pleosaturate) to the lower limits of the planet's ecosphere. Penetrated bodies of water (including the ocean) received flow, wave, and eco-continuance mechanisms on the habitat so that in relocation these water systems would operate somewhat as they did on Earth.

PHASE 3.04: Hovering in the ionosphere above the center of the project at Oakland, California, we extruded a tough, lightweight pleodome, bonding this with the base. Our ship, sealed in the dome apex, became the center of habitat weather control, with seventy-eight robots remaining aboard. The project was now ready for propulsion into space.

—Arionnese Student Team Report

Rachel's mother-in-law was the noted San Francisco councilwoman, Granmère Liliane Fouquet. These women detested one another, and Rachel sometimes spoke of introducing dust into the meticulous old woman's modular house to sprinkle about "in dark corners and crannies where it might breed." Rachel's imagination conceived a special variety of dust for her *bête noire*, one that would drive her mad with its stickiness and proliferation.

Recalling this incident, eleven-year-old Michelle Fouquet sat primly on the clear plastic cover that protected Granmère's green brocade French provincial couch. Glancing sidelong, Michelle saw her mother, Rachel, sitting in semi-drunken erectness in a wrinkled brown dress, her back arched to exaggeration, on the opposite end of the same piece. Rachel's left hand held a long, lipstick-smeared cigarette aloft, and the elbow of that arm was supported on the upturned palm of her right hand. It almost caricatured the parlor manners of Granmère's *beau monde* friends, but Michelle thought it unintentional.

Michelle perceived in her mother a certain tattered and sodden regality. Every few moments Rachel moved the cigarette to her mouth and worked at it, glaring all the while into the kitchen that was straight ahead of her, where Granmère busied herself preparing Sunday dinner. Michelle smelled the delicious aroma of roast lamb.

At the edge of her awareness, Michelle heard children's voices (those of her younger brother, Renney, and toddler sister, Coley) coming from the arch-doored music room, interspersed with the deeper tones of her father, Henry, and of his father, Michelle's beloved Granpère Gilbert. Michelle wished Dad hadn't forced Mom to come, for there would be the inevitable quarreling between Mom and Granmère. Then Michelle would feel sick to her stomach, longing for an end to the bickering and viciousness. Already she felt a little queasy—a slight rolling emptiness as if her innards were tumbling upon themselves. She noted numbness at the temples too, and near dizziness. These sensations passed.

The chairs in the living room matched the couch, and were also plastic-encased. Plastic strips with curled-up edges ran along the carpet as well, protecting the most traveled areas. The sidetables were dark-stained cherrywood, with curved, hand-scrolled legs. Dainty porcelain lamps sat atop them, touched by cool November sunlight that slanted into the room.

Mounted on each wall were heavy fabric straps in green and white *petite fleur* designs, arranged for the heights of children and adults. These were to be held when "riding the rooms." Of typical modular design, the room arrangements could be altered at will, using a hand-held transmitter that activated a flowing system of changeable windows, walls, floors, doorways, and staircases (the furnishings and other personal belongings being floor-, wall-, table-, or countertop-secured beforehand).

Granmère and Granpère were constantly hiding the transmitter from one another, for Granpère loved to shift things around on a regular basis. She was in the habit of scolding him about this, asking him where he had put the bathrooms and commanding him for all time to leave her kitchen where she wanted it. Michelle thought that the present arrangement corresponded roughly with Granmère's wishes, although only a month earlier the kitchen had been on a different side of the living room.

To Michelle it seemed that Granmère's house had all the stiffness of a museum where objects couldn't be touched, and in this respect she empathized with her mother's discomfiture in the place. It wasn't their only point of agreement when it came to Granmère.

"Michelle, where are you, Michelle?" Granpère called out, his frail voice straining. Presently she saw the old man smiling at her gently from the arched doorway. He was tall and slightly stooped, with long and thick gray hair that overhung his forehead rakishly in the fashion of a much younger man. His eyes danced with a pixie liveliness that set him apart from the stodgy, businesslike demeanor of Granmère. His clothes were airy and cheerful, of the golfers' pro shop variety: short-sleeved yellow shirt open at the collar, with an eagle pocket insignia; white, perfectly creased slacks; white loafers with pointed leather flaps draped across the tops. He waited for Michelle's response, seemed to notice her immersion in thought.

Behind Granpère in the music room stood his massive grand piano, an awe-inspiring burnished white instrument of another century that he maintained impeccably but played only rarely. Granmère invariably criticized his keyboard skills, purporting to find tiny flaws that no one else heard. Michelle was certain that he polished and waxed the piano in part to please Granmère's demands for spotlessness, for she was the unquestioned ruler of the household and he the working prince. Michelle wished he would stand up to her just once, and it occurred to her that he probably did, in private. But to do so in front of the family: what a memorable occasion that would be! Beyond his apparent subservience, the girl knew her grandfather polished his piano because he loved it.

Granmère the perfectionist: the supreme nit-picker, with more demands than those of ten normal people. Rachel didn't stand a chance.

But Granpère did. He was an innately happy man, and even with all her sourness Granmère could not take that away from him. He fairly lit up the living room now for Michelle as he shuffled toward her arthritically, drawing her out of her ruminations. She bounded into his arms.

"I love you, Granpère," Michelle murmured, nuzzling against his slender midsection.

"We have an hour before dinner," he said. "What do you say we go for a little drive?"

Michelle looked up, nodded briskly.

"Don't be late getting back!" Granmère squawked, as the girl and her grandfather tried making it to the side door unnoticed.

In the background someone picked at the piano—Renney, Michelle decided, recognizing a tune the boy had composed. He and his mother had artistic talents, and both were sensitive, but in different ways. Renney seemed less fragile than his mother.

"Not to worry!" Granpère shouted back, in the saucy tone of one whose greatest pleasures lay beyond these walls. With that they threw on their coats and slammed the door shut behind them in a great flourish, scurried across the porch and bounded down the motionless electric stairway like schoolmates, hand in hand. A black button at each end of the stairway would have activated its escalator mechanism, but that was not for Granpère. Nor for that matter was it something Michelle had ever seen her grandmother use.

"It'll be nice in our old age," Granpère liked to say.

As Granpère led the way past his vegetable garden along one side of the house and through the iron grand gate to the street, he complained good-naturedly about Granmère's bossiness. Michelle heard brittleness in his octogenarian voice that troubled her, and as she moved up alongside him she thought his skin looked paler than usual. Still, when he glanced down at her his eyes sparkled reassuringly. They were happy, youthful eyes. But it seemed to Michelle that his voice echoed more how he really felt, and oftentimes she suspected him of buoying himself for her benefit.

"Thick fog rolling in," he said, pausing on the sidewalk to look up. "Can't even see the sun anymore. Button your coat."

While doing as she was told, Michelle followed his gaze to swirls of dark gray mist that rolled around treetops and Tudor roof lines.

Michelle had seen her grandfather looking far more sickly than he appeared to be now, but during the past three years she had noticed increasing vocal frailty. Each time that his voice came back (to a degree) after a viral or bacterial beating, it never seemed to reach the peaks of strength that it had before. Each new valley of illness seemed lower too, as if his body were trending downward.

Granpère's white sedan was old, but polished to the same high gloss as the piano. The vehicle's finish was about that shade of creamy white as well. She watched him use his ever-present yellow chamois cloth to rub a blemish from the driver's side of the hood. He smiled at her as he pocketed the cloth, revealing big overhanging front teeth. In that posture he lacked little more than a change of rainment and a sliver of straw between his teeth to seem like a farm boy.

"Hop in," he said.

When Michelle was inside and harnessed into the passenger seat, she experienced a guilt pang at not suggesting the inclusion of Renney and Coley. But it was only the faintest sensation, and soon passed. Michelle enjoyed her times alone with Granpère. They shared secrets.

The motor purred on, leaving its afternoon nap without complaint. A golden brown maple leaf on the fender trembled.

As Granpère Gilbert punched course instructions into the vehicle's computer, Michelle swiveled her bucket seat to investigate the rear passenger compartment. The car was a small limousine from another age, with a chrome-plated soda dispenser mounted in the center, between the front and back seats. In the rear one sat on a curving divanlike affair that followed the contour of the passenger compartment, providing enough room back there for four adults. Sometimes Granpère placed wrapped presents on this seat for Michelle and her siblings, but not today. She was only mildly disappointed.

As she swiveled forward, she saw that the car was proceeding along Geary Boulevard in the slow lane. They passed colorful sidewalk flower carts and fruit stands, set against a backdrop of reconstructed Victorian storefront houses. Many buildings had gas lamps, ornate European mailboxes, or wrought iron gates, and artsy wooden shop signs hung over the sidewalk.

A small computer screen in the center of Granpère's dashboard flashed bright green letters: DESTINATION: GOLDEN GATE PARK. Under Granpère's command, the sedan went as slowly as he would have driven it had he chosen to operate it manually. Virtually every other car, truck, bus, and bicycle on the pavement passed them. Ahead, one of the new adjustable-width cars contracted to squeeze through a narrow space between stopped vehicles and the right-hand parking strip. The car expanded back to full width after it was through the perilous slot, and made a right turn.

As Granpère's car stopped and waited for a light to change, Michelle realized that her grandmother's parting shot hung in her mind, ominously:

"Don't be late getting back!" Visibility was dropping in the fog, and most vehicles had their headlights on.

"Pea-souper comin' in," Granpère said. He flipped a toggle, and Michelle saw the reflection of his headlights on a bumper ahead of them.

Golden Gate Park was only a few blocks away, and within moments they were on one of the park's winding grass and tree-lined thoroughfares, passing areas where old men played cards, checkers, and bocce.

"I'm sorry there's no present for you today," Granpère said. "I'm still working on it."

"It's something you're making?" Michelle felt the inanity of her words as they escaped her lips. He'd said so, hadn't he?

"Yes," came the reply, with infinite patience. "I hope you like it."

"Oh I will! What is it?"

"You want me to tell you what your gift is? Don't you realize how that spoils the fun for both of us?"

"Suspense can drive a person crazy. Just give me a hint, Granpère. A teeny, tiny little hint, that's all."

Granpère chuckled weakly. "It's a concept I first came up with thirty-three years ago, toward the end of my hitch in Moon War IV. I kinda laid it aside for most of those years. It's nothing dangerous, of course, and I think you'll like it."

"That's not enough of a hint!"

"It's all I'm going to tell you, child. Don't mention this to Granmère. She likes to know everything I'm up to, but a man needs a certain amount of space for himself."

"Okay, Granpère." Silence. Then: "I don't really need gifts at my age. I'm happy just being with you."

"You're too old for gifts? How can such a thing be?"

"You know what I mean!"

He looked at her pensively, as if trying to decide how patronizing her tone had been. She knew how she must look to him. Her green and yellow floral print dress had the dull tones of something worn many times without laundering, but he wouldn't blame her for that. Michelle's mother should take care of such matters. Michelle had strawberry blond hair tied in a ponytail by a green ribbon. Her prominent cheekbones stood high on her face like those of her mother, but the nose most resembled that of her father, Henry Fouquet. It was squat and wide, with a little bump beneath the bridge. She, her sister, and her younger brother were quite thin, which their grandparents often spoke about with concern. In their own ways Granmère and Granpère did what they could for the children.

Michelle hated to admit it, but in some respects Granmère seemed like a mother to her. She was gruff, but she cared, made sure Michelle ate properly at least once a week, gave her dresses, shoes, blouses, even toothbrushes and dental floss. Nagging accompanied these things as a matter of course, but whenever Michelle felt most forgiving she knew her grandmother acted toward her and the other children out of love.

Granpère couldn't replace Michelle's father, even in part. Granpère was more of a friend, the best she had in the whole universe.

"Have a mint soda, Michelle," he said. "We won't tell Granmère."

Michelle smiled as she swiveled back and punched one of three buttons on the soda dispenser, selecting "mint." A glass dropped into a bracketed claw, and she heard liquid gushing inside the machine. Then with eager eyes she saw the foaming green fluid rush from chrome spigot to glass, filling the receptacle just past the halfway mark.

As the dispenser clicked off, Michelle lifted the glass to her lips. The aromatic bite of mint filled her nostrils and she salivated. She took a long sip as her seat came back around and popped into place. The soda was quenchingly cold and thick, mixed exactly the way she liked it.

"Do you know the difference between a sip and a sup?" she asked.

"Why, no. I don't believe I do."

"A sip is a teeny taste. But a sup—that's like this!" She tilted up the bottom of the glass and drained most of its contents into her mouth, swallowing with an unladylike gulp.

Granpère chuckled.

As Michelle swallowed the thick, soothing drink, she recalled the queasy near-dizziness she had experienced on Granmère's couch. It had been an odd sensation, extending from the pit of her stomach to her head, and now she recalled having felt that way before—while taking off in a plane on a secret joyride arranged by Granpère.

Granmère had to know about this soda bar and disapprove of it, although she probably rode in the sedan only rarely, preferring her city-provided luxury autos and helicopters. The old woman could never have enjoyed a cold mint soda, even as a child. She must have always been wrinkled and crotchety. But here was the soda dispenser nonetheless, evidence that she at least allowed Granpère some leeway in his life.

They stopped at a shrub-terraced hill that sloped off to a pond, and fed crackers from Granpère's glove compartment to the ducks. A cool, brisk wind rippled across the water, and on the birch-lined, hazy opposite shore men and boys were bringing in their model sailboats and powerboats, heading home because of the fog.

Sometimes Granpère brought all of the Fouquet children here—even Michelle's nineteen-year-old brother, Joseph—and they fished with simple plastic poles that had strings tied primitively on the ends. Granpère built the poles in a computerized hobby shop in his basement, and once Joseph had asked why they didn't simply use wooden sticks instead.

"I need to justify my fancy hobby shop, don't I?" Granpère said, and Joseph didn't have a retort.

Granpère loved gadgets. He even had a diamond-point fountain pen with thirty-seven functions, and a headset television receiver that sported a tiny microwave dish on top. Many of Granpère's things were outlandish, impractical, or both, and Michelle never caught any fish with him. But it didn't matter to her.

She saw him studying the swirling gray sky and looking across the pond, apparently gauging visibility. Cars with headlights on moved slowly along the roadway near the area being abandoned by model boaters, and Michelle could no longer see the entire shoreline.

"We'd best get back," Granpère said, furrowing his eyebrows.

"What's the matter?" Michelle asked.

He didn't say anything more until they were in the car and out of the park, pulling onto a city street.

"I'm probably just a silly old man," he said. "But that fog was giving me a funny feeling, closing in around the pond like that. It was eerie. What am I saying? Frightening an eleven-year-old!"

"I'm not frightened. Besides, you always said I think like an adult. Don't worry, Granpère. There's nothing to be afraid of."

She patted his age-spotted hand.

Her grandparents had been in a hotel fire in Honolulu the year before, where twenty people died. Ever since he had suffered nightmares, although the incident didn't seem to affect Granmère. It occurred to Michelle now that the fog billowing in toward him around the pond might have reminded him of smoke. Conceivably he felt trapped there, and maybe even now, as if he were inside a burning building. Uncertain, she decided not to mention this. It was a wound she didn't want to disturb.

Granpère switched on the radio, but couldn't get reception on any station—only disconcerting and annoying buzzes and crackles of static. Once inside the house he tried a radio in his bedroom and the television set in the parlor, both with the same result. He went to the dinner table muttering and scratching his chin, a worried expression on his face.

"Fastest appearing fog I've ever seen," he said. "And we can't get a lick of news about it."

He found his place at one head of the table, farthest from the kitchen. Michelle sat to one side of him where she always did, opposite the empty place of her brother, Joseph, who was on a date. Everyone had his or her established place at the table, and even Rachel, who defied virtually all tradition, seemed content to sit in the same place two down from Joseph's— on those rare occasions when she came to Granmère's.

The crystal-chandeliered dining room was off to one side of the kitchen, and as always Granmère had out her finest dinner settings. The long cherrywood table was covered in an exquisite handmade white lace cloth, topped by silver, crystal, and Rouenware. There were ornate carved candles at each end, and glasses of red wine all around, even at the places set for Michelle and Renney. Children received diluted wine, an old country practice according to Granpère.

Henry and Rachel had argued in the car on the way over. As usual, she didn't want to come. He had the temerity to ask Rachel to promise that she would go out of her way to avoid incurring Granmère's wrath.

"You're talking impossibility," Rachel had said. "My mere presence agitates the old lady. She'll start it, you watch, and I won't take her guff."

Michelle agreed with her mother. Invariably it went that way.

Nine-year-old Renney sat between Joseph's place and the chair occupied by their mother. Renney was Rachel's favorite. Michelle reached to her right, helped Coley onto a booster seat atop a chair.

Noticing the angry red eruptions of fleabites on her little sister's arms, Michelle thought, *I'll have to spray her room again. Did Granmère notice?* No indication that she had.

Henry was busy helping Granmère, bringing food and utensils to the table. She ordered him about, using the French pronunciation of his name, much as it must have been when he was a little boy. With a pockmarked round face and only a fringe of gray-brown hair around his pate, Henry looked like an aging weightlifter. His tree-trunk arms were as big around as the legs of most men.

"What were you saying, *Père*?" Henry asked, addressing his father. This form followed one of Granmère's many rules, along with the use of certain common French terms in her presence, usually for salutation and departure. Henry set a tray of small crystal glasses, each containing apricot juice, on the table.

Those already seated took glasses for themselves or passed them to others.

Granpère repeated his comment about the fog and the lack of television or radio reception, adding, "It came on like gangbusters while Michelle and I were out."

Henry looked out the lace-curtained window, whistled in a low tone. He squinted, said he could barely make out details of neighboring houses.

Coley wasted no time in spilling her juice. This produced a squeal of disapproval from Granmère, who ran in from the kitchen with a wet dish towel and wiped Coley's dress, the tablecloth, the chair, and the carpet.

During this commotion, Rachel sipped from a glass of red table wine, seemingly unconcerned about her daughter's gaffe. Michelle saw her grandmother fire a disdainful look at Rachel but didn't think Rachel noticed.

Michelle helped her father and grandmother bring out salad and dressing, sourdough French rolls, and butter.

When all were seated and the salads were served on gold-edged glass plates, Granmère drank her apricot juice, the aperitif. This was the signal for everyone to eat, without any prayer.

While partaking of her salad in the most proper manner, Granmère stopped suddenly and closed her eyes.

"Oh!" she exclaimed. "I'm not feeling at all well. My stomach . . ." She lifted her eyelids, blinked. "Strange . . . whatever it was seems to have passed."

"I felt it too," Henry said.

"So did I!" Michelle exclaimed. "I felt it before dinner too. Like being in an airplane taking off."

"What do you know about airplanes?" Henry asked. "You've never been in one."

Michelle couldn't reveal the secret flight Granpère had taken her on, and picked at her salad.

"The child's right, anyway," Granmère said. "It *was* like a takeoff."

Everyone except Coley and Rachel said they had felt briefly queasy and dizzy, both before dinner and moments earlier, when Granmère spoke.

"Earth tremors?" Renney offered.

"Not like any I've ever felt," Granpère said.

"The ground around here can roll in funny ways," Granmère said, breaking open a dinner roll. She glared at Henry as he sliced his roll in half with a steak knife.

Behind Granmère on the wall by the kitchen doorway an antique gold-framed photograph depicted Henry as a boy, his blond hair cut pageboy short. He wore a feminine white lace blouse with elbow-length sleeves, white shorts, and white, tightly laced boots. Granmere had raised her only son in the "proper" manner, teaching him daily how polite people spoke, how they broke open their rolls, how they selected suitable mates, even how they looked at one another. As Michelle thought about it, she realized that Granmère's gaze of disapproval had been precipitated by more than Henry's faux pas with a dinner roll. He must have seemed a complete failure to her. This time, however, the old woman said nothing.

"Maybe it was like flying," Henry said, speaking with his mouth full. "I remember when I was in the National Air Service, and we'd pitch, roll, or yaw and everyone felt like dumpin' their cookies."

"Henri!" Granmère exclaimed, in her most severe tone.

But Henry, with his eyes bulging comically, tightened his lips over his upper and lower teeth and said, with intentional exaggeration: "Mebbe dish housh ish flyin', huh?"

Michelle and Renney laughed.

Henry was a fairly well educated man, having attended a fine university for three years and done well there. He knew how to speak correctly, and frequently when he didn't do so his eyes would twinkle in Michelle's direction, as they did now.

Henry's mispronunciations occurred for the most part beyond the hearing range of his mother, although he enjoyed dropping occasional mangled phrases to agitate her. Often his words and phrases suggested tangential, intriguing concepts, and many of them came so close to correct pronunciation that gems could go right by a listener who wasn't paying close attention.

Some of Michelle's favorites, from this very table: at a Little League baseball game, a player made a "head face slide"; a person with Alzheimer's disease had instead "oldtimer's disease"; cardiac arrest became "hardiac arrest"; pronunciation was "pronounciation"; altitude shifted to "altitoad"— and whenever Michelle heard this one she envisioned toads flying through the air, as she had heard they did at times during violent storms.

As Michelle reminisced fondly and smiled at these (which the children called "Henryisms"), she noticed suddenly that her grandmother was staring directly at her with those dark, penetrating old eyes. Michelle felt blood rush to her face, and she straightened her mouth.

"You should get a decent haircut, Michelle," Granmère said. "Then you wouldn't have to tie it in a ponytail."

I'll keep it forever! Michelle thought, staring at her plate.

Soon this incident passed in Michelle's mind, like so many similar ones before. She, her siblings, and their father ate voraciously, while Granmère and Granpère proceeded more deliberately, the way gentry behaved in fine restaurants. Rachel seemed to have little interest in her food, but by

Michelle's count she consumed two glasses of burgundy by the time everyone else finished the salad.

Michelle loved Granmère's food. The green salad included generous portions of fresh tuna, avocado, and hardboiled egg, all doused in as much tangy vinaigrette dressing as a person wanted. Granmère served real butter with the sourdough rolls too, not the whipped, watery margarine that the children sometimes had at home, when Mom allowed them into the food.

Between bites, Michelle sneaked glances at her grandmother. The old woman's bespectacled face had a weathered hardness to it (despite the plethora of moisture creams she employed), and heavy creases on her forehead and neck ran horizontally, almost in parallel. Vertical parallel lines that ran down her cheeks and the bridge of her nose made Michelle fantasize about what her grandmother would look like if the vertical lines ever extended themselves and crisscrossed with the horizontal ones, making her a walking tic-tac-toe board.

There were no laugh or smile notches around Granmère's eyes or mouth, for she rarely displayed happiness. The eyes behind the brown-framed glasses were cold and black, like those of a predatory bird. Her political opponents referred to her as "French Steel," but with considerable admiration and respect. Michelle experienced such emotions for her grandmother herself, for at times the aged battler seemed capable of carrying the entire problem-riddled Fouquet family on her shoulders. Mostly, though, Michelle feared and hated her grandmother.

Love also entered the complicated equation of emotions Michelle felt for her grandmother, and the girl, despite her youth, recognized this. As Michelle looked around the table she realized that, as callous as it sounded, she loved everyone at the table with varying degrees of intensity. Her feelings for each person were different, individual and special. Perhaps she loved her mother most, even more than Granpère Gilbert, despite the myriad shortcomings in that woman.

Rachel was thirty-four years younger than Granmère but looked nearly as old. Once a beautiful redheaded Irish colleen, Rachel's features had been creased and seared by alcohol, by Granmère, and by the ravages of mental illness with all of its concomitant mind-deadening drugs. This woman lived much of her life in deep, shadowy regions, unrevealed for the most part to anyone. She emerged for brief flurries, making guerrilla attacks on the world orally or with sensitive, tormented poems that she wrote on slips of paper.

She was subject to sudden bursts of rage if she failed to take her medications. Michelle witnessed one occasion when her mother screamed obscenities at Henry and hurled a small table at him after ripping it from its floor mountings. Michelle didn't know the proper terminology for Rachel's ailment, and wondered if that mattered much anyway. She understood her mother, knew her in ways no doctor could.

There were many facets to Rachel's personality, and she kept people who opposed her off guard by her unpredictability. One moment she could be insipid and stupid (faking, Michelle thought), flaring in the next instant to a rapier edge of devastating wit. The unfortunate woman had a loving side too, one she revealed on occasion to Michelle and always reserved for her favorite, Renney.

Granmère's third course was squash soup, with croutons served on the side that were supposed to be dropped in a few at a time to keep them from getting soggy.

This was followed by leg of lamb, mixed peas and carrots, and mashed potatoes that had carrots mixed into them. Granmère had prepared a rich and delicious gravy from lamb drippings, and Michelle poured it generously on her plate from the gravy boat, covering even her vegetables.

Rachel and Granmère were avoiding one another thus far, listening instead to Henry and Granpère as they speculated on the causes of the fog and of the interference with radio and television communication.

As Michelle and Renney heaped more lamb on their plates, Granmère exclaimed, "Goodness! You children eat as if it has to last you a week!"

By the silence and abashed expressions that resulted, she must have sensed how true these words were. Granmère knew something of the way her son's family lived. Too much, Rachel always said. Those piles of garbage and dirty laundry at Henry's house, along with the chronic overflow of food-scabbed dishes and clutter around the place distressed the old woman no end. But no one, not even Henry with all of his grievances, complained to Granmère about Rachel. This left Granmère to draw her own conclusions, which she was quick to do.

By the time Camembert cheese and *pâté de foie gras* were served, Michelle was cautiously optimistic that Granmère and Rachel would avoid crossing swords. The natural grouchiness brought on by hunger had passed, and while Rachel had consumed four glasses of wine she had eaten a good portion of her food as well.

Then Granmère, while slicing a piece of soft cheese for herself, said in her most precise tone, "I have something very important to discuss with all of you. The children especially should hear this." She stared at Coley and Renney, who weren't paying attention.

"Colette! René!" Granmère said, her nose twitching angrily.

All eyes shifted toward Granmère.

"Never sleep with your head under the covers," she said, "for that restricts the oxygen you breathe, cutting down the necessary flow of oxygen to your brain. This causes brain damage."

"Is that a personal testimonial, Liliane?" Rachel asked, coming out of her stupor and projecting her voice nasally. "Don't do as I did?"

Renney suppressed a snicker, but Michelle closed her eyes, waiting for the explosion.

"Certainly not!" Granmère said. "I read it in one of my magazines!" She tapped the center post of her computerized glasses, where a tiny magazine disk could be attached, enabling her to read printed words on the inside surfaces of her lenses if surrounding illumination wasn't too bright.

"I suppose you connected the magazine disk to your word processor too," Rachel said, "and we can look forward to receiving our usual copies of the article."

"I find your tone offensive," Granmère said, haughtily. "You didn't stay on the plastic runners either when you came to the table. I watched every step you took."

"I stepped in some birdshit outside," Rachel said. "Just for you." She took a gulp of wine, betraying little emotion in her expression.

Granmère gasped.

"Don't send us any more newspaper or magazine articles, Liliane," Rachel said, working at her wine.

The table was hushed, with onlookers either staring motionlessly at their plates or sneaking furtive glances at the combatants. Then Coley threw a hard piece of roll at Granmère. It bounced off Granmère's shoulder, to the floor.

Granmère shot her angriest glance at the toddler, who was readying another missile.

"We don't want to be like the plastic people in your goddam articles," Rachel said. "We want to be human, not perfect."

"When I spoke of oxygen starvation," Granmère said, her words flowing with the practiced diction of an experienced city councilwoman, "I wasn't addressing you, Rachel. Your brain is too far gone to worry about."

Michelle felt sick to her stomach. She pushed her cheese plate away.

Coley's subsequent toss left butter on Granmère's chin.

"Isn't there someone here who can control this child?" Granmère raged, using her napkin.

"Coley, stop that!" Michelle said, moving the food arsenal out of her sister's reach.

"I don't like Granmère," Coley said, pouting.

Someone clinked a piece of silverware against a plate, and the sound seemed to echo around the room.

Michelle stared across the table at her mother, who appeared to have withdrawn from the skirmish. Rachel was humming, and the soft melody escaping her lips carried her off to another dimension, making her smile in the sweetest fashion that Michelle could imagine. Hypnotically, Rachel poured more burgundy from the carafe near her, then took a sip from her glass. She seemed totally unaware of anyone other than herself.

"You'd better get some help for her, Henri," Granmère said, in a low, hostile tone. "Is she taking her medication?"

"I think so," Henry said.

Abruptly Granmère rose and stalked into the living room, where she retrieved Rachel's big, worn purse from the floor by the couch. Granmère rummaged inside and withdrew three prescription bottles, shaking each as she brought it out.

"Empty," she reported, tossing them back in the handbag.

Michelle noticed that her mother, still humming, was watching Granmère dully out of the corners of her eyes without smiling.

Granmère withdrew a half-liter sized clear glass bottle from the purse and held it aloft. The bottle, which had a red label, was half full of the clear alcoholic beverage called Snowfly Extract, or "Bug Juice" as it was more commonly known. Michelle had seen empties secreted at home in the clutter of back porch trash. Rachel couldn't resist the stuff. Cheap and popular among skid row alcoholics, it was extracted from the antifreezelike bloodstreams of Arctic insects and then flavored with lemon squeezings.

Granmère tossed the purse on a side chair, and without another word took the bottle into the kitchen. By the sink, she touched a wall button. A large round lid on the floor by her feet yawned open, into which she dropped the bottle. This was the public garbage system, connected to every house in the city, including Michelle's. Something had partially blocked their line though, preventing the disposal of anything but the smallest items. Like other mechanical devices around the Henry Fouquet household, in all probability it would never be repaired because of inattention and lack of money.

"Snowfly don't bother me," Rachel sang, staring all the while at Granmère. "Snowfly don't bother me." The tune sounded vaguely familiar to Michelle, but the words weren't right.

"I'll get her to the hospital right now," Henry announced.

He went to Rachel and with firm gentleness helped her to her feet. She didn't resist, but repeated the words of her song, in a voice that alternated between harsh nasal tones and the softness of lullaby. By the time she was being escorted out the door, Rachel had internalized the melody. Her lips continued to move with no sounds issuing forth.

"*Au revoir, Granmère et Granpère,*" Michelle said at the door. Only Granpère was there, kissing her on the cheek and squeezing her hand. Granmère remained in the kitchen, where she rattled pans, utensils, and dishes.

"We're in America," Rachel said, her tone loud and nasal as she descended the steps with Henry. "Don't talk like a foreigner, Michelle."

The door shut crisply behind Michelle. It was frosty outside, and so foggy that she could barely see her father's car in the yellow light cast from the house.

TWO

We had planned to take off surreptitiously, but a number of "glitches" appeared. It took nearly seven times longer than projected to depart their atmosphere. On two occasions the drive mechanism ceased and then surged on, giving many inhabitants a physical sensation of movement. This was regrettable. Aided by the delay, National Air Service jets gave chase, and the scene on the surface after we pulled away must have been somewhat chaotic. The jets did not fire on us.

—Alien data system notes

After debarking the subterranean hypersonic train, Stu Kroemer crossed the passenger terminal, half listening to his footsteps as they clicked on the mosaic tiles. He thought back on the thirty-three-minute trip he had just made from New Orleans to San Francisco. That ceiling speaker by his seat had provided a constant flow of information, some of which he had absorbed despite his overriding concerns: top speed 9280 kilometers per hour; fifteen percent weight increase felt by passengers at each end of the link, during acceleration and deceleration; no additional weight sensation at maximum thrust, due to compensating centrifugal forces.

The blare of a terminal loudspeaker announcing the delay of an inbound Tokyo nonstop interrupted the boy's thoughts. He became conscious of body and clothing odors from transients, mostly older men, who occupied nearby dark hardwood benches. They lay asleep or sat leaning and half awake, like neglected shanties. Some held stubby cigarettes or cigars, and a number of brown paper bags were in evidence. A massive, brass-numeraled clock perched regally and far out of reach on one wall of the high-ceilinged terminal, but it seemed to Stu that time carried no significance for many of the people in this place.

For others, time was of the utmost. Here and there families and individuals stood by their luggage, waiting. They shifted on their feet, moved hands in and out of pockets, crossed and uncrossed their arms, all the while glancing at their watches and at the big wall clock.

The boy passed unnoticed.

More train delays were announced, and near a ticket window Stu overheard one clerk tell another that the New Orleans Superliner was the last to get through, inbound or outbound. Stu didn't care about any of that, and hardly gave the clerk's patter any thought at all, despite the urgency and confusion he heard in the man's tone.

Zipped into an inside pocket of his brown leather jacket Stu carried a worn and folded letter from his birth-father, Henry W. Fouquet. He didn't have to look at it again. The letter, which had been sent to Stu's mother in New Orleans, bore a return address that Stu had imprinted in his brain. None of the letters from his father had spoken of Stu's parentage, and the boy had read all of them. He knew the truth nevertheless, having overheard conversations between his mother and stepfather.

Now he was to be an unannounced visitor, and with time to think about it he didn't like the idea so much any more. But he wanted to see his father, *needed* to see him. There were matters they should discuss. Stu would tread lightly to avoid an embarrassing scene.

Stu asked directions from an attendant at the takeout fast-food outlet in one wall. An elevated tramcar would get him within a couple of blocks, the woman at the counter estimated—if the trams were running in the fog. While she spoke, she adjusted a bobby pin that secured her white and orange paper cap to her hair. She said she had never seen anything to match this mist over the city, and admitted that it frightened her. Everyone was talking about it, she said.

Thinking about the lousy time he had chosen to arrive, Stu rode an escalator up to street level. With an icy breeze cutting through his clothing he ascended a fog-shrouded stairway to the elevated tramstop.

There were four green and yellow benches here in a line, illuminated by sterile fluorescent light from the underside of a metal roof that ran the length of the benches. With no side walls it wasn't much of a shelter. He selected a bench nearest the top of the stairs and sat hunched over with his hands in his pockets and his back to the wind, feeling the frigid bench through his trousers.

Something moved on his left, and Stu turned his head to see a big swarthy man in a dark overcoat emerge from the fog. He walked stiffly in Stu's direction, then turned and went off the other way, disappearing from view. Soon he reappeared and repeated the performance—apparently pacing to keep warm while awaiting the tram. As Stu squinted in that direction he made out the contour of another shelter immersed in the mist, unilluminated.

Would there be a tram this night? What about a taxi? Did he have enough money? Stu thought no to all of these. His knees knocked together. He thought about walking around to get away from the chill of the bench, resolved to walk across town if necessary. Maybe he should have telephoned ahead before leaving Louisiana. But the blowup he'd had with his mother and stepfather had been conclusive, the result of nearly three years of unrelieved tension since her marriage to that man.

He saw no point in calling his father to make arrangements, then or now. Stu could live by his cunning in the streets if necessary. He'd done so for nearly two months after running away the last time, until the police apprehended him and forced him home. Nonetheless, the cold fog that whipped against his face and permeated his inadequate clothing imparted a sense of urgency to him. He wanted to get on with his life and establish himself, wherever that was meant to be.

Ten minutes later he was inside a tramcar, speeding through the fog toward the Henry Fouquet house.

Korpunkel's Psychotherapy Center occupied the highest elevation of Twin Peaks, and had red aircraft beacons flashing atop it. On most evenings the structure (in a former public park) stood out as an illuminated beacon for the mentally ill, observable from all over the city. San Francisco, long a mecca of insanity, kept Korpunkel's humming with activity. Tonight, however, Michelle could not see it for the fog. She rode in the backseat of the car driven by her father as it wound up Twin Peaks Boulevard to the top, having just gotten past an accident where police, firemen, and ambulances forced them into a thirty-minute wait. Henry was still cursing under his breath.

The situation with Rachel exacerbated the difficulties of travel. She didn't want to go to the hospital and didn't want to take her medications any longer. Repeatedly Henry reminded her of the court order controlling her behavior—the result of a drunken house-wrecking binge in which she and her alcoholic friend Jennie had ridden the rooms in Henry's house until they burned out the mechanism—no small feat, considering the durability of the equipment. It left their rooms in jumbled disarray, a condition that had not been repaired. And nosy old Mrs. Meley down the street had filed a complaint, bringing in the police and Child Welfare authorities.

Now Rachel threatened to reopen that troubled chapter.

"Take me back to Ireland like you promised," Rachel pleaded, from the front passenger seat. Through an open side window that chilled the interior of the car she leaned out.

Michelle, Renney, and Coley huddled together in the back, afraid to complain of the cold.

"You ain't nebber been ta Ireland," Henry said, lapsing wearily into mispronunciation. He sounded almost drunk, but Michelle knew he wasn't. "I didn't make no promises! What kinda crazy talk izzat?"

"Liar! You did promise! When we were married, you said we'd visit first thing."

"I don't recall."

"Well, I do! My blood is Irish. Mama was born there, and I have a hundred-year-old great-grandfather who still lives in County Kilkenny."

"Your mama was nuts, just like you. Dat's in your blood, too."

The comment cut through Michelle like the icy wind that surrounded her father's words. Would insanity appear in Rachel's children? If so, in what form?

Michelle had always tried to see her mother's good points, which were many, in the girl's opinion. Sometimes Michelle sat and went over all of the good things about her mother that she could think of so that they would not be overlooked, especially when Rachel was having one of her "bouts," as Granmère termed them. But with her brain numb from the cold and her parents arguing in the front seat, Michelle could recall nothing from the list.

"We ain't goin' ta Ireland," Henry said, "no nebber mind what you say I promised twenty-six years ago. Promises dat old ain't collectable."

Using the dashboard steering toggle, he took a corner too quickly, squealing rubber. Michelle kept her little sister from toppling over.

"Turn this car around!" Rachel said.

Henry muttered something.

Michelle felt the car accelerate.

"You're making me crazy!" Rachel shrieked, her head, shoulders and arms out of the vehicle. "Stop the car! Let me out right here!"

"Get back inna car, you stupid bitch."

Rachel cut loose with a terrible scream that made Coley cry.

"It's all right, Coley," Michelle said, hugging Coley tightly and rubbing her back soothingly. "Mama's gonna be all right."

Rachel slumped back into her seat, leaving the window open.

"You wanna go ta Ireland on some kinda goddam lark," Henry said, "an' I'm workin' t'ree jobs already."

"Then pry some loose from the old biddy. She's got tons of boodle, I hear."

"You know she won't gib me a damn penny. Not while I'm wid you."

Michelle had heard this before. Granmère was threatening to disinherit Henry if he didn't leave Rachel. To his credit Henry was staying with his wife, through every hardship. But there had to be a limit, and Michelle wondered if her father might give up at long last under the continuous pressure. She hoped he wouldn't, but couldn't avoid noticing that her father was being drained of energy, of emotion, of love. She worried about his health, felt helpless to aid him.

"Get a job," Henry said.

"I've got a job, On-ree." The tone was nasal and cutting. "I'm a home-maker."

"Don't gib me any o' dat shit. Our house izza goddam mess. An' don't pronounciate my name dat way ebber again!"

"Why not, On-ree? It's the way *Maman* says it. Don't we have to say Colette and not Coley in her presence? And René," Rachel added, rolling the *r* precisely, "never Renney."

Michelle heard menace in her mother's tone. It was always there when Rachel spoke of Granmère.

Renney reached forward and patted his mother's shoulder. "It'll be all right, Mom," he said. "Let Dad get you some help."

Rachel did not respond. Moments later she touched the button on her armrest to close the window. Neither she nor Henry said anything further, even when they pulled into the parking lot of Korpunkel's.

"Stay here," Henry ordered brusquely, throwing words over his burly right shoulder at the children. "An' keep da doors locked."

Through the windshield moments later, Michelle watched her parents slide into horizontal Plexiglas admission tubes at the building entrance. These tubes, bathed in red light so that Michelle could see her parents lying supine in them, were creations of the Hospital Workers Union, protecting medical personnel against injury by their patients.

Michelle watched the enclosed tubes slide through a wide security entrance. Heavy double doors swung shut over the opening after her parents entered, blocking Michelle's view.

Somewhere inside the ninety-story structure, Michelle knew from asking her father, attendants were standing on a glass floor looking down at Henry and Rachel, questioning them and punching entries into electronic clipboards. They would let Henry out immediately since he wasn't a patient, and he would sign the electronic admission board, releasing the therapy center from responsibility for anything that might happen to Rachel. Then Rachel would be dispatched in her tube to a diagnostic and medication room. It wouldn't take long, and she'd probably be sent right home.

Korpunkel's knew how to process people.

After her parents had been inside the imposing tower for twenty minutes, Michelle heard a commotion of loud voices. One of the voices belonged unmistakably to her father, and she saw him at a little door off to one side of the main entrance, struggling with two big men in gray smocks. Shocked, she opened the car door and told Renney to watch their little sister.

"Daddy!" Michelle squealed, running toward him. Reaching the bottom of a chipped concrete staircase, she heard one of the men yell inside the building for help. Both attendants were bigger than Henry, but it was apparent that they had underestimated his strength.

In pale yellow light from two light posts at the head of the stairs, Henry's face was a fierce, dark mask. He backhanded one of the men, sending the hapless fellow crashing against a wall. With his other hand he had the second attendant by the throat.

"I ain't da one dat's nuts, you son-ubba-bitch!" Henry bellowed.

"Leave my daddy alone!" Michelle screeched. She ascended two steps.

"Michelle," Henry said. "Tell deez fools I ain't crazy. I can't beleeb dis! I come to check Raich in an' dey wanna put me inna nut house!"

"You're choking me, Mr. Fouquet!" the attendant in Henry's grasp gasped.

Rachel appeared in the doorway behind Henry. Four beefy attendants in gray smocks stood just behind her, like her private guard. "Get him," she commanded. "Before he gets away. And hand me the keys in his pocket so I can drive home. He took them away from me."

Michelle interjected as the attendants moved toward Henry. "Daddy's telling the truth," she said. "He brought Mom here to get her more medicine. She ran out of it."

"Da woman's been here before," Henry fumed. "Aintcha got no records?"

He released his grip on the attendant and the man stumbled to one side, rubbing his throat.

"Like I told you inside," the man who had been knocked into the wall said, "our computer's down. Your wife here made sense and you didn't. You shouldn't have broken out of the admission tube, sir."

"Aw, shit, you pack o' idiots. Raich really did it dis time, Michelle. She tol' deez guys I needed ta be committed, an' dat none o' da medicines wuz workin' on *me*."

"It's my mother who needs help," Michelle said, climbing the stairs and taking a position next to her father.

"Computer's back on line!" a woman yelled from inside the building. "Mrs. Fouquet's the one, not her husband!"

Rachel glared down at Michelle, using the penetrating, hateful gaze the girl had seen directed so many times against her grandmother. Rachel's pupils seemed to extend from her head like frozen ropes, and she held the gaze a frightening length of time.

Michelle moved partially behind her father, peeking around him.

Rachel's eyes softened abruptly, and she seemed to stare beyond Michelle, at the fog-immersed parking lot. Michelle detected resignation in the eyes, an acceptance of what was to come.

"Wait inna car, Michelle," Henry ordered. "We're gonna try again. Dat is, if deez guys got da message." He shoved out his jaw and glared, eyes bulging, at the attendant he had been choking. "You heard what da lady inside said, didn't ya?"

"Yes, Mr. Fouquet. We're very sorry. Your wife is most convincing."

"Enough o' dis jabber," Henry said. "It's late, I'm tired off my ass an' my kids is waitin' inna cold. Can we get on widda reason I came here?"

Henry paused for dramatic effect, then leaned closer to the attendant, adding, "*If* you don't mind."

The man lost his composure and stammered something Michelle didn't understand. He escorted the adults back inside while Michelle returned to the car.

A few minutes later Henry returned to the car with Rachel. She was moving phlegmatically, evidence that she had been medicated, and Henry helped her into the car, letting a blast of cold air inside. He tossed a bag of medicine on the seat.

Renney and Coley were asleep, on the rear seat and floor respectively, while Michelle was sitting alertly, pumped by adrenaline and the temperature.

Renney stirred as Rachel slumped into her seat.

Henry slammed the door fortissimo, causing Renney to sit up, dazed.

Henry went around to the other side, plopped heavily into the driver's seat, and slammed that door too. "I can't face no more," he said. "Dis wuz too much."

Michelle leaned forward and massaged the top of her father's balding head the way he liked. She did this for him at the end of each day, soothing the stress of the three jobs he held simultaneously.

But he shook her off this time as he started the car, mumbling something about having to make certain that Rachel took her pills. Michelle promised to help, but he didn't acknowledge.

Soon they were proceeding home, in a fog so dense that it reflected the headlight beams back into the passenger compartment. As Henry inched the car down the incline, he rattled off a steady stream of expletives.

Michelle did her best to block out his words, reminding herself that he wasn't a bad man just because he swore. She drew a parallel between these thoughts and those about her mother. To some people, Michelle realized that her father seemed crude and her mother bizarre. They were somewhat correct in these estimations, the girl had to admit.

But these personalities held more that others could not or would not see—the sensitive, loving sides and the humor both of them were able to find in difficult situations. It wasn't the outright side-splitting variety of humor, or even the more subtle varieties that many people might recognize. It was a Fouquet variety of its own, but one that Granmère Liliane apparently did not see. Michelle could not recall ever having seen her grandmother smile. She felt the fog and the weight of the day's events compressing her thoughts, pressing her into a vapid, dormant state before the advance of sleep.

While the Fouquets and Stu Kroemer advanced separately across San Francisco toward the same destination, yet another vehicle fell into competition. This one carried Michelle's nineteen-year-old brother Joseph, but not inside the passenger compartment.

Draped across the hood of the car, Joseph clung to the hood ornament, with the toes of one tennis-shoed foot inserted into the windshield-wiper well and his long tawny hair streaming behind him in the wind.

"Speed it up!" Joseph slurred in a loud, drunken tone. "I can see at leas' four feet ahead. Go ahead and floor it!"

The driver, Joseph's best friend Kenny March, was only a little less inebriated. He accelerated, laughing wildly.

"You're nuts, Joseph!"

"Hit t'e brakes an' make a left!" Joseph instructed.

Kenny was slow responding, and the car skidded past the intersection where his lookout wanted to turn.

"Ne'er back up," Joseph said. "Thassa firss rule o' drivin'. Turn at t'e ness corner instead."

"Aw, to hell with that," March responded, leaning out the window. "We're goin' to Thyla's. I want your strait-laced girlfriend to see the real Joseph Fouquet. The shitty drunk one."

"Donshou dare! Whattaya mean? I ain't no alcoholic!"

"I'm gonna take your cognac-soaked face over there and get it over with for you. You won't need to worry about hiding from her anymore when you get booze on your breath. Don't worry. She'll understand."

"Like hell!"

"Hang on!" March warned. He made a hard right turn, scraping the side of a parked van. Joseph held on with difficulty.

Joseph wasn't a heavy drinker, despite what March had said. Nor was March, and as a consequence the young men didn't have much resistance to the few drinks they did have. Joseph wanted to go home. He wanted sleep.

"Turn aroun!" Joseph screamed. "Turn aroun!"

After two blocks of screaming back and forth, March went into a sideways skid that nearly sent Joseph flying. Only Joseph's superior strength kept him from being dashed to the pavement, and he was struggling to sober up, wishing he weren't in such a precarious position. Where were they? Was Thyla's house close? He couldn't identify the neighborhood and realized he was in no condition to recognize much of anything.

Fleeting glimpses of reality frightened him. In one he saw himself mangled, with transients picking his pockets. In another he reeled and staggered before Thyla while she looked at him disapprovingly.

If Thyla saw him now he would lose a great deal, far outbalancing the raucous evening he and March had enjoyed. She wouldn't understand. One look and Thyla Dunlap would remove herself from his life forever. He wanted to get away from this place, wherever it was, and hide somewhere until he was sober enough to sneak home.

But by the time Joseph had thoughts of escape, the car was traveling at high speed back the way they had come. He debated whether he should jump free anyway. Injury and even death seemed preferable to facing Thyla.

To Joseph's relief he began to recognize landmarks from his own neighborhood. There was the abandoned hamburger stand on the corner, and ahead he saw Mrs. Meley's house with the lights on. When Joseph was fifteen, he broke her window intentionally with a rock after the old grouch yelled at him and his friends for sitting on her lawn one warm evening.

March's car swerved to the wrong side of the street and narrowly missed clipping Mrs. Meley's parked sedan, then swung back across the street and onto a section of sidewalk, which he drove upon as if it were a narrow road. Then into the street again and a skidding right turn onto Joseph's driveway.

"I betcha I can make you fall off!" March shouted.

He slammed on the brakes and then threw the car into reverse, backing into the center of the street, which fortunately was empty of other traffic.

Before Joseph could find a good place to jump off, he felt himself being propelled in a moment of screaming, screeching acceleration toward his driveway like a human warhead on a rolling missile. March hit the brakes and swerved left onto the grass next to Rachel's old parked car that she called "Putt-Putt."

Joseph let go and pushed himself off to one side. He rolled across the scrubby, uncut lawn into a high English hedge.

March was a laughing maniac at the wheel. He spun the car around and screeched down the driveway, waving wildly out the window. In only a few seconds the lights of the car disappeared in the fog.

Joseph composed himself as much as he could and staggered into the house, nursing scratches. He was the first to arrive.

THREE

We apologize for not obtaining trip and project permits before departing, but you see there were no categories for what we had in mind. It occurred to us that some stupid, unimaginative bureaucrat would have blocked us for sure, asserting that our concept didn't fit any of his forms. We plan to set the San Francisco tourist facility down on unused state land, as shown in the enclosed chart. If all goes well, we suggest that you take full credit. In the event of failure, we are prepared to accept complete responsibility.

—Excerpt from a message left by the
students for the Triumvirate of Arionn

Joseph had immersed himself in a spiritus frumenti slumber by the time his father reached home. Henry knew something was amiss when he carried Coley up the front stairs, ahead of Rachel, Renney, and Michelle.

"Da fuckin' front door's wide open," Henry groused, wearily. "Da house is prob'ly fulla t'ieves."

"Nobody would want our junk," Rachel said.

No one noticed a boy standing in foggy shadows on the sidewalk, trying to read the home's address.

After placing Coley in her urine-saturated crib on the uppermost, tiniest floor of the house, Henry went down one level to what used to be the master bedroom. Now it was shared by Michelle, Renney, and Joseph. With Michelle and Renney trailing him, Henry switched on the light and crossed the clothing-littered floor to the bed on the east wall. Joseph's bed had an odd lump in it, with blankets and sheets piled atop it and hanging over the sides in peculiar fashion.

Without hesitation, Henry yanked the blankets and sheets away. Michelle saw her older brother's face turned sideways beneath the thin upper mattress. He was lying on his back with one of his muscular arms sticking straight out, vulnerable.

"Hey Raich!" Henry shouted, in truculent glee. "You gotta see dis! I ain't ravin' needer!"

Rachel did not respond.

Henry's repeated bellowings caused Joseph to stir. In the dim light from a single overhead fixture heavy with dead insects, Michelle saw Joseph's eyes open. They were heavy-lidded and glassy, and soon closed.

Henry leaned close to his eldest son, and in his tight-lipped way Henry whispered, "Sleep soundly, drunk. Tomorry ya can pull weeds fer dis one. Whenner ya ebber gonna get a job?"

The eyelids barely twitched.

Joseph dreamed that he had a heavy weight on his chest, one he couldn't lift. He was hot, terribly hot, and his clothes were drenched in perspiration. Somewhere a voice alternated between whispers and booming tones. It called his name mockingly, reminded him of the perennial punishment: weeds!

Joseph despised pulling weeds.

They were the curse of every home occupied by his family. Despite all the yard work Joseph had done, the front and rear yards remained the ugliest he had ever seen. Joseph's vision of hell was overgrown with weeds.

Bumper, chained in the back yard, was barking, and Henry shouted for Michelle to find out what was wrong with the animal. When Michelle reached the bottom level, she heard a tapping at the front door. Presently she encountered her father in the kitchen and told him a boy was outside, asking for him.

"Tell whoever it is ta come back tomorry," Henry said. "I ain't talkin' ta nobody."

"He says he came all the way from Louisiana, and that it's very important."

"Loosyannie?" There was a pause, and Michelle saw her father's large eyes harden. Then she thought she detected fear, but only for a moment.

"Aw, shit," Henry said, brushing past Michelle and going to the kitchen cupboard where he kept his cigars.

Because Rachel had ridden the rooms to the point of mechanical burn-out, the kitchen was adjacent to the small bedroom occupied by Henry and Rachel. The porch behind the kitchen was on the main floor, half a level lower than the kitchen and Henry's bedroom, and was reached via a three-step staircase identical to another leading down from the other side of the kitchen to the living room. Like an interior designer's nightmare, the basement was stuck on the main floor between the living room and the front of the house. At the very front of the house was what Granmère termed "the hallway going nowhere" that now constituted the front porch, the original having been crushed in the stampede of cubicles. When Granmère heard about it, she said the porch had committed suicide.

One bathroom, the dining room, and the family room ended up on the lowest level, where the displaced basement module used to be. The three bedrooms were stacked to one side like an afterthought, joined by staircases and stunted halls. Remarkably, the flexible modular equipment left every room (except the crushed front porch) accessible. And since there were no electric wires (the home was equipped with microlec beams), all of the us-able rooms had electricity. The plumbing was adaptable as well: when the rooms settled down, the pipe ends stretched, found one another, and locked into place. Since the pliable windows were on horizontal tracks, they ended up on exterior walls. Everything met the building code.

The only more unusual house Michelle had ever seen, that one from the outside only, was in the North Beach district—owned by a notoriously pe-culiar sculptor. People unfamiliar with the Fouquet family thought an ec-centric artist must live in this house as well. From some perspectives, if Michelle squinted her eyes and held her head just right, the front of the Fouquet house didn't look too bad. And with her poetry that she wrote on scraps of paper Rachel was an artist of sorts.

From the kitchen Michelle and her father traipsed down the abbreviated staircase to the living room, then passed through the junk-clogged basement to the fraudulent front porch. Rachel was standing by the front door with a boy who wore a brown leather jacket.

The boy had long black hair, a rather rough-hewn, bony face, and had his arms crossed. "He says his name is Stu Kroemer," Rachel said, looking sidelong at the boy. "Sounds like a Nazi name to me. If you are Nazi, you'd best turn and run. My man killed hundreds of your kind in Moon War V. He's got a gun around here that he uses especially for Nazis, and I know where it is."

Stu looked at Rachel with an apparent mixture of wonderment and sur-prise. "I ain't no Nazi," he announced.

"Get out of here, Raich," Henry ordered. "This is Willie and Marie Kroemer's son—friends of mine from the stratobase where I was stationed."

"They're not my friends," Rachel said, retreating into the bowels of the house.

When Rachel was gone, Henry said to Stu, "Don't pay no attention to her. The docs have 'er doped up."

"I see."

"Get to bed," Henry said to Michelle.

When Henry and Stu were alone, the boy spoke first, in a subdued tone: "I know your family doesn't know about me . . . that I'm your son, I mean. I won't say anything to them."

Henry led the way into the living room, motioned the boy toward a heavy-winged old armchair. Henry settled into his favored recliner, a threadbare ochre unit that squeaked when he lifted the footrest. He relit a stubby, nearly spent cigar.

Stu, dwarfed in the big armchair, told of overhearing the truth about his birth and of finding letters with Henry's address on them. He mentioned the train and tram rides, the cold weather and the fog, and asked for a place to stay.

"If you don't want me to stay with you," Stu said. "I'll understand." He watched his father belch smoke inartistically, and added: "It looks like you've got your hands full here, and you don't seem to have a lot of money."

Henry scowled, forming deep furrows on his forehead. "We're doin' fine."

He studied Stu, noted the boy's dark, oily hair and olive-pit eyes, like the eyes of his mother. The chin was strong and wide, the mouth small. Stu spoke with only the slightest hint of drawl, and Henry recalled the boy's mother, Marie, writing that Stu was a quick study, able to adapt his accent to particular locales. His mother had such a talent herself, as Henry learned during their wartime affair. She had been single then, expressed no animosity when she learned Henry was already married. Soon afterward she married Willie Kroemer, a corporal in Henry's unit.

"You met Mom on Stratobase Nineteen Alpha," Stu said, feeling a need to demonstrate his knowledge. "She worked in Logistics there, making certain the barracks and mess halls were supplied with matériel. She had a little room near the ballfield, and you . . ."

Henry coughed, leaned to one side, and pulled an ashtray on a side table closer to him.

"I'm not here to embarrass you," Stu said, keeping his voice subdued. "Can I stay with you . . . kinda like a visitor? Things didn't work out for me in Louisiana. I couldn't get along with my stepdad, and Mom took his side."

Henry tapped his cigar on the ashtray, stared at the floor. "I don't know. I'd better call your mother an' let 'er know where you are."

Stu didn't reply but watched his father fight his way to his feet and rumble up the steps to the telephone on the wall just inside the kitchen doorway.

Soon Stu heard Henry experiencing trouble with the line, asking an operator for assistance. Then the receiver thunked into its cradle, and Henry clumped heavily back to his recliner.

"Local calls only," Henry said, plopping himself on the chair. "Can't get t'rough." He stared at the boy so intensely that Stu was forced to look away.

Henry wondered how he was going to deal with this situation. Problems seemed to breed more problems, and he never seemed to get enough rest to deal with them intelligently.

The boy was looking at him again. Dispassionately, it seemed to Henry.

"You don't know nobody else in this damn town 'cept me?" Henry asked.

Stu shook his head, still without apparent emotion. He seemed prepared for rejection.

"Just hang onna minute an' we'll chitchat awhile," Henry said, feeling himself soften. "Kinda catch up onna years, so to speak. Then I'll try that phone again. It ain't no picture phone as you can see, but not cuz we can't afford one. I just don't like lookin' at people's ugly mugs while I'm talkin' to 'em."

Stu saw through this, and it seemed to him that with everyone so tired his father should just let the day end and put him up for the night. It would be two hours later in Louisiana, not a good time to expect civil conversation from the other end. But this was Henry Fouquet's house, such as it was, and from the strength of the man's presence he didn't appear to be anyone with whom to argue. So Stu went into detail about his difficulties in school and at home.

When Henry's cigar became too short to handle, he smothered it in the ashtray, then rummaged around in his trouser pocket until he found another. This one was new, still in its wrapper.

Unable to sleep, Michelle sneaked downstairs into the kitchen. A sliding door leading to the living room was shut, and she heard low voices through the barrier—her father and the visitor.

Through the open doorway of her parents' bedroom she saw her mother sitting at her dressing table, looking in the mirror. She held a pile of papers on her lap.

"Is everything okay, Mom?" Michelle asked, moving to her mother's side.

"I found some of my poems on the floor and others stuffed in the cubbyholes behind the telephone," Rachel said, her tone nasal. "People were using them to jot down phone messages. They shouldn't do things like that."

"I didn't do it, Mom."

Michelle recognized the compact penmanship of her father on some of the sheets. Rachel's poems were always scattered around the house, on tattered, stained pieces of paper that were kicked around on the floors, shoved under and behind things. They had coffee and food stains on them, footprints, even Bumper's teeth marks. But while the writings were neglected and sometimes abused, no one threw them away or carried them out of the house. It was an unspoken law of the place: Rachel's poems were important.

Michelle didn't understand most of what her mother wrote, and what she did understand seemed sensitive but not that well done. None of that mattered. She knew the verses were a release for Rachel's innermost anxieties and frustrations. Occasionally the unfortunate woman went collecting the scraps of paper as if she were on a deadly serious treasure hunt. She crawled around, opened drawers and looked behind them, pushed things out of the way, and generally shuffled the family mess around. Then she would leave her collection of writings on the kitchen table or somewhere else unsafe, and they would be disseminated again throughout the household. Rachel was not an organized person, although perhaps she longed to be.

"I'm not worthless," Rachel said, her tone soft. "I could be somebody. It's still not too late. As long as I have a breath left in me, it's not too late."

Michelle had never heard her mother speak this way before, and was stirred by her words. But looking at the reality of the broken-down woman, Michelle didn't see how Rachel could haul herself out of the mire.

"Are you going to compose a famous poem, Mom? Is that what you mean?" Michelle heard disbelief in her own words.

Rachel's hazel eyes glistened in the way that often preceded tears, and she stared straight ahead into the mirror. Did she see reality there, or was she fantasizing, looking beyond the silver metallic backing? Michelle couldn't tell.

Rachel's lips moved, ever so slightly, and Michelle thought she heard something.

"What did you say, Mom?"

Rachel swallowed hard, and the vulnerability in her eyes remained, tears withheld.

Michelle told herself that her mother had heard insincerity in her question about the poem. She wanted to apologize, clarify, or simply affirm that she believed in her mother's abilities. But that might make the situation worse.

Michelle leaned over, retrieved a fallen sheet from the floor. "Here's another one, Mom," she said, lifting her mother's hands and sliding the sheet onto the pile beneath them.

Rachel smiled wanly toward Michelle in the reflection, and the expression went beyond anything she might have heard in Michelle's question. It reflected pain from the leavings of life she had received. Rachel's eyes looked worn, and sat in deep hollows, like those of a ninety-year-old. But she was only forty-four. Deep creases ravaged her face and neck, and there were dark splotches along her forehead, near the rootline of her thin and scraggly gray hair.

Granmère is to blame for this, Michelle thought, letting her bitterness flare. *That tyrannical, domineering, stubborn old hag.*

But it was Rachel who looked more the hag. It seemed to the imaginative girl that her malefic grandmother must have cast a sorceress's spell on Rachel, causing her to age prematurely.

"Would you like me to brush your hair and make it pretty, Mom?"

Rachel crossed one forearm across her midsection and rested the other elbow in that hand. She began rubbing the bridge of her nose between a thumb and forefinger, humming an unidentifiable, plaintive tune—probably something she had made up, Michelle thought. Her mother had entered the melancholy safety of an interior world.

Multiple personality disorder was Michelle's best guess, based upon a news cube she had read. Father wouldn't talk about the diagnosis, if he knew it himself. All that medicine was supposed to control whatever she had. But no matter how much medication Rachel consumed, she seemed always to retain her ability to withdraw inwardly. Internalization didn't seen dangerous to Michelle, but doctors interviewed in the news-cube story expressed concern that such "journeys" made it more difficult for subjects to return to reality. What did doctors know, anyway?

Michelle brought a brush from the adjacent bathroom and passed it through Rachel's hair. When the brush snagged Michelle worked it gently, holding hairs near the roots with her other hand to prevent their coming out unnecessarily.

A tender smile passed over Rachel's face and remained there for a time before fading. She dropped her hands to her lap and continued humming. It was a forelorn, doleful tune.

"Are you making that song up, Mom? It's ever so pretty."

Rachel behaved as if she were all alone in her own special universe. Michelle's brush strokes became smoother, and in the lamplight the girl thought she saw the hairs shimmer an exquisite shade of red. Once this had been a strikingly beautiful woman. Michelle had seen the pictures, and her father spoke of her lost beauty with great remorse. Surely he could see that his own mother had done this to his wife! Perhaps not, Michelle realized. He too had been shaped by Granmère, in a different but nearly as ruinous manner.

No one in the family escaped that woman.

As her mother hummed, Michelle tried to fit the pieces together. Somewhere in Rachel's soul, in a sheltered place no one could destroy, there existed a realm of grace and simple delights. Rachel composed melodies there and reposed in serenity, created her own verse. There she smelled things of great significance, touched them, tasted them, and lived as she could nowhere else.

Renney experienced some of that himself, with his exceptional natural drawing ability. Occasionally he would tell Michelle of his own private place, a cocoon he crawled in to create. Rachel recognized this similarity, and protected the boy. Renney was her favorite, her soul mate, and Michelle never could occupy such a position, no matter how hard she tried.

Renney's words, so often spoken, came back to Michelle: *"I'm the best, Ma, huh? I'm the only good one, huh?"*

But Renney, even with his favored position, didn't seem to see their mother the way Michelle did. In time, Michelle thought, perhaps he would.

Michelle passed her hand through her mother's hair. It was coarse and bristly, and this returned Michelle to immediacy. The hair wasn't red any longer, and stood as a lumpy gray scruff of unbrushable ugliness in the lamplight.

At the telephone in the kitchen doorway Henry muttered something to the operator that Stu, from the living room, couldn't discern.

Stu stood awkwardly, awaiting his father.

Henry returned the receiver to its cradle, roughly. "Still can't get t'rough," he announced, looking down at the boy. "Awright. Sleep onna

back porch tonight. There's a mattress you can t'row down, an' I'll rustle
you a blanket."

"Thanks."

Shortly after Henry went for the bedding, Stu heard loud voices in another room. First Henry telling Michelle to get back to bed. Then Mrs.
Fouquet objecting to the order. Stu saw Michelle cross the kitchen and
disappear through another doorway.

Stu heard his father tell Mrs. Fouquet that "the boy" was staying a while,
"mebbe a few days." He asked her where the extra blanket was. She didn't
seem willing to help him locate it, and objected vehemently to Stu's presence.

"We don't need another warm body in this place!" she shouted, her voice
a hostile rasp. "We're already going crazy here!"

"Shadup an' take yer medicine!" Henry retorted, so loudly that it sounded
to Stu as if his father were in the same room with him. "He's the son o' my
service buddy, Willie Kroemer, an' I'm takin' 'im in for a while. There ain't
nuttin' you can say about it."

After considerable shouting, Henry returned to Stu carrying a thick brown
and red blanket. He said it was the only extra they had, and handed it to the
boy.

"It's fine," Stu said.

"Porch is back t'rough there," Henry said, pointing toward the kitchen.
Stu nodded.

"Don't pay no attention to my wife," Henry said, his tone apologetic.
"She rages all the time. Little t'ings t'row 'er off. She can't cope, the doctors
say. It's why our house is such a goddam mess. She never cleans, cooks, or
nuttin' else aroun' here. Mostly she lies aroun' with her Biblecorder."

"I see." Stu felt out of place hearing these things.

With few additional words his father was gone and Stu was on the back
porch mattress, lying beneath the blanket. The living room and kitchen
lights were off, but to one side Stu saw a stream of illumination from the
stairway that led upstairs. The house was near the corner of two busy arterials, and he listened to the horns, whooshes, hisses, and motors of traffic
outside. Once he went to the side window, wiped away frost on it, and saw
that the fog around the lights didn't seem as thick as it had been.

He lay awake after that, turning from side to side. Finally he settled upon
a position away from the window, his head supported by his folded jacket.

Up on the small wooden waveshack mezzanine of her bedroom, Michelle
adjusted the controls of Joseph's infrawave transceiver. She sat in the bright

narrow beam of light thrown by a wall-mounted Tensor lamp, wearing a set of earphones. Her older brother had purchased this equipment and constructed the low mezzanine with the earnings of last year's summer job. He had since lost interest in I-wave transmissions, leaving the set for Michelle.

She thought back a few minutes to when her father ordered her back to bed. His tone had been weary, carrying with it more than the fatigue of a long day. Then there was the argument between her parents, building up as she scurried upstairs. It seemed to have died down now.

Michelle tuned in to an excited voice on the transceiver. A man was saying that the fog layer had lifted, but remained high over San Francisco and the surrounding communities. The fog never entirely blocked I-wave equipment, according to the man. Some rigs had been powerful enough to get through, but only for a few kilometers. In some unexplained fashion, he said, the fog had entirely blocked other forms of radio or television communication, but local transmissions were now possible. They still had no communication of any sort with the world beyond the Bay Area.

Michelle adjusted the tuner, searching for more information. She had never heard of anything like this.

When Henry crawled into bed, Rachel was there, slouched against two pillows with her Biblecorder on her lap. A lighted fiber-optic scanner traversed the open page, transmitting words to Rachel via a wire that led from the unit to the silver and black earphones she wore. Henry heard the low, monotonous murmur of a minister's voice from the machine and made out: "The Holy Bible, Old and New Testaments, Copyright 2037 by Bookcorder International."

Rachel always listened to the title page before proceeding to the text.

"Philippians Two," Rachel said, speaking into a tiny microphone that protruded from the binding.

This microphone was connected to the base of a flexible plastic tube that dangled over the open pages. The business end of this tube was an electric-eye scanner, and at Rachel's command the tube bent low and nudged pages until Philippians Two was beneath the electric eye. The unit also contained a computerized concordance, so that it could be instructed to find particular passages.

The ministerial voice resumed: "If there be therefore any consolation in Christ, if any comfort of love, if any fellowship of the Spirit . . ."

Henry lifted a television channel selector from the nightstand and pointed it at the small set on the dresser by the foot of the bed. The television went on, casting improperly mixed tones of blue, red, and green across the bed. He groused about fuzzy reception, turned up the sound. It was a rebroadcast of the Academy Awards presentation held a month before. A man who greased the car that was used in an award-winning stunt was receiving his Oscar and bowing to the audience. He went on to say that he used triple-A 12/40 oil, nine liters of it.

"You watch too much of the boob tube, On-ree," Rachel said, her nasal tones drowning out the program. "It fries your brain."

Hearing this from her, whose brain he considered long overcooked, Henry was incredulous. Out of pity he tempered his retort: "You read that book too much, Raich."

"The Bible isn't a *single* book, you consummate fool! It's many volumes combined. There are more books here than you've read in your whole life-time."

"You don't do no work aroun' here," came the response, almost automatic. Henry felt himself locking into a familiar pattern of confrontation, one he was helpless to prevent. "Alla time lyin' aroun' with that stupid Biblecorder. This place is a friggin' mess."

"I'm doing the Lord's work, On-ree. Nothing comes before that."

"Call me Henry, you stupid bitch."

She began to discourse, but Henry turned up the volume of his program. Although he didn't focus on her words, her tone penetrated, preventing him from concentrating on the show. He knew she had won the exchange, as she invariably did. He loathed her sharp, sarcastic tongue, which lashed him as if she didn't appreciate him for staying with her through her mental difficulties.

He looked up at the stainless steel nozzle of their dysfunctional ceiling-hung antisnore mister, then across the room to a dark wooden French provincial dresser his mother had given him. Its brass handles were oxidized or entirely broken away, and it stood in scratched and chipped disrepair, with a long split running diagonally across the mirror. An empty cartridge of snore-suppression powder lay on the dresser top near his wallet, his keys, and a pile of soiled clothes. Slowly he turned his head back toward the screen. He had placed the cartridge there to remind himself that it needed replacing for Rachel's benefit, since he slept like a choking, snorting bear. She hadn't complained in a while, but he chastised himself for not remembering.

But he kept noticing the way she treated him and her utter disregard for those possessions that mattered most to him. That chest of drawers had been beautiful once, before Rachel attacked it in one of her black rages. He told himself that lesser men would have given up on their wives under similar circumstances. He had heard of divorces granted by the Catholic church, his church, and felt that with an appeal to the Pope he could obtain freedom.

I won't divorce her! he thought. *No matter what, I'm staying with her!*

Troublesome thoughts clamored for attention. No matter what? That encompassed a great deal. Was there no circumstance under which he would leave her? And if not, why not? He wondered if he was being stubborn just to show his mother, the powerful city councilwoman, that she couldn't dictate his life.

Mother. So dominant, so pushy, so demanding.

I'm fifty-three years old! he thought. He wondered if he would ever be free of *Maman*, as Rachel so pointedly called her. The children had to be considered too. They would be harmed by a divorce, especially Renney and Coley, assuming Rachel lost custody because of her medical history. Michelle had a special attachment to Rachel as well, despite the mental abuse from her mother. Michelle played both sides better than the other children, making herself available whenever either parent needed help or comfort.

Despite his fatigue, Henry recalled that there was yet another side in the ongoing battle between him and Rachel—the position occupied by Granmère. Michelle didn't play to that side, except for her relationship with Granpère, and he was mostly a neutral party.

Granpère seemed relatively independent of the power of the old woman. Their marriage had survived almost half a century, so they had to have common ground. But Henry couldn't figure out where that was, even though he as their only son should know better than almost anyone. They always seemed to tolerate one another without any show of special affection, and probably it was easier to continue in that relationship than to obtain a divorce.

Divorce. That word again. He switched the channel, to a talk show.

Joseph always took Granmère's side. Completely and unquestionably. He was the only one.

Despite all, Henry loved Rachel, and this was no small consideration. But she could be so cruel at times with her biting, devastating comments. Henry felt he didn't deserve to have such things said to him. Invariably they cut away his manhood or ridiculed something he held important, for she knew precisely how to agitate him. In a peculiar way it cheered him at times to hear Rachel make brilliant remarks, regardless of their target. They meant her brain still had spark in it. But she could change so quickly, in the beat of a hummingbird's heart, reverting to a mushbrain that hummed and communicated with no one.

One of the doctors at Korpunkel's called it in part a defensive posture that she assumed, since most people observed an almost innate taboo against attacking crazy people. The doctor felt that initially Rachel had feigned some aspects of her illness, but that this was, in his experience, a dangerous thing to do. Like the actor who eventually became like the character he played, so it was in other aspects of life, to the point where the real and the assumed become increasingly difficult to distinguish.

Henry felt the television show swimming through his consciousness, pushing away the concerns of his day and of his life. He sighed, thought the talk show conversation sounded familiar. Had he seen it before?

Rachel was immobile. Glancing sidelong at her, Henry saw that her eyelids were closed. Her partially exposed bosom heaved regularly, almost imperceptibly.

Henry shut his eyes to rest them, listened to the program without really hearing it. The volume was just loud enough to drown out the overflow of the Biblecorder, with that incessant, pedantic tone he couldn't abide. Layers of consciousness slipped away. When he opened his eyes he didn't recall having been asleep, but he couldn't recover details of his thoughts.

Rachel was asleep, snoring lightly. She had one arm across her open Biblecorder, folding some of the "read-along" pages. He moved her arm, smoothed the pages, and closed the volume, shutting off the unit. She stirred as he removed her headset and placed it on the nightstand with the rest of the gear.

Henry massaged the side of Rachel's creased neck, then slid his fingers up through the thin strands of gray hair to the side of her head. He rubbed her scalp gently and soothingly, trying to transmit serenity from his fingers to the sleeping cells of her troubled brain.

Henry didn't know what the doctors had done to Rachel's brain. She brought home so many medicines, and he never asked about side effects. He felt guilty about this and helpless. He didn't know about medicines and trusted those who did. The prescriptions did seem to work—at least they sedated her, controlled her. Usually she accepted the drugs meekly, without much complaint. Refusals were rare because she understood the consequences. If she didn't follow the hospital's orders, it was back inside, to incarceration in one of the wards.

She did seem to have run out of medicine today, or to have lost some of it. Henry didn't think it was a refusal.

Rachel had been in a ward for nearly a month the year before. When she got out, she told him in a plaintive tone, "They hurt me in there."

He hadn't asked for details.

Henry stopped massaging his wife, let her head sink into one pillow. He nudged the other pillow she had been using to the floor, where it plopped.

The noise or motion, however slight and gentle, awakened Rachel. She looked directly at Henry, her eyes fierce and bright.

With a cruel, distant smile she said, "One of these days your mother is going to wake up dead."

Henry reached across Rachel to shut off the bed lamp on her side, then repeated the ritual on his side. The room fell into charcoal tones, faintly illuminated by the orange glow from a street lamp which threw the shadow shape of the six-paned bedroom window against one wall.

In the manner of one who ignores a child's dirty words so as not to encourage that behavior, Henry made no comment. He had heard such talk from her many times before, and always it gave him a sense of uneasiness mixed with disbelief. He didn't believe that Rachel would ever carry out an act of finality against a member of the family. Henry could not love such a woman, and he did love Rachel, despite everything. Consequently he had not communicated any threats to his mother.

"I've been charting the occurrences," the man on the I-wave said, his voice hollow and distant to Michelle. "There have been nearly two hundred mysterious collisions since the fog appeared. I don't mean the normal crashes that happen in any thick tule fog. I'm talkin' about trucks, buses, cars, planes, helicopters, and boats hitting some kinda barrier out there. Even subsurface trains are smashing into something. How do you explain that? Every way out of the San Francisco Bay Area is blocked. I've got a police communications tap, whether they like it or not, and the collision coordinates I'm getting are more than interesting. They form a circle around the Bay Area, with Oakland at the approximate center."

Another voice came on the air, that of a woman. She asked a garbled question. When the man responded, this too was unintelligible. Michelle adjusted the tuner and lost the frequency.

On every channel people were discussing the fog, the collisions, and rumors of barriers. Michelle heard fear and excitement in their voices. She forgot about having to get up early for school the next morning. She wouldn't be able to sleep tonight anyway.

The faint voice of a woman caught Michelle's attention, and she tried to tune it in. Michelle heard the woman say she was standing near the barrier with a flashlight on it, just south of Stanford University. A background motor noise virtually drowned out her words.

"There's an eerie grayness here at the edge," the woman said, "and the barrier material, whatever it is, absorbs any light I cast toward it. I have my face against it now. The surface is cool, hard, and smooth, like plexform or reinforced glass. I'm returning to my plane. It's a single-seater vertical-take-off craft, and I intend to ascend the barrier surface, attempting to locate a route over it. Stand by."

Michelle surmised the woman must have a portable microphone because she heard the motor noise grow louder, then diminish.

"I'm inside the plane now," the woman reported, "rising along the surface. Lost sight of the barrier . . . immersed in thick fog . . . trouble with the instruments . . . losing all sense of direction . . ."

Michelle heard a pop followed by a burst of radio crackle, then silence. Then the excited voices of other wave operators came on the air. Michelle picked out two men and an older, throaty-voiced woman.

"You there, McKay?"

"Linda McKay, are you okay?"

"Did she hit something? Did you get a fix on her?"

They chattered excitedly. Then the throaty-voiced woman made an emergency broadcast, giving everything she knew about the flyer's last reported coordinates.

As she finished, a new voice came on, louder than the others. It was asexual and polished, speaking English precisely:

"Your attention, please! Your attention, please! A number of citizens have lost their lives attempting to penetrate the fog, which remains in outlying areas and at elevation over your cities. Be assured that we are working on the situation, and are doing everything necessary to safeguard your persons. Go about your lives as normally as possible, avoiding regions of poor visibility. Further information will be provided by television, radio, and I-wave tomorrow at six P.M."

The wave operators came back on.

"Who the hell was that? Did anyone get a handle?"

"Sounded like someone in the government."

"Yeah, but who? Those guys don't work in the middle of the night, cutting in on I-wave frequencies."

Michelle listened for another hour but heard only the confused voices of I-wavers. She shut off the set and crawled into bed.

But she tossed and turned the rest of the night, recalling that voice. Its tone had been remote, she decided, as if the speaker were not from the Bay Area. It spoke of "citizens," "your persons," "your cities," "your lives." She wondered if another nation had conquered the United States, using a mysterious fog to conceal its activities. As difficult as that was to imagine, she came up with no plausible alternative. Why the barriers? Had an enemy divided the entire country into walled sections?

FOUR

I began to realize that your mother was strange
shortly before her wedding to Henri. As her mother-
in-law to be, I invited her to go downtown and look at
silverware patterns. She wouldn't do it. Then when
your father was away in the service during the last
Moon War, she wouldn't come and live with me. It
was because she wanted to run around with her wild
friend Jennie. They hung around in sleazy bars, waiting to get picked up by men.

—Granmère Liliane to Joseph

From her snug semi-cocoon of blankets Rachel watched Henry as he sat on
the dressing-table bench, putting on his socks. He was up two hours before
dawn as usual, on the way to his subpoena route, and light from the bed
lamp threw bulky shadows against the dressing table and wall behind him.

"If I said to you 'blue out,'" Rachel asked, "what would you think?"

"You ain't makin' sense, Raich. Go back to sleep."

"I could mean b-l-e-w out, as in an explosion. Or I could mean b-l-u-e
out, as in the color blue on the outside. When it's cold you wear two pairs
of socks to work. You always wear the pair with the blue top stripe on the
outside, and they match if anyone sees."

"You're talkin' nonsense." Henry reached for one of the heavy brown
boots on the floor and pulled it on.

"No one knows you're wearing two pairs of socks unless they've seen you
dress or unless you've told them. The hidden pair might not even be a
match."

"So what? Jesus!" He worked at the boot laces.

"My blue side is out, Henry. It's the blue of sadness, of wounds, of exposed veins that ripped through the pure skin of youth. It's the blueness of approaching death."

As Henry finished putting on his boots he tried to formulate a rejoinder about her "blew out" brain, but found himself unable to string together the words sensibly. She was off on one of her wild tangents, talking riddles. But—and this troubled Henry—even when she made no sense she seemed able to run verbal circles around him.

"Inside at times I'm still a young burgundy-red rose," Rachel said, "in the bloom of life's springtime. Pink cheeks, perfect white teeth, my hazel eyes flashing and my fingernails and lips made up in the brightest, prettiest damn red that God ever came up with."

"Aw, Raich . . ."

"You *do* believe in God, don't you, Henry?"

He lurched to his feet, tucked his shirt in, and grabbed a heavy green pea jacket from his side of the bed. "Leamee alone with this shit. For Christ's sake, Rachel. Go write a poem or sumpthin'."

"I think I will. I think I'll do just that." She swung smartly off the bed and entered the bathroom, shutting the door behind her.

"What kind of a family is this?" Henry shouted after her. "You lushin' aroun' talkin' nutso an' writin' wacko off-the-wall stuff on little slips o' paper . . . Joseph inna other room drunk off 'is ass, lyin' like a dead man underneath a mattress! I'm sweatin' t'ree jobs to support this zoo. He's old enough at nineteen to get one, but all he can do is mooch offa me like everyone else. I'm damned tired of it."

Henry stalked out of the bedroom.

Henry left his personal car in the sprawling Lawservice parking lot and switched to a one-seat company vehicle for his route. He thought about the law and his place in it as he threw the little delivery van into gear.

It seemed to him that everyone in the country must be involved in a lawsuit, either as a litigant, a witness, or in a court-system support capacity. He delivered fifty-five to seventy-five subpoenas or other legal notices every day, usually completing the task before sunrise. Then he would return home for breakfast and a short rest before going off to his second job.

With its single headlight probing the darkness ahead, the pint-sized, rubber-tired vehicle ran along a narrow lane to the edge of the Lawservice compound, jerking as it reached the street. The vehicles used by Henry and other Lawservers had their own curbside lanes on every street, running between sidewalks and parked cars. This was the best position from which to ensure accurate delivery into the receptacles that were required by law on the outsides of all buildings.

Henry had been fortunate in one respect. He hadn't been to court himself in nearly eighteen months, since Mrs. Meley sued him for a window that Joseph allegedly broke. Joseph denied the deed, and the old busybody couldn't prove her case, so she lost. Henry had only been sued five times in his adult life, with perhaps twice that number of court appearances as a witness. Although urged to file litigation himself a number of times, Henry had never been a plaintiff. It wasn't so much that he didn't want to, for there was no shortage of negligent acts committed by others against him. Rather, Henry didn't have the funds or the time to become involved in every incident. The occurrences had been minor, and he'd found it easier to forget them.

The van slowed as it reached the steep hill above Space Exploration Park, and it creaked as it started up in low gear. Only a few of the homes and businesses on the hill above him were illuminated, and these sparkled clearly, undimmed by fog. That was his territory ahead, and from this distance he couldn't yet see the glows given off by Lawservice receptacles.

On the average each citizen of San Francisco made a court appearance every seventy-nine days. He knew the statistics, even some of the legal jargon. Some people who suspected imminent litigation let the lights burn out in their receptacles or set traps for the delivery men—illegal acts. Henry told himself that he knew all the tricks.

When the van reached an aging retail area on the hilltop it freewheeled for a moment before slipping automatically into a higher gear. Hugging the curb in the Lawservice lane, Henry made a right turn and traveled one block. He was on Mississippi Street facing north, with the graceful buildings of downtown looking like illuminated Oriental lanterns in the distance, beyond parklands and a comparatively flat industrial-commercial area.

Glancing at the fluorescent green address on the plastic tube that rested in a tray to his left, Henry made a left on Nineteenth Street. Pulling the torque lever by his seat, he brought the minivan to a squealing stop in front of a small all-night apothecary that had been hollowed out of an old turreted Victorian home.

Heihnson's Drugmart was robot-tended, one of the twenty-four-hour establishments that catered to drug addicts and people who weren't sick during daytime hours. It had aisles of glass-cased drug bins, with each case fronted by a chute that could be activated by a shopper's plastic card. All of the hallucinogens were here, even those that had been illegal in the recent past.

Controversial government statistics had shown that addicts committed fewer crimes if their needs were freely met. The government even provided buildings near the apothecaries in which the addicts could lie about in collective stupors. Most of these fringe people were provided with drug cards, enabling them to obtain substances free of charge, at taxpayer expense.

The system made Henry sick to his right-wing stomach, and he was glad to be delivering a Lawservice notification to this particular establishment. He wasn't certain, however, if the sealed plastic tube in the tray beside him contained a subpoena or a notice of suit.

Sighing and wishing it were a firebomb, Henry loaded the tube into a small cannon mounted on the outside of the van, then reached out the window. He clicked shut the chamber at the rear of the miniature artillery piece and touched a heat-sensitive button on the base.

The cannon swiveled to the left, zeroing in on the illuminated red electronic eye on the red, white, and blue Lawservice receptacle box to one side of the apothecary's front door. When this eye became aligned with another eye on Henry's cannon, which took only a second, the tube discharged.

A percussion crack filled the van's interior, causing a momentary dull throb of pain in Henry's left ear. He had been in the Strato Guard (a National Air Service division) during Moon War V, but the injury hadn't been particularly war-related. One of the military doctors lanced his eardrum while giving him an examination, then gave Henry the runaround when Henry tried to get it repaired. All Henry received was a pressure-balancing ear cartridge that eliminated pain while he was in an airplane or rocket. He didn't know where the cartridge was now, although they had permitted him to keep it.

Henry's ear injury seemed minor to everyone at the time it occurred. There was a war on for control of "high ground" on the Moon (the whole Moon in relation to Earth), and many men had far more serious afflictions. Henry served without complaining. Then when the hostilities were over and the war won, he allowed himself to be discharged without further medical attention. He even signed a form releasing the military service from liability. At that point all he could think about was getting home, and he assumed that the ear would improve. From a hearing standpoint he didn't think that it did improve, although he didn't seem to have lost that much auditory function. His threshold of pain seemed to have increased, however. It didn't hurt much anymore when the mini-cannon went off—only enough to remind him of another age when he had served his nation and planet.

Looking up at the roof of the drugstore, Henry saw a bright yellow light blinking on the little Lawservice tower mounted there. It would continue to blink until the capsule was removed and opened, indicating a completed service. If the tower on a structure continued blinking for more than forty-eight hours, the police investigated. Anyone away longer than that had to leave a travel itinerary with the cops for service at all times, anywhere in the solar system. No allowance was made for vacationers, business travelers, or any other variety of traveler. The legal machinery could not be delayed. If Henry made the mistake of delivering to an unattended location, it wasn't his fault. It meant either a legitimate foul-up in the forwarding system, a skip, or a foolishly forgetful person. There were stiff penalties and fines for failing to follow procedures.

Another tube with a fluorescent green address popped into the tray beside him.

As Henry threw the van into gear, he considered how unfair it was that people even got served while vacationing. He was thankful that he did not have that sort of duty, although he might enjoy a territory that served legal papers on vacationing junkies. He despised those people with a nearly murderous passion. The alleyways and drug sanctuaries of the solar system were littered with addicts. He lamented having risked his life fighting for such a society, then reminded himself of the evil, totalitarian societies that America had fought in each war.

As they sometimes did, the troublesome tales of Rachel's infidelity during his service years came back now. None of them had ever been verified, so they remained rumors. All came from one source, his mother. Liliane loathed Rachel from their first meeting, so the reports had to be discounted. Not that Rachel was above such conduct, considering how many people had affairs. She might have behaved exactly as *Maman* said she did. But if so, Henry tried to tell himself that Rachel did it only *after* Liliane started spreading rumors, assuming that she might as well behave the way people believed she did.

Henry stared at the illuminated address on the waiting Lawservice tube, set the van in motion while forming a mental picture of a white and green house on the next block. When he reached the house he went through the motions, discharging his delivery.

By the time Henry started out again for the next address, his thoughts of Rachel's alleged infidelity were gone, having been shifted into a darkened, nerve-dead tunnel of his brain. It was his way of dealing with the pain.

Standing in her nightgown, Rachel switched on the lamp by her bed, melting the predawn darkness of the room. The heinous image of Granmère

Liliane appeared before her, a ghostly apparition that jeered and made threatening faces. Rachel swatted the air, but the image remained. Then, with hatred and terror on her face, Rachel threw open the drawer where Henry kept his automatic pistol.

She waved the gun in the air, but the image didn't fade.

Tossing the gun back in the drawer with a clunk, she slammed it shut and opened the next drawer down, bringing forth a box of laser-activated matchsticks. Quickly she had a match in her hand, and she held it unlit between herself and the apparition.

"I'll burn you with these!" Rachel said. "Stay away from me!"

The image faded.

"You fear me, don't you, hag? One day maybe I'll torch you in bed!"

Rachel crept around the room with her eyes aflare, holding the unlit laser match before her as if it were a beacon. She looked behind and beneath dressers, in the closet, under the bed.

"You've gone and crawled into your devil hole," Rachel rasped in her nasal tone. "But I'll get you, biddy. You'll rue the day you riled me! Oh, Beauregard . . . are you here to do my bidding? The old hag is hiding. And there's another enemy, Beauregard . . . one who sleeps and lives in this very house. Come with me, soldier. Let's go see Joseph."

Having thus called upon the friend that Henry scoffingly called "imaginary," Rachel switched off the lamp, throwing the room into near darkness. Holding the box of matches in one hand and the single unlit matchstick aloft in the other, she swung open the bedroom door and traversed the shadow-immersed kitchen to the left, moving with the unshod stealth and surefootedness of a nightseeing cat. All the while she saw the specter of a long-dead, discontented American Civil War general moving beside her.

Reaching the carpeted staircase she crept up it, remaining close to the wall where the steps creaked less. Halfway to the top she paused, listened to house sounds. Somewhere water ran through a pipe. The whine of an electric car motor on a nearby street dominated her senses, then diminished. She detected little light anywhere, meaning that Joseph's bedroom door was closed, keeping the modicum of street light from passing through the bedroom window to the hallway.

Then she remembered the fog, and the fact that she hadn't looked outside yet. The door might be open.

Rachel envisioned a thick blanket of fog around the house, caressing it, smothering it. Her mind's eye switched channels, and she envisioned Joseph arguing with her as he did frequently, calling her a drunk, a derelict, and a loser. His imagined face was only centimeters from hers, and it was consumed with revulsion. His words deafened her:

"This house is a mess! You never do anything around here! You've ruined the place and this family! Everything Granmère says about you is true!"

Joseph had spoken these very words a week before, and with them he ceased to be her eldest son. He was no longer of her womb, but lived as the direct offspring of Granmère Liliane.

Now Joseph was drunk upstairs, asleep and helpless in his own jobless swill. Who was he to talk about her? Granmère's protégé had been out of high school for more than a year, but hadn't held a job for more than two months at a time.

Joseph was always quitting his jobs after accumulating a little cushion of money, and was forever saying that he hadn't yet found a really suitable position. It was his age to a great extent, Rachel realized. But she resented the general conception (shared by Joseph) which held that she was lazy. She'd held full-time jobs constantly from the age of sixteen until her mid-twenties, when the demands of raising a family interfered.

Rachel resumed her climb, felt General Beauregard merging into her flesh, imparting masculine strength and ferocity to her.

Do you know where I've worked, Joseph? No you wouldn't, would you? You only know what Liliane tells you. Maybe I worked in a match factory, sleeping one. Did that ever occur to you?

At the top of the staircase she began to scamper on the balls of her feet, still making barely any sound. She fantasized what her own face looked now: a ferocious beast's head with red ember eyes. The prey was near!

Holding the match box under one arm, she used her free hand to touch the door. It was closed. Her hand slid to the manual lever, and she depressed it, just slightly until she felt the tension of the spring. With the slightest noise of plastic gears, she heard the door latch click open and the metal on metal squeal of hinges as the door swung aside on its own.

In dim light cast from the street now, she swept past the beds occupied by Michelle and Renney, taking care to avoid the clutter of objects on the floor. She had no thoughts of the other children now—only of Joseph.

"Come along, Beauregard," Rachel whispered. "Let's find the enemy."

Reaching Joseph's bed, she knelt beside it, listening to his breathing. The swallows of air he took were long and unlabored, and she saw that he was still sandwiched between the mattresses as Henry had described.

She touched a partially shielded pressure pad on one end of the matchbox, transmitting a curving thread of purple laser light from the box to the tip of the matchstick held in her other hand. The stick flamed to fiery brightness, illuminating Joseph's sleeping, sodden face.

"Haaah!" Rachel exclaimed, holding the match beneath her own face to make herself look scary. "It's Beauregard!"

With these words rasping in his dream state, Joseph snapped open his eyes. In the matchlight, Rachel saw terror transform his features. He screamed and tumbled the other way into a wall, throwing the mattress that had covered him toward Rachel.

She dodged it deftly and approached Joseph ominously, her match still burning brightly.

"You shouldn't fall asleep," she said. "It's dangerous to fall asleep."

Michelle was awake now, in the darkness beyond Rachel's matchlight. Michelle sat up, heard Renney stirring nearby. He was a sound sleeper.

"Whass goin' on!" Renney asked.

Michelle saw a circular glow of purple and yellow light that emanated from her mother's hand. Rachel had one nightgown-covered knee on Joseph's bed, and there was a faint odor of sulfur in the air.

Joseph, clad only in white underpants, was seated on the other side of the bed with his back against the wall, cowering. He held one muscular arm up across his face, protecting himself from the tall, comparatively frail woman who leaned toward him. Joseph's tawny hair was sleep-wild, and from lack of combing it looked thin above the forehead. He had the roundness of his father's face, and the same wide nose with a little bump beneath the bridge. If Michelle squinted, she could see her father as a young man.

This encounter between mother and son, while different from any Michelle had witnessed before, didn't surprise the girl. Rachel and Joseph were perpetually sniping at one another.

Calmly, Rachel placed the matchbox on the bed between her and Joseph. Then, removing her knee from the mattress she stood erect and withdrew a cigarette from the pocket of her nightgown. She lit the cigarette and extinguished the incendiary laser stick by waving it through the air.

"Goddam it, Mom," Joseph said, lowering his arm. "Stay in your own room, for Christ's sake, and let people sleep."

"I was just checking on my darlings," Rachel said, her voice coming from a shadowy form. Michelle saw the cigarette ash glow as her mother inhaled.

"Sleep well, little ones," Rachel said, her tone sweet in a way that made Michelle shiver.

The ember moved past Michelle's bed.

"Come along, Beauregard," Rachel said.

Joseph slammed something into the wall, probably his fist.

"Damn that woman!" he said. "How'd we ever end up with her for a mother?"

The door clicked shut behind Rachel.

Joseph stumbled across the room to the light switch by the door, flipped it on. Finding the box of matches still on his bed, he hid them on a closet shelf, beneath a pile of soiled clothes. As he put his bed back together, his powerful hands shook.

Michelle wanted to tell him that their mother wasn't really crazy, that she only acted that way because she hurt so much inside. Joseph was terrified of Mom, and Mom knew it, Michelle realized. Now fully alert, Michelle drew an analogy. If strangers revealed fear toward her dog, Bumper, it went into a barking attack. Intimidation. Showing who was boss of the territory. That was the game, at least in part, and maybe Joseph didn't see it.

People are always talking about Mom too, Michelle thought. *Saying she's nuts in front of her and behind her back. So, she figures, why not act that way.*

Michelle smiled at the thought of Beauregard, the house ghost of Mom's imagination. Rachel had seen the name in a book on the American Civil War, told Michelle that he was a Confederate general who lost a number of key battles. "He's a Frenchman too," Mom said. "You can tell that by his name. A Frenchie loser with a tormented spirit, hiding inside our walls."

Michelle and Joseph had picked up the tale with great relish, embellishing its doubtful details. To them, Beauregard became a seven-foot giant flea, living in one of the filth-infested Fouquet closets, waiting to pounce upon any hapless person happening to open the closet door at the wrong time.

Renney didn't like to talk about Beauregard. He believed in the creature, with all of its embellishments, and had nightmares about it.

"What are you smiling at?" Joseph demanded, slapping his pillow to the bed surface. He stared angrily at Michelle, hands on his hips. "You see somethin' funny goin' on around here?"

"I'm half asleep," Michelle countered. "Half dreaming. A 'morning dream,' I guess you'd call it. I wasn't laughing at you." She slid back into bed, pulling the sheet and her single ragged blanket around her.

Joseph stalked to the light switch, threw the room into darkness. He hurled himself into bed, making a loud thump with his muscular body. Michelle heard him muttering and turning over a number of times after that.

"I'm gonna figure some way to barricade that door," he said.

*   *   *

Michelle slept fitfully, and when she rose for school two hours after the confrontation, she remembered hearing Joseph's voice, as if from a dream: "She's a time bomb, ready to detonate. And she's our damned mother. You're just a kid, Michelle. You don't see what I see."

Michelle sat on the edge of her bed, trying to get her thoughts in order for the day. How many hours had she actually slept? Did that matter so much, except as a suggestion to the brain covering how she *should* feel? How did she really feel? A little dopey, maybe. She had felt worse.

She wanted to tell Joseph what she had heard on the I-wave the evening before, but he wasn't in bed and no one was in the bathroom. Sometimes he attended morning classes with his girlfriend Thyla at her college.

The voice on the wave set came back, as if the transceiver were on next to her: "Further information will be provided by television, radio, and I-wave tomorrow at six P.M."

Today!

Who should she tell about it? But that was an open wave channel. Others had heard it—adults who would know what to do with the information. She didn't need to worry about communicating it. Her father was at work anyway, and Mom . . . well, Mom was Mom. Granmère? No. She wouldn't take a call from a child during business hours, and she went to work early. Granpère was out as a recipient as well, owing to his frailty. He shouldn't be made upset if he hadn't already heard.

The moth-nibbled gray wool blanket she sat on was scrunched around her thighs, felt coarse against them and against the butt of one hand as she rubbed it on the blanket. The striped sheet was faded and dirty, with bare threads revealing a stained and lumpy mattress beneath. The soiled pillowcase, with green and orange triangles, didn't match the sheet. The bed had no headboard, only a gray metal frame with protruding pieces that Michelle occasionally bumped her feet against painfully when getting in and out of bed.

Those few personal possessions that mattered to her were arranged upon a flimsy scuffed white child's bookcase that had but two narrow pressboard shelves—one so badly bowed that it appeared in danger of breaking. On the top shelf, off to one side, a digital clock radio and its white-on-blue numerals stalled at 9:36, with a frayed brown cord dangling halfway to the floor. Bumper had chewed the cord in two one morning while Michelle was at school, and she often wondered if her dog had been shocked. She wished he hadn't ruined her radio (a birthday gift from her grandparents), but it meant less to her than Bumper's well-being. Appliances could be repaired, and maybe someone would get around to it one day.

Her dog. Actually, Bumper belonged to the entire family. His mange-scarred old body, sagging and wobbly, was one of the unifying elements in the household. Everyone loved Bumper. Even Rachel had been known to feed him, and she detested every other pet that had ever appeared in the house. Bumper was decrepit when they got him three years earlier. He just appeared at the back door, like an escapee from a city pound truck. Joseph fed him at first, sharing whatever scraps he could find. Then the others picked up the duty alternating it with loving attention for a few months. Gradually Michelle assumed most of the responsibility. That was why she felt so close to the animal.

She washed Bumper and took him for walks through the neighborhood, especially to the playing field two blocks away. On several memorable occasions, Granmère had even brought the dog meat tidbits whenever she and Granpère visited. Michelle reflected with fondness on those peculiar scenes: Granmère in her pressed and precisely tailored clothes bending down to feed the scruffy old animal. Granmère and Rachel shared an affection for Bumper. It was something upon which they agreed—no small matter in Michelle's opinion, considering the intensity with which the women quarreled.

Michelle sighed, slowly and sadly. One point upon which to build? A mangy, not-long-for-this-world dog?

She chastised herself for nurturing silly, useless thoughts. It was the most fantastic, unrealizable fantasy to hope that her mother had paternal grandmother could ever like one another.

But Michelle held onto her optimism. Perhaps if she thought about it in greater detail she could come up with other areas of agreement. Or promote them. She needed a plan, but drew a blank for the moment. She felt these thoughts and all hope being buffeted. If she didn't hold on they would fly off and scatter irretrievably. *Intentions*, not unlike those her father had to repair things around the house. He was caught in a great malaise that set in upon him like a family-nurtured cloud, and Michelle felt its heaviness. It was the cloud of someday, fading to never.

Michelle opened the refrigerator, moved a nearly empty jar of catsup aside and pulled out a large green plastic bowl. The bowl had a fresh-tight clear plastic lid, and she pulled it back, exposing three bran muffins. Rachel had made these—one of the few recipes in her repertoire. One muffin was supposed to last Michelle an entire day, until dinner. Dad didn't know about this, or at least Michelle assumed he didn't know. She never dared discuss it with him, for fear of enraging her mother.

Rachel wasted much of the money he gave her on booze, cigarettes, and trinkets for herself. Henry, either in chronic mental fatigue or out of resignation, never seemed to notice the lack of food in the house. Rachel always made certain that the things he liked were there—his brand of coffee, longhorn steaks, potatoes, eggs, bacon, butter, string beans—but there was precious little else around that Rachel allowed the kids. Even the communion wafers at church made Michelle salivate.

But she couldn't blame her mother. Not at all. Michelle formed a horrid image of Granmère in her mind. What vicious, hateful things this old woman had done to Rachel! But as hard as Michelle tried to hold the image, it shifted to a benevolent, only slightly stern visage, looking down.

Michelle was in her crib again, looking up at the person who was as much a mother figure to her as her own mother. Granmère smiled gently, took Michelle in her arms. They were strong arms, and Michelle felt secure in them.

A taste of bran muffin brought Michelle back to awareness. How she hated those muffins! Sometimes when Michelle thought about them, she vowed never to eat another. And yet here she was early in the morning devouring one as if it were delicious, scraping muffin fragments from the bowl, and washing everything down with tap water from a mason jar.

The cold water caused a tooth on the upper right side of her mouth to throb. She pressed her tongue against the underside of the tooth, diminishing the pain.

Michelle recapped the bowl, which had two muffins remaining, and replaced it in the refrigerator.

Carrying a taped blue plastic school binder, she paused at the gut-split three-pillow couch in the living room, where her father was napping between jobs. The television set was on, and through the interference lines Michelle saw that it was a Japanese-made romance movie, with computer-dubbed Caucasian faces to accompany English subtitles. The faces weren't quite in synchronization.

Henry lay on his back with his head on one upthrust beefy arm. A half-consumed glass mug of coffee sat on the side table. Henry's face was round, stubbled, and pock-cratered, with a wide, short nose that had a bump beneath the bridge. The high forehead retained very little hairline delineation. At the sides of his head the hair remained dark brown and was closely cropped, as it had been during bygone military days. A color photograph on the mantel across the room showed the way he used to look in snappy tan and blue dress uniform, and as Michelle appraised the toll taken by years and hardship she had difficulty recognizing that this was the same man.

He wasn't the same, of course.

She realized that as she bent close to kiss his ruddy forehead, passing one hand gently across the top of his head. The sparse hairs were blond and baby fine there, felt smooth to her touch.

He stirred and grunted. His eyelids flickered but did not open.

Around Henry the dark green shag carpet was matted by dog urine, food, and only Beauregard knew what. Michelle couldn't recall the last time she heard the vacuum running; She thought it was out in the garage with other unrepaired mechanical devices. They did have a worn broom on the back porch, and once every week or so Dad told one of the children to sweep the kitchen. Rachel never issued such commands.

The house was scattered with many of Granmère's antiques, now ruined by abuse and neglect. Sometimes Rachel went around kicking or tearing at things Granmère had given them. Once, after breaking the glass out of a small portrait of Granmère, she set the portrait up again and hurled a dart at it, striking the old lady's image in the center of the forehead. The dart was still in place when Henry returned from work, and he blew a fuse over it.

That same evening Henry found one of Coley's dolls with a paring knife in its stomach. It was a round-faced male doll that had been made to look surprisingly like Henry, with beard stubble and pockmarks inked amateurishly on the face. Granmère often said the Coley had inherited Rachel's violent side, and the consensus between Granmère and Joseph about this incident was that Rachel inked the face as a sort of game with Coley and then showed the child how to plunge a knife through its belly.

Rachel never admitted to such activity, and Coley, if she knew anything about it, didn't break under interrogation. It was shortly afterward that Henry convinced Korpunkel's Psychotherapy Center to strengthen Rachel's medication.

Michelle gave her father another kiss without waking him, then ran down the makeshift front porch stairs two steps at a time.

Bumper was at the bottom of the stairs, wagging his tail. He'd broken free of his chain. She patted his hairless backside, ordered him to stay.

He whined but complied.

Michelle skittered down the weed-torn concrete driveway, rounded the high English hedge separating her yard from the sidewalk, and proceeded along the busy boulevard, passing small modern homes interspersed between comparably sized family-run businesses. The sky was an ominous shade of gray, a shapeless monotone cloud cover high overhead. She looked up as she walked, recalling the way the thick fog had moved in on her and her grandfather the day before.

Detouring a couple of steps onto a bumpy stretch of ground where roots had overgrown, she stepped through the saddle of a tree that had two trunks in a low "Y". She did this regularly for good luck, an exercise she made up one day and found herself unable to avoid.

At the stop sign on the corner she turned right, onto a wide sidewalk running along a street divided by islands of groomed grass and young hemlock trees. This took her a couple of blocks out of her way and past the "Special Purposes" lockup facility—a sixteen-story brick and stone structure painted institutional buff. There were mysterious compounds like this all over the city in a variety of buildings, all painted the same drab way and all manned by the Special Purposes Police. It was top secret stuff, and while Michelle had seen maroon SPP vans all over the city she'd never seen who they transported. The vans all had tinted windows and were low to the ground, with no wheels visible. Some of the kids at school said they were hovercraft.

"Bad people" were kept inside those buildings, according to sketchy SPP press releases. It used to boggle Michelle's mind to think how many bad people there must be, but lately she no longer believed everything the police said.

"Quit walkin' by that cruminal lockup," Henry told her more than once, in the blue-collar dialect that Granmère didn't like. "They'll think some-thin's wrong with you and scoop you away. There ain't no visitin' passes to that place."

The girl rounded the corner by Old Man Graham's house. Like some of the women on Michelle's block, Old Graham was a yeller and a busybody, a man who hated children and the noises they made. He was a miserable little man who lived in a drab little modern house that had low-cost, inar-tistically shaped bay windows. The summer before when Michelle and Ren-ney were riding homemade coasters down the hill by his house, metal roller-skate wheels clattering, he had stood smack in the middle of the nar-row sidewalk, blocking their path. Michelle had to swerve into the Lawservice lane to avoid him, and this dumped the conveyance over, skinning her elbows and knees. Renney didn't react quickly enough, ran into the old geezer, and banged him around pretty badly.

Michelle and Renney went home crying, and upon arrival found Henry in a foul mood, awaiting them. Old Graham had called and spoken with him.

Michelle got a couple of gruff words from her father and was sent to her room. Renney suffered the worst of this episode, as he did too frequently. Henry scolded him for reckless coasting, then embarked on a tangent and said "Yer growin' up to be a sissy, a momma's boy. Go out an' play baseball like a man."

From the stairway to her bedroom, Michelle heard her brother respond angrily, but couldn't make out all of the words.

She heard her father clearly, though. He was going wild, talking about "sissyboys" who eventually became something worse. He employed graphic terms, uttering a phrase so vile and suggestive that she thought about it a lot afterward, speculating on its meaning. She would never think of asking anyone for details, not even Mom. Rachel would describe anything anatomical that a person wanted to know, and often did so for Michelle's brothers. Such conversation embarrassed the girl.

Henry often insisted, but thus far not in Renney's presence, that the boy didn't resemble him in the least—in mannerisms or in appearance. The implication seemed obvious, in light of other facts Michelle had culled, for Renney was conceived during Moon War V. The question of the hour was whether it occurred during one of Dad's leaves or when he was away fighting.

Michelle felt certain that Renney was her legitimate full brother. He strongly resembled their Granpère Gilbert in the eyes, the nose, and the toothy farmboy grin—facts that Dad apparently refused to accept.

Michelle wondered if her brother might ever become homosexual, just to spite his father. That would be an attack on Henry's manhood, since Henry felt that real men did not sire such people. She hoped Renney didn't follow that course, because one rumor held that homosexuals were among the groups rounded up by the Special Purposes Police.

Michelle's first-period classroom was rectangular and low-ceilinged, with a raised platform on which the instructor stood. Mrs. Lovelace was a small silver-haired woman whose agitated, rasping demeanor kept Michelle in a constant state of disquiet. This was the worst class of the day for Michelle, and like a disliked entree she would have preferred facing it last.

Not that Michelle enjoyed her other classes. She didn't. She felt out of place, unattractive, and doltish for the most part—unable to cope with the pressures of curriculum and grade-school politics. She was an unpainted tramcar on a sidetrack, watching shiny express cars whiz by.

Mrs. Lovelace spoke into a tiny cone-shaped microphone which amplified her voice and sent it booming through speakers mounted in the ceiling near each individual student learning module.

Michelle's module, identical to the others, was an electronic study carrel having high walls on three sides and a little Plexiglas window in front that allowed her to see the instructor. The module had "eyes," a tiny corner camera that electronically graded the student's attentiveness in class. Students were graded down if they looked away from the instructor, doodled, chewed gum, wrote on the carrel walls, nodded off to sleep, passed notes, or engaged in other unapproved behavior.

A central computer connected to the learning modules recorded the curriculum taught that day and all student infractions. Twenty-five minutes of testing followed each thirty-minute lecture. During testing the carrel's Plexiglas window became a video screen, with multiple-choice questions printed on it. The student touched buttons from A to E for his answers, and had to receive a sixty percent score (along with a satisfactory attentiveness rating) to pass.

Failing students were assigned to after-school detention in the "bonehead" room, a scholastic dungeon where they listened to recorded lectures, behaved properly, and retested until they passed. On particularly dismal days Michelle had to retest as many as three classes, making her three hours late getting home. Somehow, despite her pitiful overall scholarship, Michelle was passed to the next grade at the conclusion of each semester.

She never asked why.

Jokingly, Michelle's classmates referred to the electronic carrels as "burning modules," since they were in effect hot boxes in which unwilling participants sweated until lessons were burned into their gray cells. Michelle couldn't find it in herself to enjoy the joke.

She wasn't stupid, and understood this despite the constant teasing she endured at the hands of other children. She found it difficult to concentrate at school because of the hunger pangs gnawing at her stomach, pangs that sent blocking signals to her brain. The inadequate diet left her perpetually weak, too. But she didn't complain to classmates anymore because that gave them information to use against her. Once she confided in a Hawaiian girl who seemed nice, and the girl spread the story of Michelle's single daily bran muffin around school. After that Michelle found scraps of food left by her locker—inedible things for the most part with cruel notes attached.

This was a Monday, and Mondays weren't too bad for Michelle. They usually followed a sumptuous Sunday dinner at Granmère's, and the reservoir of food energy often carried her through the next day. Fridays were the worst.

Sometimes though, even on Fridays, Michelle succeeded in overcoming her obstacles, and she would pass every test. She had to play little mind games with herself to accomplish this, and she wasn't always up to the task. Her most successful effort involved convincing herself that she was a mountain climber, out of food because of the arduous and lengthy climb she had endured. The peak was a short but steep distance above her, and she could conquer it only if she called upon a reservoir of strength available to her for special occasions. Sometimes the reserve was there and sometimes it wasn't, no matter what her fantasies.

Using this technique one midterm examination day (which happened to be a Friday), Michelle surprised the instructors and her classmates by testing higher than anyone else in every class. One instructor accused her of cheating. Then, seeing Michelle's tears and sincerity he apparently decided it must have been an incredible fluke—a lucky day in which she happened to guess correctly before pressing every button.

Another mind game she employed involved increasing her pain threshold, trying to convince her brain that there were no hunger signals emanating from her stomach. This worked on occasion, but usually for no more than a single class. Sometimes she thought about going to a doctor and asking to have herself hypnotized into thinking she was full, or about joining one of those oddball religious groups that taught people how to fast.

She couldn't go back to the same games time after time, day after day. Whenever she tried that, they failed to work. Her body had an aversion to being fooled the same way twice—at least during a short period of time. After the passage of months, she could return to an old method and again it worked passably well for her. So she was constantly searching for new methods of getting through each day, and this became such a

burden at times that she often gave up and fell into the old bonehead detention rut.

Once a tough boy who had just transferred into Michelle's school approached her in the hallway and demanded her lunch money. Another
hoodlum of his recent acquaintance happened by at the moment, and he
said, "Leave Fouquet alone. She never has any money."

FIVE

SUBJECT: Unauthorized Student Excursion, Ethical Considerations

FINDINGS: It is presumed that thousands of humans perished in the severance of the Earth coastline. Consider, however, all of the new oceanfront property created in the event: A big ocean bay resulted, one packed with choice waterfront parcels. This made innumerable survivors happy and wealthy, offsetting all death and damage. Additionally, compensating machinery was left in place on the planet, thus preventing rotational wobble. It was rebuilt machinery, however, and perhaps not the most reliable.

—From a classified report prepared for the Triumvirate of Arionn

While Michelle's schoolmates ate in the cafeteria or on the school grounds, she traipsed down the block to Rankin's General Store. Everyone at school that morning had been talking about the opaque weekend fog, and some knew about the peculiar I-wave broadcast announcing the imminent release of more information. Who would release the information and what was it? No one seemed to know, and Michelle was anxious to check the news cubes at Rankin's. She liked to go there anyway, as Mr. Rankin was a nice man who never asked her to stop loitering about the premises. Often she wondered how much he knew about her family.

The store was not large, but had been packed with a remarkable selection of foodstuffs, dry goods, hardware, and automotive products. Michelle suppressed her lunchtime hunger pangs as she passed the sidewalk fruit bins and went inside. She cast a quick glance at Mr. Rankin. A small mustachioed man wearing a green visor and a white apron, he was preoccupied with reading a computerized inventory screen by the counter and didn't look at her. She hurried by him, disappearing behind high stacks of canned goods. The magazine and news rack was at the rear.

This was unlike the super foodarama at which her father occasionally shopped. Unlike most grocery establishments, Rankin's had no bright neon displays, food sample dispensers, robot clerks, or electronic-eye price scanners. There were no voice-activated mechanical arms on the shopping carts either, Michelle thought as she scooted past a woman putting soup cans in her cart. If a person wanted something in Rankin's he had to reach it himself. The shopping carts had to be pushed too; they didn't follow the customers around. Father rarely shopped here. He said the prices were too high, and that Rankin sold old food.

The news cubes were being set up at that moment by a young black man in a navy blue jumpsuit, working between an electric cart he had brought in and a low metal store rack.

Michelle waited for him to finish.

Clear plastic and the size of a man's fist, each daily news cube was imprinted with magnifiable black lettering. The cubes clicked against one another as he unloaded superseded editions from the rack.

Michelle's father worked three jobs to make ends meet, so he didn't often have the energy to shop himself. Most of the time he turned the grocery money over to Rachel, and she promptly squandered it. Rankin's was the closest market to the house and to Michelle's school, so Michelle came here regularly on errands for her mother. Mom always telephoned her orders ahead, and when the girl arrived she asked for "Mrs. Fouquet's order." Always it was stapled shut across the top so that Michelle couldn't see what was inside. But she knew anyway.

Even after laboring at all of his jobs, Dad had to cook dinner every night. If there was little food on hand, Rachel lied to him, telling him the children had already eaten, and that "what was left" was for him. So he would prepare his own meal and eat while the children stared at him, watching every bite. Michelle believed her father wasn't very observant (possibly due to fatigue), or that he didn't have the energy to straighten the situation out. None of the children complained about this, not even Joseph, so perhaps Dad assumed that the situation wasn't too bad.

The man working at the news rack glanced down at Michelle, smiled. "I'll be out of your way in just a minute," he said.

Once in a while her mother forgot her game entirely, and Michelle heard

Dad yelling that there was no food for dinner. Whenever that happened he would either drive to the store himself or take the family to one of the budget-priced "all you can eat" restaurants, where the children ate as much as they did at Granmère's.

Michelle smiled at the thought of the restaurants they patronized. Those establishments never made money on the Fouquets. The children piled their plates in great mounds and kept going back for more, while the owner probably looked on from behind the scenes wringing his hands.

Why didn't the children tell their father when they were hungry? In part it was because each knew or sensed that he had enough problems. Beyond that they were afraid of incurring Mom's mercurial rage. She could do things to them when Dad wasn't around. As Michelle thought about it she realized her mother had never actually struck her or the other children. She threatened to, and once she chased Michelle and Joseph with a broom handle. But she never caught them, and her temper always subsided quickly. Still, Michelle feared her.

"You look like a smart little girl," the news vendor said as he completed his work and prepared to leave. "There's quite a story on those cubes." He lowered his voice. "It's why I'm running a little late. I read every word!"

"Oh," Michelle said. She felt uncomfortable talking with a black man. Her father hated people of that race, warned her never to date one when she grew older.

The man hurried away.

As Michelle reached for a cube, she heard the electric buzz of his cart. The buzz diminished, disappeared, and she held the news cube at arm's length, pressing a tiny button on one side.

It was as if she were looking into an illuminated little black-on-clear world, and as Michelle's eyes focused she saw the front page of the *Bay Daily News*, growing easier to read as her eyes adapted. She had heard that the magnifying light cast from the cube did something to a reader's pupils that made it possible to read microdot-sized pages. She wondered why it didn't hurt.

The story she wanted was at the top of page one, in the upper-left-hand corner of one cube face, which now seemed tremendously large to her:

NO WAY IN OR OUT
DID PLANE CRASH INTO SHIELD?

The lead story, spread across six columns, began: "Linda McKay wasn't going to be confined. Yesterday after walking along one perimeter of the mysterious tule fog that engulfed our region and finding a smooth barrier there, she decided to fly over it. While transmitting details by I-wave from a single-seater VTOL plane, she suddenly went off the air.

"This is but one of numerous confirmations that the San Francisco Bay Area is surrounded by a mysterious opaque shield. With fog still thick in outlying areas near the shield, military authorities have set up roadblocks to keep the curious away. There are no known openings in the barrier, which even extends to the sea and to the air above us. All air, sea, and land traffic has been confined, and there is no confirmation of any contact with the President of the United States."

Michelle took a deep breath. She half-heard voices in another part of the store and read on:

"Can the shield be penetrated? Who is responsible for its existence and how does it work? Why was it put in place? Speculation is rampant. One rumor receiving attention holds that survivalists in our region got wind of an impending quark holocaust and initiated a secret plan to protect the area. Is the rest of the world, perhaps even the rest of the star system, dead and barren? Maybe these aren't survivalists in our camp at all. Maybe they initiated the conflagration . . ."

Michelle recalled her theory that an enemy force had conquered the region and located a paragraph mentioning this possibility.

She was beginning to read a tiny feature box postulating that the affair might be a massive practical joke when the snooty voice of a woman cut in:

"Don't play with the cubes, little girl. You'll burn out their power supplies."

Michelle wanted to argue with the woman, telling her that news cubes received continuous power from a central transmitter, and that furthermore Mr. Rankin didn't mind her being here. But the voice was so authoritarian, so reminiscent of her grandmother's, that Michelle obeyed. With only an unfocused glance up (eyes that have been reading news cubes took two or three seconds to return to normal), Michelle trudged away. She didn't want to risk irritating Mr. Rankin (who might side with a paying adult), as that could prevent Michelle from coming here on her lunch breaks. Then she would have to watch the other children eat, or find a new place to hide from them.

It was early afternoon beneath a gray sky, and Henry was in the midst of his second job of the day, delivering parcels in the Balboa district. He had arranged this job through the same union responsible for his Lawservice duties, but this was a more prestigious situation, available to him by virtue of his seniority. He had been in the local for twenty-three years, eighteen of which were in various delivery support duties leading to this position. He was proud to hold it, but sometimes wished it paid more. Rachel's medical bills were staggering, and for a variety of reasons he had failed to obtain medical coverage for anyone in the family.

In truth, the ParSell delivery van was fully automated. This made him something of a monitor, although he carried no weapon. The vehicle had bells that rang constantly, like those of an ice cream wagon. When inside its territory it stopped every few hundred meters and gave off a rather pleasant chiming melody. It did this now as Henry sat smartly in a powder blue uniform and cap in the single front seat, and he knew that the large octagonal readerboard atop the roof listed the addresses of those persons on this block who had packages inside. These were products that had been ordered and paid for through computer, radio, or television terminals.

Henry counted off ten orangutan seconds, one of his diversions, then slid open the door beside him and stepped onto the running board. This was a conveyor that carried him along the side and around the back of the vehicle to the rear cargo door, which was activated by photographic identity scanners to open at Henry's presence. It slid up, revealing a small pile of packages on a shelf in the foreground, next to a robot arm that had placed them there for this block. Each package bore a luminous name and address tag, which tied it in electronically with the readerboard.

A small cluster of housewives gathered around the rear of the van, which had stopped in one of the wide street's two center lanes, separate from the parking and Lawservice strips that were closer to the sidewalks on each side. One of the women, a tall and bony lady in her fifties, smiled and bid Henry a good day.

He doffed his cap to her.

This was one of his nicer customers—a Mrs. McDuff or McSomething— he wasn't good at names, and the rooftop readerboard didn't indicate them. It was on the package just beyond his line of sight and on the luminous orange and black identification card she held up for the van's robot eyes to read.

Thinking he might like to get to know her better, Henry tried to read her card. But she put it away before he could do so, and off she went with her package.

Henry's affairs, which he could count on the fingers of one hand, didn't last long. The longest had been four months, with Stu's mother Marie on a

National Air Service stratobase. That had been the last, nearly fourteen years ago, and sometimes he lameted lost opportunities, those signals that he had overlooked and thought back on later. He was getting older and slower, losing what touch he ever had.

As each woman identified herself to the automated delivery van, the robot arm thrust forth a package. Looking up at the readerboard, Henry watched the addresses disappear. Soon it was down to one and there were no more people. The robot arm lifted the remaining parcel to a holding bin for redelivery another day, and the cargo door slid closed.

Noticing a tan and yellow diamond-printed glove on the pavement, Henry stepped from the running board and retrieved it. He had seen Mrs. McSomething with it, and looked toward her dwelling, a small blue and white bungalow constructed on a narrow lot. She was just shutting the door behind her, so Henry didn't call out. He didn't know her name anyway.

Henry scuffled between two parked cars and then across the Lawservice lane. At the top of her stairs, he returned the glove to the woman with a polite tip of his cap. She appeared genuinely surprised that it was missing, so that hadn't been a signal.

As he walked ponderously across the Lawservice lane, the angry, high-pitched beep of an approaching mini-van startled him into motion. He scurried across the lane, just in time to avoid being hit by a Lawserver he didn't know, a burly woman who glared at him.

He shrugged the incident off, climbed back into his ParSell van.

"Nothing can slow the process of the Law," the saying went. One in seven persons, including himself, worked in the legal profession or in a support capacity.

Support capacity, Henry thought, slumping into the seat and sliding the door shut. *Sometimes I think I support the whole goddam world. Oh to let somebody else do my work for a change! I'd like to sit back and drink a tall cool one!*

As these thoughts occurred to him, he felt anger toward his mother, his wife, and his children. They had boxed him in, in one way or another. His father deserved blame as well, in Henry's estimation, for the old man did virtually nothing to control the relentless, stubborn pressure of Liliane.

In thought he slipped into his alternate dialect, a dialect that allowed him to think things that would not normally have occurred to him. He enjoyed this dialect for the mental release it imparted:

Counceywoman Fouquet is comin'! Ebberyt'ing in its proper place! Prepare fer a fuckin' white glub inspekshun! Sic 'er, Bumper, sic 'er! What da hell

kin' of a guard dog are ya, anyhoo? Yer supposed ta protect da master of da
house, dammit!

On her way home from school that afternoon, Michelle saw Stu Kroemer
on the other side of the street, coming out of an alley. He noticed her
simultaneously, and after waiting for a truck to pass he ran across to her.

"Hey," Stu said. "How ya doin'?"

Michelle absorbed the boy's appearance. Although barely her height he
was a bit older than she, she guessed, with long black hair that shone
greasily. The eyes were small and dark, beneath black brows. He had a
tough, street-wise look to him, and walked with a pronounced bounce to
each step.

"Hi," she said.

"You don't talk much, huh?" Stu rubbed an earlobe between his thumb
and forefinger.

Michelle laughed. "I talk too much sometimes. To be honest, I was
thinking about the way you walk and look."

"You don't like it?" The tone was challenging.

"No, it's not that at all. You don't . . . well, you don't seem like the type
who goes to school."

"Right on, girl. I learn my lessons out here, not in a stuffy classroom. I'm
what they call a road kid. I survive on the scraps of society when I have to,
pick up jobs where I can. Scrounger yes, thief and punk no. Louisiana Kid,
I like to call myself." He caught her gaze, added, "I don't sell my body to
perverts, either."

"Well, that's good," Michelle said, not knowing what else to say.

They looked at one another as they continued along the sidewalk, and
Michelle thought she detected something vaguely familiar in the boy's ap-
pearance, something she couldn't quite identify. But he was from the
South, so far away.

"Have you ever been in San Francisco before?" she asked. "You look
familiar."

"Naw, this is the first time."

I ought to look familiar! Stu thought. *I'm your half-brother!* He wanted to
tell her, felt the secret eating away at him. He suppressed the urge.

"Since you're going to be staying with us a while," Michelle said, "I
should inform you that my family is not ordinary. It's . . . well, bizarre, to
put it bluntly. Some of the things my parents do . . ."

"I've already noticed," Stu offered. "Your mom has problems."

"So does Dad. My parents act funny. We mimic them sometimes. It helps us stay sane when everything seems to be coming apart. When Dad's real tired or upset he mispronounces a lot of words, and talks like a space-dockman who didn't graduate high school. Actually he attended three years at an excellent university. Mom graduated from a university, even did some work toward her master's."

"Let me guess. In English?"

"Right."

"Figures, with the way your dad talks sometimes. A perfect mismatch, where each one grates on the other."

"That's part of it, and my grandmother has her influence on the whole thing, as you'll learn. Mom isn't always sharp because of the medication she takes. But every once in a while she lets loose something so brilliant that everyone is astounded."

"She was humming and rubbing her nose kinda weird like when I left this morning. Up here along the bridge," he said, demonstrating. "It gave me the willies."

Michelle laughed, then felt guilty for having done so. "She goes into herself sometimes. Other times she tries to scare people she thinks are threatening her. They're her ways of surviving." Michelle's features tightened. "It's pretty complicated."

"Isn't everything."

"Dad's not home a lot," Michelle said.

At a corner they waited for a walk signal. An elderly man was pressing the big pole-mounted signal button, cursing the lethargy of the light.

Stu became impatient and ran across.

Michelle followed.

Behind her, the driver of a truck honked at the old man, who was scuttling across rather inefficiently. Michelle watched the oldster, made certain he made it to the sidewalk before she resumed her conversation.

She spoke of her father's three jobs, of the doctor's bills and the lack of medical insurance.

"Three jobs?" Stu said. "He works around the clock?"

"It's bad, but not quite that bad. Only one of the jobs is full time . . . delivering parcels Monday through Saturday. Before that each day and on Saturdays too he's a Lawserver. That takes a couple of hours every day. Then in the evenings on Mondays, Wednesdays, and Fridays he's on a semi-pro wrist wrestling team. My dad's naturally very strong, and he gets paid for doing that. I don't see how he manages, he seems so tired sometimes. But he does, and says he enjoys the matches. He wins most of the time. The matches are by age group, you know. I go and watch when I can."

"Do they use those giant arm extensions?"

"Yes. The extenders in his league are around thirty meters from elbow to hand, I think."

"Those matches are really something. I've seen them on TV."

"My dad's league doesn't get televised, so he doesn't make a lot of money at it. His matches are in big arenas, though."

Natural strength, huh, the boy thought. *I'm pretty strong myself, in a wiry way.*

"Dad swears a lot," Michelle said matter of factly. "I've learned to tune it out. He grew up in the Castro district, a rough part of town."

"That so?"

"Granmère made him wear French knickers to public school. Fancy shorts, if you can imagine, and white lace shirts that were more like girls' blouses. He had to be able to take care of himself dressed like that."

They crossed a grassy lot, following a well-worn trail that ran along a high board fence. She asked him not to reveal what she had told him, and he promised not to do so.

Presently Stu said, "I don't know how long I'm staying with you, but I'll tell you this: if anybody teases you or gives you a bum time, let me know. I'll take care of 'em for you." He hesitated, smiled stiffly and added, "I don't mean your mother. She looks too tough for anybody. I'm talkin' about kids . . . people your age."

"Thanks, but I don't think . . ."

"I don't necessarily mean beat 'em up," Stu said, interpreting her tone. "Lotta times there's better answers." He removed a small red plastic case from his jacket pocket. "This, for example."

Michelle studied the case curiously as Stu stopped and flipped it open, the hinged top swinging back. A little clear glass vial of brown liquid was inside. When he held the vial up to the light, Michelle saw that it had an applicator sponge immersed in the liquid, attached to the underside of the lid.

"A dab of this in the right place and whattaya know," Stu said. "Hair within fifteen minutes. I put it on a guy's nose once." He spun the lid to unscrew it.

Michelle stepped back. "Keep away from me with that junk!" she exclaimed. They were on Balboa Street, on a block paralleling the Special

Purposes lockup building near her house. She could see the upper stories of the structure above housetops and business roofs behind Stu.

He laughed, tightened the lid, and replaced the vial in its case. "I'm kind of a joker," he admitted. "You'll find that out about me. The stuff's harmless, anyway. The hair falls off within forty-eight hours."

"Your victims must spend a lot of time in closets."

"Some. I got this dude mail order. It's good for moustaches, too, whenever I want to look older and meaner than I am."

"I see."

They resumed walking, and Stu slipped the case into his pocket. "Does Dad," he said, ". . . your dad, I mean . . . knock you around?"

"No. He's as tough as they come but he's never hit us. Whenever we get on his wrong side he makes us pull weeds. Joseph has nightmares about weeds."

They walked in silence for a time, and as they neared home Mrs. Meley's black cat began to accompany them. Being familiar with the animal, Michelle warned Stu about it. The creature had an annoying habit of walking briskly beside a person and then crossing the person's path so suddenly and tightly as to trip him up if he didn't constantly apprise himself of its location.

Even after the warning, Stu nearly fell victim.

As they were laughing about this, Joseph caught up with them. Bulky of muscle and nearly six feet tall, he towered over his sister and Stu. Joseph appeared uneasy to Michelle as he made small talk with her, and she surmised that Stu's presence was the reason. Joseph, in his protective way, didn't like having this unrelated boy living in the same house with his sister.

Michelle was correct, for Joseph's mind was racing as he spoke. To make matters worse, Michelle and this intruder were laughing when he encountered them. They seemed to like one another. Joseph glared down at Stu, and felt from a brief locking of their gazes that Stu perceived the threat and concern. This was a tough-looking little punk, Joseph decided. One who might carry a weapon. Joseph wished his father had not allowed the boy to live with them. Their family was unstable enough as it was. An outside influence such as this could send everything tumbling down.

Joseph wasn't paying attention to the black cat, which now pranced beside his left ankle. Suddenly it darted across his boot tops, tripping him. Cursing, he fell to one knee. The laughter that ensued sent rage boiling through Joseph. He stood and administered a jolting kick to the feline's side.

The animal squealed in surprised protest, ran a short distance off, beyond the range of Joseph's boots.

"You shouldn't have done that!" Michelle exclaimed. She ran to the wounded cat, knelt, and reached for it. It backed off a step, then waited, trembling. Michelle ran a hand caressingly through the fur on its back, felt a shudder course through its little body.

"You've hurt it," she said angrily. She glared up at Joseph, who stood to one side. Joseph's dark brown eyes reflected a paradox of emotion. She saw parental hardness there, of the Granmère Liliane variety, along with a degree of confusion and vulnerability.

"That was a terrible thing to do, Joseph," Michelle said, her tone scolding. "I don't like you anymore!"

As Joseph stalked off, she could not recall her last argument with him, despite their difference of perspective concerning Mom. This was Joseph's fault, she told herself. He shouldn't have kicked the cat. As she delved into the seriousness of the breach with her brother, she recognized Stu's part in it. Joseph was being overprotective, behaving foolishly. He had taken out his frustrations on a small animal.

Soon the cat was purring in Michelle's hands. But when she let it go and walked with Stu the short distance remaining to her house, the creature was up to its old tricks.

Michelle had been home from school for less than a half hour. With Stu off in another part of the house, she stood on the back porch, leaning over a full plastic sack of garbage that she had just opened. Their public disposal system being partially blocked, they could only get the smallest, smelliest items into it. These things in the sack were the bigger items, to be hauled off periodically by Dad's friend Phil Cartucci, who had a pickup truck. Michelle made certain the bags were kept sealed and also sprayed the area with bug killer and disinfectant, which Dad bought directly from another friend. It didn't smell too bad here now, and there were only a few flies. It was worse in summer, when the days were warmer.

With a little picking through the contents she withdrew a clear glass liquor bottle and read the red label. It was Bug Juice (Snowfly Extract), like the bottle Granmère had found in Rachel's purse. The label had a snow-covered mountain on it, and for diversion Michelle never tired of reading the explanatory label on the back:

Snowfly Extract is taken from the bloodstream of a certain species of snowfly that uses alcohol as its antifreeze. The particular insect we favor is laboratory-fed on the sweetest, tastiest airborne pollens known to man or snowfly. The unique patented flavor of our sectohol cannot be duplicated by any competitor. And our selective filtering method guarantees absolute purity while retaining those ingredients necessary for flavor. Accept no substitutes.

50 PROOF

Michelle often wondered how pure Bug Juice really was, or if it contained bug parts . . . wings, leg fragments, mashed brains. Selective filtering. What did that mean?

As Michelle considered this, she heard someone behind her. Startled, she stuffed the bottle back in the garbage, then looked back. To her relief, it was Stu.

"Havin' a snort?" Stu asked.

"Certainly not! Keep your voice down. Mom's napping in the living room."

"Yeah, I saw her." Stu hadn't lowered his voice. "She's lights out. On that stuff?" He gestured toward the refuse sack.

Michelle nodded. "Probably."

"I've had Bug Juice myself," the boy said matter-of-factly. "Lots of people drink it."

"Yeah. Skid row bums."

"That brand isn't so bad. I've had it myself. You should try it. There might be a little left in the bottle." He reached into the sack, retrieved it. "Sure enough," he said, holding the bottle to eye level.

Michelle saw a small quantity of clear liquid in the container. Impulsively, she took it from Stu and lifted it to her lips. After only the briefest hesitation she poured the sectohol across the top of her tongue and swallowed. For an instant her throat and sinuses burned. It had a sweet, aromatic aftertaste.

"Not so bad," she said.

Stu jammed the bottle back in the trash, located the wire tie, and tied the sack shut. "Don't want my bedroom to smell bad," he said, with a wink.

Michelle told him about the spray cans and showed him where they were kept on a bottom shelf.

She experienced a giddy sensation, the way she felt occasionally at Granmère's house after drinking the small glass of diluted French table wine that Michelle, Renney, and Joseph were allowed to have. It was a traditional old country practice, and afterward while the adults talked she and Renney would confide to one another how drunk they were, comparing silly symptoms. The children had to speak with the utmost of discretion, for stodgy old Granmère did not tolerate overt displays.

As Michelle stood on the back porch with all of its informality she didn't have to worry about "stodgy old Granmère." That was Rachel's term for the old woman, and in Michelle's opinion it fit perfectly. No prancing about in drunken silliness at Granmère's house. No sir, not there! But here, in this falling-apart wreck of a home with her mother asleep . . . why not? With a burst of enthusiasm Michelle threw open the screen door and clattered down the shaded wooden staircase to the back yard.

"Where are you going?" Stu called out.

"I'm a snowfly!" came the response, gleefully. Michelle extended her arms to each side as if they were wings and waved them up and down as she skipped across the weed-infested, mole-mounded grass. "I can't go in the sun! Snowflies melt in the sun!"

While Stu sat on the steps and watched bemusedly, Michelle dodged sunbeams and ran around in the house, fence, and tree shadows. She flattened herself against one side of the rickety board fence that encompassed the yard and moved within a narrow band of shadow there, stepping gingerly on dead flowers and high weeds. Seeing no way across a sunlight-splashed section of fence, she turned back.

"That one almost got you!" Stu shouted from the steps. "Flee, snowfly! Flee!"

Fluttering her arms desperately, Michelle leaped across a nearly dead azalea bush and landed face down on a sunny stretch of grass. "I'm dead," she moaned.

She shriveled and twisted her face, turning onto her back with her arms and legs extended upward, in the manner of cartoon pictures she had seen of dead bugs. But now as she thought about it, Michelle realized that few of the cockroaches, fleas, or flies she had seen around the house died in this fashion. They died on their sides, or on their stomachs with their feet crushed beneath them, having been smashed by shoes or rolled magazines.

She heard footsteps on the porch, and the pig squeal of the screen door.

"It's Beauregard!" Michelle wailed without looking. "Come to jump on me and mash me!" She screamed and rolled away.

"Such a pleasant day. The sun is back." It was her mother's nasal voice. "Why, Michelle, what are you doing down there?" Her tone became openly hostile: "Get up here and find my Biblecorder for me, right this instant!"

"Yes, Mother," Michelle said abashedly as she jumped to her feet. Leaving fantasy behind, she trudged up the steps past Stu and slid by her mother into the house.

It took Michelle ten minutes to locate the Biblecorder, which settled her mother down. By that time all of Michelle's giddiness had worn away. She remembered her homework reading assignment, which she wanted to get out of the way before dinner.

"Who's Beauregard?" Stu asked. He and Michelle were on the second level, outside the door to her bedroom.

She told of the seven-foot flea purportedly living in their midst. "Joseph knows a lot about Bo," she said. "He tells us about Bo when it's dark, but Renney gets scared and covers his ears. He's more afraid of Bo than any of us."

Then she said, mimicking Joseph's voice: "According to legend, a giant flea named Beauregard inhabits the dirtiest region on Earth . . . our house. We've created the perfect breeding ground for the heinous creature. Beauregard is as tall as a door and can open his ferocious jaws wide enough to eat a small child in one gulp. Because he doesn't like to be seen, no one should search for him . . ."

She cleared her throat, spoke normally. "It goes on like that. Mom started the whole Beauregard thing when she said he was a Confederate Civil War general whose spirit was tormented by the battles he lost. I used to think she made it up from something she read in a book but I'm not so sure anymore. Once I heard a strange man's voice in my room while I was out in the hallway. And . . . like in an old movie . . . the click of a gun hammer being cocked, and a sword swishing through the air."

"You were on Bug Juice that day."

"No, I wasn't. Today was my first time."

"Then somebody left a tape recorder in there. Joseph maybe, since he likes to tell stories. I understand tricks like that, you know."

"I don't think it was a trick. Mom is . . . well, tuned in to things we can't always see or hear." She laughed nervously. "Maybe it was just my imagination." She nodded her head briskly. "Yes, I'm certain that was it!"

Stu detected an element of fear in the girl's voice. He was trying to formulate something to say when she said, "I have to study. I'm not doing well at school. Today I don't feel as drained as I often do, so I'd better take advantage."

After she went into her bedroom and shut the door behind her, Stu explored the littered house. From the top level of the bedroom "wing" he marveled at the worst floorplan he had ever seen. Michelle had mentioned something about the home's floorplan modification system being stuck, and that it remained like this because of a lack of funds. The top level had a bathroom and a single bedroom (Coley's), reached via an extruded plastic staircase that was only partially carpeted and had several cracked, dangerous-looking steps that he skipped over during ascent. It smelled strongly of urine in Coley's room, but that didn't bother him. He had lived in dirty places before.

There were clothes and broken toys scattered all over the toddler's quarters. A crumpled and torn rollup shade lay on the floor beneath the window, having fallen there some considerable time before, since now it looked like an archeological artifact. An overflowing cardboard box full of paper trash and toy remnants rested atop one side of it, leaning back against the wall. All four drawers of the blue and red dresser were partially open and overhung with stained, torn clothing. A doll whose rubber face and body had been scribbled over with crayons lay on the dresser top, one arm in the top drawer. The crib had once been fancy, perhaps a gift from the rich grandmother he'd heard about. It didn't look recent, probably had been handed down from one child to another. The crib had a matronly "storytelling nanny" hooked to one side. There was a bead-tipped cord on one side of the nanny's head that the child could pull to hear a story, but the cord hung extended and limp, as if the whole mechanism were jammed. Like the doll, the nanny's face was scribbled over.

Stu pulled the nanny cord, confirming the inoperability of the device.

Ignoring the powerful ammonia redolence of urine, Stu crawled under the crib to examine the nanny, pushing dirty diapers and broken pieces of plastic out of the way. These were longtime dirty diapers, dry and crusted with baby excrement. As Stu popped away a panel beneath the nanny, he decided that Coley no longer wore diapers. She looked to be four or five years old.

Stu used a long thin piece of scrap plastic to push a trip lever on the side of the nanny's clear plastic voicebox mechanism. He heard the cord snap itself free of obstacles as it rolled back into the unit.

One side of the voicebox held a cassette cartridge, and Stu pressed a button marked "Eject" to pop it out.

"Goldilocks and the Three Aliens," he said, reading the cassette. He grunted.

A small shelf by the cassette orifice held two more cassettes. Upon investigation Stu discovered that one was another fairytale, while the second was designated "Parent's Favorite Stories." In fine print beneath that, Stu read instructions for recording on the blank tape.

This was better than he had hoped for, for it was now unnecessary to modify an existing tape.

Following the instructions with an increasing sense of prankster's glee, he pressed down the green lever on the voicebox, marked "RECORD." He popped the recordable cartridge in, then crawled out from under the crib. Standing by the nanny, he pulled her cord to full extension, keeping it all the way out as he spoke.

"Grrr!" Stu said, in a deep voice calculated not to sound like his own. "I'm Beauregard the Monster and I'm gonna get you! No more wetting the bed, do you hear me you little shit? Clean up this pigpen, Coley Fouquet, or I'll bite off one of your legs!"

The story, if it could be called that, went on in this vein for nearly fifteen minutes, interspersed with Stu's wildest, most macabre beast sounds, threats, and epithets.

When he was finished Stu let the cord roll back, then flipped up the green voicebox lever. Then he listened to his story. Each new pull of the cord continued the recording where it had left off. Reaching the end, Stu thought of something to add. He was about to reset the mechanism when Coley sauntered in, carrying a one-armed doll.

"This is *my* room," she announced, authoritatively.

"Sorry," Stu said, sliding around her and backing out the doorway. "Look, Coley!" He pointed toward the crib. "I think Nanny wants to tell you a story."

"My nanny works again?" The child's eyes were open wide. She climbed over the low side rail and into the crib, seating herself by the matronly, scribble-obscured face.

Stu ran, cackling gleefully when he saw Coley reach for the cord.

SIX

The Henry Fouquet family, like virtually every other family in the Bay Area, huddled in front of the LCD television set, awaiting the six P.M. broadcast that had been promised so mysteriously the evening before. The TV hung low and a little crookedly on one wall. It was shortly before the appointed time, with Coley whining that she wanted to watch cartoons.

Renney told her to shut up, and Michelle listened with impatience as two local anchormen speculated on the contents of the broadcast. In their opinion, a military authority would appear to declare martial law for one reason or another. All military officials in the region had been refusing press inquiries.

Henry, puffing on a cigar and taking occasional sips from a tall can of budget beer, concurred in mutters with this viewpoint. He was plopped on his big recliner at the room's center, commanding the best view of the nearly flat television. Slumped in a dozing position on the couch, Rachel had only a partial view that she didn't seem intent on using. She slipped in and out of consciousness, emitting great sleepy snorts that drowned out some of the words of the anchormen. Joseph was cross-legged on the floor by his father, while Michelle, Renney, Stu, and even Coley sprawled bellies down before the set, their faces resting on elbow-supported palms.

Each vehicle that passed on the busy thoroughfare outside shook the walls and sent dark interference lines horizontally across the screen. Michelle could estimate the size of the vehicle by the amount of interference. Buses and large trucks caused the most havoc, and it was during the passage of one of these that the anchormen concluded their remarks.

Through the filter of the horizontal lines, Michelle saw the outline and then increasing detail of a gigantic building in the shape of a golfball with dimpled, black concave windows. The picture became clear again.

"What the hell?" Henry exclaimed, lurching forward on his seat so suddenly that he slopped beer on himself. "That's in the Mission district, right next to the Warehouse of Thingamajigs or sumpthin'. I was by there yesterday, and there was a bunch o' ol' hotels an' junk right where that big building is!"

"Maybe you were driving with your eyes closed," Rachel said, from her sideline position.

Turning so that she stretched the muscles in her lower back, Michelle looked up and saw her father glaring at her mother, his jaw firm and his lips curled in over the teeth. His large eyes bulged at her, and he had a way of leaning toward an adversary that said with body language what he couldn't think fast enough to vocalize.

"I ain't ravin'," he snapped. "I tell you, I know what I'm talkin' about!"

But Rachel's eyes were heavy-lidded and she peered straight ahead without response, toward the fireplace mantel beyond Henry's chair. Michelle wondered if her mother might be thinking about one or more of the family pictures that crowded the mantel, some in front of others. Rachel's eyes closed and Michelle looked back at the set.

She heard her father's chair squeak as he settled back into it.

Something was happening around the golfball building—golden aircraft were coming out of hatches near the top, flying down toward news cameras that were projecting from positions near the base of the structure. The aircraft looked so small and so distant that Michelle was struck anew with the immensity of the building.

Henry's chair squeaked again, and out of the corner of her eyes Michelle saw that he was sitting on the edge, a perplexed expression on his face.

"That hummer's hundreds of stories high!" he said.

Michelle counted six bubble-shaped flying ships, descending in a nearly perfect horizontal line, like fat golden bees but without discernible wings or control surfaces. As they neared, Michelle saw that they were small, with flat bottoms and curving windshields. Seconds later they were within a few meters of the cameras, setting down in the midst of a big concrete plaza that was rimmed with ponds, fountains, and small trees in planter boxes. Now Michelle could see a noseless gray face behind each windshield. One on which she focused had two eyes, and the eyes were odd—full of dots, it seemed. The mouth (set in the approximate position of a human mouth) was small, but with thick, red-veined lips.

"Some kinda robot deal," Henry said. He took a swig of beer.

Dark interference lines and a static crackle threatened to steal the reception, and Michelle estimated that three or four large vehicles were passing on the street by her house in close succession. She heard the roar of big engines, and when the engine noises faded the picture cleared.

Each craft had landed, and they now formed a neat line. Then in near synchronization two sides and the front of each ship swung open like inverted tulip petals, revealing creatures that were the precise shapes of their enclosures and very nearly as large. They were bee-fat and nearly round, except for a flat lower portion from which protruded a number of exceedingly short legs. Michelle could not count the number of legs, but saw three across the front and more behind those. A dozen, maybe. She discerned no arms.

The front portion of each ship became a ramp, and the single inhabitant of each scurried the short distance to ground level. Cameras recording the event switched back and forth to show different angles.

"Is the movie on yet?" Rachel asked, drowsily.

"Shadup, Raich," Henry growled. "They're robots, just like I told ya."

The snoutless creatures did look something like robots to Michelle, but they moved with a fluidity she didn't think such devices had. Their eyes were most intriguing. Each socket held an ovular collection of what looked like multicolored atoms from someone's physics experiment. She couldn't tell in which direction the eyes were looking, and it occurred to her that they might be multipupiled, capable of focusing in several directions at once. Their bulbous bodies were an off shade of white, and upon closer examination she detected the fabric lines of one-piece, nearly featureless suits. She theorized that these suits protected the mechanical men against corrosion.

Michelle realized suddenly that the television set had no sound whatsoever, and that it had been silent since the announcers went off the air. Inside the ships that were more like shells than ships she saw no instrumentation on exposed surfaces and no concealed spaces that might hold rocket engines.

Mechanical men? Why not *women?* But men seemed a more comfortable category to Michelle, although she discerned no identifiable sexual features whatsoever and certainly robots were asexual by definition. Unless they were androids. Michelle hardly ever though of such matters, and surprised herself by instantly calling forth the proper terminology. She had learned about androids in a movie, but androids without arms? She found herself stretching to the limits of her restricted knowledge and experience, trying to fit her observations into comfortable niches.

There was nothing comfortable about this scene. The robot men stood silently, looking straight into the main bank of cameras with those damned weird atom eyes. Michelle didn't see any ears. Unless those sets of portholes on each side of the head were ears. She counted three holes to a side, lined up horizontally with the ground. Weren't androids supposed to resemble humans in appearance and function?

What else could they be?

One of the robot men at the side showed that he did have arms. Two of them, with oddly elongated hands. The arms popped out from right and left side compartments that had been invisible to Michelle. She saw no elbows, but there was a compensating pliability to the arms. She counted six fingers that also were pliable on each of two hands and watched as one set of fingers reached into a marsupial front pouch below the protruding belly line and withdrew an irregularly shaped black plate. The robot man held it in front of himself, just beneath his veiny lips. Then he let go, and the plate remained suspended in the air.

The television set began to transmit background noises. Engine sounds came from somewhere in the distance, and she identified the smooth, flowing sound of a turnpike. Someone near the camera spoke in a low, inaudible tone—probably one of the reporters or cameramen.

Then the maw began to move, making odd, pliable shapes. Unsynchronized words issued forth, in coordination with deaf-mute-type hand and finger gesticulations. The words were loud and in precise English diction: "I will be succinct. Time, despite the technological advances of my people, remains a finite commodity, one to be managed with utmost care. This is an announcement only. No questions will be entertained."

Michelle decided that the curious black plate was a translator or amplifier. She began to have doubts that these were robots or androids, and recognized the voice. It was the one that had come across the I-wave transceiver, through fog the night before.

She thought again about the apparent lack of ears. Maybe that was why they would entertain no questions, if they couldn't hear. A silly, facetious thought, she realized. This was a serious situation.

"The black sheet of alloy suspended before me is a finely tuned lighter-than-air translating mechanism, enabling you Earthers to understand my words. We are Arionnese—students at the City College of Grappus, to be more precise. This portion of Earth known to you as the San Francisco Bay Area is no longer of Earth. That is to say, it is a fully enclosed experimental habitat traveling under its own power through what you refer to as deep space."

"Jumpin' Jehozephat!" Henry said.

Michelle saw him glance at Rachel, and now Rachel appeared to be fully alert, leaning to one side to get a better view of the television screen. Her expression was intent.

"We are going to be in space for an additional twenty-four Earth days," the spokesman said. "Traveling to Arionn. That is the principal planet of my people. Let me assure you of one thing. You are in no direct danger from us. We mean you no harm, and apologize should misfortune befall you."

"Thanks a lot," Henry said. "Students? That's all the hell we need. A pack o' alien hippies callin' the shots."

"Barring an unforeseen catastrophe, we do not plan to alter your lives. You may go about your daily tasks as you always have. Your system of local government is essentially unchanged. State, national, and solar governments have of necessity been interrupted. For that reason those taxes will no longer be collected."

"What a crock," Henry said, taking an angry tug on his cigar.

"Many of you experienced slight sensations of motion sickness when we lifted off yesterday, and for a few of you this feeling has not entirely passed. We apologize for this discomfiture."

"Look at that creep's mouth," Henry said. "He ain't got no teeth."

Michelle saw her father's gaze dart toward Rachel. For the most flickering of moments Michelle thought she detected remorse in his face, as if he regretted hurting Rachel's feelings with the comment. Rachel didn't have many teeth left to lose. But the woman appeared not to notice and stared straight ahead at the photographs lining the top of the fireplace mantel. She seemed suspended in the wreckage of her life, transfixed by pictures of the past and mental images of the way things might have been.

We're being hurtled into the future, Mama, Michelle thought, feeling great tears coming on. *Can you understand that?*

Michelle looked back at the screen.

"Every business on this habitat will discover that it can reorder any product it has obtained in the past. I speak of food, merchandise, and any other commodity characteristic of your civilization—whether or not such articles have been generated in this region in the past. An artificial billing system has been established, since we don't need your money. Merchants will have to pay for goods nonetheless, and we will employ collection agents if necessary. You will never notice the difference."

"I'll notice," Henry snarled. "I ain't your damn fool."

"He's talking about shopkeepers and middlemen, Daddy," Renney said. "People who do the ordering."

"Shadup an' run to your mother," Henry said.

"We will now switch to our own cameras for a spaceside view."

In a fraction of a second, Michelle saw the Golden Gate Bridge, Alcatraz Island, and the high-rise buildings of San Francisco (including the massive golfball-shaped one) through what looked like refracted glass, looking down. Scattered clouds drifted in the sky, and they looked peculiar seen from above.

"There should have been a warning before this show," Rachel said, her tone nasal and tinged with displeasure. "This could frighten a lot of small children."

"This is *real*, Mom," Renney said. "It's not a movie."

"Real?"

"Shadup, bowda yuz," Henry snapped.

The television screen darkened. Presently the pair of news anchormen was back on, making observations about what they had just witnessed. They referred to the alien structure as "the Arionn Building."

"You were kidding, right, Renney?" Rachel said, her voice cracking. "This isn't real, is it?"

"I told the truth, Mom," Renney said.

Glancing back, Michelle saw the most worried expression she could recall on her mother's face. Renney must have seen it too, for he went to sit by Rachel on the couch. Michelle wished she could share the special position in Mom's heart that Renney dominated, in order to help her. It was the position Michelle held with their father, and she would share gladly with

Renney if Renney would do the same. But that didn't seem likely, for Renney and Dad were galaxies apart—much farther apart it seemed than Michelle and her mother, despite the barriers Rachel constructed.

"This isn't real, is it?" Rachel said again.

Again Henry told her to shut up.

Finally Michelle interjected. "No, Mom. It's make-believe. You're right. It isn't suitable for children. It's terrible, some of the programs they put on nowadays."

As Michelle spoke she saw her mother's expression shift, to a smiling mask of horror. Rachel loved horror shows.

"Twenty-four days to Orynon or whatever they call that place," Henry said. "We arrive the day before Thanksgiving. Mom was gonna fly to Paris and have it with her sisters this year."

"That'll be a neat trick," Rachel said, with startling alertness. "Tell the old witch to use her magic broomstick this time."

"Shet yer trap, Raich. No one wants yer two-bit opinion."

With the thumb and forefinger of one hand, Rachel began rubbing each side of the bridge of her nose, emitting a low, groaning hum as she did so.

"Is she okay?" Stu asked, from the floor near Michelle. "That's what I saw her doing this morning."

"She does it all the time," Michelle said. An answer of sorts.

Rachel's eyes were in a trancelike state, and it seemed to Michelle that her mother might be faking much of the time while listening in on what people said about her, so that she could sort friends from enemies. It would explain the quick changes in her demeanor.

Michelle tuned out the television commentary and reflected on the hardships she had experienced in her eleven years. She could not recall her mother ever hitting her, but there was a constant sense of threat emanating from the woman—as if she were about to go berserk at any instant. Rachel had directed considerable violence toward Henry—those instances every so often when she swung at him with anything in her reach. Michelle tried to recall the last time she had seen her father and mother kiss. They had done it in front of her, but when? It seemed like a long, long time ago. For that matter, it seemed to Michelle that she had lived much longer than eleven years and three months.

Michelle's thoughts were interrupted when she heard Coley protesting going to bed. "I don't like my room anymore," she told Joseph, who was trying to escort her away. "There's a scary monster in there."

Joseph laughed as if she were just coming up with an excuse. He dragged and then carried the struggling child into the kitchen.

Stu ran after Joseph, and within earshot of Michelle said, "Uh, I fooled with that nanny thing . . . put a scary story on it. I wasn't thinking, I guess. I'm sorry, Coley. I know how to fix your nanny. Would you like me to do that for you?"

Coley stopped yelling. "Yes," she said, her tone whimpery.

"C'mon," Joseph said to Stu. "You're gonna be with us for a while, what with this space journey thing, and I'll help get you straightened out. Jeez! I can't believe this is happening to us! It doesn't seem real just seeing it on TV, but it must be. Holy shit!"

Stu and Joseph conversed as they ascended the stairs on the other side of the kitchen, but Michelle could no longer pick up the words. Joseph didn't sound angry, and Stu was trying to make amends. Maybe things would go smoothly between them after all. Stu was tough, but he had a soft spot.

"Stu's gotta go to school now," Henry said, watching Michelle flex to her feet. "He can't go back to New Orleans, and I can't call there, unless I miss my guess about the phone system."

Michelle had difficulty visualizing Stu at a classroom learning module. He wouldn't enjoy that, might run away, as he had done before. Michelle tried to tell herself that this didn't matter much now, in light of the Big Announcement. None of the Fouquet problems and squabbles should matter much anymore. Maybe this event would draw the family members closer together . . . even Rachel and Granmère.

SEVEN

Get some experts to go over the videos. Pronto. I
want to know why they talk and use sign language at
the same time.

—Memo from General
Toshio Oso (Commandant of Hamilton
Air Service Base) to his adjutant

Since it was Monday, Henry had a wrist wrestling meet in the evening, one
of three weekly that his team had almost all year round. It was one of the
sports that had no season, like bowling, and even his Fifties Plus League
drew respectable crowds. At fifty-three Henry was one of the younger con-
testants, which compensated somewhat for his feelings of fatigue much of
the time. Then too, maybe his best friend Phil Cartucci was right when he
said Henry was stronger on his worst days than a twenty-year-old medalist
on his best days.

As Henry sat alone in the wrestling cage mounted high on one wall of the
arena, he felt the exhilarating flow of adrenaline. He was the star of the
team, and basked in that position. The others looked up to him, despite
admissions from Henry that his strength was natural, that he had never
exercised a day in his life. Joseph was like that too, but had never expressed
an interest in wrist wrestling.

Joseph's my boy, Henry thought. *Ain't no doubt about that. Renney's a
different matter. Kid don't look like me, don't act like me, don't talk like me,
don't do nothin' like me . . .*

Henry reached for the pair of high-powered miniature binoculars on the
ledge beside him. Technicians were still adjusting the giant arm extensions
connected to the cage and to the cage of his adversary. Through the binoculars he looked past the mega-scale mechanical forearms, and saw the opponent just entering his cage, on the opposite wall far across the arena. He had

the dark skin of sun-drenched aeons, with high cheekbones and massive arms and legs. He wore a loincloth for theatrical effect, went by the moniker "Indian Bill."

Henry, known as "Frenchie" in the league, had his own prop: a floppy red beret that was at that moment perched atop his head. Indian Bill was mostly show, and Henry usually beat him—unless the arm extensions weren't adjusted fairly, which happened on occasion.

With a few moments to spare, Henry's binoculars scanned the men in the crowd. People were still filing into their seats, and Henry was searching, as he did frequently, for the face that looked like Renney. It had become an obsession with him, and he used lulls in his schedule such as this one in a manner he considered productive. He wasn't certain exactly what he would do if he ever located exactly the right face, the one that, combined with the features of Rachel, had to be the guilty party.

He focused the glasses on a dark-haired, buxom woman, then on a young blonde with knee-length straight hair. Henry sighed, felt his vision and memory glazing over. He tried to remember how Rachel used to look, framed a hazy image of her in the lenses of his binoculars. She became the blonde he had just seen, but with a different, more classic face and long red-orange hair that cascaded to the small of her back. Rachel had been spectacularly attractive.

Then she started boozin', smokin', and goin' nuts, Henry thought, sadly.

Henry half-heard the cage door squeal open behind him. Then the voice of Phil Cartucci bent around the barriers Henry had erected. These two saw a lot of one another, on the wrist wrestling team, in taverns, and at the ParSell Delivery Company, where Cartucci was Henry's supervisor. Disjointed words found their way into Henry's mind, followed by increasingly complete sentences.

"You're driving yourself crazy, Henry. Come on, give me those glasses. It's almost time to wrestle and you'd better concentrate."

Without looking back, Henry held the field glasses tightly, just beyond his friend's reach. They were in front of Henry's mouth, and Henry imagined his own wild spittle peppering them as he spoke: "If I ever find out who shacked up with her, I'll kill him. Worse than that, I'll murdalize him."

"You're going on rumors, fella." Cartucci kept his voice down to prevent embarrassing his friend in front of their teammates, who sat on benches in the wings, a few meters away. "Ten-year-old rumors, with no evidence whatsoever."

"Lotsa stories came in about her," Henry said, through taut lips.

"Don't try to snow me. I've known you too long. The only things you ever heard were from your own mother . . . those tales of Rachel hanging around in servicemen's bars with her friend Jennie."

"You callin' my mother a liar?"

Henry recognized the futility of his effort. If Rachel did have an affair it might have been with anyone, from anywhere. Renney's real father might even have died during the war. Still, in his irrational, consuming jealousy and rage Henry searched the faces, never considering for an instant that he might be wrong in his suspicions.

"Give me the glasses, Henry." Cartucci's beefy hand was on Henry's shoulder.

Henry swatted it off.

"The kid looks like your dad, you idiot. When are you ever gonna admit it? Listen up, dummy. Genetic characteristics often skip a generation. Take a close look at both of them, as I have. You can't miss the similarities."

The hand was back on Henry's shoulder. Henry sighed, passed the binoculars back. The hand took them.

"I don't know about none o' that," Henry said. "All I know is the kid don't look like me, an' that tells me sumpthin'. Shit in an egg carton, the kid looks more like my dog Bumper than me."

"Aw, for Christ's sake, Fouquet. You're getting worse. I didn't think it was possible. Pretty soon if you don't watch it everyone on the team's gonna know what you're thinking about in your twisted little mind. Then you'll be the laughing stock of the whole outfit, maybe even of the whole league."

"I'll bash all their noses, an' yours too."

Henry whirled sideways on the metal bench, and with one leg across the benchtop stretched his neck to face Cartucci. Henry had searched these features before, but maybe there was something he had missed . . . an angle he hadn't seen . . . the way shadows played on features. The shape of Cartucci's cheekbones, maybe. He was tall and bony, with a narrow, snubby nose, olive skin, and little black eyes that seemed to laugh at a person. Even now, with a scowl across Cartucci's wide mouth, the eyes seemed to be laughing.

"It might even be somebody I know," Henry said, his tone accusatory.

Cartucci shook his head. "I'm not the one. You know that. And even if somebody else was, you're talking about ancient history. Forget about it. I'm telling you this as a friend, for your own good."

Henry's eyes bulged, and he thrust his jaw out. "Never!"

Cartucci tilted his eyes upward in exasperation, spun, and walked away, carrying the binoculars.

Hearing the anticipatory noises of the crowd, Henry turned on his bench, facing the arena once more. He adjusted the French beret, stared at a black Plexiglas box that was mounted in front of him on the cage. Known as an Archimedes Box, the unit was capable of transmitting tremendous leverage from a human arm inserted inside it to the giant mechanical extension that rested on its elbow on the dirt floor of the arena. The long arm that extended on the other side of Henry's Archimedes Box was muscular, covered with black hair, and towered above the cage almost to the arena ceiling. Its skin was slightly darker than Henry's own, with a leathery, dead look to it.

From Henry's vantage, the Archimedes Box looked small and devoid of the electronics he knew it had to have, and for a moment he marveled at it. On the other side, Indian Bill had his arm in the box and was making clenched fists with the huge hand connected to his arm. The crowd was responding.

"Get your arm in there, Henry," one of Henry's teammates called out from the Blasters' bench behind him.

Henry wondered who ever came up with that team name, and for that matter with any of the other names around the league. Tonight they were meeting the Hard Guys. He tried to psyche himself up, gazed down along the nearly full viewing stands along one side to a radio announcers' table that ran along the edge of the arena floor. The announcers—six of them— were looking up at him, saying unknown things about him into their microphones.

Henry tipped his beret, then replaced it on his head and thrust his tree-trunk arm into the black box. When he made a fist, the crowd roared its appreciation, vibrating his cage. Inside the Archimedes Box there was no sensation of feeling whatsoever—no hot, no cold, nothing to touch. He couldn't have touched the walls of the box had he wanted to, for the mechanism was set to repel his hand from all areas except the exact center, where he had to keep it to activate the giant arm. From his experience on the circuit, Henry understood that the Archimedes Box contained a series of electronic eyes on finely tuned wavelengths that transmitted each movement of his hand to receivers in the giant arm. There was no discernible delay whatsoever.

Henry gave his opponent the finger and received a response in kind.

The crowd began clapping, jeering, whistling, and pounding their feet, transmitting a frenzy of vibration through the building. Henry smelled dust, popcorn, and hot dogs.

Theoretically each giant arm was equal to the other, making it in reality a glorified contest between humans. The stronger, more skilled, or more devious man would win. But Henry and others to whom he had spoken had noticed differences in the equipment from day to day—differences that seemed too great to be ascribed to chance. There were suspicions that the matches were rigged, or at least that some of them were. No one on the Blasters seemed to have any evidence of this, so it remained a suspicion with them, one that affected other members of the team more than Henry. They complained of losing to unworthy opponents, and every once in a while someone would go to the media. These stories rarely reached the public, at least not in a serious context. It was a hoary subject, long bantered around and no longer considered newsworthy. Sure it's fixed, the public seemed to say, and everybody knows it. So what?

Some Blasters said that Henry didn't have so much trouble since he was the star of the team, the one expected to win most of the time. Henry couldn't support the team by himself, so the gamblers and fixers allegedly did their work on the other team members, swinging matches on total team points.

Beneath the towering arms, a brave judge in a long white coat and tails strolled to the center of the pit of combat. Had Henry or Indian Bill moved their appendages at the wrong moment, the fellow might be squashed—and there had been fatalities of that nature. Henry had witnessed one from the players' bench, when Samoa Jack, then a member of the Blasters, moved his elbow and mashed Judge Renaldo Griffin. An investigation ensued, and some of Jack's enemies around the circuit assumed that he must have done it intentionally because of some alleged animosity toward Griffin. No one developed the facts to prove murder, but Jack was barred permanently from competition in any league.

As Henry recalled these events, he placed his elbow as far down as he could in the Archimedes Box, well toward himself and away from the box center that corresponded with the judge's location. While he couldn't feel the bottom of the box, he had been informed by a box serviceman that he was within a micrometer of the surface, but that the mechanical elbow attached to his box did actually rest on the floor of the arena. With an expert cock of his wrist, Henry formed a tight "V" with his upper arm and forearm, opened his hand to do battle, and waited for his opponent to do likewise.

Indian Bill wasn't finished with his gesticulations, and used his extension to flail the air with clenched fists, karate chops, and dive-bombing obscene gestures. He was a crowd pleaser, and the more the audience cheered the more Indian Bill acted up. Finally the judge had seen enough, and he used his lapel microphone to call for order.

Grudgingly, Indian Bill's arm settled down and went into a tight "V" for maximum leverage.

When the giant hands touched, Henry felt flesh against his own hand, an illusion he had been told, for Indian Bill's fleshy hand remained far across the arena, in his own Archimedes Box. Both men maneuvered for an advantageous grip, trying to lock the opponent's wrist underneath in the process. Through a speaker inside his cage, Henry heard the judge barking out commands, from his vantage point precisely beneath and far below the giant maneuvering hands.

"Indian Bill, relax your grip . . . Okay, try again . . . No, not like that! . . . Both of you relax grips . . . All right, now slowly grip again . . . You guys know the rules, so quit the tricky stuff . . . Elbows on the deck at all times or you're disqualified . . . No holding on with your free hand . . . You know about the spotters monitoring your cages . . . Get ready . . . This is a go! . . . Three . . . two . . . one . . . wrestle!"

Setting his jaw, Henry thrust his hand hard against Indian Bill. The opponent went over a little, then fought back to the starting point.

The din of the crowd enveloped Henry's cage, shaking it until it seemed likely that the bolts securing it to the wall would give way.

Henry gritted his teeth.

Now the opponent was thrusting, and Henry felt the power of it forcing his forearm over. The fatigue of the day and of Henry's lifetime threatened to overwhelm him, and people were stomping their feet in anticipation.

Henry's surrogate forearm and knuckles were almost flat against the arena floor.

As if from far away, Henry heard the faint chanting of his stage name: "French-ie! . . . French-ie! . . . French-ie." It grew louder, crowding away all other sounds reaching Henry's consciousness.

In a vision, Henry saw Indian Bill calling upon the spirits of his Cherokee ancestors to win, and through narrowly open eyes he saw a thousand Indian Bills inside a thousand wrist-wrestling cages on the opposite wall.

Henry called upon his own spirits, for his was a God-given strength. In a mighty surge of Christianity, he brought his arm up and back once more to the middle.

The roar of "French-ie! Frenchie!" shook his cage and sent chills down his spine.

Again Henry called upon his deepest reservoir. In a tremendous thrust, he rammed Indian Bill's mechanical arm all the way down, causing a mini-earthquake as the equipment hit the arena floor.

Henry's teammates mobbed him and pulled him out of the cage.

Henry barely had enough adrenaline left to enjoy the moment. Every muscle in his body, not merely in his fighting right arm, felt the fatigue of a thousand pitched battles. His beret flew off, and someone retrieved it, pressing it back on his head. In unison with the appreciative crowd, Henry's teammates shouted "French-ie! French-ie!" They pushed him back inside the cage for two curtain calls, and Henry bowed stiffly, swinging his cap close to the floor.

Then the cacophony died down and Henry was sitting on the Blasters' bench. Cartucci, seated next to him, said something about the paltry money they earned in the "wristling" racket, that for the participants it was mostly an ego pump. He mentioned a radio reviewer who the year before had termed the proceedings "enthusiastic amateur night."

Cartucci and a Blaster named Miner Mike began talking about the days when Miner Mike had wrist-wrestled in his twenties. He had made good money in those days, as had half the men on the team. Most of those fellows had invested their money and done pretty well, while others who hadn't wrestled in their early years did well in other pursuits. No one needed the money from this league, what little there was, as badly as Henry did, and as Henry eavesdropped he thought about this. He was like the others in one respect, however. Every one of them was in the game to reassure himself that the old body still worked.

Henry enjoyed these nights out with the boys, too. He could have obtained a higher-paying third job, but not one with the comaraderie and fringe benefits of this one. Two years before, one of those fringes, a big one, came up. A promoter offered to pay Henry's expenses on a national exhibition tour, and Henry had been the only Blaster member invited. The guy even said he'd spoken with Henry's other employers and that his salaries for those positions would be continued during his absence, with the jobs waiting for him upon his return. But Henry declined the offer, since Rachel was going through one of her lowest points and required constant attention.

Like an insect caught by a predator's web, Henry saw strands leading away from him in all directions. To his fatigue-fogged mind, these became the paths of his life that had led him to this place. Each strand shape-shifted into a long tunnel, through which he had passed. The tunnelways bent around in the distance, and somehow they all led to one place, to his youth. He wished he could re-enter the tunnels, following each back to a golden time, to a moment when all of life's wonders lay before him resplendent, awaiting his selection.

But the tunnels were blocked, and he was stuck helplessly in the web of circumstance. It was that way for Rachel too. He longed for a tremendous surge of life's adrenaline for both of them, one that would endure for all of their remaining years together. With strength they could cope.

"This is an obscene telephone call," Stu said, using the phone mounted on the kitchen wall by the doorway. "You can hang up now or remain on the line. My first offering will be composed of vintage street or gutter talk, in disgusting, graphic detail, including a number of alternative terms for the various sexual parts, functions, and toilet activities. I will follow with the brand names of American condoms, and in closing will entertain requests . . ."

Stu could see Rachel dozing on the deep-cushioned, torn old couch in the living room. She had her Biblecorder on her lap, the earphones of which were secured to her head. Her head flopped to one side, and every so often she snorted, straightened, and half-opened her eyes. Once while Stu was delivering his most articulate barrage of filthy language, she seemed to look at him. Stu thought he detected a faint smile at the corners of her mouth, but if it was there it faded quickly and her eyes closed again.

Three of the people that Stu called at random that evening listened, and one of them laughed. Five others hung up on him before he could get to the prurient portions of his presentation. Bored at last, Stu carried a nearly spent jar of peanut butter into the parental bedroom and smeared the insides of Henry's socks.

Stu recognized the personal danger in this, targeting the head of the household, his own father. It would have been far safer to have chosen Michelle, Renney, or even Rachel. (Coley and Joseph didn't enter his mind for the moment.) But Stu liked Michelle and pitied Rachel. That left Renney. A series of pranks he might employ against Renney tumbled through his impish mind, but none seemed particularly appropriate. Leaving Henry's violated socks inside a dresser drawer where they were likely to be used, Stu replaced the now empty peanut butter jar in a kitchen cupboard.

He felt a twinge of guilt for wasting food, and there was the troublesome incident with Coley in which he had been too cruel. He wouldn't target her anymore.

He tried to analyze his own motivations. His own father? This was the person responsible for taking him in off the streets. The house wasn't much though, and he was also the accursed man responsible for bringing Stu into this crummy world in the first place. For these infractions, Henry deserved to wear peanut-buttered socks.

Renney had to be next, and now as he so often did, Stu forgot about justification. Mostly Stu was a creator of pranks for the sake of pranks and the ongoing battle against boredom. A fine joke stood on its own. It was a creation, an art form.

Stu's mind whirled with devices and setups as he walked up the staircase and through the littered, worn, and scribbled hallway that led to the bedroom shared by Michelle, Renney, and Joseph. Renney was the only occupant of the room when Stu entered, and was lying on one of the beds, drawing on lined schoolpaper with a heavy black pencil. Renney's strokes were bold, interspersed by shading, done with the pencil edge. He was copying from a hologram comic book, which lay open next to him.

Stu paused just inside the doorway.

Renney glanced up at him, then returned to his drawing. The piece of schoolpaper had been paperclipped to a magazine for backing.

Stu looked around the room. For the most part it was as scattered and untidy as the rest of the house, with shirts, trousers, underwear, and dresses slung here and there on chairbacks and bedposts or dropped on the floor in heaps. The large room boasted only one chest of drawers, cheap pinewood with round wooden knobs that hung loose or were entirely gone. The unit, adjacent to a messy bed by one wall, had been painted white and the knobs red—a long time before, judging from the chips and scratches. As in Coley's room, all the dresser drawers were open and overhung with messy contents.

Renny's bed and its immediate environs were an oasis of impoverished neatness. The old yellow bedspread was nearly smooth around him, and tucked beneath the pillow. A small wooden table with a single shelf beneath it held many of Renney's possessions—an inexpensive brown clock radio, a creased and oil-darkened baseball glove, two hardballs (one used, one new and covered with autographs), a shoebox, a half dozen books, a cracked blue vinyl school notebook worn at the corners, and a mason jar of drawing pencils, inserted with their sharpened points up.

The first thing occurring to Stu was that he could break all of the pencil points in such a fashion that they could be inserted back into the pencils, making the pencils look as if they were ready to use. He should find the pencil sharpener as well, and gum that up.

He went around behind Renney and studied his drawing. It was a caricature of Bumper, showing the mange-bald dog leering rapaciously at a pretty white poodle as she strolled by arrogantly, her head held high.

"That's pretty good," Stu said, reminding himself that he wouldn't stoop so low as to deface artwork. Even pranksters had their standards.

Renney looked up. "You really think so?"

Stu nodded.

"Thanks." Renney shaded an area on the back of Bumper's neck.

"Where do you keep all your drawings? I mean, if you're this good you must have more."

"Under the bed."

"Can I look?"

"Sure, why not? Pull the box out."

Stu located a low but wide cardboard carton. Holding a flap, he pulled the box toward him. It grated against the hardwood floor on a small rock or something else that Renney, despite his fastidiousness, had overlooked.

Renney continued working as Stu knelt over the box and perused its contents.

The kid's a neat freak, Stu thought. *Crackers in the bed are an old standby, and I could short-sheet him, slitting the sheet a little at the fold so that he rips right through. Too bad they're out of peanut butter . . .*

"Hey, these are good," Stu said, fingering the mismatched sheets.

Some drawings were on heavy art paper, of varying sizes, with both sides utilized in most cases. Others were just little torn scraps with sketches on them—Coley on her tricycle, the house (before and after the rooms went berserk), an old man polishing his sedan with a cloth. Most involving people appeared to be caricatures, and Stu judged these to be the best.

"I don't see Beauregard anywhere in here," Stu said after a time, recalling a comment Michelle had made with respect to Renney and the house ghost.

Renney's deft pencil strokes paused, then resumed. "I don't like Beauregard," he said.

"Now here's a good one, Renney."

Stu withdrew a large color drawing from the bottom of the carton. It depicted Henry through a half open bathroom door sitting on a toilet, reading a copy of the *Union News.* His pockmarked face was covered with dark stubble, and he had an insipid, vacant look on his face. A lit cigar was wedged over one ear, with its ember end burning the fringe of hair there, sending curls of smoke overhead.

Renney's eyes became saucers when he saw the drawing. He flushed, leaned over the edge of the bed. "Put that one back!" he snapped. "I don't want Dad to see it!"

Armed with valuable information from an unwitting victim, Stu did as he was told. As he slid the box back under the bed he formulated yet another prank in his agile mind. He knew from experience that the best practical jokes explored or played upon a weakness of the victim. In the growing scenario he envisioned two victims brought to ground in one brilliant maneuver.

Michelle had been caring for Coley most of the evening, and now with the toddler in bed Michelle slumped on the living room couch, exhausted from the rigors of the day. Earlier Rachel had appeared in a nightgown at the kitchen doorway to announce, "Jennie was visiting Las Vegas when this habitat took off. I'm never going to see her again." Before Michelle could respond, her mother turned and trudged off to bed.

Jennie Parker . . . "Wild Jennie," Granmère called her. "A bad influence on Rachel, if such a thing is possible."

When Rachel spoke of her lost best friend, her tone had been one of resignation, more matter of fact than sad. Maybe Rachel felt as Michelle did, that it was for the best. Michelle hoped her mother would find a new and better friend, one who would encourage her to stop drinking.

Michelle wondered if she might have misinterpreted her mother's tone of voice. Maybe her mother was keeping the hurt inside, absorbing it in the shell-shocked fashion of one who already had endured terrible inhumanities. This seemed more logical, Michelle had to admit.

Her mother had only one friend in the universe.

Michelle let this tumble through her mind, separating it from the prior reality of "only one friend in the world." Now Rachel's predicament took on a larger scale, more cosmic reality, one that isolated her even further from the mainstream.

I'm a loner too, Michelle thought. *Sure, I have a few friends at school. But they never come to visit me here . . . I never invite them. And they never invite me over to their houses. Maybe it's the way I disappear at lunchtime or the way I cut conversation short with them. I look away or hurry away, as if I'm occupied with something else. Actually I'm constantly occupied with eluding people, afraid to reveal things to them anymore, terrified that they'll laugh at me and tease me.*

She drew a parallel between herself and her mother, with each hiding from the world (the universe, now) in varying degrees. Was she becoming more and more like her mother, and with too much stress would Michelle too go over the proverbial edge into full-fledged mental illness? What was Rachel like at Michelle's age?

It occurred to Michelle that her mother had more than one friend, whether she knew it or not. Renney was her friend. So was Henry. And, to a lesser degree since Rachel wouldn't let her in, so was Michelle. Michelle drew a mental spectrum of the bonds of family and friends, with ties emerging like groping, desperate hands from the Henry Fouquet household to the members of other households. But to a large extent other families rejected the Henry Fouquets, for obvious reasons. Oh, Joseph had his fancy girlfriend, but he didn't have a job and didn't seem comfortable with his life. Thyla wouldn't remain with him long, and sometimes Joseph behaved as if he were participating in a self-fulfilling prophecy. Henry's jobs weren't really jobs, compared with what he might have done. And so it went with others in the household, including mangy old Bumper.

These thoughts troubled Michelle, and she gazed toward the television set for escape. Using the remote control she flipped on the set, volume high. A police show blared across her wounded gray cells, causing a surge of pain across her temples. She switched the sound off, imagined to herself what the characters were saying. Upstairs, Stu and Renney were talking. She heard water flow through the pipes in the walls, probably Joseph in the bathroom up there.

A vehicle pulled into the driveway outside the house, casting the glare of headlights against one of the living room's side windows. From the electric purr of the motor, Michelle recognized it as her father's car. She gave it only a passing, weary thought as the headlights went off and the engine stopped. Back to her show.

When after a time she heard no further sounds from outside, she looked away from her program, letting the story line she had fantasized drift away. She went to the front "porch," pulled the sheer curtain aside and looked out.

Half illuminated in the light thrown by a street lamp, Michelle saw her father's beige Plymster parked in the driveway. The car was a little out of position, with the two passenger-side wheels on the lawn. This concerned her, and she ran to the front door, hurling it open.

She bounded down the steps, taking three and four at a time. Through the passenger window she saw her father slumped across the steering wheel, his face turned toward her. His eyes were closed, features slackened in a deathly pall.

Michelle suppressed a scream, jerked open the passenger door.

"Daddy, Daddy! Are you okay?"

Henry stirred, and his eyelids lifted as if held down by weights, revealing pupils that rolled upward.

"Are you okay, Daddy?"

"Sho tired," he slurred. "Hel' me ta bed."

Michelle breathed a tremendous sigh of relief, recalling a time the year before when he had come home in a similar state. Now, as before, Michelle helped her father out of the car and into the house.

As she held his arm and they ascended the front stairs, she saw what she had not seen during her rushed exit: a hideous drawing thumbtacked to the outside of the partially open front door.

Instinctively, before her father focused on it, she swung the door wide open, placing herself between him and the drawing.

What a thing for Renney to do! Michelle thought. *With Daddy so tired, that's all he needs!* She recalled telling her brother to destroy the awful caricature several months before.

Her mind raced angrily as she guided her father into his bedroom and helped him sit on the double bed where her mother was asleep. The adjacent bath's light was on and the door ajar, revealing the toilet from much the same angle as that depicted in the drawing. She couldn't imagine Renney tacking up that horrible drawing, despite having created it in the first place. He had taken care to conceal it from his father, showing it only to his siblings.

Did Rachel run across the drawing and perpetrate this? She could be cruel at times, and conceivably she might have urged Renney to create the drawing in the first place.

Michelle helped her father remove his shoes, then guided him fully dressed underneath the covers.

"Get da light, Michelle," he said, burrowing his head into the pillow. "Love ya."

Michelle smiled tenderly, kissed him on the temple.

After clicking off the bathroom light and emerging into the kitchen, Michelle shut the bedroom door behind her, feeling as angry as she could ever recall feeling. With the strongest urge to rip Renney's drawing into little pieces, she stormed across the kitchen. At the base of the stairs leading up to the next level she encountered Renney.

Seeing the expression on her face, he stepped out of her way.

In an angry whisper, Michelle chastised him.

"I didn't put it up!" Renney protested.

"Well, somebody in this house did! You should never have made the damned thing, and I wish I had the guts to tear it up! Art, ha! You call that art?"

Renney shook his head in bewilderment.

"Hide it better this time!" Michelle husked. "Better yet, destroy it! I hate it!"

Flustered, Renney hurried to the undecorous gallery on the door, cursing the misfortune that nearly had befallen him.

Michelle followed.

For a long moment, Renney stood in front of the caricature, staring at it intently.

"Get rid of it!" Michelle snarled. "Or I will!"

"Stu!" Renney said. "I showed it to him today, and I thought I saw a gleam in his eyes. He did that thing to Coley's talking nanny too. It had to be Stu!"

Renney removed the thumbtacks carefully and took down the drawing. With Michelle close on his heels, he stomped back to their room, where they searched for a hiding place.

The room had one dim lamp light on, and bright light from the bathroom pierced the opening beneath the door. Michelle heard water running in there: Joseph taking a shower. He took so many showers.

"Where'll I hide this thing?" Renney asked. "I feel like going out on the back porch and pounding Stu in his sleep."

"He isn't there. I don't know where he went."

"I can't destroy my drawing. Can you understand that?"

From the doorway, Michelle stared at him icily.

Renney dashed by her into the hallway, where he stood before one of the hall closet doors, staring blankly at it.

They had three closets in this hallway now, since Rachel had broken the home's room arrangement mechanism, and the one receiving his interest was a linen closet with the lower shelves missing. Michelle recalled the interior, which had a pile of soiled bedding on the floor, a loose wall panel behind that, an air space beyond, and then another loose wall panel that led into the closet in her bedroom. She had discovered one of the loose wall

panels while playing hide-and-seek with Coley, and later had worked at the
other one to free it as well. She didn't think Renney knew about it, but the
space between would be a perfect hiding place for his drawing. She didn't
have anything in there at the moment but didn't want to reveal its existence
to him, not for his despicable sketch! He could find another place for that!
Some day she might keep a diary in there, if she got around to starting one.
There would be plenty to write about in this family.

Another closet, just to the right of Renney, was so full of junk that no one
opened it anymore. It was also one of the terrible places said to be fre-
quented by the giant flea, Beauregard, for it was one of the dirtiest regions of
the dirtiest house on "Earth."

Renney rolled up his drawing and secured it with a rubber band from his
pocket. Flying in the face of the great fear Michelle knew he held for Beauregard, he opened the junk closet door and shoved the drawing in, pushing
the door closed in the blink of an eye before anything could tumble out.

"Stu doesn't like me," Renney said. "Why, I don't know."

Michelle wondered if Stu was like Dad, another person who equated
Renney's artistic talents with homosexuality. Such foolish, shallow thinking!

"You should be more cautious in the future," Michelle said. She recalled
confiding in the Hawaiian girl about the daily bran muffin, and the embarrassment when this information was spread all over school. "You have to
learn to expect this sort of thing."

Renney shrugged and went sluggishly to bed, his head down.

As Michelle shut off the television set in the living room, she enumerated
her own friends. Most were in her family, and she found nothing wrong
with that. Granpère headed the list. So what if her best buddy was old? Her
mother, despite an enigmatic nature, was right up near the top, maybe on
top, depending upon how Michelle felt toward her on particular days.
Michelle felt more than obligatory love for her mother. It went to *need*, to
the very core of friendship. If Michelle kept herself available as a friend long
enough, Rachel would respond in kind. Rachel was a sensitive person who
wrote poetry, who saw things others couldn't see. She would recognize
Michelle's efforts, undoubtedly already had to a great extent. Maybe she was
testing Michelle in that realm beyond obligatory love.

Michelle added her father, Renney, and Coley to her list, then gently
chastised herself for being so clinical, so objective. It seemed to her that
friendship by nature should be a spontaneous affair, something that a person
didn't think about in such a conscious, detached manner. But here she was
anyway, adding Mr. Rankin to the list for letting her spend lunch periods

reading news cubes in his store. He was her friend for giving her something important. She would take him a gift one of these days, maybe something Granpère helped her make.

When Michelle thought about all the people who needed her, she told herself that she didn't have time for any more friends. For the first time in a long while, she felt satisfied with herself and with the position she occupied in the universe.

EIGHT

Since the alien broadcast less than three hours ago, we've experienced a rash of murders and suicides all over the habitat. Early telephone interviews taken on a random sampling of the populace indicate that many people can't cope with the stress of not knowing if they'll ever see loved ones on Earth again. A large number of persons, particularly the elderly, are panicked at the thought of flying through deep space. They wonder about the integrity of the habitat—if it can break apart, if the atmosphere might leak out, if we're likely to be struck by a meteor. Granmère Fouquet recommends the establishment of a mental health task force, one that will operate efficiently and discreetly, reporting directly to the mayor's office.

Our sampling indicates a degree of sentiment in the other direction as well—persons who might otherwise have committed suicide find now that their lives suddenly are more interesting, more exciting. They can't wait to see what will happen next, and especially what awaits them on Arionn. To them we are on a Grand Adventure. Thus far this group is a decided minority, outnumbered fifty-four to one by the other end of the spectrum.

—Staff report to San Francisco's
Mayor Wilde, delivered just before
her emergency city council meeting

Far into the night in the City Office Tower, Mayor Peninnah Wilde held session with her council members. A slender, aging spinster, seamed of face and snarly of voice, Wilde was not at her questionable best on this occasion.

Since the appearance of the artificial fog and the revelations of the Arionnese, she had broken out in a terrible case of hives that threatened to cover her flesh in red bumps. To make matters worse at the moment, as she stood trying to bring order to the room, she had contracted a nasty case of hiccups.

Councilwoman Liliane Fouquet, better known even in public life as Granmère Fouquet, was leaning forward and arguing across the conference table with Big Jack Brittany, an immense man with long gray hair opposite her. An animated man, Brittany pounded his fists on the table and stammered somewhat incoherently as he repeatedly slammed his bulbous belly against the table edge, adding physical threat to his words.

At precisely the right moment, Granmère sat back hard against the padded leather chair and gazed at Brittany with an accomplished, condescending sneer. This was for show. She had practiced it in front of a mirror. Brittany worried her, for many reasons. By virtue of his seniority and political connections he was the third most powerful presence in city government behind Mayor Wilde and Granmère. Granmère resolved that she would command her staff to intensify their fact-finding efforts against him. She suspected that he was gay, and that made him a candidate for inquiry by the Special Purposes Police.

Brittany under lockup. What a delicious thought! But she needed hard evidence.

Granmère glanced at Mayor Wilde, who continued hiccuping worse than before. Wilde's face radiated purple, with fresh hive eruptions across her forehead. Her eyes were feral, frantic.

"Are you all right, mayor?" a balding man next to Brittany asked. This was ex-businessman and third-term Councilman Nellie Conrad, invariably with an unlit pipe in hand, since his doctor had ordered him to stop smoking. He pointed his pipe at Mayor Wilde.

"I'll . . . hic! . . . be all . . . hic . . . right! Just leave me be for a while!" Wilde's diaphragm went berserk, preventing further words.

"Excuse me for asking," Conrad said.

In the absence of Wilde's leadership, the other council members, who thus far had been conversing among themselves, began shouting at one another. John Aronson, a young black with designs on the mayor's office, told Granmère in the loudest voice of all that she should stop starting arguments with Brittany. Thereupon Wilson Domenicco, an olive-skinned little fellow with ink-dark hair who was seated next to Granmère, came to her support, asserting that Brittany had been entirely at fault.

"That damned Italian-French connection again," Aronson growled, refer-

"That damned Italian-French connection again," Aronson growled, referring to the predominant constituencies and nationalities of Domenicco and Granmère. "Don't you two ever disagree?"

While Granmère and Brittany glared across the table at one another, the rest of the participants flew into an uproar, going off on emotion-laden tangents.

"Stop this!" Mayor Wilde screamed finally, slamming a fist on the table at the height of pandemonium. "You're arguing over who called whom a name first! What's the matter with you people? The Arionnese! Don't you remember why I called this meeting?" She waved a sheet of red-bordered paper in the air. "You've seen the report on murders and suicides! What are we going to do about it?" She thrust back her chair and stood, looking decidedly unwell to Granmère, although the convulsions had abated.

The room grew quiet. Granmère felt fatigue set in, saw it as well on the drawn faces of the others. Her eyeballs felt grainy in their sockets.

"Take over, Fouquet," Wilde ordered. "As President of the City Council, you're acting mayor. I'm checking myself into the hospital. This is worse than before."

Granmère nodded, suppressing any outward display of her pleasure. Watching the mayor shuffle toward the door, Granmère recalled the prior incident that required hospitalization, some five years earlier. It occurred during another crisis, when angry city government workers threatened to storm the City Office Tower over a pay and benefits dispute. Granmère had assumed the duties of acting mayor then, too. There had been other more minor hiccuping and hive attacks over the years since then, each kept secret from the press and the public.

"Shall I coordinate an announcement through your press secretary?" Granmère asked, insolently. "We can't say you've been called away to Sacramento on urgent business this time, can we?"

Someone tittered weakly.

Mayor Wilde stopped near the massive French chalet door leading to the corridor. She turned, holding one hand on the door frame for support. Her eyes, ravaged by debility, scanned the room, looking for disloyalty. Then she gazed away, toward the bank of bay windows looking out over the lights of her city. To Granmère it seemed as if the mayor identified everyone in the room as her enemy, to one degree or another. At the same time they were all allies, holders of positions in the city's political nucleus. Everyone in the room knew or suspected things about the others that would damage political careers, but they maintained a code of silence out of self-interest, realizing that the slightest revelation could precipitate a bloodletting that would bring all of them down. It was a precarious balance.

Mayor Wilde smiled faintly. "It would be a neat trick to see the governor this time, wouldn't it?"

The council members broke into a short burst of controlled mirth, with the exception of Granmère. She gazed stony-faced at Mayor Wilde, and felt already the weight of the duties that had been thrust upon her.

"We'd better not make up anything about your going off to a military conference either," Granmère said. "That could worry the Arionnese, and we don't yet understand the scope of their power."

Mayor Wilde nodded. She shifted position, leaned against the wall. "What about the truth?" she asked.

"The truth?" Granmère blurted. She felt her facial muscles slacken.

"Did she say the *truth?*" Felicia Robinson, a first-termer from the Mission district, asked.

To the last person the council members were astounded. No one had ever before suggested such a thing. And coming from Mayor Wilde made it even more surprising, as she had the most to lose in the present circumstances.

As Granmère studied the mayor's hiccup-racked body, it seemed to her that Wilde was infinitely tired of everything, perhaps weary enough to accept whatever fate lay in store for her. This had to be the crisis of all time for the chief executive of any city, one that did not lend itself to solution by the powers at the disposal of the office. Granmère felt helplessness seeping into her own mind, and the sensation angered her. She steeled herself.

"We'll come up with something, Peninnah," Granmère said. "Don't worry about it. A simple announcement of illness will suffice. No details."

"Thank you," Mayor Wilde said. Moving to one side of the carved chalet door, she touched a button on the door frame. The door swung inward without a sound, then closed behind her as she disappeared into the corridor.

Now Granmère tried to focus the remaining energies of the assemblage, and for a time she succeeded. At Granmère's insistence they agreed to establish a mental health task force, with Robinson as overseer. They speculated about who the Arionnese really were and why they had appropriated a large chunk of the state of California. Were they terrorists, planning to hold eleven million hostages for an immense ransom? Or were they uncaring, thoughtlessly joyriding aliens on a universe-scale lark, with limitless technology at their disposal?

DeForest Lindholm, a first-termer from Ingleside, suggested the establishment of a contest among the populace to see who could come closest to guessing the truth about the aliens. He felt it might draw the Arionnese out in some way, causing them to make their intentions public.

Mulling this over, Granmère pulled the skin of her chin between a thumb and forefinger, then worked in reverse, smoothing the skin back. "The Arionnese would have to become involved," she said, "or no winner could be declared. Short of that, though, it would at least provide us with a list of options concerning their reasons."

"We can think for ourselves," Brittany snapped. "We don't want the public thinking that we don't know what's going on."

"You're right," Granmère conceded, without delay.

"What about mass hypnosis here?" Aronson asked. "I mean, maybe we're not in deep space at all. This could be a big practical joke."

"It's no joke," a tenor voice said, from the big chalet door. Unnoticed by anyone, an Oriental National Air Service officer decked in the tan, blue, and gold regalia of high command stood just inside the chamber, the door partly opened behind him. He carried a bulky black valise.

"Who let you in?" Granmère demanded. "We're in the midst of an important meeting." Then she shouted: "Security!"

"It was urgent that I reach you," the officer announced. "I have placed a contingent of crack troops around and inside this building. My personal Tyrolean sharpshooters are on the roof. Your 'Security,' as you call it, proved to be pathetic . . . only three men that I saw . . . easily penetrated. I merely spoke with them to get in."

"This is General Toshio Oso," Brittany said. "Commandant of Hamilton. We've met, General, at the . . ."

"I recall," came the response. A crisp, dismissive tone.

"What's going on?" Granmère asked, rising. She felt anger coming on, worked to control it. "Are you staging a coup of some sort?"

General Oso laughed, making his epicanthically enfolded eyes tinier than normal. It was a brisk, officious laugh that ended abruptly. "Nothing of the sort. I am informed that you are the acting mayor of San Francisco."

"That is correct," Granmère said, haughtily.

"So this is the City Office Tower," Oso said. "COT Tower, where the government sleeps."

"A bum rap," Granmère snarled. "Why are you here?"

"Confidential," General Oso said. "I must ask you to meet with me now, privately."

"But I'm in the middle of an important city council meeting! You can't expect me to . . ."

"It is most urgent, Madame Mayor," the general said.

Granmère heard something in his tone that told her he wasn't about to be denied. Beneath the polite exterior she sensed a demanding, forceful personality. This irritated her, for it was normally the position she liked to be in, compelling the actions of others.

But the council meeting wasn't getting anywhere, and this officer said he had troops stationed all over the building. Yes, there were matters of importance to discuss with him.

"Leave us," Granmère said, scanning the council members. She stared at Brittany and added, "Go home all of you, and get some rest."

Brittany looked away, muttered something under his breath, and then trudged heavily from the room.

The others followed, and the chalet door to the corridor clunked shut behind them, leaving Granmère and her visitor alone.

"As leader of the most important city in the habitat," General Oso said, "that makes you my new commander-in-chief."

"You mean like the President?"

"Precisely."

"But I'm just acting mayor, not even accustomed to everything involved with that. There's a full-fledged mayor over in Oakland, Jimmy Sunvold. What would he have to say about my being in charge?"

"Nothing that matters. I have coordinated this decision with all military leaders in the habitat, and we are throwing our collective might behind you. A decision had to be made, for the sake of order. Without one leader, we might fall into chaos."

"I'm listening."

"I took the liberty of coming here in force without calling ahead in case the telephone lines were tapped. We don't want any counter-governmental types getting entrenched around here. My men answer to you. In the present emergency, I offer my services to you as general of your guard. Accepted?"

Granmère smiled. "Most heads of state only get a captain of the guards. I am honored, and accept of course, if you feel all this is necessary. Commander-in-chief? Do we really need to use that title for me? I'd prefer to scale down this situation somewhat. If we stiffen our defense and attitude too much, that could cause trouble with the aliens. They're in total control here as far as I can see, whether it's through mass hypnosis or a real trip through space."

"I assure you, we are in deep space," General Oso said. "This has been confirmed to me by astronomers at Cal Berkeley, although they're having difficulty pinpointing where we are."

"*Ça n'a pas de nom!*" Granmère exclaimed. The situation was almost beyond belief to her.

"Continue to call yourself mayor if you wish," General Oso said. "That doesn't matter." He set the valise on the floor, pointed at it discreetly, and quickly placed his forefinger across his lips.

He's telling me the place is bugged, Granmère thought. *I'm not to mention the bag.*

The room was silent, except for the carefully chosen words and rustlings of the general.

Oso glanced around the room with wary, dark eyes, focusing momentarily on the uncovered bank of bay windows.

Casually, Granmère strolled to the windows and drew the drapes across them.

General Oso placed his valise on the conference table. Speaking about how nice the Arionnese-controlled weather had been that day, he released two valise snaps carefully and quietly. The case flopped open, revealing a small brown briefcase inside, which he also opened. It contained an electronic keyboard with an oval screen. It sat atop another valise of approximately the same size, this one dark blue with black straps. Maybe it wasn't a valise after all, Granmère decided, studying it closely. She didn't see a carrying handle in the midst of all of those straps.

"Madame Mayor, I do not believe we should pursue military action against the Arionnese," Oso said, touching two buttons to illuminate the screen in amber. "They're obviously too potent for anything we might throw against them."

"I suspect you're right about that," Granmère said.

She studied the electronic unit, which displayed black lettering on the amber screen, reading: "Sicom Silent Communication Unit, Model 001605½. Made in the U.S.A."

Leaning over the communicator, General Oso said, "Protesters have been gathering all evening in front of the Arionn Building."

"We know and were just about to discuss it," Granmère said, lying. She cursed under her breath at the delay in learning this and said, "It's one of the reasons we're burning the midnight fluorogas. We don't want those fools angering our hosts."

"Hosts? Ah, yes!" Oso cut a terse smile. "That's appropriate, I judge. We are aboard their habitat."

Making a mental note that he had employed the word "judge," Granmère wondered if this might indicate that Oso was not in fact making himself subservient to her. Granmère would be no one's puppet. Testing, she told him to take a seat at the table.

"Thank you, no," he said. "The mind has a tendency to sleep, sitting, you know? I prefer to stand." He thought momentarily, then: "Those protesters are a mixed bag—some peaceful, some potentially violent. Six members of the crowd have a history of bombings, always some public building and for a variety of reasons." He looked at Granmère, and she sensed that he was reading her face.

She took a deep breath, noting dark circles under his eyes.

"You didn't know about the bombers, did you?" General Oso said.

Sheepishly: "No."

"Well, you'll get intelligence like that when it's hot from now on, and we can move against them together, civilian police and military. I'm tying you in with military intelligence and all those federal boys around here that came along for the ride to Arionn. You've got a state of emergency here with no governor to call it. I'm talking bombers and potential riots."

He fingered a noiseless keyboard at the base of the sicom screen, producing this message: "THE HELL I AM! IT'S THOSE ALIEN BASTARDS THAT I MEAN!"

Granmère pursed her lips.

"We don't need to concern ourselves with the formality of declaring an emergency," Oso said. "Any fool can see what's going on out there. An undeclared state of emergency is better for a while anyway. We don't want folks panicking, and if I read the Arionnese right they don't want that either."

"They did say our lives should continue normally," Granmère said.

"That's right," the officer said. "Might I obtain a drink of water here? I'm parched." As he spoke, he keypunched: "UNDER PRESIDENTIAL ORDERS SIGNED 19 YEARS AGO, EVERY MILITARY BASE IS FIBER-OPTICALLY WIRED TO DETONATE SHOULD THE NEED ARISE, THUS PREVENTING ENEMY MISUSE OF U.S. PROPERTY. THE PACK BENEATH THIS COMMUNICATOR CONTAINS THE DETONATION TRANSMITTER, ENTRUSTED TO ME PERSONALLY BY THE PRESIDENT TO HAVE REPAIRS PERFORMED ON IT IN DALY CITY. KNOWN AS THE BUTTON PACK (NOT TO BE CONFUSED WITH THE BLACK BOX), IT IS OPERATIONAL ONCE AGAIN. I AM UNDER ORDERS TO TURN IT OVER TO THE COMMANDER IN CHIEF."

Granmère felt her face slacken. Inquisitively, she touched the center of her chest with one hand. Was he trying to turn this thing over to her? She retrieved a pitcher of water and a clean glass from a side table and placed them within his reach.

General Oso nodded, shutting his eyelids deferentially before looking up. The gesture struck Granmère as Oriental, and she reserved judgment about its sincerity. If he was subjugating himself to her, that was as it should be, civilian over military. But she almost wished he had come to stage a coup.

As Oso's fingers danced across the keyboard, Granmère squinted to read the message:

"OUR LOGIC AND TECHNICAL BOYS HAVE STUDIED VIDEO TAPES ON THE ARIONNESE PRESS CONFERENCE. THROUGH VOICE STRESS ANALYSIS, OPTICAL MOVEMENT PROBES, AND PURE COMMON SENSE WE'VE DECIDED THAT THE ARIONNESE WANT THIS HABITAT PRESERVED. WHY, WE DON'T KNOW YET. BUT YOU COULD FIND IT NECESSARY TO THREATEN THEM WITH DESTRUCTION OF THE HABITAT . . . A DANGEROUS TACTIC, BUT ONE THAT MIGHT WIN IMPORTANT CONCESSIONS."

Granmère moved closer to the screen and noted that she and Oso were around the same height.

Oso's glance flickered at her, and then he was back at the keyboard: "WE'VE SENT MECHANICAL PROBES BURROWING UNDERGROUND TO THE LOWER LIMITS OF THE HABITAT AND INTO THE AIR TO THE UPPER LIMITS, ASSUMING THERE'S A TOP AND BOTTOM TO THIS SETUP WHILE WE'RE IN ZERO-G. THERE'S SIMULATED GRAVITY ABOARD ANYWAY, SKILLFULLY AND MYSTERIOUSLY INTRODUCED. WE DON'T KNOW HOW THEY DO IT. ACCORDING TO THE PROBES, THERE'S ONLY ONE ALIEN SHIP ON THE HABITAT—BONDED INTO THE DOME AS A WEATHER CONTROL CENTER. THIS MEANS THAT UNLESS THE ARIONNESE CAN FREE THAT THING FROM THE DOME THEY'RE LIKELY TO MEET A FATE IDENTICAL WITH OURS."

Granmère found herself unable to accept what was happening to her. She looked at Oso, shook her head.

"USE SICOM TO RESPOND," Oso keyed. He poured himself a glass of water. Removing two red and white pills from his pocket, he washed them down. Aloud, he said, "With your permission, Madame Mayor, I will remain with you until my aides confirm that these premises are secure."

"Please do so," Granmère said. She keyed: "PREFER YOU KEEP BUTTON PACK. IT'S MILITARY."

The response was quick: "NOT PROPER PROCEDURE."

"SHOW MANUAL VERIFYING THAT," Granmère demanded.

"MADAME MAYOR, THIS IS A CLASSIFIED MATTER, AS YOU CAN APPRECI-

ATE. ONLY THE PENTAGON AND THE PRESIDENT HAVE COPIES OF THAT
MANUAL. I'VE BEEN BRIEFED ON IT, BUT CANNOT PRODUCE IT FOR YOU."

"HOW CONVENIENT."

He shrugged.

"I'M MAKING A NEW LAW THEN, GENERAL. I ORDER YOU TO KEEP THE
BUTTON PACK."

"PRIOR INSTRUCTIONS FROM HIGHER AUTHORITY SUPERSEDE. NOT MY
JOB TO KEEP."

"THIS HABITAT IS A NEW NATION, AND AS YOU SAID YOURSELF, I'M COM-
MANDER IN CHIEF. DO AS I COMMAND, YOU PETTY BUREAUCRAT!"

Hesitation, then: "THERE ARE FORMALITIES REQUIRED IN DECLARING A
NEW NATION. I BEG TO DISAGREE. HIGHER ORDERS . . ."

Granmère slapped his hand aside. "I SUBMIT TO YOU THEN THAT THIS
ISN'T A NATION AT ALL, AND SINCE IT ISN'T A NATION IT CANNOT HAVE A
COMMANDER IN CHIEF."

Granmère set her jaw and awaited his response.

Obviously troubled, Oso reached for the keyboard, but withdrew his
hand.

Granmère stamped one foot angrily. *The damn Button Pack's like a hot
potato!* she thought. *No one wants it. This guy's afraid of it himself. What a
chickenshit general! If those bases detonate, the whole habitat undoubtedly
goes with them. Yes, I see that on his face. Better that I have the thing than
this twerp. Get your stuff together, Liliane!*

"EXPLAIN DEVICE TO ME," Granmère keyed.

Leaving the communicator as a separate unit on the table, General Oso
lifted the Button Pack and held it with one hand in front of his stomach.
With his other hand he adjusted the straps, then inserted both arms through
them and reached behind his neck to connect a Velcro tie piece between the
straps. Another Velcro piece was secured across his lower back.

Granmère noticed that he took a deep breath, as if he didn't want to make
a mistake.

He passed one hand over the top of the pack, causing a hinged lid to flop
open in front of him. He folded four more hinged sections open from this
lid, revealing an intricate electronic panel that gave off a faint mauve glow.
Lifting a golden stylus from its bracket at the base of the board, he showed
Granmère that the stylus tip would fit into any one of hundreds of num-
bered little pegboard holes on the panel. He never actually inserted the
point during this demonstration, and upon close examination Granmère
determined why.

Along the dark brown edges of the board, etched in scrimshaw-thin lettering, she located the numerical key. Each number corresponded to a different military base: 106 designated one of the Equatorius submarine bases on Jupiter's moon, Europa; 721 and 722 were Fort Ord and Camp Pendleton, respectively, both in California but not aboard the habitat.

General Oso keyed an explanation that verified this, and when he touched a panel button the edges of the board rotated, revealing more numerical keys underneath. In his explanation he said that only this particular transmitting stylus could activate destruction commands. One unnumbered hole in the center of the panel, surrounded by a red circle, would detonate every base simultaneously.

"Would you like coffee or fruit juice?" Granmère asked, for the benefit of any electronic eavesdroppers present. (A beverage dispenser was mounted on one wall.)

"No, thank you."

Granmère realized with a rush that she had to be conscious of security on a level that was mountaintops above anything she had ever before considered. She wondered whether she should say anything to Oso about Brittany, then decided that Oso would already know about him. Besides, in a true crisis she felt even Brittany would set aside a personal quarrel for the sake of habitat security.

A true crisis? Wasn't this a true crisis?

Oso replaced the stylus. Then he leaned awkwardly over the sicom on the table and keyed: "ONLY ONE PERSON CAN OPERATE THE BUTTON PACK. PRESENTLY THAT IS ME. THROUGH A PARTICULAR PROCEDURE, I PASS THE MANTLE OF OPERATION ON TO THE COMMANDER IN CHIEF. ONCE THAT IS ACCOMPLISHED, I CANNOT AGAIN OPERATE THE PACK UNLESS THE COMMANDER IN CHIEF PERSONALLY FOLLOWS THE IDENTICAL PROCEDURE TO RELINQUISH IT TO ME."

That relieved some of Granmère's security concerns. The pack knew who was wearing it, she thought. It probably read Oso's finger and palm prints when he passed his hand over the top of the pack to open it. Undoubtedly there were additional reading mechanisms inside the stylus.

Via the communicator, she asked about these, and Oso confirmed them. He said the unit also picked up circadian and other biological rhythms characteristic of (and unique to) particular persons.

"WHAT ABOUT VOICE ANALYSIS, RETINA PRINTS, BRAIN SCANS, AND CELL SKIMMERS?" Granmère asked.

He answered that these were unnecessary complexities. The machine

never failed in making an identification. Also: "THE STYLUS SENSES VOLI-
TION. IF ANYONE ATTEMPTS TO FORCE THE PACK OPERATOR TO USE IT
AGAINST HIS WILL, IT DOES NOT FUNCTION. IT FOLLOWS THAT NO ONE
CAN KILL THE PACK OPERATOR AND THEN HOLD HIS OR HER HAND OVER
THE STYLUS TO SIGNAL DETONATIONS."

Granmère felt that she was about to swoon. Her thoughts scattered, then
regrouped. She felt awed and honored at the tremendous responsibility with
which she was being entrusted. If she played this correctly, her ace in the
hole was the power to destroy the habitat. The off-worlders wanted it intact,
but to what purpose? She couldn't play this incorrectly, not by one iota. No
empty threats. It would require meticulous planning, perhaps consultation.
Suddenly the council members seemed like mental lightweights to her, incapable of dealing with the scale of crisis. The military? A possibility. But
this general, who seemed to know more about the Button Pack than anyone
else, was scared of it. Someone had built it, maybe at the Daly City facility
he said had serviced it. But Granmère didn't want technical advice now.
She wanted a tactical and strategical brain trust.

I'll run an ad, she thought, using humor to kill her concentration momentarily.

She hadn't yet accepted the Button Pack. She could step aside, tossing the
hot potato. If not Oso, who would get it? Brittany, her archenemy, stood
next to her in the line of succession, and that would never do. What about
Mayor Wilde, patched together and jittery on drugs? That one might hiccup
at the wrong moment, plunging the stylus into the red-encircled hole.

Just considering my own safety, Granmère thought. *I have to take it. Did
General Oso wait for Wilde to hiccup herself out of here before appearing?*
Noting an expectant, thoughtful expression on his face as he gazed across
the Button Pack at her, Granmère surmised that he did. This chamber was
double-bugged, then, in all probability—by the Arionnese and by the U.S.
military.

My military, she thought. *What's left of it.*

"REMOVE YOUR BUGGING DEVICES FROM MY OFFICES, FROM MY VEHI-
CLES, AND FROM MY RESIDENCE," Granmère keyed, glaring fiercely at
General Oso.

If I'm truly in command, let's push it right now, she thought.

Oso, caught off-guard, hesitated before keying his reply: "OK."

As Granmère stared at these letters on the screen, she imagined Oso had
voiced them, and she heard them internally, in the meekest tone: "OK."

"TRANSFER THE BUTTON PACK TO ME," she ordered.

General Oso bowed his head in that Oriental manner again, removed the pack, and helped Granmère into it. With the unit folded open before her Oso removed the stylus and placed it upside-down into the largest hole on the panel, at the upper right corner. Subsequently he moved his open hand laterally across the entire panel, four times around the perimeter and then back across the surface twice, from corner to corner. The stylus glowed bright red.

"REMOVE THE STYLUS," Oso keyed, "GRASP IT IN YOUR FIST FOR A MOMENT AND THEN REPLACE IT IN THE BRACKETS. THE PACK WILL THEN BE AVAILABLE FOR YOUR USE. THE UNIT HAS ABSORBED MY VOLITION, KNOWS YOU ARE TO RECEIVE IT."

Now it was Granmère's turn to use the communicator on the table while wearing the Button Pack. She felt a lancing lumbar pain as she leaned over the table.

"THE STYLUS LOOKS RED HOT," she protested.

"IT IS, FOR ANYONE EXCEPT YOU. EVEN I CANNOT TOUCH IT NOW, FOR THE TRANSFER DECISION, ONCE MADE, CANNOT BE REVERSED BY THE TRANSFEROR. THE CLOCK IS TICKING. MOVE QUICKLY OR THE DEVICE WILL SHORT-CIRCUIT INTO USELESSNESS."

Another out, Granmère thought. *I can just let this thing die.*

Impulsively, she took hold of the stylus and squeezed it with all her might. Her hand and all of the muscles running up her arm ached. Her eyes ached as well, for she squeezed the lids shut around them, expecting the pain of a scorching burn. But the stylus, despite its appearance, was cool to her touch. Gradually, becoming conscious for the first time of a murmur of voices from the other side of the chamber, Granmère relaxed her grip. When she opened her eyes, she was staring at the golden stylus in her open palm.

"IT IS DONE," Oso keyed. "NOW IT MAY NOT MATTER SO MUCH IF THE ARIONNESE HEAR US. NO ONE CAN TAKE THE MECHANISM AWAY FROM YOU AND LIVE, NOT EVEN AN ARIONNESE, I SUSPECT. THE PACK HAS WHAT OUR ENGINEERS CALL 'KILLER WAVES.' DON'T ASK ME TO EXPLAIN, JUST KNOW THAT THEY EXIST. THE SAME HOLDS TRUE FOR ANYONE—EXCEPT YOU, PERHAPS, I'M NOT SURE—WHO ATTEMPTS TO TAMPER WITH IT."

Leaning carefully to avoid the lumbar pain, Granmère responded: "I DON'T CARE ABOUT THAT. I CERTAINLY DON'T WANT TO TAMPER WITH IT. COULD I THROW IT AWAY IF I WANTED TO? JUST CHUCK IT INTO BLACK SPACE?"

Angered, Oso stood militarily erect. He started to speak aloud, chewed at his lip, and leaned back over the sicom. "GIVE IT BACK TO ME BEFORE YOU DO THAT! I ASK THIS RESPECTFULLY. YOU MUST UNDERSTAND WHAT I'VE BEEN THROUGH GETTING THIS HUMMER REPAIRED, NEVER LETTING IT OUT OF MY SIGHT, LIVING ON BENNIES . . ." He withdrew his hand from the keyboard, stood erect again, and stared at the floor.

So that's what he popped, Granmère thought.

"OK, GENERAL, DISREGARD MY QUERY AND GET SOME SLEEP. WHAT'S THE TRANSMITTING RANGE OF THIS BABY? I MEAN, COULD I DETONATE BASES ON EARTH IF I WERE CRAZY ENOUGH TO WANT TO?"

General Oso tilted his face toward the ceiling, lids over his eyes, as if the question were patently ridiculous.

Quickly his features became emotionless and he returned to the sicom: "THE TRANSMITTING RANGE IS A BIT LESS THAN 200 MILLION KILO-METERS, WHEN BOOSTED BY RELAY STATIONS IN OUR SOLAR SYSTEM. WE MUST BE MILLIONS OF LIGHT-YEARS FROM THAT REGION, AND THERE-FORE CAPABLE ONLY OF EXPLODING BASES ABOARD THIS HABITAT. I HAVE DIFFICULTY GRASPING THE SCALE OF OUR JOURNEY MYSELF. NONE OF THE ASTRONOMERS WE WERE LUCKY ENOUGH TO BRING ALONG CAN EX-PLAIN THE ARIONNESE SPACE DRIVE AND G-FORCE CONTROL SYSTEM. IT MAY BE TIED IN SOMEHOW WITH THEIR GRAVITONICS, WHICH WE ALSO CAN'T FIGURE OUT."

Hearing two sharp raps at the door, Granmère caught Oso's gaze.

"I'll get it," he said.

A brief conference at the door ensued, between the general and another officer. Presently Oso announced, in a loud voice: "The building is secure, Madame Mayor. Will there be anything else?"

She told him that was all and thanked him.

He bowed and departed.

Granmère dimmed the lights and opened the drapes. From her chair at the table she looked around the room and across the lights of the spaceborne city. She felt like a captain on a doomed ship, protecting it to the last instant for corporation, for country, for honor and posterity. And this *was* a Great Ship, cast into the coldest, most unforgiving sea of them all. Granmère was, however, a captain without control over destination.

Destiny was a different matter. There she might exert some influence—at the proper moment, with the utmost of care.

A fatigue-laden thought found its way to the surface of her consciousness. It seemed strange to Granmère in this scenario that one of the citizens of her city might still wander into the Tenderloin district and get knifed. That didn't seem plausible in the shadow of super-technology, as if every aspect of life should be lifted by the bootstraps and cleansed for the new order. But apparently it wouldn't work that way. Some things would never change. So here they were, millions of humans kidnapped across countless star systems, replete with dirty laundry, murderers, hangups, and bathroom odors.

When at last Granmère stepped into the corridor, infrared sensors in the council chamber flicked off the lights behind her.

NINE

They tell us to go about our lives normally. Maybe
their weird alien graphs and projections show this is
possible. But let's focus on outdoor recreation for a
moment, just one area of our lives. As a species, we'll
go nuts without it. Fewer parks and natural areas are
available to us than before, meaning that any parcels
of undeveloped land on the habitat are at a premium.
Some people are going to get rich who wouldn't have
had a chance before the intervention. All this assumes
Zero Population Growth, an ideal we've never at-
tained. It may be that we'll have to ration public park
usage, setting up a coupon system like they used to
do with fuel during wartime. In lieu of that, usage
might be coordinated by time and name: If your last
name begins with "F" through "M," you can be in the
park between 10 A.M. and noon.

—Report submitted to acting Mayor Fouquet
by one of her aides

"Joseph, wake up! I'm frightened!"

Joseph turned on the sore shoulder that bothered him chronically when
he slept. Someone whispering . . . Thyla . . .

He saw her sitting up nude on the bed next to him, her small breasts and
strong chin silhouetted against moonlight passing through the bedroom window. Artificial moonlight, he reminded himself. They were nowhere near
Earth. Would it be like this on Arionn, when they arrived in a little more
than three weeks?

"I've been thinking about everything," Thyla Dunlap whispered. "There
are people on Earth we'll never see again. What if these monsters torture us
on Arionn? They must be cruel, taking us the way they did."

Joseph replied in full voice: "We don't know that for sure. Maybe they're just thoughtless. They'd have done more to us by now."

"Sssh! My parents will hear you! Maybe there aren't enough Arionnese here to completely control us yet, and they'll do terrible atrocities when they outnumber us."

"Don't be silly. What time is it?"

"Four-thirty. When is Kenny picking you up?"

"Five-fifteen."

"You reminded him not to come near the house? His car is dreadfully loud."

"A block and a half away. Don't worry." Joseph's eyelids felt leaden.

"Go ahead and nap," she said. "I'll get you up in time. I can't sleep anyway."

Joseph dropped his head back into one of Thyla's down pillows, closed his eyes. He drifted in and out of sleep.

When she nudged him on the hour, he was up, dressed, and out through the window of the one-story house in eight minutes, carrying her parting kiss into the chill morning. The Arionnese had even duplicated November weather, hadn't missed a detail in that respect. As he watched his moon-shadow ahead of him on the sidewalk, he wished something could be done to change the weather. It might be nice to have summer all the time as a sort of consolation.

As Tuesday dawned artificially on the habitat San Francisco, Granmère Liliane Fouquet began her first full day as commander in chief. A paper title she wouldn't use. Even "mayor" bothered her. When all was tallied, history might hold her accountable somehow for the debacle. Wasn't that the real motive behind General Oso's transfer of the Button Pack to her? He didn't want to be *blamed*.

History. It was Earth history that concerned Granmère, and probably Oso as well. But how would the facts be transported back, across an entire universe? Maybe she was worrying needlessly, and she might as well take the helm of the human population.

There were practical reasons for avoiding the title "commander in chief." One she had recognized immediately when it was thrust upon her: the holder of such a position might draw fire from the aliens. There was the classic security problem as well. Oddball humans were in no short supply on the habitat, drawn to the city by the bay in a mutant mass. Some would be more likely to threaten the family of a national leader than that of a mere councilwoman or even an acting mayor, and the crisis would make them worse.

Recalling the "moon" of the night previous and the effect the real orb was said to have on aberrant behavior, she wondered if "lunatics" would continue to proliferate on moonlit San Francisco nights. The most widely accepted theory held that it was the moon's gravity that caused the phenomenon, tugging at the fluids of the brain. But Granmère wondered now if it might be more of a primal thing, with the mere appearance of the moon bringing back ancient, savage memories to the most sensitive individuals. Maybe someone would do a study on that.

This was such a small nation, albeit an unofficial one. How did the habitat's area and population compare with the tiniest nations of Earth? She didn't know. Her people had to be under more stress per capita than anywhere else, and on the whole they weren't the sort who could tolerate it. Already they were leaping from the Golden Gate Bridge in droves, although the first contingent of guards would be stationed there and at other popular suicide spots within an hour.

The two-seater helicopter in which she rode sped along the "sunlit" side of the golfball-shaped Arionn Building, into a drizzle. Squinting through fine mist toward the pink-and blue-framed fireball that hung low on the horizon, she could not distinguish this sun from the real one she and her fellows had left behind. She wondered if it looked as authentic to observers on the edge of the habitat nearest sunrise, and decided it might be very different there. Unless these ingenious kidnappers had a method of projecting the sun into a region of near space, in the manner of a hologram. She wanted to look into that one day, and into the lunatic question, when she wasn't so busy. Beside her the pilot, a pint-sized mulatto man, chattered nervously.

"I don't like this, Madame Fouquet," he said, adjusting the window-wiper speed. "Not one little bit. I mean, the creatures might consider this controlled air space. They could blast us right outa here."

"We are not in a military craft, my dear Mr. Tubbi. The Arionnese know what's transpiring and why I'm here. We pose no threat to them whatsoever."

Granmère's unsubstantiated words were for the pilot's benefit as well as for the aliens, if they were eavesdropping. If Oso guessed correctly about the council chamber, they undoubtedly had a tap on this helicopter as well. She was struck by the utter absurdity of her craft as a threat. The Arionn Building towered above any other structure in the city, a mini-moon that probably bristled with concealed weapons. Her craft wasn't even a tick in comparison.

"Take us lower," she ordered.

Tubbi muttered something but nudged the control stick without delay. The nose of the craft tipped downward, and Granmère heard a change in the vibration of the rotors.

She estimated eighty or ninety demonstrators in the center of the tree-rimmed plaza by the building, carrying flashing electronic protest cards. Some had umbrellas or umbrella hats. She couldn't make out the slogans and demands, and heard occasional unintelligible bullhorn blasts above the drone and clatter of the helicopter. Knots of onlookers milled nearby, kept separate from the protesters by police lines.

"Land over there," Granmère said. She pointed to a space in an apartment building parking lot a short distance from the plaza.

Granmère released the shoulder harness and put her arms through the black straps of the Button Pack she had been carrying on her lap. General Oso's assurance that no one else could gain access to the pack's instrumentation didn't assuage her worries, and she brought it along anyway. It struck her as foolhardy to leave a device such as this with anyone, or even to hide it. Someone might find it and in turn conceal it from Granmère, or hurl it into space. Oso hadn't mentioned a method of electronically pinpointing its location or whether the behavior she had imagined would activate the defensive "killer rays." She would need to consult with him further.

I'll call it a communications pack if anyone asks, she thought.

Tubbi banked the craft and set it down as ordered.

Umbrella in hand, Granmère stepped from the running board to the parking lot. With the rotors whining to a halt in her ears, she saw two men running toward her from the direction of the plaza. One carried a video camera.

Reporters, she thought, opening the umbrella. *They'd better step aside when I bark.*

"What's that funny-looking thing you're wearing?" the man without the camera shouted. Tiny window wipers swung back and forth on the lenses of his eyeglasses. He gestured for the cameraman to move around to one side.

"A communications pack," Granmère said. *Oh, the predictability of these fools!*

"Keeps you in touch with everything, eh?"

"Right."

"Kind of an ugly thing."

"It's utilitarian," Granmère said, haughtily. She stalked past the reporter and his man, heading toward the throng.

It is rather an unsightly contraption, Granmère thought. *I'll put someone to work designing the case more stylishly. What do military functionaries know of style anyway? Nothing, obviously. An arrangement on my back? Perhaps, but the instrumentation must be available to me within seconds. As Oso said, this might be useful against our captors. Maybe the rig could spin around my body to the front, locking in place where I can get to everything.*

The reporter and cameraman scurried to keep up.

"What do you think about the murder-suicide rate in the last twelve hours?" the reporter asked. "Is it true that you're going to station plainclothes police officers on the Golden Gate Bridge to keep people from jumping off?"

"No comment," Granmère said, out of the side of her mouth.

A leak, she thought. *What else does the press know?*

"What do you think about these malcontents blocking the vans?"

"I don't know what you're talking about."

"I'm talking about civil disobedience," the reporter said. "It's one thing to protest, quite another to block commerce."

"Vans, vans, what are you talking about vans?"

"Three of 'em—gray and unmarked. Just twenty minutes ago, they tried to drive through the plaza to an entry in the building. Bringing something the Arionnese want, I suppose. What about that, Councilwoman Fouquet? Do our laws protect the Arionnese? What if they're hauling in military gear?"

"I'm acting mayor. As for the . . ."

"What's wrong with Mayor Wilde?"

"Illness. Nothing serious. She'll be back to work soon."

"What a time for her body to go gunnysack! What's the matter with her?"

"As I told you, nothing serious."

"Stonewalling, eh?"

"*Certainement non!* There will be announcements. Now, as for the vans, I'll look into the situation. I assure you our visitors do not need military gear. Don't you understand the scope of what they've done?"

"I do, but as acting mayor you should understand the scope of what's happening in the plaza. They started forming twelve hours ago, and I'm told you didn't learn of it until late last night."

When Oso told me, Granmère thought.

She shot a vicious glance at the reporter and noted a half-sneer on his ruddy, bespectacled face. She felt like ripping away one of his windshield wipers. "Don't be impertinent," she snapped.

How does he know these things?

The protesters were marching in a long oval adjacent to the fluted white columns that supported the Arionn Building. Beyond the columns, Granmère saw a gold teelike pedestal which she surmised housed elevators. How many creatures were inside the structure? The workmanship looked exquisite from this vantage point, and it had gone up so quickly!

Through openings in the crowd, she was able to read some of the programmable electronic demonstration signs:

"SEND US HOME!"

"DOWN WITH THE CREEPS!"

"MAYOR WILDE, WHERE ARE YOU?"

"YOU MAY AS WELL KILL ME. MY FAMILY'S IN ST. LOUIS."

"You didn't know about the vans, either," the reporter said, dogging her. "Don't you have a radio in that chopper?"

"Get away from me, you insolent fool. It wasn't working right, that's all." Actually, with all of her other concerns Granmère had not thought to turn the radio on. After a quick shower and a change of clothes at home, the helicopter had brought her directly here. She hadn't slept all night. Funny, though—she didn't feel particularly tired. The reporter was right. She should have been on top of intelligence reports from "the front."

It was a battle front, she told herself as she pushed her way through the multitude, trying to reach a police command post that had been established on one side of the protesters' marching oval. Spying an opening to her left, she moved toward it quickly, before it could close. Beyond the voices of those nearby she heard rhythmic, chanted slogans.

General Oso said there were professional protesters here. And bombers. Has he arrested the hard core people? I wouldn't think it would be his jurisdiction. Dammit, that intelligence hotline he promised me better start working!

The reporter was still right behind her, peppering her with questions. "Did you send someone to tail those vans? You didn't, did you, because you didn't know about them, did you?" The tone was childlike, taunting.

"Listen, *andouille*," Granmère said, raising her voice. "The police are here because I told them to monitor the situation." A *lie, but plausible.* Then: "They're following the vans, you can rest assured of that."

"I don't think any of us are going to be able to rest assured for a long, long time. On-what? What did you call me?"

"She called you a chowderhead," the cameraman said.

The reporter let Granmère continue alone. When she was delayed a short distance ahead by a knot in the crowd, she heard him speaking into the video camera: "There you have it, folks. We have an acting mayor who insults people in an arrogant, *alien* tongue and doesn't know what's going on in this city. Let's hope she learns her job quickly. This is no place for amateurs."

Resisting an urge to turn and administer a verbal thrashing, Granmère pushed her way through to the police command post. As she neared it, she heard the static pop of a public address system, with a female voice running through the time-hackneyed inanity of testing the system.

"This is the police! Testing, nine, seven, two! Can you hear me over there, Sergeant Wilkins?"

A youthful police captain hurried to greet Granmère. She had seen him before but refreshed her memory by glancing at his brass name tag: Captain Linnell.

"Right this way, Councilwoman Fouquet," Linnell said, taking her firmly by the arm. "Step aside, step aside. Coming through!" Some of the onlookers seemed to have taken root in the concrete aggregate, directly in Granmère's path. Sluggishly, they moved out of the way.

"Is it true that you're acting mayor?" Linnell asked.

"It's true."

"These demonstrators are angry. They want to see Mayor Wilde. Should we start locking them up?"

"Not yet. Where's the microphone?" Granmère put a hand out from under her umbrella. Feeling no rain, she closed the umbrella and slid it under one arm.

A policeman thrust a microphone toward Granmère, and she seized it.

The air smelled clean from the rain, and she felt her heart palpitate with excitement. She cleared her throat, depressed a button on the side of the microphone.

Somewhere behind her, static shot out of a big speaker.

"Listen to me!" Granmère said, hearing her amplified words made deeper by the speaker. "This is acting Mayor Fouquet. Please disperse immediately. You can only worsen the situation. Return to your homes, and rest assured that we are doing everything possible to rectify the situation."

From the midst of the protesters' oval, a bullhorn responded: "Rectify? You mean you'll get us back to Earth?"

"If possible. I don't want any of you to get your hopes up, but we will explore that avenue. Perhaps arrangements can be made to send some people back whose families are still on Earth . . . or arrange to bring family members here. No promises, so don't hold me to any of that, but we realize how distressing this is for many of you. In the meantime, we'll find food and places to live for every visitor who happened to be in the Bay Area when it was . . . uh, lifted."

Some of the crowd chuckled at her choice of words, and she expected someone to ask why she had specified the entire Bay Area. Wasn't she just the acting head of one city?

The question didn't arise, for the moment.

"Not enough!" a bullhorn blasted. "Send us home now! Send us home now! Send us home now!"

The protesters joined in the chant, and as it continued Granmère noticed to her dismay that many of the persons she had counted as onlookers were participating in the chant.

The movement was growing.

"Please stop!" Granmère shouted, feeling the uselessness of her words.

"Save us!" a woman screeched, nearby. Granmère could not locate her face.

People were massing close to the police command center, pushing the limits of the police lines. Tempers flared on both sides.

Granmère clicked off her microphone. "Bring in more officers," she ordered, looking at Captain Linnell. "Arrest anyone who becomes violent or who incites violence. No vandalism, either. Now help me back to my 'copter."

Back from his predawn Lawservice route and feeling more weary than usual for the hour, Henry decided to shower. It might perk him up. Shuffling past the unkempt double bed occupied on one side by Rachel, who remained asleep, he thought how pleasant it would be to don clean underclothes. Had Michelle done his wash? It had been piling up more than normal the past few days.

Henry slid open the top drawer of the dark mahogany chest of drawers his mother had given him. Nudging a tangle of unmatched socks out of the way, his hand touched something solid in the rear of the drawer. He identified it without looking: the family Bible his mother had brought to America from France. He hadn't opened it in a year, but found its presence reassuring.

He was able to locate only a clean pair of boxer shorts. No T-shirt, but the fresh shorts were more important anyway. He would wear the unlaundered shirt a while longer.

Henry pulled his clothes off, left them on his side of the bed with the pair of shorts he wanted to wear, and sauntered into the bathroom.

At that moment on the floor above, Joseph was just getting his day in motion, preparing to attend Thyla's liberal arts classes with her. He had no clean underwear and couldn't find his belt. Mostly naked, he conducted a hurried and unsuccessful search of the house and yard for his belt and couldn't locate Bumper, either. Bumper liked anything made of leather that he could rip into with his teeth. He carted them off to clandestine doggy places and buried them. He dug them up, chewed them more, and reburied them. Once when Joseph was pulling weeds for punishment he found a shoe of Dad's snarled in the root system of a big dandelion plant.

At great peril, Joseph slid into his parents' bedroom, grabbed his father's clean boxer shorts, his belt, and removed fifty dollars from the old man's wallet. Joseph knew full well the extent of the rage that would ensue, but decided to take the risk anyway. Nothing was more important to him than being with Thyla and having the money to do things for her. He showered in record time, dressed, and fled the house. As he was going down the front stairs, he heard the first booming tones of his father's anger.

"Who da fuck took my belt? An' where da fuck are my shorts? Shit! Can't a guy eben take a damn shower aroun' dis place? Joseph! Joseph, come here! Rachel! Where da fuck is Joseph?"

"What is it this time, Henry?" Rachel asked, slipping into an old gray terrycloth robe.

He was in the midst of a rolling boil, stalking around their bedroom in only a threadbare T-shirt. The rainment only partially covered his drooping, protruding belly and rode atop it, well above the belly button.

"It ain't nuttin' I done. I can tell you dat! Looky here!" He pointed at the bed, lowered his voice. "I ain't ravin', needer, so don't start none o' dat. I went inna goddam shower, an' when I come out all da clean clothes I'd arranged onna bed wuz moved aroun'." He spoke faster and faster, became very loud again. "My friggin' belt an' shorts is gone! Dey're gone! Izzat ravin'?"

Rachel rolled her eyes.

Henry rummaged through clothes, roared, "Where's my wallet?"

He located the billfold, bent it open. "I t'ink I had more dan fibe bucks in 'ear too. Shit! Yeah, goddam it. I had a fipty." He confronted her with bulbous, angry eyes, his lips puffed to ridiculous proportions and his jaw so taut that it nearly concealed his double chin.

Rachel shook her head in dismay and stared right back at him.

"You know anyt'ing about dis?" Henry asked.

"It's not exactly the crime of the century, Henry."

"Where's Joseph?"

Rachel shrugged. "I dunno." She leaned over and pulled on her slippers. The heating mechanism in only one of them worked, and its warmth felt good against her skin. As she moved around the bed to leave the room, she saw that her imperturbable attitude was enraging him further. Henry was melodramatic, she believed, and liked to generate reactions in people.

"What kinda place we got here?" Henry demanded.

"I have things to do. Do you suppose you might dress yourself?"

"Bitch! Listen, bitch. Call up Cartatucci an' tell 'im I ain't comin' ta work. I ain't got no unnerpants!"

With her back to him, she said, "It's Cartucci, Henry. Not Cartatucci. Your *Maman* says you should pronounce things correctly. Enunciate, On-ree. Speak with precision."

With tattered grace, she flowed from the room.

"Ya bitch! Ya hear me nunshiate dat? Bitch! Come back in here, ya bitch! Call Cartatucci, ya hear me?"

Standing in the kitchen, Michelle heard every word.

Rachel swept by toward the living room and didn't hesitate at the telephone mounted on the wall by the doorway. "Your father's in there with his dong hanging out," she said, flatly.

Michelle had heard such talk before in this house, and it never failed to numb her.

Television sounds began from the living room, a morning exercise program. Michelle had never seen her mother performing the exercises, and once when asked why she watched such shows, Rachel admitted, "I like to watch muscle men."

Henry slammed around in the bedroom, sending reverberations of rage through the house. Something heavy thudded against a wall.

Michelle plopped into a wooden chair by the glassed-in rear porch and bent over, burying her head in her hands. The chair legs wobbled. The tastelessness of the situation embarrassed her. She was certain someone passing by on the sidewalk or a neighbor in his own yard could hear her father booming obscenities. Maybe they could even see him and his private parts through the bedroom window, since the curtain was left open much of the time. Michelle longed for a normal family, one that wasn't subject to such outrageous scenes. The chemistry was all wrong, it seemed to her, irretrievably so. Despite that, despite everything, she reminded herself how much she loved everyone in her oddball family.

She leaned one elbow on the window sill, noticed that Stu wasn't on the back porch mattress. Through a dirty, cracked glass pane, she saw Bumper burying something in the back yard.

Under the dresser, Henry located a pair of striped boxer shorts, which he held to his nose. They were tolerable, and he pulled them on roughly, right leg first. He heard a seam pop but paid it no heed.

Henry located another belt on the floor of the walk-in closet, under a mishmash pile of shoes. This belt was black and dark brown, in alternating, nearly indiscernible squares, and he recalled why it had been tossed aside. It was a diet-enforcing waistband, a birthday gift from Rachel. It had an electronic buckle that measured caloric intake through hairlike probes that pierced clothing to touch skin, comparing the food intake with body size and condition. He loathed the belt, the way it spoke to him rudely whenever he tried to relax and eat.

It would be different this time, he vowed.

Placing the belt on the bathroom floor, Henry used the scale as a hammer, smashing it repeatedly against the buckle. He hadn't attempted that before.

"Indestructible mechanism," a whining electronic voice announced, from the stainless steel buckle. "Nothing can prevent performance of assigned duties. Put belt on or face immediate injury from cowhide upon backside."

Something hypnotic in the tone compelled Henry's obedience. He needed to get out of the house, and this appeared to be the only way to hold his pants up. It would drive him mad sitting around all day with Rachel. Tremulously, he slipped the belt through the loops of his trousers and pulled them on. The belt was engaged by feeding the loose end into its buckle in the manner of electronic calculator tape. By touching a button on top of the buckle, Henry adjusted the fit. He threw on a plaid sport shirt, left it unbuttoned, and wandered into the kitchen.

Barely noticing Michelle on the side chair by the porch, he prepared a cup of coffee in a one-cup "Java-Jammer." The belt made no comment, even when Henry dropped two big sugar cubes into his cup and stirred them to speed dissolving. He knew why the belt remained silent. It would take a few minutes for it to gauge his body and set up a diet.

He quaffed the brew without incident.

Clumping heavily into the living room, he retrieved the television channel selector from the table by Rachel with barely a glance at her. He folded his thick body into the recliner in front of the set.

Rachel didn't protest when he flipped to a morning talk show. One of the silly, hair-sprayed young actors from a nighttime soap opera was being interviewed. Nearly gagging at the sight of the fellow, Henry nudged a switch on the selector to douse the sound. Frequently they had sports personalities on this program and he would wait, keeping an eye on the screen.

Rachel crossed between him and the television and left the room.

"Fat cell alert!" the belt said. "Dangerous expansion! If subject touches another sugar cube, this mechanism will cinch his belly so he cannot breathe. Required lunch today, considering weight, body type, and improper caloric ingestion: Twelve centiliters of lean fish, without bone, nine centiliters of boiled green beans or carrots, a slice of unbuttered whole wheat toast, and a twenty-two-centiliter glass of unsweetened grapefruit juice."

Henry's stomach growled.

He didn't care what the belt said. He had a plan to get rid of the infernal gadget that very morning.

After Michelle kissed her father good-bye at the front door and he departed for his second job of the day, she carried a paper bag full of garbage that wouldn't fit into the impaired trash chute on the back porch. Sealing the refuse into one of the large plastic sacks there, it occurred to her that Stu's nearby mattress wasn't a very nice place to sleep, scrunched as it was in a narrow space between two walls, with heaps of dirty clothes and sacks of garbage that had to be negotiated to reach it. The room smelled pungent, and she sprayed it with disinfectant.

These trash sacks had been here too long awaiting a trip to the dump, and she wondered how many rats might have chewed through the plastic where she didn't want to look. She saw them on occasion, running for cover at the sight of a human, and envisioned whole families of them traveling labyrinthine passageways in the trash. They had names, personalities, and problems, just as her family had. She pictured the Fouquets sitting around the dinner table in the rubble of this house, all of them with rodent snouts and tiny, dark eyes. The head rat, Granmère, wore a spotless pale green suit, and she issued squeaky commands. Granpère Rat and Henry Rat leaped around doing her bidding, carrying to her trays of scrap food, arranged on beds of brown lettuce. All of the little rats laughed and laughed and laughed.

She repeated the scenario, and everyone was a flea.

Then the front door slammed, and she heard quick footsteps. They weren't the familiar footsteps of her parents, or of her brothers, which left but one logical choice.

Michelle entered the kitchen through one door as Stu came in another.

"Did you sleep here last night?" she asked.

"Naw."

"Is the porch too dirty for you? I could help you clean it after school."

"Naw, don't bother. This one's a road kid, remember? I've crashed in worse pads." He opened the refrigerator, looked inside.

"You should get ready for school, Stu."

"Nothin' to eat around this joint." He slammed the refrigerator shut, stared pensively at Michelle. "I been out all night, girl, getting to know the streets o' this burg. You don't survive if you don't know the streets."

"You can have my bran muffin."

"I don't eat stuff like that. I'll go out and scrounge around, and when I get things goin' in a few days I'll bring in some groceries."

"You don't have to do that. It's more important that you attend school. I'll help you enroll, and we'd better be on our way in a few minutes."

"Forget it, girl! I ain't goin'!"

"Whass goin' on out here?" Rachel hovered in the doorway at her bedroom, holding her Biblecorder under one arm. The book's headset was around her neck, earphones forward. From the way she leaned to one side and hung her head, eyes tilted toward Stu, it was apparent to Michelle that her mother had been drinking Bug Juice.

"Nothing, Mother. We're just getting ready for school."

"Not me," Stu said. He folded his arms across his chest.

"So you don' wanna go ta school, huh?" Rachel said, leering at Stu.

"No, I don't!" He eyed the available exits.

"Well, thass awwright. Whass ta learn 'ere anyhoo? I don' care if you go ta school or not."

Abruptly, Rachel stood up straight and pulled together her sagging facial muscles. "You thought I was drunk, didn't you? Well don't believe everything Michelle tells you about me. I fooled you, isn't that so? I know everything that's going on around here. I even know where Beauregard hides, and if you're not good little boys and girls I'll turn him loose on you!"

Stu forced a smile, glanced uneasily at Michelle, then looked back at Rachel. "You mean I can live here and not go to school?" he asked.

"Sure," Rachel said, magnanimously. "Why not? I need an errand boy now anyway, and that's more important than classwork. I'll call in my order. Michelle, show him where Rankin's General Store is on your way to school."

"But is that legal keeping him out?" Michelle asked.

"Legal schmeegal," Rachel said, with a contemptuous sniff. "I'm no legal beagle. What do I care about laws?"

Stu laughed, and on the way to Rankin's he told Michelle she had a "funny" family, whatever that meant. He also told her he would see her at school after delivering Rachel's groceries.

"But you said you didn't want to go," Michelle said. They were on the block paralleling the Special Purposes lockup. She didn't have time to go that way this morning, though it was her favorite route to school.

"Maybe it'll be different this time," he said. "Who knows? I'll give it a chance, and if I get bored I got options, you know?"

A maroon Special Purposes Police van rushed by, red lights flashing and sirens wailing. It turned left at the next corner, heading for the lockup. She wondered if the rumor about homosexual roundups was true, and worried about what would happen if Henry went berserk and denounced Renney as gay. The boy was not that way at all, having confided to Michelle his interest in a girl, but the word of a parent would carry strong weight. It might happen when Henry was crazy-angry with Rachel.

"There's Rankin's," Michelle said, pointing the store out. It was just ahead, on the other side of the street. "Go inside and ask for Rachel Fouquet's bag. She pays once a week, and that's not today. The bag'll be stapled shut across the top."

She detected a momentary, knowing glint in his eyes.

They parted a few steps farther along, agreeing to meet in the vice-principal's office in an hour.

"The school is two blocks down this street and a block to the right," Michelle said, glancing back. "I'll ask for time off to help you get registered."

Stu waved, waited the passage of a truck, and crossed the street.

In the vice-principal's office Michelle introduced Stu to one of the elderly secretaries, Miss Norman, as her "new brother."

"New brother?" the woman exclaimed, looking over bifocals from the other side of the counter. "What on earth do you mean? He's your age, child."

"I'm thirteen, actually," Stu said. "She's only eleven. She means I'm kind of adopted by her parents. Mine are in Loosy-anna, and I was visiting the Fouquets when all hell broke loose."

"We do not employ language of that sort here, young man," Miss Norman said, raising her silvery eyebrows in displeasure. "I will overlook it this time, but only this time."

Michelle saw Stu glance away, toward the doorway and freedom. He had done that in the kitchen with Rachel, too, surveying the escape routes. Stu thought ahead. He was probably envisioning himself bolting through the doorway and down the hall.

Miss Norman switched on the computer terminal atop the counter. "Your guardians will have to appear here with you," she said.

"I don't have no guardians no more. I'm not in reform school now."

"You misunderstand. Oh my, reform school! I'm talking about Mr. and Mrs. Fouquet."

"Dad's always at work and Mom's sick," Michelle said.

Miss Norman sighed, as she had some acquaintance with the family. "All right," she said. "Have them come in as soon as possible, Michelle." She adjusted her spectacles, looked at Stu. "Why were you in reform school?"

"I . . . uh . . . me and some friends broke into a warehouse and took some stuff."

"Have you ever attended an English class?"

"What do you mean?"

"You'll find out." She stared at him sternly. "There will be no breaking and entering around here. Understood?"

"Understood."

"Very well." Miss Norman pressed two keys on the terminal, glanced sidelong at Stu. "Your full name and date of birth, please."

"Stu Kroemer. March 7, 2072."

Haughtily: "Pay attention. I said your full name. Is Stu short for S-t-e-w-a-r-t or S-t-u-a-r-t?"

"Neither one," Stu said. "It stands for Studebaker. I was borned inna backseat of a 1951 model onna way to the hospital."

"Borned." She shuddered. "What on earth is a Studebaker?"

On earth, Michelle thought. *Will sayings like that survive on our new planet?*

Stu was replying, and Michelle heard his words with part of her brain. "A car," he said.

"A 1951 car was still running in 2072? That's amazing."

"It's still running, lady. Uh, Miss Norman. I seen it just a few days afore I come to Frisco."

Miss Norman shook her head, predictably. *"Saw it . . . before . . . came . . . San Francisco, never Frisco."*

"Frisco is like Crisco and has bad connotations," Michelle thought, recalling a remark of her mother's. What did it mean?

Miss Norman keypunched his first name in full, and Stu saw it in black letters on amber. "Middle name," she said.

"None. How about shortening my first name back to 'Stu' and tossing in the middle name 'Baker?' I think Stu Baker Kroemer sounds better, and I don't want nobody laughin' at me."

"It's 'I don't want anybody,'" Miss Norman said. "And we're not in the business of *making things sound better.* I'll fill in your full name, such as it is."

The telephone rang at a nearby desk, and Miss Norman went to answer it.

"I wish I'd lied to her about my name," Stu said to Michelle, in a low tone. "If the other kids ever found out, I'd have to fight my way outta here. I'm plenty tough but not very big. I'd probably go after heavyweights and they'd cream me. It's happened before."

"Over your name?"

"Yeah. And other things come up a girl wouldn't understand."

"Try me."

"Just walking down the sidewalk, for example. It's a territorial thing with some guys. There's squares and a center line usually, and when you're walking toward a guy he crowds over onto your side. You've gotta either get out of his way or bump him. I don't back off. On a bus seat too, a guy'll crowd his legs and his butt over on your side, making you sit all scrunched up."

"That's ridiculous."

"No it isn't. It's survival. As I said, you wouldn't understand."

Michelle listened to part of Miss Norman's conversation. Then Michelle said, "Your speech patterns vary, Stu. You can speak correctly when you want to, and like a spacedock worker at other times. Why do you suppose you do that?"

"I dunno."

Michelle smiled.

"Miss Hotsy-Totsy over there *is* in the business of making things sound better," Stu whispered. "Hear the way she kept correcting my pronunciation?"

"Uh-huh. You were doing that on purpose, to get her reaction."

"Maybe. I should have opened up on her and smarted back, though."

"You were wise not to. So that was your poor little street urchin routine, huh?"

Stu cut a crafty smile.

"Demonstrating that you don't really belong here?"

"Don't dig too deep, for crying out loud. I was just having a little fun with her." Under Michelle's relentless stare, he broke and admitted, "I suppose I was. Yeah, you're right."

TEN

Their language is, to say the least, complex. Utilizing special sound segregating equipment, we recorded their sketchy public announcement, the one made from the Arionn Building plaza. When the effects of their translating plate are removed (assuming this particular spokesman is typical of the race) it is apparent that they make peculiar consonanted utterances, like "glppz," "frtnl," and the like. The hand gestures are either signs for the deaf/mutes of their race, or, more likely, an integral part of their language. We believe that the hand gestures are vowels or the equivalent, which accompany spoken consonants.

—Confidential message sent to General Oso,
from the Language Department, U.C. Berkeley

On her way to third-period class, Michelle noticed a group of students milling around a fat boy by the lockers. The boy at the center of attention was Roland (Roley) Peterson, an eighth-grader and the smartest kid in school. He held a large black-and-white glossy photograph and was explaining it.

Michelle moved closer to listen.

"My uncle works for the *Bay Daily News*," Peterson said, with gushing pride. "This is a shot of the map that's going to be in tonight's news cube."

Michelle saw a circular map, with San Francisco, Berkeley, and Oakland near the center.

"This shows the extent of the Arionnese theft," he said. "A circular section of Earth, with a diameter of 80.46 kilometers . . . extending just east of Mount Diablo . . ." His hand slid around the perimeter of the chart. "To the south, Woodside is near the edge . . . in the north, Vallejo is comfortably aboard . . . Novato to the northwest and Pittsburg to the northeast barely made it."

The students were in awe.

"Wow," one said.

"Incredible."

Michelle, no exception, described it as "unbelievable." She felt a stirring of excitement in her chest.

"Look here," Peterson said, pointing. "To the west. We've got a whole panful of the Pacific Ocean aboard, extending 22.5 kilometers west of San Francisco. This part is really amazing. Sea waves are hitting shore as they always have. We even have tides, faithfully following the heights and patterns they achieved on Earth. The weather's even normal for this time of the year, and you've all seen the 'Moon' and the 'Sun.'"

"Yeah," a short, bespectacled boy from the sixth grade said, "They towed 'em clean out of our solar system."

"Really?" a little freckle-faced girl said.

A boy guffawed, and then another boy exclaimed, "Holy shit, this is wild!"

A tittering of nervous laughter ensued, and Michelle heard a girl explaining to the naive, freckle-faced one that a sun and a moon couldn't possibly be in tow, no matter the technology of the Arionnese.

Michelle wondered if there was in fact a limit to what the Arionnese could accomplish.

Peterson slid another glossy photograph out from behind the first. "This shows the exterior of the habitat from space," he said. "It's the same view you saw on the alien news broadcast. They released it to us."

"How'd they take the picture?" the boy from the sixth grade asked.

"I guess they have cameras mounted on the habitat's exterior," Peterson speculated. "Or maybe they've got an escort ship out there."

"Has anyone seen their ships?" Michelle asked.

"No. Uncle Roy thinks there might be a huge fleet out there, maybe on the underside of the habitat where we can't see it. He doesn't think we're moving under our own power, either—he says a powerful space tug might be way out ahead. I kinda disagree with him. My bet is that they installed a powerful space-drive mechanism inside and underneath the Arionn Building, extending through the ground to the 'bottom' of the habitat. There's really no top or bottom in space, you know. We just think there is because of the artificial gravity system they installed."

As the group dispersed and hurried off to class, Michelle thought about the way fat old Roley Peterson was being treated with new respect. Before the Great Theft he had been an outsider, so smart that classmates were hesitant to approach him. Now it seemed that he had something important to offer. The old social distinctions were disintegrating.

Henry knew he would have to be quick and deft, or the day would be ruined. It was late morning, and with his stomach knotted in hunger pangs he entered Uchiyama's Clothing Emporium. So as not to alarm the diet-enforcing belt, he ambled toward the men's furnishings department. They had belts in that area that held a man's pants up without telling him what to do, but Henry tried not to think about them. Nothing he had heard about diet-enforcing belts indicated that they could read minds. As far as he knew they simply reacted to the presence of food and barked out consumption commands to the wearer, having established by body size and condition how much and precisely what the wearer could eat.

Bedtime would be the easiest time to get rid of the annoying device, when he removed his trousers anyway. But that would require an entire day under mechanical tyranny, and Henry couldn't bear the thought of that. Preparing for battle, he placed his wallet and all the other objects from his pants pockets into a jacket pocket, zipping it shut.

Henry's amble had become a nervous, rapid march toward the men's room and the fruition of his plan. He skirted the men's furnishings department, saw the lavatory door looming ahead. Salvation lay beyond that door.

He straight-armed the door, and it bounced in a squeal of protest against the restroom wall. People sounds from the store diminished, replaced by water that ran somewhere through a pipe. The room smelled antiseptic.

There were three stalls on the right, and he made for the one closest to the wall. Once inside, he was careful to leave the cubicle door barely latched. This was important, as he might need to effect a rapid escape from an angry belt. He loosened the belt, dropped his trousers and boxer shorts, and plopped onto the cold toilet seat. Casually, he pushed his shoes against one another to lift his heels out of them.

Then, gripping the waistband of his shorts with one hand, he jumped up and out of his shoes and trousers, taking the shorts with him and crashing out of the stall. With his shorts around his thighs, Henry rolled across the floor like a parachutist completing a fall, an injury-avoidance method he had learned in the National Air Service.

The sink hadn't been accounted for in his desperate plans, and he thumped the middle of his back into it. The bruised area shot a sharp pain through his nervous system.

This being the moment for someone to appear, the restroom door opened. Henry was crouched by the sink pulling on his shorts when he noticed an impeccably dressed man in a gray tweed suit standing just inside the doorway, staring aghast at the scene before him.

"I was havin' a little trouble with my trousers," Henry said, feeling the hotness of blood that rushed to his face. He straightened, adding quickly, "Just in case you're thinkin' funny business is goin' on here, look around. There's nobody else in here."

The man stared at Henry disdainfully.

Henry went blank with rage and embarrassment, said, "I ain't no damn queer!"

"Indeed!" the man exclaimed. "Perhaps you were expecting someone!" With a snooty toss of his head he turned and departed.

That was one of 'em, Henry thought. *A flamin' queen if ever I've seen one!*

Inside the stall, Henry's belt-propelled trousers were leaping about, slapping against the floor and toilet. "Where are you, Fouquet?" the belt asked, in its irritating mechanical whine. "Escape alert! Escape alert!"

Henry tiptoed to an adjacent stall, and with two quick thrusts under the side wall retrieved his shoes. His original plan had been to attack the belt at this point and use his considerable strength to wrench it free of the trousers. They had served him well, and deserved a better fate than flopping around in a toilet stall.

But what if the belt got a death grip on him, around an arm, a leg, or even his neck?

Henry retreated.

Resigning himself to the loss of his trousers, he put on his shoes and strolled into the men's furnishings department to make two purchases. That clerk by the cash register had better not laugh if he knew what was good for him.

When Michelle skittered down the steps of Paddington Elementary School at the end of the day, she was surprised to see her grandfather's shiny black sedan parked on the street, beyond the wide lawn. He only appeared like this on special occasions, and Michelle's heart skipped with joy. She completed the staircase and bounded across the grass, books under one arm, her ponytail flying in the wind she made.

When she opened the car door, he greeted her with his toothy farm-boy grin. She pulled the heavy door shut behind her, leaned across the console, and kissed his cheek.

"Buckle your seat harness," he said.

Michelle did as she was told and would have done it anyway.

"You're my special girl," Granpère Gilbert said as he started the car. "There's a present for you on the back seat." He reached back before she could swivel her seat, handed her a gleaming metal box.

"Oh, Granpère!" she gushed. "Thank you!"

The box was heavy for its size, about as big around as one of her father's cigar boxes but twice as high. It was cool to her touch. As she turned it over she saw a number of geometric-shaped inlays on each surface, in a variety of metals, mostly brass and stainless steel, she judged. There seemed to be no top or bottom to it.

"It's solid?" she asked. "It's so beautiful. You made it, Granpère?"

"It's not solid, dear," he said, guiding the sedan manually into traffic. "Of course I made it!" Michelle detected goodnatured agitation in his tone.

"I love it."

"In my old age, I've been tinkering with things more and more. I've had the inclination and the time. I think I told you I was in a cryptography unit during Moon War IV."

"Yes, you did."

"Most of the fellows were involved in code work, setting up or deciphering secret messages. A lot of our messages went out by radio, but they were forever getting intercepted by the Nazis, no matter how elaborate our signal scrambling mechanisms were. The Nazis had the same problem, and we picked off everything they sent. Finally one of our generals decided to put our messages on parchment and transport them by courier rocket. You with me so far?"

"Yes."

Michelle watched a shaggy cocker spaniel by a Lutheran church rummage for food around a garbage dumpster.

"Of course those rockets weren't labeled 'Courier Ship' on the sides or anything like that. They looked like or actually were civilian craft. That's where I got involved, designing secret message compartments in which to hide classified documents."

"It sounds terribly exciting."

"Maybe it was exciting for the couriers themselves. Me, I was ensconced in a nice safe bunker working with drafting tools and prototypes. It was challenging, that's for sure, and I felt some excitement whenever I learned how well my compartments made it through. The object was to assume that our rocket would be captured, as many of them were. I had to hide a message aboard where their experts wouldn't find it, no matter how hard they looked or how much they took apart. It got kind of involved, of course, because we had to have people on the other end who knew my methods."

"You had an important job."

"That I did." He rubbed his eyes, and looked fatigued to Michelle. She heard frailness in his voice as he continued: "We set up decoy compartments some of the time, so the enemy thought they found what they were looking for."

"With fake messages, right, Granpère? Stuff that threw the enemy into confusion or sent them in the wrong direction?"

"You'd have done well, Michelle. You're absolutely correct. Each message went into a box like you're holding, except the boxes were much smaller, so small that they could be concealed inside bars of alloy, behind painted surfaces, that sort of thing. My boxes were as small as a speck of dust, and as you can imagine they required special equipment to open them. They were designed so that even if the bad guys found them they wouldn't be able to get inside."

"Did you rig them with explosives? I mean, was that practical for things that small?"

Granpère Gilbert smiled. "No, as strange as it sounds, we had a code of honor preventing that. Cryptographers on the other side were just like us, and each side played similar games at my level. It was a mental challenge for everyone involved, despite the stakes, meaning the Moon."

"Nazis with a code of honor? I can't believe that."

"All the people in their war machine weren't necessarily in the Party. Most were just citizens, conscripted into the fray, fighting for their nation. They were caught up in it, I guess, and didn't recognize the evil of their own government. Cryptographers on either side were a special breed, the sort of people who enjoyed mathematical puzzles and gadgets. We didn't think about philosophy, human rights, and all that. We just did our jobs."

"It almost sounds like fun."

"Oh, it was. To show that we had broken into a code box, we sent it back to the other side, opened and empty of its submicroscopic contents."

"Did any of your boxes come back?"

"Two. They figured one out, and a crazy that slipped into their midst blasted the other one open, destroying its contents." Granpère smiled. "The one they blasted was a toughie, the forerunner of the beauty you're holding."

"This one's even tougher?"

"Well, it's easier in a sense, by virtue of its size. Things could be done to get into yours. But if yours were real small like the others they wouldn't crack it legitimately. I was working out the design for it when the war ended, then laid it aside for thirty years and came back to it only last year." His voice betrayed pride in the completion of an important effort. "Sent a copy of it by military express just yesterday to what they call 'Habitat HQ.' It's our counterpart of the Pentagon, and I thought they should have it."

"Granpère, is there something inside this box?"

"Maybe. Go ahead and take a look."

"I can't open this!"

"Then you'll never find out what's inside."

Michelle discovered that some of the geometrically shaped pieces moved along each surface, either rotationally or through sliding maneuvers. But she discovered no pattern, and soon gave up the effort, declaring she couldn't get anywhere with it.

Granpère removed a folded sheet of paper from his cardigan pocket and handed the sheet to her.

As Michelle accepted this from him, she realized that he was stopping the car. They were in the parking lot of the Catholic church that he and Granmère attended every Sunday, sometimes with the rest of the Fouquets, except for Rachel. Granpère's car was the only vehicle on the lot.

"Let's review the instructions," he said. "After you've memorized the steps, I'm going to destroy the sheet."

Michelle felt herself being drawn into a new world, beyond the countless wonderful moments she had theretofore shared with her grandfather. It was as if they were in a war together, sharing the knowledge of his arcane panels, hiding important secrets from the enemy. And who was that enemy? Why, everyone else, of course. Everyone other than Michelle and her grandfather.

"The box is an elaborate arrangement of moving panels, buttons, and removable pieces," Granpère Gilbert explained. "There are six pieces which must be removed as you proceed, and they are replaced subsequently in different positions. All pieces must be reconnected before the box will open. Just imagine doing this with a speck of dust!"

Michelle unfolded the instruction sheet, which was quite large and printed on both sides, depicting steps and sketches that concerned the six sides of the puzzle box.

"It's designed with so many variables that I don't believe anyone could open it unless told how," Granpère said. Note the many fine marks along the edges of the pieces that must be aligned precisely. There are 22,305,116 variables."

"Wow," Michelle said. "How neat!"

The instruction sheet listed forty-six steps, which at first glance seemed mind-blistering to Michelle. As her grandfather leaned toward her and went over each step with her, however, she felt the intricate procedure sinking into her brain with startling clarity. Never before had she experienced such effectiveness of concentration, and she heard an urgency in his tone that drove her. She imagined that unfriendly persons wanted to know the secrets of the puzzle box.

"I can do it, Granpère," she said at last. "Let me go ahead and try."

"All right."

Glancing back and forth from the sheet to the box, Michelle's fingers slid across the sides of the box with increasing ease. Slide here, remove there, slide two more, replace the removed piece and spin it to the third marking . . .

"Perfect, perfect," Granpère said. "I knew you could do it!" Then he chuckled. "Maybe it isn't as difficult as I thought."

"It's difficult! It's terribly difficult!"

Her fingers faltered. She felt torpidity in her brain, re-examined the instruction sheet.

"Uh-oh," he said.

"I'm sorry, Granpère. I got mixed up, just when I thought I had it."

"You were doing fine, all the way through step thirty-seven." He slid back the last panel that Michelle had moved, a rectangular brass piece. "I should have cautioned you to go more slowly, but you were doing so well. Unfortunately that mistake you just made is now imprinted in the synapses of your brain, and you're likely to repeat it each time. Also repeat the correction I've made. You understand it?"

"Yes, Granpère."

"Make the mistake again now, and then correct it. There is a learning process in the fingers, and you must do it yourself to learn."

Michelle again slid the brass piece in the wrong direction, then returned it.

"When I studied the clarinet," the old man said, "my teacher always told me to perform each exercise slowly at first, because once made, mistakes tend to be repeated. He said the brain had gotten itself programmed incorrectly."

"I didn't know you played the clarinet," Michelle said, studying the instruction sheet again.

"Not for fifty years I haven't. I still have my instrument, though. My mother loved the sweet sound of it and insisted that I never get rid of it."

"I see what I did wrong," Michelle said. "I had the right piece, but instead of sliding it I should have pressed it."

"Very good. Proceed."

She pressed the piece, then found a square stainless steel piece on an edge of the other side that could now be removed. She popped it off, glanced at the instruction sheet, and twisted that entire side of the box as a unit four times all the way around and replaced the piece.

Her grandfather grew silent as she completed the last steps.

When at last she had followed all the instructions faithfully, Michelle found that she was able to slide one of the sides of the puzzle box as a unit. She turned the box so that this side was on top and was sliding it open when Granpère snatched the box from her and moved everything around so that it wouldn't open.

"Run through the whole thing again," he said. "Go as far as you can without looking at the sheet, but when you're uncertain, look back at the sheet. Try to go farther and farther into the procedure without looking at the sheet. It's going to take you a while, so I'm going into the rectory to talk with Father Colbert."

So engrossed was Michelle in the puzzle box that she heard his words in a fog, barely noticing him as he stepped from the sedan and closed the door behind him.

Gilbert activated the vacuum door-locking mechanism to seal the car, administering a gentle, percussive thump to Michelle's ears.

Michelle went through the whole thing a second time, then scrambled everything according to the instructions without opening the box and did it again, feeling her grandfather wouldn't want her to look inside until she could do it without a crib sheet.

On her twelfth pass, Michelle completed the steps without a single error. She had to concentrate extra hard to get by step thirty-seven, but she made it.

She folded the instruction sheet, stuffed it under the seat of the car where she couldn't see it, and began anew. Her fingers built up a tempo and moved deftly, as if they had independent eyes and brains. Never before had she learned anything so quickly, but her achievement did not particularly amaze her. Michelle was doing it for her grandfather and for herself, calling upon their shared strength. She was halfway through. This time she deserved to learn what was inside. Faster and faster she worked.

Granpère returned just as she slid the lid off and placed it on the dashboard. It looked like a bookcorder inside the box, bound in fancy red leather.

"Remove it," Granpère said, edging into the driver's seat. "Go ahead, look at it."

Michelle removed the volume, found that it was not a bookcorder at all but a standard nonmechanized book. She lifted the front cover and saw a pastel yellow envelope inside bearing her name. She left the envelope in place and turned the page. There, next to a handwritten title page bearing only Granpère's name, was a picture of him as a young man. He wore a funny brimmed hat, and his clothes fit him too loosely.

"I snatched that from one of our picture albums," Granpère said. "The old woman never liked that shot anyway; she said the suit didn't fit me."

He touched a heat-sensitive tab on the corner of the photo, and the image did a little thousand-frame jig, clapping its feet and tipping its hat at the end before returning to the original pose.

Michelle giggled, touched the tab, and watched the jig again.

Michelle had seen the picture before and liked it. To her, it represented the way he really was at heart . . . an unadorned, simple man who liked to dance. Granmère had changed him in many ways. Michelle was certain of that. But this simplicity and immense good-heartedness still showed in the man.

Michelle turned the pages. It was written entirely in French in her grandfather's firm hand.

"It was easier for me to compose in French," he said. "It flowed. And I thought it was nicer to leave it in my handwriting than to have it printed."

"It's beautiful." Michelle recognized only a smattering of the words and couldn't make sense of very much.

"It's about the old country," he explained, "and about San Francisco when we came here during the European depression more than a half century ago. Your grandmother used to yell at me for spending so much time at my desk, so I got in the habit of rising at four A.M. to write."

"But Granmère's so busy herself. How could she feel that way?"

"Unfortunately, I only felt like writing when she was around, or at least when she was in the house. She was in the old country with me, and we came here together. It was inspirational having her nearby."

"You really love her, don't you?"

"Yes," he said, revealing emotion in his tone.

"So much in your book to read. I'll study my French very attentively now, Granpère."

"That's good." His chin bobbed slowly in the preoccupied manner of an old man. "I had the pages professionally bound, and thought the book should be kept inside a nice box, so that someone wouldn't be so likely to throw it away."

"Oh, Granpère! Who would ever throw this beautiful book away?"

He smiled. "I don't know. It just seemed to me that it stood a better chance inside a pretty container. The rambling writings of an old man, you know. In a foreign language, too. You'll keep it in the box always?"

"Of course I will," she promised, seeing worry in his expression. "This should be passed on to my children at the proper time, don't you think?"

"That's up to you, sweetie."

"Your book is full of family information, and should be shared." She examined the pages closely. "This is the original, isn't it?" She looked at him.

"The one and only. It's yours, to do with as you wish."

"I could make copies of it someday if I wanted?"

"Sure."

"Do you have a copy, Granpère?"

"No."

She saw him studying her closely, asked him, "But what if this is lost? All that work and no other copies? Aren't you worried about that?"

The toothy grin glimmered and faded. "What about you, Michelle? You're one of a kind, aren't you? No copies of you around that I've noticed."

"You can't compare a person with a book!"

"Well, you could, with a little imagination. This book represents the outpourings of a person, making it a living thing in a sense. But when you think about what's really important, you're right. The person's far more important. I say, worry about people, not about books."

"I didn't mean your book wasn't important."

"I know you didn't."

Michelle was not entirely certain she understood or agreed with what her grandfather was saying, but he was old and she decided not to agitate him with questions. She would figure it out later if she could, when she was alone with the book.

"I'll keep these things safe," she said. "Forever. I think I'll make copies for my kids, and by then I'll be able to read French so I'll read to them . . . I'll read from the original, and they'll hold bound copies. That would be nice. But they won't learn the solution to the puzzle box while I'm alive.

That will be sealed in a safety deposit box, to be read with my will. I'll set aside funds to preserve the original book and its beautiful box somewhere."

Granpère chuckled. "A girl of your age shouldn't make such plans!"

"I've had to grow up fast in some ways."

"True, you have. There's a little something extra inside the envelope for you. A fifty-thousand-dollar Face-Plus check. Emergency money only, I'd suggest."

Michelle caught her breath. So much money! Then she recalled her father saying once that $50,000 wasn't so much anymore. It barely bought a good automobile. Still, it was a lot to her. Think of all of the candy and cupcakes it would buy! And the kids wouldn't laugh at her anymore for not having lunch money. But he said emergency money. Granpère's money should be spent intelligently.

"What does 'Face-Plus' mean?" she asked.

"Face amount plus interest, honey. Take it to any bank. I got it only last week, so there isn't much interest accumulated. It's a little savings certificate for you basically, but like a bearer bond. Granmère doesn't know about it." He smiled.

Michelle smiled in return, and for a moment she saw the Gilbert Fouquet of the photograph—the young immigrant in loose-fitting clothes who had just arrived in a new land. Suddenly she felt frightened and alone. Michelle envisioned him standing in his immigrant suit before God, hat in hand.

"Hide the box, the book, and the money well, Michelle, and don't tell anyone in that house about them." He paused. "It's up to you, I suppose, whom you tell. I just prefer . . ."

"I understand. Thank you, Granpère." She felt privileged, and a little guilty. Michelle wanted to ask, 'What about Renney, Joseph, and Coley?' But she didn't speak out. Tears were approaching.

"Where are the instructions?" Granpère asked.

She retrieved them from under the seat and handed them to him.

Granpère tore the instruction sheet into little pieces and stuffed them into a little plastic bag in his pocket. "I'll burn this later."

"We're the only two people in the universe who know how to open this box," Michelle said. Then she recalled the information he had sent by express to the military, and was about to comment on it.

He mentioned it, adding that he had thrown a couple of variations into the puzzle box Michelle held. So they were, after all, the only two people in the universe with the secret.

Michelle felt very special and very sad. She tried to look beyond her frail old grandfather to a time when she wouldn't have him anymore, to a time when she would be alone with his puzzle box, crying. It would be a poor substitute for him, and for a moment she hated the box, wanted to stuff the book and the check in it and hurl it out of the window.

Granpère rubbed his eyes.

He didn't sound or look terribly bad, she decided. Better than he'd been two months before.

"We'd better be getting you home," he said.

As Granpère started the sedan and pulled it into traffic, Michelle saw a new dimension of the delicate, complex puzzle box. Its workings were an extension of Gilbert Fouquet's brain, an intricate passageway his mind had traveled. Michelle would share this passageway each time she opened the box. As her fingers worked, she would see the image of her beloved Granpère's face before her, gazing tenderly upon her in the way she would always remember. In some manner she might pass the secret of the box on to her children. Or she might not.

Michelle took a last glance at the photograph, slid the envelope into the book, and replaced everything inside the box. When the lid was back in place and the mechanism scrambled, Michelle turned the box over and over in her hands. It was a wondrous object to behold, glinting from all of its intricate facets. She saw the blurry reflection of her own face, of the dashboard instruments, and of Granpère as he guided them safely through traffic.

That afternoon Michelle secreted the puzzle box in the air space between the hall linen closet and her bedroom closet.

ELEVEN

It's an ugly tale, but someone has to tell it. I've actually seen her flying around our house on a broomstick, and she visits me in hideous nightmares.

—From a Gestaltobot's interview with
Rachel Fouquet, Korpunkel's
Case #SL397684-1

Late that afternoon, Granmère Liliane received an anonymous tip that television reporters were on their way to her son's house, purportedly to obtain his opinion about how she was handling the Arionnese crisis. In reality, according to the tipster, Big Jack Brittany, her primary enemy on the city council, had hatched this plot to embarrass her, knowing full well that Henry and Rachel would come off as buffoons on camera.

Granmère tried to call ahead and have the premises cleared, but the line was busy, there was no "call waiting" service, and a problem with the phone company's equipment prevented an emergency interruption. She considered contacting a neighbor to relay a message, but decided against that tactic. She didn't know which neighbors, if any, could be trusted.

Granmère didn't waste any time. The mayor's private helicopter sped her across the city and set down on a baseball field four blocks from Henry Fouquet's house. The pilot hit a large orange button on the instrument console, and within five seconds the props were tucked into rooftop compartments, converting the flying machine into a land vehicle.

The helicar sped across the grassy field, through an open gate, and down the street that led to her son's home. When they pulled up in front of the house, it was only moments behind Channel 800. Two women were standing by a tan and blue car, waiting for a cameraman to remove his gear from the trunk. The women were pointing, and Granmère could tell from their incredulous, bemused expressions that they hadn't seen too many homes like this one.

Granmère wished she'd had the foresight to have the home repaired. There must be a way of jamming the room riding mechanism to prevent Rachel's tamperings. Too late for such thoughts now. Granmère would have to make the best of the situation. Putting on her most pleasant expression, she stepped gingerly from the helicar and headed straight for the front door of the house, pretending not to see the media representatives.

"Hey!" one of the women yelled. "Aren't you Councilwoman Fouquet?"

Granmère paused, and with uplifted nose and her most distant tone replied, "I am not accustomed to responding when someone shouts 'Hey!' at me." She feigned a first notice of them. "Oh, you're reporters." A broad smile enveloped her face. "Are you looking for me?"

"We came to interview your son, Councilwoman," one of the women, a tall brunette with heavy cheekbones, said. "Would you care to participate?"

The query sounded insincere to Granmère's experienced ears, and she delayed a moment to study the woman's reactions. Very often this brought nervousness to the surface, revealing interesting things.

The reporter was edgy. "I mean, do you have time or would you prefer that we wait until you've left?"

Granmère smiled knowingly to herself. *You don't want me around, do you? Didn't expect to see me here, did you? Well, like you I have my sources! Prepare for battle!*

Granmère noticed that the cameraman had the video recorder on, trained toward her. Calmly, she adjusted the Velcro neck strap of her Button Pack, expecting at any moment to field a question about it.

"It just so happens that I always have time for the media," Granmère said, sweetly. "It's important to communicate with the people, you see, so that they understand the workings of government. I'll take a moment from my busy schedule to talk with you."

"Thank you, Mrs. Fouquet," the brunette said. This woman appeared to be in charge. The other woman, also a reporter it appeared, was much younger and carried an electronic notepad. She spoke into it occasionally, apparently describing things that the video recorder might not pick up.

The brunette's face looked familiar. That slightly cleft chin. Granmère had seen it before. There hadn't been time to review surveillance files on

Brittany before running out the door, but this face . . . was it in those files? What was this woman's connection with that corpulent faggot?

In a display of artificial effusiveness, Granmère led the way up the front steps, cringing privately at what lay ahead. Surely they noticed already that this porch was a hallway turned sideways, stuck eternally in an untoward position, pleading for death. Then, with journalistic fervor and Brittany-induced glee, their eyes, human and electronic, would drink in the basement, jammed as it was against the living room. She sighed.

"Someone has arranged this home in a very . . . artistic manner," the brunette said. "Oh, forgive me. I'm Patty Wissner, and this is my trainee, Joanne Muir. Over here's my cameraman, Nelson Stigman."

At the head of the stairs after what seemed like an interminable climb, Granmère nodded to each. She pressed the doorbell. Wissner . . . Did those files mention a Wissner?

Henry swung open the door, and said in a surprised tone, "*Maman!* I mean, Mother." He preferred calling her "Mother" in front of other people. Henry's expression, initially one of irritation at the interruption, changed to confusion. Clumsily, he tucked in his shirt.

"Did you just get home from work, Henri?" Granmère asked, hearing the background whining of Coley.

"Uh, yes, I did."

"Why don't you step outside, son, and talk with these reporters?" She stared at him intently, importuning obedience.

"Uh sure, lemme grab my shoes."

"We'd rather come inside," Wissner said. "There's a lot of traffic noise out here, and our video recorder is quite sensitive."

"Sure," Henry said, before his mother could intercede. He moved awkwardly to one side, held the door open.

Granmère stalked into the house first, having momentarily lost control of her disposition. This had to be the most embarrassing moment of her entire life! What could she say to these people to save the situation? She passed through the "hallway going nowhere" and into the odorous, littered basement. What could be said? Who could possibly come up with an excuse for any of this?

She heard footsteps behind her, and the whir of the everpresent, abhorred video camera.

What to say? I've got to say something!

"The modular room-designing mechanism went out of control here," Granmère said. "On its own, and left quite a mess. The insurance company has been slow settling my son's claim."

"There's coverage for that?" Wissner asked.

Uh-oh, Granmère thought. *She knows about an exclusion.*

"They had a special policy on it," Granmère said.

"Which company?"

"It would serve no purpose to drag them into the media now," Granmère said, glancing back. "There's a claim to be settled, and publicity might irritate them."

"Publicity has a way of doing that to people," Wissner said.

Granmère was searching desperately for the best place to stop. It had to be either the living room or the kitchen. As bad as they were, the other options were horrendous. Surely the reporters saw that the utter mess and neglect all around went beyond any insurance matter.

Seeing Rachel on the tattered living room couch, dozing with her Biblecorder on her lap and the earphones over her head, Granmère paused at the entryway and turned to the others.

"Mrs. Fouquet hasn't been feeling well," Granmère said, watching the Biblecorder's lighted scanner traverse a page. "Please pass quietly through to the kitchen." Granmère caught Henry's gaze. They were on the same wavelength, to the extent possible.

"We've been planning to rebuild the whole house," Henry said. "And with my wife's illness and my work things have kinda been let go."

Granmère detected disappointment on Wissner's face. These people had come here on a mission of embarrassment, and Wissner saw her story falling apart. These Fouquets might elicit sympathy from the television audience, not the emotions she wanted to produce.

Even to Granmère's critical eye, the kitchen didn't look too terribly bad. She had seen it much worse. Michelle stood at the sink, rinsing dishes and piling them by the dishwasher. Coley was next to her, sucking on a baby bottle. The table had been cleaned, the chairs arranged neatly around it, and the floor swept. Granmère wanted to run over and slip a hundred dollars to Michelle, for she appeared to be the one responsible.

"We can talk in here," Granmère said.

The reporters and Granmère sat at the table, while Henry and the cameraman remained on their feet. Granmère kept her chair away from the table to allow room for the pack.

"What do you think of your grandmother as acting mayor?" Wissner asked Michelle, having caught the girl's gaze.

"I wasn't aware that . . ."

"It's best to leave the child alone," Granmère said. "She has chores to finish before she can get to her homework."

"Chores," Wissner said. "How quaint. There appear to be no servants in this home, despite the political position occupied by Granmère Fouquet. Such old-fashioned, unassuming people."

"What's she talkin' about?" Henry asked, looking at his mother with wide eyes. "You're mayor of something?"

"That's why I came by, dear. Your telephone's out of order, and it all happened rather quickly last night. Mayor Wilde is ill . . . in the hospital."

Wissner addressed Henry, and as she did so Granmère saw the cameraman shift position to obtain a side view of Henry's protuberant, beer-bloated belly. "Mr. Fouquet," Wissner said, "you didn't know your mother was acting mayor?"

"I just said he didn't," Granmère said, her tone frosty.

"He looks like a *big* boy," Wissner said. "I'm sure he can answer for himself."

Granmère saw anger building to a quick crescendo in her son. Wissner had cast an aspersion upon his manhood, and Henry was not one to fend off such remarks skillfully. Granmère knew why, and that to a large extent it was her own fault for dressing him in what Rachel, damn her, called "Little Lord Fauntleroy" clothes. This despite the fact that out of necessity in those years Granmère and her family lived in the hoodlum-infested Castro district. Henry had become tough and coarse to survive, and before Granmère realized what was happening her son was far down the path toward becoming precisely what she didn't want him to be.

"It's just like she told you," Henry said to the reporter, tersely. Henry was fighting to keep his enunciation under control.

"Do you mean *Maman?*" Wissner asked, hitting the precise diction and accent of Henry's surprised utterance at the front door.

Henry did his best to maintain himself, but he sputtered something unintelligible. To Granmère, he looked like a bulging red pressure vessel, about to burst.

Wissner asked him to repeat what he said, as it was too low to be picked up by the recorder. She was pressing him, and the camera was only a meter from his face. He pushed the camera away.

"Tell yer man ta stand back," Henry said, with the skin of his mouth tight across his teeth. "He's gettin' too close, an' I don't like dat. Whatter ya here ta ask me, anyhow? I wanna be cooptertive . . . cooperative, I mean."

Henry shrugged and spread his arms effusively, a gesture of openness. Miraculously, the color in his face became almost normal, and the pressure appeared to have subsided.

"You're a very physical man, aren't you, Mr. Fouquet?" the trainee said. "Do you hit people?"

Such sweet features, Granmère thought, looking at the brown-haired young woman. *Hiding sharp teeth.*

Henry leveled a ball-bearing stare at the trainee. "Naw," he said with a wide smile. "Only reporters, and they aren't people."

Touché! Granmère thought.

"Mr. Fouquet," Wissner said, "what is your opinion of the manner in which your mother is handling the crisis? Permit me to rephrase that, since you were entirely ignorant of her position in the matter until just now. Almost everyone in San Francisco knew before you did. Don't you find that irritating, Mr. Son?"

"Not in the least," Henry said, calmly. But his eyes smoldered. "Get to the point, please."

"Very well. What do you, as the son of the acting mayor, think of the situation in which we find ourselves? I speak of our alien overlords, Mister . . . Fouquet."

"Oh, you're here to talk about the aliens, eh? Well my opinion of that is that the Orinneesh are gonna do what the Orinneesh wanna do. There's nothing any of us can say about it." A look of bewilderment crossed Henry's face, probably concerning the name of the aliens that he couldn't quite remember.

"Rather curiously put," Wissner said. "And not so inaccurate, it seems. A very astute observation, sir."

Henry set his jaw and leveled his death stare at her. "Who are you callin' stupid?"

"I said 'astute,' sir."

"Yeah? Well I thought I heard you say . . ."

"Shall I play it back, sir?"

"Naw. Forget it."

To Granmère it did not seem that her son could hold on much longer. These reporters were trying to make him blow his stack for the television audience. How awful that would be! Granmère compared Wissner with the reporter who had hounded her that morning at the Arionn Building demonstration. Like a mosquito, Wissner wouldn't back off until she drew her fill of Henry's blood.

"By the way, sir," the trainee said. "It's Air-ee-uh-nees, not Oar-uh-neesh."

"Aw who gives a flyin' crud?" Henry said. He puffed up his chest and arms, turned his head toward the cameraman. "Didja get dat, or ya wanna retake?"

The cameraman didn't respond, but Granmère saw fear in his eyes. Henry was beginning to make his physical presence known, and his upper arms were as big around as the cameraman's thighs.

"Is 'crud' really the word you meant to employ?" Wissner asked. "Our viewing audience can stand worse."

Granmère heard Michelle speaking in a low tone to Coley, keeping the toddler quiet.

"Ya wanna make a fool outa me onna ebening news," Henry said, taking a menacing step toward Wissner. "Datch why yer bein' sech a pest. Well, put it onna air. Da whole t'ing, if ya hab da guts, an' ebberyone will see how rude ja is. Dere's my wife in dere sick, and we're obveeshly habbin' some misfortune aroun' here an' look atcha. Yer a real sensitib one, ain'tcha?"

Granmère hated his dialect, but this time saw no harm in it. She saw that Wissner was thrown off guard, as reporter and trainee exchanged uncomfortable glances.

Granmère didn't bother to conceal a smile, but realized that careful film editing might still produce a segment she wouldn't want to air.

Wissner focused on Granmère, absorbed the smile, and attacked right back. "I've been meaning to ask you, Coun . . . acting Mayor Fouquet, what's that hideous contraption you're wearing?"

Granmère held her smile. This upstart was no match for her. She could barely handle Henry. "I answered that question for a reporter this morning. Channel 755, I believe. Why don't you tune in?"

"I saw the broadcast," the trainee said. "It's a communications pack."

"Would you show us how it works?" Wissner asked.

Granmère saw the video recorder lens zoom in on the pack.

"No, I'm sorry. Not today. Perhaps another time."

"As you wish. I have some additional questions, but we'd like to get some good frames of mother and son outside before we lose daylight. It's looking a bit dark out there. You should protest to the Arionnese and ask them for longer days."

"These days are perfectly seasonal."

"But they could provide more daylight, if you would only . . ."

"I'm protesting nothing to the Arionnese!"

"Don't you have the interest of your people in mind?"

Granmère felt the jaws of a trap closing around her. "*Certainement* I do," she snapped. Then, pleasantly: "Let's get those pictures."

Wissner smiled, making the cleft that divided her chin more pronounced. "The backyard is best at this time of day," Henry said, having regained his composure. "Excuse the back porch. I haven't had time to straighten it up."

"Curious the way you alternate speech patterns, Mr. Fouquet," the trainee said.

But Wissner didn't pursue this, and instead smiled in an almost friendly way at Granmère. "You look so young to have a son this old," Wissner said. "You look more like sister and brother than mother and son."

Involuntarily, Granmère beamed.

"I'll bet you have a youthful figure too," Wissner gushed, "behind that dreadful pack thing."

Trying to appraise the reporter's motivations for flattering her, Granmère drew herself to her feet. The pack wasn't particularly heavy, but it was awkward. Henry hadn't fared too poorly on the hot seat, bless him, and Granmère decided that Wissner had altered her attack stance to put her victims at ease for unexpected thrusts.

Henry was leading the media people down the three steps to the porch, one of the most disgusting areas of the house, in Granmère's opinion. She shook her head in dismay, resolved to make the best of the situation. Henry's three jobs hadn't been mentioned yet, and might be used to Granmère's advantage. Obviously she wasn't funneling money to him. The reporters could be told how proud he was, that Granmère was not a wealthy woman herself. Comfortable, yes, but there was a difference. No crooked politician here, skimming from the tax coffers.

She would mention these things in the backyard, with the video camera rolling. To complete her victory, however, she wished she weren't wearing this infernal Button Pack. She would come off looking so much better without it.

I'll just slip it off for a moment and set it on the porch, she thought. *This won't take long.*

"There's a dog back here," Wissner said, from the top of the outside stairway. "Mother, son, and dog."

Mangy dog, Granmère thought. *Oh well, I'll turn that to my advantage, too. Plenty of people have decrepit pets they love too much to turn over to the Humane Federation. I can make the ordinary viewer identify with Henry's family. Watch out, Wissner.*

Granmère undid the neck and lumbar Velcro straps, slipped her arms out of the pack, and set it to one side on the porch floor, pushing an old raincoat over it for good measure.

She hurried to catch up with the others, who were now on the splotchy, weed-savaged lawn. She pattered down the wooden steps, nearly tripping as she tried to hold her head high and to be businesslike.

At Henry's side, Granmère was just about to put her thoughts into words. Then she recalled what she had read in the surveillance file about Wissner! Her name wasn't Wissner, and this was no lady, in any sense of the word!

I'll end this farce straight off, Granmère thought, taking care not to step in a pile of dog excrement.

"I'll have a word with you privately, *Miss* Wissner," Granmère said, taking Wissner by the arm. "Alone. No cameras."

Wissner was startled, but she signaled the cameraman to keep his distance and went with Granmère to a bare patch of ground by the garage.

"This absurdity is concluded," Granmère announced. She heard power in her words, and she delighted in the perplexity apparent on Wissner's visage. "Give me your film and leave!"

"What are you talking about? This is a free country. I can interview anyone I please."

"Your name isn't Wissner. I don't recall exactly what it is, but I have it in a file on you and Brittany."

Blood drained from Wissner's face. "I . . . I don't know what you mean."

"If you attempt to continue this trumped-up interview with my family, if any other reporters return to my son's house, or if you broadcast anything concerning the personal aspects of my family I will reveal that you are really a man and that your lover is Big Jack Brittany!"

A *bluff,* Granmère thought. *But a good one, judging from Wissner's expression. We've no proof of illegality, but I'm sure I've seen this face as a man, in Brittany's file. There is something fishy here.*

Wissner let out a deep sigh, looked away.

"Big Jack sent you here to embarrass me, not realizing the extent of my information. Your clandestine liaisons, while cleverly plotted, did not escape surveillance."

"Lies!"

"Would you care to attend my press conference?"

"No. I, uh . . ." A heavy shrug, and: "Okay. You win."

"Bring me the film and the cartridge out of that electronic notepad. Now! Move it!"

Wissner followed this command, then scurried away.

Granmère delivered a parting shot: "You're protected only because Brittany and I have an understanding. I can change that understanding in an instant, so don't push me."

A *few dirty deals*, Granmère thought. *That's all Big Jack has on me, and I could ride out that storm.*

Within moments the news team was around the side of the house and heading for their car.

Bumper shuffled to Granmère's side, wagging his nearly hairless tail.

She leaned over and patted his head. "Sorry I didn't bring you anything this time, boy," she said.

"What did you say to those reporters?" Henry asked. "Why'd they give you their film and notes?"

"Their interview didn't go as well as they'd hoped." Granmère straightened, brushed her hands together briskly to rid them of fine dog hairs. "Don't speak to any reporters, Henri, because they're always out to trip somebody up. They need us, but we don't need them. Remember that."

A movement on the back porch caught Granmère's eye. She lunged toward the stairway. Someone near the Button Pack, and it had what Oso called "killer rays" to take care of anyone tampering with it! Who was on the porch? The windows were dirty and piled high around them with clutter. She couldn't quite see.

Granmère broke into a flat-out run, hit the steps and roared up them to the screen door. Bursting inside she saw, to her complete horror, Rachel wearing the Button Pack. She not only had it on, but had the instrument panel spread before her. And she was alive!

"Don't touch anything!" Granmère said, her voice breaking.

"I already have. Such pretty little buttons and lights."

The transmitting stylus was upright in one of the holes and glowed ember red. Calmly, Rachel moved it to another hole. It didn't burn her, didn't transmit killer rays. What had happened?

Oso, you fool, what have you done?

Granmère listened for the sounds of distant, habitat-breaking explosions, but heard nothing except traffic sounds from the nearby arterials.

"Every time I put the pen into a hole," Rachel said, "All kinds of pretty lights go off." Her face was illuminated in color like a child's by a Christmas tree.

Granmère inched closer, letting the screen door go behind her.

Henry was there and kept it from slamming shut. "What's goin' on?" he asked.

Granmère didn't respond, narrowed the gap between her and Rachel. Impulsively, Granmère grabbed for the glowing stylus and got hold of it. The stylus came out of the hole easily, didn't burn her hand.

Granmère waited for killer rays, if they existed, to strike her. Nothing happened. The mechanism wasn't supposed to allow anyone other than Granmère to tamper with it. How could this have happened?

"How many holes did you put the stylus in?" Granmère asked.

"You mean that pretty pen thing? Twice, I think. Or was it three times?"

"Which holes? Quickly, show me the numbers."

"I'm not sure." She moved the pinky of her left hand over one side of the instrument panel. "Somewhere here, I think."

"Somewhere there? You foolish woman, take that off!" Without considering the possibility of risk to herself, Granmère released the Velcro straps and jerked the pack away from Rachel.

"You had it hidden under a coat," Rachel said, defiantly. "I saw you put it there. What is it?"

"None of your business!"

"Secrets aren't nice, Liliane. You aren't a very nice person."

Noticing Michelle on the kitchen threshold above them, Granmère demanded, "Why didn't you keep her out of my things?"

"You didn't say anything to me. I didn't know I was supposed to watch anything."

In a frustrated rage Granmère replaced the stylus in its clip, closed the panel, and snapped the pack over it. Carrying the pack in one hand, she bolted past Michelle and out of the house, cursing General Oso for inflicting such a sorry contraption on her.

From her airborne helicopter, Granmère reached General Oso by radiotelephone. Sputtering her words, she recounted events.

At the first mention of the Button Pack, he reminded her of security, that this line, while scrambler-protected, was not impregnable.

"Hang keeping this pack secret!" Granmère boomed. "If any of those round men with funny eyes are listening, get this, fellas: I have a device that could blast this habitat into the next galaxy! Give me a damage report, Oso. My daughter-in-law got hold of the Button Pack and stuck the stylus in two, maybe three holes."

"There have been no explosions on the habitat," Oso said. "You have the pack back?"

"I do."

"Then I suggest you calm yourself."

"Calm myself? You said this rig had killer rays. My demented daughter-in-law got into it, and she's still walking around. How do you explain that?"

"You left the instrument panel unlatched."

"I don't think I did. Anyway, shouldn't she have died if she touched the stylus, especially if she inserted it in the holes?"

"Yes, I think so."

"You aren't sure?"

"After this, no. Anyway, the stylus sent no signal. No one except you can activate one of the buttons beneath the holes."

"The damn thing was glowing, Oso. That means the system was operational, right?"

"The stylus was glowing?"

"What in the hell do you think I'm talking about?"

"That surprises me, a lot. Still, there is no apparent damage."

"Luckily she didn't tap the buttons that would have blasted us. But she sent signals through space that could blast bases to smithereens on Earth."

"We're way beyond transmitting range. I don't think signals were sent, but if they were and reached Earth they'd be too weak to activate anything."

"Somehow I'm not reassured. The way I see it, we've got a major problem here. I'm bringing the infernal gadget to you right now, and I want it repaired immediately. Is that understood?"

"It's understood, but impossible. Unfortunately the only man aboard capable of such technical work is no longer with us."

"He's on Earth? From what you said, I thought you had key technicians in the Bay Area . . . Daly City, I think you said . . . and that's why the Button Pack had to be brought here for servicing."

"Correct, madame. The team supervisor, an essential person, is not on Earth. He's with us but not with us."

"Don't pitter-patter with me."

"He committed suicide this morning. A problem has developed among servicemen, it seems. Acute depression, even more pronounced than among the civilian population, since such a high percentage of servicemen left their families on Earth. We're setting up a mental health task force somewhat like yours, but ours is in-house. Since everything is breaking so fast, I took the liberty—on your behalf and on ours—of having my staff contact the media about this, asking them not to carry stories on the subject. Stories might trigger panic and more suicides. You've been on the move today, and I had trouble reaching you."

"I didn't want to be in charge anyway," Granmère said. "The news moratorium is fine, a good decision. Look, maybe it's time we chucked this pack into the cosmic icebox."

"I think it's still functional, Madame Mayor, except for the security aspect, where it does sound like something's haywire."

"If something's haywire there, the whole rig could be messed up. Or worse. It could send signals just by jiggling it. Do you want to risk that?"

"No, but I do have men capable of testing the apparatus. They worked with the dead man, and I'm certain they can handle it. Before we go any further, you should know there's backup security in that pack, wired independently. Since we're talking openly, I'll ask if you recall my telling you that the pack senses who is operating it?"

"Yes. You said the pack made identifications and that the stylus sensed volition, making it impossible for anyone to hold my hand over the stylus and force me to use it."

"Correct. It's actually more complex than that. I didn't go into all aspects due to the late hour, but had planned to do so later."

"You don't know all the aspects, General. We just established that."

"True, but consider this: If anyone does succeed in taking the pack away from you, ostensibly they've either penetrated the primary security system or it isn't functioning. I say os—"

"Sure, which leads us to backup security, which is necessary because the main one isn't worth *merde*. You've probably got backups for the backups, too."

"There are multiple backups, but . . ."

"Why not design the damn system so well in the first place that it doesn't need backups? Did that ever occur to anyone?"

"You speak of an impossibility. No system, however advanced, is failsafe."

"Well, your system sure broke down easily."

"We're in the far reaches of space. There are any number of factors out here that may have contributed to the problem. Unusual cosmic radiation patterns, for one."

"All right, get to the point!"

"You took me off it. Remember I said, 'ostensibly they've either penetrated the primary security system or it isn't functioning.'"

"Yeah, so?"

"Under a certain scenario, Rachel might not have gone past primary security. The Button Pack has a pulse sounder primary security system, which the layman can best understand by envisioning an electronic beacon. The highly sensitive pulse sounder transmits continuous signals, and if the nearest body is not you—identified by your characteristic, rhythmic pulse—then a circuit closes."

"Yeah, which leads us to the backups, none of which will ID her as the proper user of the pack, and eventually killer rays should have—"

"Don't be so quick to assume any of that."

"Hell, man! Isn't it obvious? Rachel—my daughter-in-law—had the pack on, as I told you! She was using the stylus! All circuits should have closed, activating the rays!"

"In and of itself, a closed circuit does not signal activation. This one in primary security is but a first step in the process."

"I can't wait to hear what's next."

"Once that particular circuit is closed, the Button Pack determines whether or not the wearer is hostile to our political interests."

"You've got to be kidding."

"I'm not."

"It reads minds?"

"In a sense. It reads intent, from signals given off by the body."

"Well, Rachel is sure as hell hostile toward me."

"Personal animosity does not enter the equation. The Button Pack is larger than personalities. It didn't perceive Rachel as a threat or as the representative of a threatening power."

"Then it perceived incorrectly. That woman's not only a threat, but she's dangerous, with a violent streak you wouldn't believe."

"Perhaps. But did she understand the significance and power of the pack?"

"No! Hell, you don't understand the damn thing! How did she get the stylus to glow?"

"I don't know, but I'll mention that when it goes in for testing."

"Stop the habitat! I want off!"

"What do you mean?"

"Nothing. A moment's giddiness, that's all."

"To minimize jostling of the pack mechanism, Madame Mayor, I suggest that you transport it directly to your office. Tell your pilot you want the smoothest landing in history. I'll meet you at your office within the hour with the men who will perform the test."

"You fry my tough old ass when you keep talking about *men*. Don't you have any *women* in your command?"

"Quite a few."

"Well, elevate them to important positions! Things like this might not happen if you did!"

"I'll look into that, Madame Mayor."

An answer that could be interpreted a number of ways, she decided. This Oso was irritating, but she would try to overlook his personality. In many respects he seemed quite competent.

But as the helicopter set down on the roof of the City Office Tower, Granmère felt nearly out of control, nearly frantic. She preferred people and situations that moved within rational parameters, making them somewhat controllable. But she wasn't naive, and she realized life's unpredictability. Sometimes surprises stimulated her. Yes, even stodgy old Granmère Liliane, a woman set rigidly in her ways and opinions. To her it was part of the human experience.

But the Arionnese were not human.

Might they nevertheless commit errors, as humans did so prolifically? She hoped the aliens were perfect in the efforts they had devoted to designing and constructing the multi-city space habitat. But she wanted a limitation on their excellence, one or more apparent weaknesses that she and humans allied with her might turn to advantage.

Granmère was impressed by the testing procedure. Shortly after returning to her office, General Toshio Oso and three uniformed NAS men arrived, carrying large gray cases. Oso sealed the office, drew the blinds, and ordered his men around with hand gestures, while Granmère sat at her desk, watching. The procedure did not take long.

They opened the Button Pack, and with the instrument panel in operating position placed the whole unit into the largest of the cases they had brought with them. Sliding away a panel on the case, they revealed the Button Pack inside, visible through thick transparent material. Then they interlocked all the cases end to end, forming an E-shaped arrangement with the largest case at the center bar of the E. The smaller cases all had sliding tops with instrument panels beneath, and the technicians worked alternately at the controls, touching buttons and levers to test the circuitry of the Button Pack.

Granmère saw a tiny ray of vertical orange light that moved inside the largest case around the Button Pack's board, penetrating holes in the manner of the stylus. Each time it entered a hole, the board lit up in a multicolored display, as it had in front of Rachel. Granmère didn't ask, but it seemed obvious to her that the cases were constructed of signal-blocking materials.

The technicians, who might have been mutes for all Granmère knew, completed their work in short order, then used a sicom to relay their findings to their superior.

General Oso in turn placed the communicator on Granmère's desk, and keypunched, on the noiseless board: "ALL SYSTEMS OPERATIONAL. IN-TRUDER DIDN'T SEND SIGNALS. GLITCH IN STYLUS THAT CAUSED IT TO GLOW HAS BEEN CORRECTED."

As the military men departed from her office, it occurred to Granmère that the testing procedure might have been a hoax. She had no way of verifying what she had been told. Not a hoax to convince her that an unsafe Button Pack was safe, for that wouldn't make any sense. The fate of the military was intertwined with that of every human aboard the habitat. But the Button Pack itself might be nonfunctioning—a bluff weapon on which Oso had leaked false information to the aliens. Thus Granmère and the Arionnese might be pawns in the general's scheme.

Granmère had the police and the local offices of the FBI and CIA at her disposal. She could order surveillance of the general's activities. But she didn't feel confident in that approach. The position of commander in chief was new to her and would require study and absorption. She would remain alert, playing along for a while with whatever the general had in mind. But she wouldn't be anyone's fool. She would learn her options, get to know the federal people, solidify her position on the habitat. Then, when she felt confident, she would see how far she could push Oso.

After dinner that evening, Michelle didn't join the others in front of the television. As if drawn by a magnet, she made straight for her bedroom closet, shoved aside the clutter on the floor, and pulled free the wall panel. It smelled musty in the tight little enclosure, but she hardly noticed.

Michelle's hands trembled as she held the puzzle box. She compared the emotion to those occasions, now and then, when she obtained chocolate or another treat and secreted what she couldn't consume someplace around the house, usually here. It was the sole hiding place that her siblings hadn't yet discovered, and in a large family with limited resources that meant a great deal.

Crouched on the floor of the closet, Michelle went through Granpère's forty-six puzzle-solving steps. Just before sliding the top away she felt an immense sense of satisfaction and accomplishment. Even though she hadn't yet moved aside that last group of pieces forming the top to reveal the contents of the miniature chamber, her mind held no doubts. It would cooperate, as it had in the car.

But the puzzle box surprised Michelle nonetheless. It began to glow a softly translucent shade of lime green as she slid away the top, and in a moment's fright she nearly dropped the box. Then Michelle realized that her grandfather wouldn't give her anything dangerous. Tremulously, she completed the procedure to reveal the book inside, bathed in such strong green light that it had lost the redness of its cover and was for the moment one with the light.

She lifted the book out with a good deal of trepidation, and as she did so saw that it glowed in its own right, distinct from the glow that continued to emanate from the box. Michelle set the box aside and spread open the volume on her lap. Each page radiated translucently, so that it highlighted Granpère's firm black penmanship like words on a computer screen.

Pulse quickening, Michelle drew the closet door shut and found a better place to sit amid the clutter, with her back supported by a pile of clothing. The puzzle box glowed beside her, casting warmth against the flank of one leg. She began to realize that the book was warm to her touch as well, but not uncomfortably so, and back to her came Granpère's words about the book as a living thing, filled with the outpourings of a person.

The little room became toasty, and as Michelle turned the pages reverently she saw words floating from them in a black-on-green mist, dancing in midair before her eyes. Since they were French and she had neglected the tongue she didn't understand a lot at first, but every few seconds Granpère's whispery old voice from the mist pronounced a floating word or phrase for her, and with these pronunciations Michelle absorbed their meanings.

"Quel brouillard, et il fait froid . . . Liliane est malade . . . Je parle anglais un tout petit peu . . ."

Michelle learned of difficult times experienced by her grandparents in New York City when they were young immigrants living in unheated rooms. Granmère nearly died of pneumonia in the bitter winter of 2037. Jobs were hard to come by, but when they worked they saved, largely because of Granmère's foresight and sense of organization. Eventually they had enough for economy seats on a hypersonic transport, and they began anew in the warmer climate of California.

As the words were spoken and translated, they flashed and disappeared from the air, as if seared away. She felt them imprint in her mind as they faded from sight, knew they would be available when she required them, just like the solution to the puzzle box. The mist hung in the air without words at the conclusion of the first chapter, and for several moments Michelle repeated the hundreds of different French words she had heard, pronouncing them correctly and translating them to English, complete with conjugations.

"That's enough for today," Granpère's gentle, susurrous voice said after a while. "A chapter at a time, and soon you will be able to hold your own with Granmère."

Michelle was eager to absorb every word her grandfather had composed, to know him more completely, and with him, Granmère. She felt her grandfather's presence in the snug enclosure, and together they shared a thought. It wasn't so far from France to the United States, not in terms of the distance their habitat had traveled from Earth. And the French language itself, which once seemed an insurmountable chore for Michelle to learn, wouldn't be so difficult or so distasteful after all. She envisioned France and the United States melding into one, with their languages homogenized into new combinations.

She held the glowing book on her lap and reflected upon the profound differences she had observed in her grandparents. They seemed universes apart now, so utterly contradictory as to make them seem more like opponents than lovers. And yet they had been lovers and possibly still were, despite divergences and the ravages of time. The distinctions of nations, of people, and of words amalgamated in her mind. She became her grandfather and he became she, speaking as one in English.

"I am going on a journey," Granpère said, through Michelle's mouth. "In a few days everyone will think I'm dead, but you and I will know the truth."

"The truth?" Michelle spoke in her own voice, across the same lips.

"I came up with a novel method of remaining alive."

Michelle found herself unable to read Granpère's mind. But he was there in her flesh, very near her thoughts. "An invention?" she asked.

"Of sorts. Do not despair, child. Remember always that I love you and that I am with you. Go on about other matters and I'll be around one day. It's our little game, yours and mine."

"When will you contact me?"

"I will contact you in due course."

"I don't think I like this game, Granpère. It frightens me."

"Don't worry."

Michelle felt one of her eyes wink, involuntarily.

"I need a little vacation from Granmère," he said. "I love her dearly, but, well . . . you know."

Michelle forced a smile. "Oh, I see. No, I don't see. Isn't this cruel to the people who love you?"

"Unfortunately there is no other way. I must ask you not to mention this to anyone and to trust my judgment. What I am doing is for the best."

"Yes, Granpère."

As the conversation closed and she felt her spirit separating from that of her grandfather, Michelle wanted to cry. The familiar patterns of her life were shifting and would never again be the same. But her eyes, pleading for the relief of tears, remained dry. They ached.

Michelle's consciousness rushed to fill the spaces in her mind, and she came to realize that hers was not a finite presence after all, physically or spiritually. When she closed the volume, replaced and sealed it in the box, and the warm green glow was gone, Michelle sat in darkness, gathering her thoughts and planning the balance of her life, as far as she could see it. She was bonded to the needs of others: to Rachel and Coley particularly, both of whom required her care; and to this new and paramount secret from her grandfather, with all of its ominous solemnity.

She became one with the darkness around her, a speck of dust traveling through space. In the distance a pinpoint of light awaited her arrival. It gave her hope, instilled Great Meaning to her life, and she looked forward to it.

TWELVE

Sometimes I tune out, and when I do I don't hear Coley whining any more. I look at her and suddenly she isn't dirty, her nose isn't running, and she's smiling kinda sweet-like, as if she knows where I am, where I've been, where I'm going. And it's as if I represent all of humankind, and she does too. We're molecules reflecting one another, and I see our images stuttering off into the distance.

—Rachel Fouquet, in a letter to herself

Two days passed, and with the habitat still intact Henry catnapped in his recliner, oblivious to Michelle's massaging fingers as they worked at his scalp from behind the chair. Soon company would arrive, and the duty of preparing dinner would fall upon Henry's already overburdened shoulders. He smelled of perspiration and cigars.

Michelle wasn't a good cook by any stretch of the imagination (despite her efforts in the kitchen), and Rachel's culinary skills were abominable. Sometimes Michelle suspected that her mother really could cook more than just bran muffins, and that her professed ignorance was exactly that—professed. If it was a sham, initiated to avoid work or for some deeper reason, Rachel performed it flawlessly.

Michelle spent much of her time thinking, piecing together fragments of information to form conclusions, mostly about the real intentions and sincerity of people around her. Despite her youth, she knew to observe the actions of people first, their utterances second. Often the two correlated, but where they didn't the former always held. No one taught her to do this. Like many other things she had discerned it on her own. Grownups usually didn't confide in children, and even Granpère withheld information from her.

To Michelle it seemed that her mother's deeper reason for avoiding kitchen duties might go beyond laziness or even depression. Consciously or unconsciously she might be doing it to get at Granmère through her son. By making it harder on Henry, he was more certain to fail, and this was certain to devastate the old lady. It would be a convoluted and potentially self-destructive line of reasoning if it existed, but Rachel's hatred for Granmère knew no bounds.

Seeing her father's eyelids move, Michelle said, "Remember when we used to go on vacation to Lake Mendocino, Daddy?"

He grunted, stretched, and tilted his head briefly to glance up at her.

"It would be nice if we did things like that as a family again," Michelle said, continuing her massage. "It's been almost three years. I saw a map of the habitat at school, and Lake Mendocino isn't with us. Mount Diablo State Park is, though. Do you know anything about it? Is it nice?"

"I guess it is. Don't think there's much water around there, though."

"That wouldn't matter."

"I'll look into it one of these days." He glanced at his wristwatch, added, "Keep rubbin' like that, Michelle, and I'll have a full head of hair before long."

Michelle had heard that working the scalp could stimulate hair growth, but that wasn't her purpose. Henry could have a maestro's mop with any number of drugstore or day surgical procedures, and he even threatened to do so on occasion "to put old Bumper to shame." Michelle smiled at the thought of a hair-growing contest between man and dog. Today as always she felt no indications of imminent hairiness. The crown of her father's head was as smooth and shiny as the banisters of Granmère's house.

Even in adulthood Henry remained one of Granmère's possessions, although he would never admit it. But Henry, despite his maternal ties, was a rough piece of creation, one who had rebelled against the dictates of "*Maman*" to an extent that had demolished his own life. And if Michelle's suspicions about her mother's intentions were accurate, Henry had considerable assistance along the path to ruination.

In Michelle's opinion, the present relationship between Granmère and Henry was cemented largely by the will of the old lady, by her hope despite all that a miracle might turn her son around and make him the suave sophisticate she so ardently desired. In this Granmère was lying to herself, failing to recognize how far from the age of short pants her son had grown.

As Michelle considered the situation, it seemed to her that her father and mother should stand together and tell Granmère off for her meddling. But the girl knew that this was impossible. The conflict worked in intricate, cancerous ways, with layers of complexity that were constantly appearing to Michelle.

Working both hands in a parallel flowing motion on the top of her father's scalp, she delved into new reaches of thought.

While Rachel and Granmère openly loathed one another and hostility brewed simultaneously between Henry and Granmère, there existed also a strong, sometimes concealed state of tension between Henry and Rachel. Not recognizing the possibility that Rachel's actions (or lack of them) might be at least in part intentional, Henry blamed her in private arguments for many of his failures and constantly reminded her of her own. Whenever Granmère blamed Rachel for harming Henry's life and career, he never let on to the old matriarch that he agreed with her. Granmère, Henry, and Rachel, connected by blood or by marriage, were bonded on a family slab going nowhere because they were incapable of working together. Henry, poor, unfortunate Henry, had gotten himself caught between two women different enough to strain the imagination.

Poor, unfortunate Henry. Michelle saw the word shapes before her eyes.

Her father was drifting off to sleep beneath her caressing hands. She heard his breathing slacken, watched the heaving rhythm of his barrel chest.

Her fingers worked over a shallow scar, evidence of a bar fight that Joseph had told her about. She massaged energetically here, imagining that the skin would smooth out like warm putty.

Noises from the front yard diverted her attention: a man talking ebulliently to Bumper, telling him what a good dog he was while Bumper yelped and whined for attention. She recognized the voice.

Michelle threw open the front door just as the doorbell rang. "Uncle Paul!" she squealed. "You're early! Daddy, Uncle Paul is here!"

Paul St. Germaine was one of those people whose height was more properly described in terms of altitude, occupying so lofty a perch that other people had difficulty ascertaining his full height. The Fouquet children regularly ventured guesses, and Michelle often suggested that St. Germaine should provide a prize if anyone hit the exact number.

"Seven feet five and one-eighth inches!" Michelle exclaimed.

St. Germaine ducked under the door frame, chuckled. His face was narrow and bony, inset with cheerful hazel eyes. In one hand he toted his ever-present tooled leather briefcase, for he didn't have the good taste to separate his business and personal lives. A man forever struggling to widen his economic horizon, he constantly dipped into new ventures that required intense salesmanship, and it wouldn't take him long to get around to the subjects he wanted to discuss that evening with Daddy.

Henry tolerated him.

"Aren't you gonna tell me if I guess right?" Michelle asked, tilting her head way back to peer at him.

"Maybe I will one of these days, if I figure it out for myself."

"You know! Come on! Am I closer than last time?"

"You do look a little taller, and I stopped growing many years ago. I'd say you are closer."

"Teaser!"

"Okay, what did you guess last time?"

"Seven feet five even."

"Keep going."

"What do you mean by that?"

"Guess."

She pounded playfully on one of his forearms, and they passed through the litter-choked basement to the living room. Once again, Michelle called for her father.

From his recliner, Henry lifted one eyelid reluctantly. The eye moved slowly, focused. "Hey, Germie," he said, and the eyelid closed.

This was a nickname that St. Germaine didn't enjoy, but one that he accepted grudgingly. In actuality he wasn't Michelle's uncle. He was a second or third cousin on her father's side; she'd forgotten which.

"Thanks for having me over on such short notice," St. Germaine said. "There are a number of insurance aspects to this Arionnese matter that you oughta consider."

"I'll get the grub on," Henry said, lumbering to his feet. He shuffled up the compact stairway into the kitchen.

St. Germaine winked at Michelle, motioned for her to sit with him on the couch.

Among other pursuits, Paul St. Germaine was an insurance salesman. She never heard of her father purchasing any of his wares, insurance or otherwise, and if this evening held true to form Henry would say, "I'll t'ink about it." Maybe they consummated deals when she wasn't around, but Michelle suspected otherwise.

Michelle didn't understand why her father had her "Uncle Paul" over so often. Maybe it was out of a sense of familial obligation, and St. Germaine wasn't close to Granmère, so that probably had something to do with it. The men never really argued, but Michelle couldn't detect any extraordinary fondness between them either. Maybe they continued the relationship for Michelle's benefit, although everyone must know that St. Germaine could never rival the position held in Michelle's heart by Granpère Gilbert.

Sometimes St. Germaine gave Michelle and the other children gadgets from his briefcase—little toys or plastic advertising novelties that didn't last long. Even if they were worthless, Michelle didn't care. He was a good-hearted man and she liked him. He was nice to Rachel besides, and that meant a great deal to Michelle. Most visitors treated Rachel as if she weren't there, but not St. Germaine. He relished engaging her in conversation, and there had been occasions when they seemed to carry on almost normal exchanges. Maybe Henry noticed this, and brought the congenial giant around to bring Rachel out of her inner worlds.

In St. Germaine's presence, Henry sometimes spoke of his fondness for the large extended family they shared, and of how nice that was for everyone involved. The "get-togethers" of the Fouquets, the St. Germaines, and the other clans on Dad's side involved nearly a hundred people, and occurred three to four times annually—usually a *fête champêtre* in Granmère's garden, where she set up long tables of food, flowers, and wine. Henry hadn't brought his household members to the last two affairs, citing as an excuse Rachel's illness and the care she required.

"You're so immersed in thought," St. Germaine said, patting one of Michelle's knees. "What a serious little girl!"

"I'm not a little girl. I'm a young woman." She craned to look at him defiantly, retaining a softness in her eyes that betrayed affection.

"Of course. How undiplomatic of me. And you are growing into a beautiful young lady."

Michelle beamed. She heard her father toiling in the kitchen, thunking a cleaver against meat on a board.

"How has your mother been?" St. Germaine asked, looking around.

"She's lying down. Oh she's been, well . . . not so bad."

"And not so good either?"

Michelle nodded.

There was a long silence. Then St. Germaine said, "I paid my house off a couple of months ago, you know that? I'd be a pretty good catch if the right lady happened along."

"Uh-huh."

"I don't actually own that house after all, you know that? What if I didn't pay my property taxes a couple of years running? That tells you who owns it. I'm just a caretaker."

"Right."

"And what about this Arionnese situation? How's that going to affect the title?"

"I don't know."

Michelle envisioned a physical confrontation between her father and Uncle Paul. Height meant nothing in that arena: Henry could snap St. Germaine like a pretzel. She scolded herself for thinking so crudely. But it was an inevitable perspective around Henry Fouquet, a physical, blustery man who got into fights. Michelle had never witnessed one of his fisticuff sessions, but Joseph had. Usually they occurred in blue-collar drinking establishments, and one related by Joseph involved a nearly tragic case of mistaken identity. Her father had been sitting at the bar one evening with Cartucci when a man came up behind Henry and crunched a quart bottle over his head, shattering glass all over . . .

"I have something for you I forgot in the car," St. Germaine, said, unfolding his body from the couch.

She barely glanced at him as he strode from the room.

On an errand to inform Henry of one of Rachel's spells, Joseph happened to wander into the bar just as Henry was smashed upon the crown. After absorbing such a blow, lesser men would have dropped straight to the floor, many of them stilled permanently. But not Henry W. Fouquet, he of thick skull and bones. He shook his head a little to clear it, saying "What? . . . Wha' da hell?" Then he jumped from his stool and faced his attacker, a man much taller and bulkier than he.

In sudden, retreating surprise, the man mumbled something about having the wrong person and tried to proffer an apology. But Henry grabbed hold of the man's jacket lapels with one hand and lifted him from the floor against a wall, holding him there.

Blood streaming down his forehead, Henry issued forth a stream of expletives. To his credit he threw no blows. Joseph said that his father kept shaking his head and trying to clear it, while holding fast to the rag doll man. Everyone in the place gathered around, and a number of the more belligerent drunks urged Henry into battle. But instead he let the man down slowly and released him. Embarrassed beyond salvation, the fellow disappeared, never to be seen in those parts again.

As Michelle ruminated, the event seemed almost legendary to her, and comically so. Her father seemed to be an indestructible man physically, with "natural" strength. Joseph had strength of that caliber too, and to Michelle's knowledge neither of them ever exercised. She wondered how powerful they might be if they did so.

Who would win a contest between Joseph and Daddy? Joseph was taller and better proportioned, but Henry had used the slam-into-the-wall routine against him more than once. Not in three years, though, she estimated.

St. Germaine returned with a plastic novelty, a clear little enclosure full of pale maple liquid in which a section of lacquered wood had been immersed.

She accepted it, turned it over. The piece of wood, which had "Arionnese Eucalyptus Association" printed on two sides, followed apparent gravity, always dropping in its syrupy little chamber to the apparent bottom, depending upon how Michelle held it.

"The Arionnese have eucalyptus trees?" she asked.

"Don't worry your head about that!" St. Germaine said, kneeling on the floor beside her. "Just take it and play with it."

She stared at him dispassionately, wondering how he could speak to her so cruelly. Had her intermittent taciturn spells irritated him?

"Oh, all right," he said. "I'm helping organize a brand-spankin'-new wood products group, and we're going to approach the round guys for support, extolling the many benefits of eucalyptus, an aromatic treasure from Earth. Plants are continuing their growth patterns on this habitat, you know."

"You expect the Arionnese to invest? What if they don't deal in terms of money?"

"Well, they must deal in terms of something, mustn't they? I'm a wheeler-dealer and I'll just have to discover what that is. The times they are a-changin', Michelle, and I plan to adapt."

"That's wise, Uncle Paul."

"I'm glad you think so, sagacious one."

Michelle heard mock condescension in the tone. One of their infinite games.

He kissed her on the cheek, said, "I'll go see how my cuz is doing in the kitchen. You've got some thoughts to complete, as I see in your face."

"You're not angry?"

"Naw."

But he was hurt. She saw that in his face.

When he was out of sight and she heard men's voices in the other room, Michelle considered the technological Everest the Arionnese had achieved in their theft of the entire San Francisco Bay area. The scale of that feat boggled and jarred her for an instant. Then she felt it slip to the hindmost folds of her mind, overridden by other concerns.

The habitat event should dominate all family affairs. It should be the topic of dinner conversation and the paramount concern in their lives: "Did you hear the latest? . . . Are the astronomers still confused about exactly where we are? . . . What are the Arionnese sexual habits? . . ."

But it wasn't happening that way around Michelle, except sometimes at school where others held forth. As incongruous as it seemed, the problems of her family loomed far bigger before her than anything else, far more immense even than the universe itself. She tried to conceive a day when this foreground of Fouquet clutter might disperse, revealing a beautiful panorama beyond. But such an image would not form in her mind.

Joseph and his girlfriend Thyla Dunlap arrived precisely at dinner time, just as Michelle, Renney, and Stu were bringing chairs and stools from around the house into the kitchen.

The six chairs of the hoary, dilapidated dinette set were of the electrically adjustable variety, and at one halcyon time they allowed the person sitting upon one to raise and lower his seat to a comfortable level. Now only one chair functioned, and that was the one St. Germaine got, since he was so tall that he preferred lowering it quite a bit. When Joseph and Thyla entered the kitchen, St. Germaine was crawling on the floor between the wall and the table, plugging in his chair.

"The charge ran down," St. Germaine said, as he straightened and saw Joseph.

Henry stood in front of the range, pan-frying chuck steaks on all four burners. "Joseph," he said with a chortle, "you have a nose for food. All the Fouquets have a sixth sense tellin' 'em when supper's on."

Joseph smiled, and Michelle thought about how nice he looked in his gray and white vee-neck sweater.

"You got my underpants on again, boy?" Henry asked, staring at Joseph in mock anger. "If you do, pull 'em off right here an' give 'em back!"

"I don't have your stuff," Joseph said.

Henry guffawed.

Joseph's face flashed red.

From beside the dinette set, Michelle studied Thyla, who was by the doorway and just behind Joseph. In a beige sweater and knee-length chocolate brown skirt, this woman of eighteen was polite and eminently proper, from a middle-class Sunset district family. She had a petite bone structure, and classic, lightly retouched features. Her father, a space cargo broker, hadn't made it very far up the management ladder, and not at one of the prestigious Montgomery Street firms. Despite this, Thyla bore the aura and manners of high social quality, a never-ending source of embarrassment for Joseph whenever she visited his family. Thyla pushed for such visitations, expressing an interest in getting to know the Fouquets better.

Tonight Henry had prepared what he termed a "special gourmet feed," as it was one of the evenings he didn't have to participate in a wrist-wrestling meet.

Exerting pressure on his chair with one knee, St. Germaine tested the electric mechanism. His knee went up and down.

"Is it working okay?" Michelle asked.

He nodded.

Michelle watched the assemblage move toward the table as Henry approached with a plate of dark, obviously overcooked steaks. Henry considered himself a chef in the tradition of his mother, whose kitchen talents were considerable. To Michelle's knowledge he had in fact adopted but one of her culinary rules—a prohibition against catsup and steak sauce at the table. This created no hardship at Granmère's house, where the cuisine required no camouflage. But as in other matters, a great deal had been lost in the transmission from one generation to the next.

Thyla rolled her eyes discreetly as Henry next brought forth a bowl of flaccid green beans and a chipped platter of grease-glistening fried potatoes. Renney followed with a plate of white bread and a pitcher of grape Sweeswee Juice, while Rachel fumbled in the refrigerator for a bottle of burgundy.

As the group maneuvered for places around the table, Michelle held back and saw her mother staring at Thyla, making Thyla uncomfortable. Taking Joseph by the hand, Thyla led him around to Rachel's side of the table (opposite a windowless wall) and sat three chairs from Rachel, next to Henry's spot at the head of the table. This reduced the staring effectively.

The last to choose, Michelle was left with a stool across from her mother that nobody else wanted.

Rachel's worn, dark blue eyes were wine-and Korpunkel-glazed, set in a sodden, hang-jowled countenance of loose skin that reflected mental strains beyond the normal allotment for a forty-four-year-old. Her face bore an unhealthy yellow pallor, not unlike the shade of those few teeth remaining in her custody. She held a long cigarette beside her head and drew upon the fag occasionally, between raspy coughs and sips of wine. Whenever an ember tumbled to her purple and yellow dress, Renney (seated beside her) whisked it away with a napkin.

Henry plopped into his chair, and a traditional silence of nearly thirty seconds ensued. This was a chair-squeaking period in which the participants were supposed to utter private, silent prayers in gratitude for the food they were about to eat. Michelle, despite her love for her father, considered this ceremony a farce in which he never actually offered any form of gratitude to the Almighty. He never clasped his hands, never lowered his head or his eyelids, never moved his lips. He was not a religious man in the formal sense.

Following upon the first plate-filling frenzy by many of those present, St. Germaine touched upon the perennial matter of his career. He said the insurance companies were pumping out fresh exclusions that would appear on all renewal policies. Certain cosmic events, such as damage from meteors and asteroids, would no longer be covered. Essentially, he chuckled, they were excluding most events that could happen and covering most events that could not.

"While I'm not your agent," he said, "I should examine your policies to make certain you're getting the best deal. I'll work up some numbers of my own, and who knows, maybe we can do business."

His words hung in the air unanswered. No one so much as looked at him.

Then Rachel began singing coarsely, to the tune of "Tannenbaum":

> Oh Ireland, my Ireland,
> Take me back to Ireland;
> Oh Ireland, my Ireland,
> Take me back to Ireland.

"Shadup, Raich," Henry said.

Rachel looked at St. Germaine, who sat at one end of the table to her immediate left, and said, "Twenty-six years ago Henry promised to take me on a visit to Ireland. I have Irish blood, you know. He hasn't kept that pact, and since it was agreed upon just prior to our marriage, he broke our marriage contract. Our marriage is null and void."

"You're outa your mind," Henry said.

"Did you promise or didn't you?" Rachel asked. "Deny it!"

"I ain't discussin' this subject."

"Not now, maybe, but we will discuss it, and I'm not waiting another twenty-six years."

"Sure, Raich, we'll catch the first express to Ireland. Does anyone have a rocket ship schedule handy?"

A deathly silence, broken at last by St. Germaine. "When do your insurance policies expire, Henry?" he asked.

"I ain't certain. Month or two, I guess."

"He's lying through his shorts," Rachel said, her tone nasal and acidic. "We don't have any policies. Haven't had any for fifteen years."

St. Germaine gasped. "Is that true?"

"Naw. Raich don't know nuttin' about nuttin'. I take it back, she does know about nuttin' because she is one—a nut. Har! I gotcha there, Raich."

"Everyone at the table recognizes the really stupid person present, Henry," Rachel retorted. "Go get the policies."

Henry turned a shade of purple that generally is reserved for ripe plums. "Dis is my table," he said. "An' I don't wanna talk about in*surance*!" He fairly shot out the last two syllables, then glowered territorially around the table.

"Whatever *shall* we talk about, Henry?" Rachel asked, sipping her burgundy.

Henry thought for a moment and then began speaking in an unkindly fashion about one of the customers on his Lawservice route. He reached a point where he wanted to swear, said, "Dat f . . ." His mouth locked, and at a sidelong glance from Joseph he didn't complete the word.

"Dat wop Martinahelli," Henry said, beginning anew, "he lept his gate open dis mornin' on purpish and his goddam dog nearly tore my arm off when I reached outa da van ta shoot a cartridge."

"It's Martinelli, Dad," Renney said, between gulps of Sweeswee Juice. "Not Martinahelli. I know his kid."

Renney removed a slice of bread from the plate at the center of the table and looked around for the margarine. He had taken up his mother's cause.

"Martinahelli, Whatahelli, Cockahelli, I don't gib a shit," Henry snapped, spraying food particles and saliva from his mouth onto the plates of those seated nearest, including Thyla and Stu.

Henry's propensity to shower persons at the table was not unknown, so others there within range, including Coley, covered their plates quickly with their hands, fending off a good deal of the bombardment.

Stu hadn't been briefed, so his hands weren't quick enough.

At point-blank range, Thyla didn't even try. Appearing nauseated, she stared at the table.

"All I know is dat Cockahelli's a goddam a-hole from way back," Henry said, oblivious to the reactions around him. He swallowed a morsel of chuck steak so large that his adam's apple bulged.

Joseph whispered something apologetic in Thyla's ear.

Just as Thyla seemed ready to detonate, St. Germaine took on a whimsical expression and began lowering the seat of his electric chair. Soon Michelle saw his head nearly disappear beneath the table top, showing only his forehead and the blond, tightly arranged curls of his hair.

Michelle giggled.

The others watched, stunned.

Then, like a mountain rising from the sea, St. Germaine re-emerged.

Everyone laughed except Thyla. She appeared more uncomfortable now than nauseated or angry and sat with her hands beneath the table on her lap.

"Do it again, Unka Paul!" Coley squealed.

"No," St. Germaine said with a broad grin. "I'd hate to have the chair stick with my rear on the floor."

But Coley pleaded and whined, to the point where Renney had to quiet her down.

When the cadence of utensils clicking against plates reached a somewhat comfortable level (except for Thyla), Henry shook his barren head and wiped a hand across his brow. "Damned hair's always gettin' in my eyes," he said.

Peals of laughter rang around the table. Even Thyla hinted at a smile.

When Henry repeated his routine, Michelle noticed that Rachel wasn't laughing. With a pained, angry expression, Rachel poured more wine from a liter bottle into her glass.

After a sip, Rachel said in a loud, biting tone: "Stop that, Henry. You're making an ass out of yourself."

This had the effect of a bomb in the center of the table.

But Henry tried to recover. "Grass don't grow on a busy street," he said.

"Your whole life is a cliché," Rachel said.

"What's a cliché?" Renney asked.

"An overused, stale expression," Rachel said. "Mental lightweights use clichés like crutches for their enfeebled brains. They take the place of original thinking."

"Shut the fuck up, Rachel," Henry said, glowering at her.

Rachel's countenance shifted. Without so much as glancing at Henry, she lowered her eyelids and raised the corners of her mouth into a gentle smile. She began to hum, a low and dulcet melody from her innermost private world.

The clatter of utensils resumed, but it was a choppy cadence, punctuated by Henry's angry mutterings.

Michelle considered her mother's assertion about her father's life and disagreed. Despite his behavior he was a wonderful, loving man—a man who had stood by Rachel loyally through all the turmoils of her malady. Why then did Rachel turn on him so unexpectedly at times? Michelle recalled other days and other words, those spoken by her father in rage, and these came to the forefront:

"I coulda been sumpthin' if not for all the time I've hadda spend takin' care o' Rachel."

Now Henry was speaking in his angry, butchered dialect, in an increasingly loud tone: "Why da fuck do I hab ta put up wid dis? If she'd take her fuckin' medicine regular, we could hab a pleasant meal 'round here once in a while."

He turned his attention on Thyla, said, "My langwich bodder ya, young lady?"

"As a matter of fact, Mr. Fouquet, it does." She didn't look at him.

"Ya ain't eatin' da food I prepared spetchul. Ya too good ta dabble wid my stuff?" Eyes bulging, he leaned toward her across his plate.

"It's not that," she said, looking sidelong at him.

"Dad," Joseph interjected. "You spit all over it when you were talking."

"Spit! Da hell ya say! I did not, ya smart-ass little shit!"

Henry leaned even closer to Thyla, and incredibly his eyes seemed to bulge even more. "Too good fer us, ain'tcha? Huh, lady? I'm right, ain't I, huh?"

"That's enough!" Thyla snarled. She pushed her chair away from the table, making an angry squeal of chair legs on linoleum, and stalked from the kitchen.

Joseph hurried after her, and moments later the front door slammed.

"She thinks I don't have any upbringing," Henry said in an erudite tone, looking at Stu. Henry sat back and wiped grease from his chin. "I'll have her know I wasn't always like this. I wore the finest of silks. I had gold on evv-erry tooth. I even had my asshole plucked."

Michelle tried not to think of her father's words. Rachel continued humming, and Michelle almost wished that she too had an interior place in which to hide. If only Michelle could enter and leave voluntarily. Did Rachel have that option? It seemed to Michelle that she did, and if she did and it was therapeutic, didn't that cast doubts upon the general opinion that she was mentally ill?

I'm playing with words, Michelle thought. *She is sick, and maybe it's hereditary, waiting to strike me.*

But Michelle felt she might make a pretty convincing case to the effect that the onset of her mother's problems came not at birth but with her introduction to Granmère Liliane. True, Rachel's mother had been "high strung," and Rachel was that way herself when off medication, but that didn't mean she was insane. In a sense it resembled the "chicken or the egg" argument to Michelle, or the discussions she had heard in church about whether man was innately evil or innately good, and the effects society had on the equation.

To help her mother Michelle needed degrees in law and psychology. Those cigarette burns on Rachel's dress, for example. Were they purely accidental, or did they emanate from some subconscious intent to destroy herself?

Henry dumped the contents of Thyla's plate onto his own. As he tore into her steak and chewed it, he glared from face to face, searching for the slightest indication of disapproval concerning his words or actions.

Receiving none, he ordered Stu to apportion Joseph's meal among the children.

"I don't want any," Michelle said in a soft voice, as Stu went around to Joseph's place.

"Me either," Renney said.

"Save Renney's share for Beauregard," Henry said. "Renney, take it to old Bo yourself."

Startled, Renney peered at his father.

"Coley, you want some of this?" Stu asked, looking at the toddler.

"More potato," she said.

Stu slid what she wanted onto her plate, then divided the remainder, taking half for himself. He placed the plate with Beauregard's "share" next to Renney.

"I don't wanna feed Beauregard," Renney protested.

"I'll do it," Michelle said, feeling a curious urge to discard this food at the first opportunity. She didn't want to waste food, but wasn't about to go in search of Beauregard!

"I tol' Renney to do it," Henry said, with his mouth full.

Renney began whimpering, leaned against his mother's shoulder.

Rachel stopped humming, and glared at Henry with the eyes of one contemplating murder.

"I thought that would bring you out of it, Raich," Henry said. "An attack on sissyboy, right?"

Without a word, Rachel stared Henry down.

Renney ran from the kitchen and went upstairs, sobbing.

Michelle wanted to defend her little brother. Just because he was close to his mother and artistically inclined didn't make him a sissy! But she held her tongue.

"Come back here and get this plate!" Henry roared. Then, to St. Germaine in a conversational tone: "I gotta ask you to leave the house. We've got some things to go over here that ain't suitable for outsiders."

St. Germaine wiped his mouth, thanked Henry and Rachel for the meal, and left without glancing at Michelle.

"Should I leave too, Mr. Fouquet?" Stu asked.

Disregarding the query, Henry said to Rachel, "I ain't the big fool you think. That queerboy in the other room ain't mine, and it's high time you admitted it!"

"The only bastard in this family is still at the table," Rachel said.

"Ya talkin' 'bout me?" Henry said, leaning toward her and spraying spittle with his words.

"Daddy spit on my food!" Coley said. "I can't eat it now!"

"Hush, Coley," Michelle said. "Come on, let's go play in your room."

When Michelle, Stu, and Coley left the table, Henry and Rachel were engaged in a ferocious stare-down. Halfway up the stairs, Michelle heard a kitchen chair topple over. Then something bigger fell, shaking the house. Her father's heavy, clumping footsteps ensued, and the front door slammed hard.

"Be quiet for a minute," Michelle said to her companions.

She heard her mother shuffling across the kitchen, humming melodically. To her knowledge, Michelle's father had never struck her mother, but in blind rages accidents were always possible.

Coley pattered ahead to the next level, continued on up another flight to her room.

"I think your mother was referring to me," Stu said. "I was the bastard at the table. I'm illegitimate."

"She wasn't talking about you at all," Michelle said, "not the way she was burning Daddy with her eyes."

"I'm your half-brother, Michelle," Stu whispered. "Your father and mine are the same. I promised him I wouldn't tell, but it just seemed like, well . . . I thought you oughta know."

"An affair?"

Stu nodded. "During Moon War V, at Stratobase Uriah."

Stu related everything he knew, and at the end asked her not to tell anyone.

"Another secret's all I need," Michelle said. She sighed. "Okay, I won't tell."

She moved slowly up the stairs. Coley was waiting.

THIRTEEN

Efficient management is a process requiring minimal opposition. Identify known and potential enemies, and either undermine them or keep them at bay. To the extent possible, reduce the odds of them getting dangerously close to you by finding your own key subordinates, as opposed to letting them seek you out. Seekers often have ulterior motives.

—From a cassette recording
of Granmère Liliane's thoughts

Michelle felt the television drawing her into its screen, to worlds within. These were worlds dominated by the problems and fantasies of other people, and for the moment they comprised the only universe in her consciousness, all other experiences having been anesthetized by the device.

Something bumped her leg, imparting a sharp but brief pain.

"Move over, Renney," she snapped, not turning from the screen, which became unfocused. She envisioned her little brother as he lay like her on his belly before the set, chin propped on upturned palms.

She heard him sliding on the carpet.

"Where's Stu?" Renney asked. "I haven't seen him since Thyla stormed out of here."

Reality encroached. Saturday now, Thursday then. On to Arionn!

"He wasn't at school yesterday either," Michelle said. "Truant officers'll be on his tail, he keeps this up."

Rachel, on the couch behind them, didn't enter the conversation. She, Stu, and Renney faded from Michelle's consciousness, replaced by a statuesque redhead who was demonstrating a Foodalizer. The size of a conventional microwave oven, the appliance enlarged and cooked concentrated food pellets that were placed into it.

"Wish we had one o' those," Renney said. "I'd put leaves, rocks, all kindsa stuff in it to see what happens. It moisturizes and stretches cells, you know."

"Rocks?" Rachel said. "Don't be silly, child. What would you do with a moisturized rock, anyway?"

"Maybe I'd use it in the desert, sucking water out of it."

Michelle felt herself drawn into the fanciful discussion, and heard her mother say, "Too heavy to be practical. Besides, I don't think a rock could be foodalized."

The telephone rang, and the children watched their mother, in a threadbare indigo terrycloth robe, shuffle up the mini-staircase to the kitchen entranceway.

"Ye-ess?" Rachel said, telephone receiver in hand. Then, shouting: "Oh, On-ree! It's *Maman!*"

Henry stomped across the kitchen, from his bedroom. "Gimme da phone, bitch!"

With only four concise words, Michelle realized, Rachel had devastated Henry's masculinity. Photographs from Granmère's house flashed in Michelle's mind, of Henry in short pants and glistening black button-up boots, his hair cut pageboy fashion.

Henry had the receiver, and after a pause, said, "Oh God! When did 'e go?"

Granpère! Michelle thought. In a daze she was up and away from the narcoma of the television, holding onto her father's free hand.

But the hand pulled away, unaware of Michelle's presence.

Recollecting Granpère's words, spoken through her mouth in the green-lit closet, she reminded herself he hadn't really died.

"*I need a little vacation from Granmère . . . I will contact you in due course . . . Do not despair . . .*"

His face ashen, Henry replaced the receiver on the hook and addressed Rachel, who was back on the living room couch. "My fodder jusht died, ya bitch. Duzzat make ya feel good?"

Without looking at her mother or listening for her response, Michelle fled upstairs, to the hiding place where she kept her puzzle box.

"Thyla doesn't want to speak to you," the voice on the other end of the drugstore picturephone said. Joseph didn't look at the screen, and stood just beyond range of the transmitting camera so that Thyla's mother couldn't see that he had been crying.

"Please tell her it's important, Mrs. Dunlap," Joseph said, in a valiant attempt to keep his voice firm. But it cracked toward the end of his sentence. He was in the shopping mall three blocks from his house, since his father had the house line tied up talking with relatives about Granpère.

"She left explicit instructions with me," Mrs. Dunlap said.

"My grandfather just died. I need to talk with her."

"Just a moment."

Joseph blew his nose.

As he finished, Thyla came on the line. "Joseph, is that true? Granpère Gilbert is gone?"

"It's true."

"How awful. I'm so sorry."

"Look, I hate the way Dad acted with you, but you can't keep blaming me for it. I'll never be like he is, I promise."

"I know your father's a loving man in his own way, and he works hard for his family. I hope you are like him in some ways."

"In darned few, I hope."

"Step in front of the camera so I can see you. Have you been crying?"

Joseph moved in front of the lens, looked down to conceal the redness of his eyes.

"I care for you, Joseph, and I have to tell you that it's not just your father that has me upset. Yesterday I learned about your wild, drunken episode. Kenny March told Nancy Wilson, and she told me."

Joseph stomped his foot angrily at his friend's careless conversation.

"How could you take chances like that, Joseph? Hanging on the front of a car? You must have an absolutely crazy streak that I don't understand."

"Like mother, like son, you mean?"

"Your mother has severe problems, and from what I understand, the alcohol aggravates it. You need to abstain from alcohol. *Totally*. Or stay away from me. I care for you a great deal, too much to watch you go down the drain."

"I'll never take another drink."

The words flew out impulsively, and as they discussed other matters Joseph found himself going back to this pledge in his mind. Consequently he stumbled over words, connecting them only partially with his thoughts.

They talked about Granpère's funeral, which would take place the following Tuesday at the Catholic cemetery where one of Granpère's brothers was buried. Thyla had her own "family matters" to take care of in the interim, she said. But she would attend the funeral.

After concluding the call, Joseph remained motionless, considering the implications of Thyla's words, intonations, and facial expressions. That comment about her own family matters sounded like a lie, an excuse not to see him. How much of it had to do with the antics of his father, and how much with his own misbehavior? It was inevitable that she would find out about Joseph's drinking bout (the only time he had ever really gotten soused), and he knew it wasn't the sort of behavior approved in the circles she wanted to travel. But the ultimatum made him angry, and he remembered the old saw about lips that touch wine. She was domineering, importunate, and stubborn.

She was also right, he admitted to himself. He considered briefly the possibility of a genetic legacy from mother to son in this regard, then denied vehemently being anything like her. One incident didn't prove a thing. He told himself that he could stop drinking at any time and Rachel couldn't. With her it was compulsion; with him it was choice.

But now Thyla wasn't giving him any choice, and he wasn't certain he wanted to quit drinking just yet, at his young age. The change seemed drastic, somehow.

"Are you finished with the phone?" a voice asked. "May I use it now?"

Joseph slid by the man without looking at him, received the vague image of someone elderly and weak. He moved by other faces that didn't register, found himself on the sidewalk outside in a shower of cold rain. He zipped his coat and headed into the downpour, staring at the suddenly wet pavement and the markings of the parking lot.

Someone honked at him as he crossed a parking lot arterial, but Joseph kept going and didn't look. A vehicle squealed to an angry stop, a hulking, unfocused peripheral form. It spoke with another bleat, then accelerated after Joseph passed.

Michelle sat in the musty, stygian blackness of her closet, holding the open puzzle box and book. Her fingers found the envelope bearing Granpère's check, and she left it in place, between pages in the back of the book. This time no translucent green light illuminated or warmed her little enclosure, and she shivered violently.

Desperately, she struggled to bring forth her grandfather's voice on her own lips, the way it had happened last time, in this place. No words came other than her own grunts and pleadings, so she tried to speak in phrases that he might have selected. But she couldn't recall his precise tone and diction. Even the features of his face, once so familiar, seemed horribly fuzzy, and she begged him to restore her memories.

"Where are you, Granpère?" she called out, plaintively. "Please talk to me. Please help me understand."

But she heard no voice other than her own.

She wondered if she had imagined all of it before—the green mist with French words and phrases floating upon it, Granpère's pronunciations and definitions, the way he spoke to her through her own body. Had the last of Granpère's spirit been in those moments, gone forever now with his passing?

But he hadn't passed. It was as he said it was, a journey from which he would return, for her. She needed to be patient, and he would contact her "in due course." That could be quite a while. He must be traveling now, getting to the place where he would hide from Granmère.

Rachel had her own hiding places from that *bête noire*, and Michelle felt the limitations of her knowledge about them. It was like that with her grandfather's place of concealment as well. It existed, but that was all she knew. She despised every thought of Granmère, that terrible old woman who had driven her grandfather away and her mother into internal, secret realms.

Secrets. Those of her own creation and those of others, entrusted to her. She wanted all of them out in the open, so they would no longer be a burden. Get them all out, the pleasant and the unpleasant alike. It occurred to her that a law should be enacted forbidding secrets, so that people could never again be harmed by them.

Following her line of reasoning to its logical conclusion, she knew she should share the puzzle box, book, and check with her family. But she didn't want to do that just yet, despite an awareness of the harm generated by Granpère's supposedly benign secrets. Secrecy was of itself an attack upon an outsider.

Why am I thinking this way? Michelle thought, staring at the unbroken darkness before her. *Am I angry with Granpère for leaving, trying to spoil what he left for me? Don't do it, Michelle! Keep what he left you for yourself!*

In frustration and confusion, Michelle replaced the book in the puzzle box. She had a chapter full of French words in her mind, with definitions and conjugations, and this would be a good basis for her to proceed through the ensuing chapters. She had the words and phrases culled from Gran-

mère's Sunday dinner proddings as well, and if the green mist and Granpère's words didn't come back she would learn French in its entirety the
hard way, on her own.

Tears for her grandfather moved to Michelle's eyes, but she wouldn't
let them fall. After all she had nothing to cry about yet, nothing requiring,
in its finality, tears. Whatever came, whatever was meant to be, she would
be strong. Granpère was of her childhood. He took her to fantasy places,
guided her through days of ducks, of ice cream sodas, of gifts for little
girls.

FOURTEEN

If unabated, Mayor Wilde's around-the-clock hiccuping (singultus) condition will damage her heart. Medical personnel are treating the matter with all seriousness. A number of remedies have been attempted, including carbon dioxide inhalations, the administration of Coramine, morphine, and sodium Luminal—all to no avail. The mayor has been checked for gastritis, stomach tumors, strangulated hernia, coronary thrombosis, appendicitis, pancreatitis, peritonitis, syphilitic meningomyelitis, and a host of other conditions that might contribute to the convulsions. She suffers from none of these, so we've called in a team of psychologists to work on her during waking and sleeping hours.

—Summary of Mayor Wilde's medical file, stolen by a reporter

Ready for her grandfather's funeral early, Michelle stood in the front yard awaiting the others. A cool morning breeze rustled her lavender and lace Sunday dress and whipped her hair across her face, stinging one cheek. She brushed the hair aside and moved into the wind shelter of the hedge, adjacent to the family car and Rachel's "putt-putt" car.

A movement on the sidewalk at the other side of the hedge caught her eye. Presently Stu came into full view and sauntered up the broken concrete driveway, looking as if he had slept in his clothes.

"Where have you been?" Michelle demanded, moving into the wind to confront him. "My grandfather died!"

He looked startled, said: "I been around."

"Where?"

"If you really need to know, I got wind of a party Friday night and flopped there. I bummed around all weekend, getting to know the streets. When Monday rolled around I didn't feel like going to school."

"The truant officers are gonna be after you." The lace that Michelle had paper-clipped to one sleeve of her dress came loose, and she tended to it, bending the clip so that it was tighter.

"So what? I can outfox any 'trew' what was ever born. I want my freedom more than they want me. They're not on commission like bounty hunters, kid. If they were, it would be harder."

"Go inside and get cleaned up for the funeral."

"I never met the man. Not that I wouldn't mind going, if that would please you. Are you sure it's okay?"

"Positive, and Dad won't dare say anything. Granpère was your grandfather, too. You're part of this family, Stu Kroemer, and it's about time you started acting like it."

Granpère Gilbert's funeral didn't resemble the images Michelle had formed. There were no black banners or morose, black-suited men in top hats. It wasn't held in the midst of urns and caskets in a musty, windowless room rife with the odor of embalming chemicals. There were no weepers hurling themselves prostrate before the coffin. All her preconceived notions were shattered when she stepped into the church, behind Renney, their father (who carried Coley), and Joseph. Stu trailed the others wearing one of Joseph's old suits, and Rachel didn't attend.

On the ride over, Michelle had considered her mother's absence. While Rachel and Granpère never quarreled openly, it was common knowledge that he did not approve of her because of her neglect of the children.

This Catholic church, which Michelle had attended on holidays with her grandparents, hadn't been where she thought the funeral would take place, and it occurred to her now that she must have confused the goings-on of a funeral parlor with those of a church. It was airy and bright here, smelling of sweet flowers. Sunny bouquets had been placed alongside every pew and abundantly around the coffin at the altar. A boy in a white surplice guided them to the front row near the coffin, and they slid uneasily into their seats.

"Is Granpère in the same place as Beauregard?" Coley queried, looking up at her father.

"No. Now hush."

Joseph left for a time to speak with Thyla, who was sitting with her mother in the back of the church. Presently he returned to his seat, just before the ceremony began.

The realities of the ceremony passed through Michelle's senses with numbing indistinctness. She recalled kissing her grandfather's forehead and placing beside him a tiny fishing pole that she had made. His skin had been frightfully cold against her lips, and as she withdrew from him she winked at the thought of their Big Secret. There was no response. In a daze, Michelle kissed her grandmother, and the old woman's skin was as cold as Granpère's. Granmère stood stiffly, staring through Michelle without apparent emotion or recognition.

What game was Granpère Gilbert playing? Why hadn't he winked back at Michelle discreetly or found some other manner of reassuring her that he wasn't actually dead?

Patience, she reminded herself. *I must have patience.*

In the limousine with her siblings, father, and grandmother on the way to the cemetery, Michelle sought refuge in fantasy. She imagined Granpère's coffin covered in glass so that the body could be viewed. But this was a box of his own invention, covered in magnifying glass to conceal the fact that the body had been dehydrated and shrunken to a length of less than two centimeters. Something to do with limited burial space on the habitat. A green mist escaped the box, nearly blew Granmère over, and disappeared through an open doorway, where it was lifted to freedom on a sweet-smelling breeze.

No one seemed to notice the green mist, with the exception of Michelle. But she wasn't the only one who knew the secret of Granpère's dehydration.

Bursting into the church while the priest was reading the eulogy, Rachel shrieked, "What would happen if someone here just up and swallowed old Gilbert? Like a vitamin pill?"

A hush fell across the fantasized assemblage. Some stared angrily or in disbelief at Rachel. Others gazed away in embarrassment, trying to pretend she wasn't there.

"I didn't mean anything by that," Rachel said, her tone genuinely apologetic. "He was a nice enough man. Something of a weakling, though, the way he wouldn't stand up to Liliane."

Then Michelle and her mother stole Granpère's little body and escaped with it to a Foodalizer display at an appliance store. With the police in close pursuit and shouting about limited burial space, Michelle placed Granpère's body inside the Foodalizer and pressed a button. The unit exploded, and in a flash of white light Granpère appeared, full-sized and alive, holding the fishing pole Michelle had made, now enlarged.

"Let's see how the fish are jumpin', eh, girls?" he said with the biggest wink Michelle had ever seen. And off the three of them went, whistling and laughing, while the police and stunned onlookers moved aside.

The pain of something hitting her leg brought Michelle back. Green. So much green. But this was the green of grass, stretching to the very limits of the horizon, it seemed.

A wind blast burned her face, and in an awakening haze she saw that Renney, to her left, was reaching to his left across Coley, pressing the button of the door's power window. Renney had kicked Michelle in the leg.

"You stink, Coley," Renney said.

Michelle was near the middle of the wide seat beside her father looking beyond the heads of Renney and Coley at the low grassy hills of the cemetery. As her eyes focused, she saw more than green, and the punctuating, startling shapes of gravestones. There were more flowers here, and elegant cypress and pine trees whose branches swayed in the wind.

Fast forward. Slowly, painfully, Michelle's gaze lowered, to the wreath-adorned casket of her grandfather. Cut with *fleurs de lis* and other French carvings, it seemed overworked, not something Granpère would have chosen for himself. Granmère, in profile to Michelle, stood by him for the last time, shifting on her feet, clasping and reclasping her hands, looking around.

Granmère was bored, Michelle decided. No sadness or remorse after forty-nine wedded years, only boredom! Michelle loathed her.

Granite-faced Granmère, with her skin saturated by moisturizing cream. How could cream penetrate such a surface, and why did she bother? Certainly not for Granpère. For herself then, or the public? What about another man, someone waiting in shadow at that very moment, oozing to her furtively in the night? Michelle admitted to herself that with all she knew about her grandmother she didn't actually know her at all. Probably no one could. She had anger as her primary emotion, and a disapproving, condescending manner of looking at things, as if nothing and no one could meet her standards. Always she was there with the white glove, locating the speck of dust.

Almost by definition, life is imperfect, Michelle thought. *Why can't you recognize that, Granmère, and accept it?*

The most tenderness Michelle had ever seen in her grandmother had been toward Bumper, when occasionally she brought him food and toys. A dog! Michelle loved Bumper herself, assuming Granmère felt genuine *love* in this example, and not mere affection. But to express herself best to an animal? Granmère must have given love and tenderness to Granpère as well, sometime during their life together. He'd told Michelle that he loved Granmère very much. Maybe chapter two of Granpère's book went into that, to their early years before Granmère began turning to stone. Michelle found herself looking forward to the formidable task of translation. She likened each product of his pen to a gem, envisioned herself turning words to the light for their facets. Things new, things remembered.

She sighed and felt the tightness in her shoulders release.

Then Michelle thought she saw sadness in Granmère's eyes and a downward wrinkle to her mouth, as if she were about to cry. A sheen came over the eyes, as from tears beginning their flow. Granmère blinked, looked away, and when Michelle could again see her eyes the old woman seemed to have composed herself.

Joseph and Thyla, who stood by Michelle holding hands, whispered to one another and looked at Granmère. Had they noticed the same thing?

A gentle rain began to fall, and with it came the priest's first words here. His demeanor seemed suddenly false to Michelle, and it must have been that way in the church too—as if his words had been selected too hastily and spoken too many times. He was an emotionless bureaucrat reading from a form, his mouth making hideous shapes in the drizzle, failing utterly to touch upon the essence that was Granpère.

She heard the past tense in her thought and switched it to present.

Michelle wanted the priest to cry out in anguish and look away from his reading, doing and saying something sincere, as if the passing of Gilbert J. Fouquet had been significant and memorable. But the man in black didn't alter his drone, and soon, after the sickliest of fanfares, Granpère's casket was lowered into the ground.

Michelle wondered if future generations of humankind would be interred in the soil of Arionn. There had been a grain of truth to her fantasy of a shrunken corpse. The land available on this habitat could not long sustain traditional graveyards.

A man with an electric spade scattered dirt in the hole, and Michelle saw it turn to mud on the casket surface.

It seemed to Michelle that Granpère should provide her with a sign of some sort, a signal that he was all right despite appearances. But as she watched mud run down the sides of the dark box, Michelle felt her hopes melting with the sod, turning to anger. Why had Granpère lied, promising to return for her? How could anyone return from *this?*

She knew this day had made itself a permanent place in her mind, and that she would return to it frequently. It hung upon her like a great turgid object.

The rain abated at the conclusion of the ceremony, and her father shook hands with the priest, thanking him for his (miserable) presentation. She wished her father had the guts to say precisely that, assuming he agreed with Michelle, shocking this religious charlatan to his foundations! But Henry didn't say it, and gave no indication that he even thought it.

To one side Michelle noticed her mother standing on a nearby knoll, viewing the assemblage. Rachel was dressed in her Sunday finest, a yellow suit, and with one hand kept a wide hat on her head from being blown away by the wind. It didn't particularly surprise Michelle to see her mother present, for the woman had sensitivities that others didn't understand. She looked fine in that suit, standing erect and with the dignified presence Michelle had always known was there, beneath the surface.

A powerful gust of wind bent the Monterey pines to one side on the knoll, and Rachel fought to hold her hat and dress in place. Then her feet seemed to lift from the ground and her body billowed, flattening and fading as its molecules joined those in the sky and became indistinct from them.

Michelle looked around. None of the others looked toward the knoll or showed the slightest signs that they had seen anything out of the ordinary. Anyone Michelle told about this would undoubtedly contend that her mother hadn't really been there, that it had been a stress-induced apparition. Viscerally, Michelle knew otherwise. Her mother had been present to pay her respects, in one of her forms.

Nearby a distantly related woman was commenting about Michelle, thinking the girl out of earshot: "Strange, she didn't cry once. I was watching her, the poor child. She shouldn't hold it in like that or she'll end up like her mother."

Thyla told Joseph that she had to go somewhere with her mother, that she would talk with him later.

In the limousine on the way home, Granmère held a black address book open on her lap. "You know what these marks mean, don't you?" she said, holding up an open page so that Michelle could see. Most of the names had been crossed out, each time with the use of a neat red *x.*

"I was going to cross out Gilbert's name," Granmère said, without waiting for a response, and she said his name in the French way. "Then I saw he wasn't in my book. Foolish of me."

She returned the book to her lap, flipped solemnly through the pages, and said, "I must write letters to people in France. Of course they cannot be mailed, but I must compose them nonetheless. It is the proper thing to do."

The limousine dropped Granmère off at her office first as she was in a hurry, then took Henry and his children home.

With her hair a feral, uncombed knot of gray frizz, Rachel met them at the living room doorway. She watched as Henry trudged by in the lead and headed for the back of the house, without a word or a glance in Rachel's direction. Michelle couldn't recall ever having seen the thin, wrinkled yellow robe that covered her mother's emaciated body. Undone at the front and revealing an opaque, poorly fitting nightgown, the robe seemed to be something Rachel had retrieved from the bottom of an old clothing pile. It reeked of musty sourness when Michelle drew near.

"Hi, Mom," Michelle said.

No response, but a glare toward Joseph, who had entered just ahead of Stu and Michelle.

"Joseph, I've been searching for you," Rachel said, her tone harsh and chafing, in the manner of a child teasing another.

From behind her, Rachel brought out a long hatpin that gleamed silver, and held it high overhead, as if she were going to stab Joseph with it.

He had his back to her.

Michelle's throat constricted. She couldn't make a sound.

Apparently detecting menace in his mother's tone, Joseph turned, saw the gleaming hatpin, and lunged to one side to get away.

"I'm so glad you're home, Joseph," Rachel said calmly, picking at her hair with the pin. "Would you help me with my hair, please? I'd like to look just right today, with everyone dressed so nicely."

Joseph caught his breath as if from a bad fright. His eyes were wild and he stood well away from his mother, shaking his head in dismay.

"It must almost be time to leave for the funeral," Rachel said. "Just let me finish my hair and I'll be right with you."

"The funeral's over," Joseph said.

"It is? Oh I swear, it takes me so long to get ready nowadays! Well, I'll make it a point to attend the next one."

A *veiled threat?* Michelle wondered.

"Let me fix your hair, Mom," Michelle offered, without approaching her mother. "I'll make it pretty for you. You've got the wrong pin there. That's for a hat."

Michelle revived the graveyard image of her mother, seen atop the windy knoll holding onto a wide hat. Had Rachel come home to get the hatpin?

Could that have happened? For a moment, Michelle feared losing her own grip on reality. The way Michelle watched television, so absorbed by it . . . that was a public realm, though, she reassured herself, and had to be government-approved, safe. But she was entering other realms, events she was afraid to discuss with others. Were there realms of supposedly private fantasy where spirits touched? Had Michelle seen into one of Rachel's secret worlds at the cemetery, and if so what did that bode for Michelle?

I am of my mother's womb, Michelle thought. She bit the inside of her lip, hard. *But everyone has fantasies. There's nothing wrong with that. I'm stronger than Mom, different from her.* Michelle's lip throbbed.

As her mother wielded the hatpin dangerously, alternately moving it gracefully through the air between herself and Joseph and then stabbing at her hair with it, Michelle wanted to go to her. But the constriction of her throat had metastasized throughout her body, and she couldn't move.

"Be careful with that, Mom," Michelle said.

"I want Joseph to help me with my hair," Rachel said. "Joseph never does anything for me, do you, Joseph? Did you talk about me today?" She took a step toward him.

He took one backward.

Michelle had felt fear in her mother's presence before, and this was as acute as ever. Even when Rachel wasn't outwardly hostile, Michelle had a constant underlying anxiety that her mother might suddenly not recognize her, might strike out at her without warning in a sightless rage, thinking Michelle an enemy. Her mother's eyes were glassy now, like the eyes of killers Michelle had seen on electronic wanted posters at the post office. It was as if a film went across the vision of such persons, making them perform insane acts.

Michelle looked around for her father, but he had disappeared into one of the other rooms. Couldn't he hear the discord in here?

Should I scream for him? Michelle wondered. *Better not, could set her off. God, why doesn't her medication keep her from being this way? We'll have to force pills down her every day, as if she were a baby. I can't do it by myself.*

"What did you say about me, little Joseph?" Rachel said. "Bad things? You're not supposed to say bad things about your mommy."

"I don't talk about you," Joseph said. "I try not to even think about you."

Michelle shot a fiery glance at him, moved to her mother's side. Taking her firmly by the arm bearing the hatpin, Michelle led Rachel into the parental bedroom.

"Sit in front of the mirror, Mom," Michelle said, taking the hatpin.

Peripherally, Michelle saw the bathroom door ajar, heard the toilet flush. Henry emerged, buttoning his pants.

"I'm gonna take a nap before I go to work," he said. "Go do that somewhere else."

As Michelle and Rachel left the room with a hand-held mirror, Michelle wondered if her father would ever take the time to understand his own wife. He remained with Rachel through trying times, to be certain, but it seemed to Michelle that he did it primarily to spite Granmère, thwarting any plans the old woman ever had for him. It was his way of getting even with his mother for the prissy impositions of his childhood. He needed either to make an effort to know and help Rachel, or, as difficult as it might seem, he needed to divorce her.

Michelle couldn't believe she was thinking this way, that her parents should split. But it seemed to her that the involvement of Granmère was destroying everyone in the family and causing people to take sides, mostly against Rachel. Joseph was one of the casualties, falling into battle against his own mother under Granmère's standard.

Not that Granmère's cause was so innately wrong. Who could criticize a mother for desiring the best for her only son? It was Granmère's methods that Michelle despised, her utter insensitivity to the plight of an emotionally fragile woman. And in the complicated scheme of things, Rachel had done little to endear herself to Joseph, threatening and teasing him the way she did. Rachel brought much of her misery on herself.

Michelle hated analyzing blame, even when it highlighted Granmère's central role in the misery of the family. Strangely, Granmère was in many respects more of a mother to Michelle than her own mother. Even with her icebox personality, Granmère occupied the role of protector in the family, a final formidable line of defense through which no malevolent outsider could penetrate. Beside the one good meal a week at her house, Granmère occasionally provided clothes for the children—times that made up in warmth or utility what they lacked in style.

Sometimes in her analyses Michelle felt whipsawed by cause and effect, blame and motivation, good and evil. Whenever she seemed to discover accountability, it had a way of turning sideways on her so that she couldn't attack it, and so many mitigating circumstances appeared that she had to go back and start all over again. It was that way even with her grandmother.

Michelle didn't allow Granmère to remain in the "good" column very long. The old woman had a way of saying ugly, hateful things, and Michelle catalogued every one she heard. They reached a dimension of nastiness that seemed unimaginable in a human being. One came to Michelle's awareness and forced itself upon her, like stink from a cesspool: "No man will ever be attracted to you, child, because the minute he sees your mother he'll think you'll be just like her."

From one perspective that might have been a sympathetic remark, Granmère feeling sorry for a little girl with such a mother. But the way she phrased it, and Granmère's own involvement!

The whole situation made Michelle ill to her stomach, and all too often she wished she had never been conceived. Life as she knew it was so complicated, so much trouble.

To console herself later, Michelle removed her puzzle box from its hiding place and sat with it in the closet. She made no effort to open the box, and with it in her hands she shut out the world of her household. She didn't hear Stu in the bedroom calling for her, didn't even see or hear him when he opened the closet door, throwing harsh white room light on her.

"Michelle," he said. "What are you doing in here?" He saw his half-sister sitting on the floor of the tiny cubicle, holding an intricately designed metal box on her lap.

"Oh, Granpère," Michelle moaned. "Don't be gone, beautiful Granpère. I need you!"

Stu noticed the loose wall panel behind her. "Are you okay?" he asked.

Michelle was in a trance, staring straight into the light like a blind girl staring at the sun. "You said you weren't dead," she said. "You promised!"

Stu moved his hand in front of her eyes, raised his voice: "Michelle?"

But she continued her strange plea in an apparently unsuccessful seance attempt.

Astounded and worried, Stu clicked the door shut.

That afternoon, when her father had gone to work and her mother was napping on the living room couch, Michelle heard a commotion in the parental bedroom. From the doorway, she observed Joseph in a rage, tearing apart sheets of Rachel's poetry.

"Stop that!" Michelle shrilled. She rushed in, tried to hold his arms.

He was much stronger than she, but acquiesced. "Where's that hatpin?" he demanded.

"You don't need to tear up her poems to find it."

"Where is it?" he repeated.

"Why do you want it?"

"I'm going to hide it, and everything else that's sharp in the house. I hid Dad's automatic pistol too."

From a dressing table drawer Michelle produced the hatpin and handed it to him.

Joseph's eyes narrowed. "Keep her away from stuff like this," he said.

Michelle wanted to tell him as she had before that their mother wasn't as bad as people imagined, but she couldn't form the words. She began gathering the torn pieces of paper into a pile.

Joseph stomped from the room. A short while later Michelle saw him hiding a pile of potential weapons beneath one of the bottom built-in drawers in the kitchen. He made Michelle swear she wouldn't reveal their location to Mom and promised he would explain the matter to Dad.

"Do you know where any tape is?" Michelle asked. "I'm going to fix those papers you tore up."

"Those worthless poems? They're sick, like she is. No, I don't know where any tape is. Furthermore, I don't care where any tape is."

He stormed into the living room. "You hear that, old lady? Did you hear what I said?"

Michelle saw her mother stir on the couch.

Not waiting for an answer, Joseph roared out of the house, slamming the front door so hard that it shook walls and windows.

Rachel swung her legs to the floor and sat on the edge of the couch, rubbing her eyes.

Her poems! Michelle remembered. She hurried to the bedroom and retrieved the pile of scraps from the top of the dressing table. She heard Rachel in the kitchen, just out of view, and hid the pieces behind her back.

"What have you got in your hands there?" Rachel asked, shuffling into the room.

"Nothing, Mama." Michelle tried to slide around her mother, found her path blocked.

"Nothing? Then open up and let me see. I believe what I see, not what I'm told." She grabbed Michelle by one arm.

The girl tried to twist away, but Rachel was too strong.

Forcing Michelle's hands to the front, Rachel found the poem fragments and took them from her.

"Now I know what you really think of me!" Rachel roared. "Kissey kissey little Michelle, always acting like you're my friend." She smiled sardonically.

"I didn't do this! I . . . I found the pieces." Michelle didn't want to bring more disfavor on her brother. "I think Bumper did it."

"A likely story." Rachel examined the pieces. "No teeth marks here, little liar."

"I was trying to find cellophane tape, Mama. To put them back together! I'd never tear up your poems. Let's find all of your poems around the house and put them in a safe place, okay?"

Rachel shook her head. "Uh-uh. I know what you're up to. You want me to show you where I've hidden my best poems so you can destroy them. I'm not going to let you do it! They're mine and no one else's!"

Rachel whirled and left the room.

A short while later Michelle saw her at the kitchen table, taping the pieces back together.

"So you've got a hidey-hole, eh?" Stu said.

Leaving the closet door ajar for light, he knelt on the floor of the cubicle. After removing the wall panel, he lifted free the intricately designed metal box and held it toward the light. The box was cold to his touch.

He shook it, felt something loose inside that bumped around dully.

He turned the box over several times, discovered that he could move some of the panels on each surface. He worked with the moving pieces for a while but found no pattern. One small triangular section of brass came off without providing a view inside, and he couldn't figure out how to get it back on. It occurred to him that there might be an instruction booklet nearby, and he felt down inside the air space to the shallow bottom of it. Nothing more there.

The wall on the other side of the air space looked a bit crooked, and he pressed a palm against it. The wall moved, slipping out of place. Shoving it to one side, Stu saw a pile of clothes and broken toys. He rummaged in these things, then realized from his position in the bedroom that he was reaching into another closet—probably one of three he had seen that faced the hallway.

Worried that he might be discovered, Stu moved this second panel back into position as best as he could from the side he was on, placed the box and its loose piece in the air space, and secured the other wall panel.

FIFTEEN

We favor stirring up public discontent against Arionnese actions, combined with a gigantic lawsuit. Think
of the class-action implications: eleven million persons deprived of their civil rights! Let's push the aliens
to the wall to discover their true nature, before they
gain the safety and strength of their home planet.

—From an internal ACLU memo

Flying in the face of Big Jack Brittany's displeasure, Granmère Liliane had
Mayor Wilde's personal possessions cleared from the mayor's eighty-third
floor office, moving in her own effects in their stead. Brittany had gone off
in a huff to notify Mayor Wilde, but Granmère didn't think they could do
anything to stop her, not as long as Wilde remained hospitalized. The statutes on Travel and Transport seemed clear in that respect: An unsound
person could not remain in charge of any air, sea, or spacecraft.

Once there had been a similar ordinance with respect to city administration, but in the absence of that Granmère found it prudent to declare herself
captain of a space vehicle. The habitat was self-propelled according to the
latest Cal Berkeley educated guess, and by the definition her lawyer had
shown her it was a spacecraft. The lives of all aboard were at stake, and
without question the situation required a strong commander. Granmère,
after much consideration, was ready to assume that position.

Such a peculiar office, she thought, staring through carved Italian doors
that led to a balcony. This ornate golden-railed balcony high on the City
Office Tower, the only balcony on the building, had been ordered by Mayor
Wilde. In the style of a grander time, Wilde envisioned herself standing
upon it addressing the multitudes gathered below. To compensate for its
remoteness from the street, technicians had fitted the balcony with a magni-

fication system, which when switched on projected an enlargement of the balcony and anyone on it across the side of the building, to dramatic effect.

But Wilde had used it only once, in her first state-of-the-city speech, for after that occasion the press ridiculed her. For a long while one local television reporter kept up a running diatribe against the mayor, denouncing the expenditure as wasteful and self-aggrandizing. "Big Building is watching you," he editorialized, and thereafter members of city government referred to Wilde as "B.B." in whispered conversations. Six years later, the controversy had died down.

But the balcony remained, and sometimes (to gather her thoughts, it was said) Mayor Wilde liked to sit outside on it, gazing across her city.

Brittany could only sputter at first after Granmère took over the office, but Granmère knew he would be back after consulting with legal counsel, bringing forth other definitions of spacecraft or the position that the Arionnese were de facto commanders, making the statutes upon which Granmère relied inapplicable.

Of course Granmère had general Oso's reference to her in an open city council session as "commander in chief" of the entire habitat, a title which Granmère sidestepped at the time. She had no regrets about that, and even now didn't desire that title. She wanted to move through the political maze under her own volition, without leaping at suggestions made by persons of doubtful motivation. General Oso had not yet proven himself worthy of her trust.

She felt comfortable moving into the mayor's office and declaring herself "captain." Mayor and captain were for this scenario nearly synonymous. Practically speaking, the "commander in chief" of the humans aboard this habitat would have duties equivalent to those of "captain." The word of either person would carry great weight, with severe penalties for disobedience. But the larger term carried with it connotations that made her uncomfortable.

Should the humans meet disaster, she would certainly be blamed by history. That caused her to hesitate, but she was coming to see that she could just as easily be blamed for not stepping forward and assuming command when the opportunity presented itself.

She considered making General Oso a powerful ally against an imminent Wilde-Brittany power play. Wilde wouldn't be able to fake a cure, not without a doppelganger, and the only way Brittany could assume control would be to prove Granmère unfit or to have her killed. Brittany *was* a sleazy fellow. Granmère's confidential surveillance file on him attested to graft and political intrigues, and hinted at an illicit relationship between him and that reporter, Wissner. But to Granmère's knowledge he wasn't a murderer. Even if he were he didn't dare take that tack anyway, not with the information on him and others that would be released if she met an unnatural end. But what if he got to the data release mechanism and compromised it? Difficult, but not impossible. These were not ordinary times.

They're going to say the Arionnese really are in charge, that even if this is a space vehicle the laws of space captaincy do not apply or are moot. They'll demand that I vacate Mayor Wilde's office, and if they succeed I'll still be acting mayor. Big deal. Let 'em force me outa here.

She peered at her watch. Nearly eleven A.M. and Oso was due. She watched the digitalized seconds approach the hour, wondered what he wanted. Was he in league with Brittany? Had he come to throw her out? Unlikely. Oso's call had come just minutes after Brittany stormed from the mayor's office, probably too soon for them to have talked.

Was the general playing both sides, though, keeping tabs on each, always prepared to step in on the side most favorable to his interests? The political intrigues notwithstanding, he might in fact be the Number One Human aboard, puppeteer of the officeholders.

She wondered again if the Button Pack was merely a prop in this drama.

It rested on the desk in front of her, instrument panel folded open. The pack was ugly, and she hadn't gotten around to ordering a more stylish carrier. She'd been busy, didn't know how to go about it anyway, and besides she wasn't thinking so much of style as she used to.

She held the stylus in one hand, ready to plunge it into one of the activating holes, touching the button beneath. No way for her to test the unit safely, except by the expression on Oso's face when she threatened to use it.

Let's see what sort of a poker player you are, she thought.

A sharp rap sounded at the door.

She touched a button on the left side of the desk top, causing the door to swing open abruptly, smashing against a sound amplification panel that focused noise on the spot where General Oso stood. A nice intimidation feature, used once by Wilde against Granmère.

Oso stood stiffly in his uniform, revealing neither fear nor surprise. He carried his sicom briefcase.

"Sorry," Granmère said, with mock sincerity. "I just took charge of this office today and don't have all the electronics figured out yet." She glanced down at the desk-top control panel. "One of these thingamajigs shoots out

an extender and slams the door *into* the visitor, no matter where he's standing. Glad I didn't hit that one. They aren't marked very well, you know."

"My condolences on the loss of your husband."

"Thank you," Granmère said curtly. She had assumed the familiar, comfortable hard shell, which concealed her emotions.

"Isn't it a bit early for you to return to work?"

"I have little time for grief, none for chitchat."

She saw his eyes flash with displeasure. He strode across the office, set the
sicom on the desk, and activated it so that Granmère could see the screen.

Granmère held the stylus just above one of the holes, watched his expression closely. "Hamilton Air Service Base," she said. "You know where that
is."

"I was just there this morning," he said, calmly. His eyes were steady,
alert.

"And tomorrow morning, if we have a tomorrow morning?"

"You aren't insane," he said. "If you were I wouldn't have entrusted you
with such responsibility."

A thinly veiled reference to the Button Pack, she decided, and to his
ability to stage a military coup.

Granmère made a motion as if to slam the stylus home, but he didn't
flinch. She half-smiled and replaced the stylus in its bracket. There would
be video tapes to analyze later with electronic detectors, revealing nuances
of expression and vocal inflection. Whether the pack worked or not, he
seemed very certain of her. And he continued to behave as if the aliens were
eavesdropping. He had that silent communication device with him again.

"I fear the protesters are annoying the Arionnese," General Oso said.
"The Arionnese seem to like sourdough French bread. They got out secret
orders to two big San Francisco bakeries, and have been receiving deliveries
by the truckload. The stuff is dumped in a hatch near the Arionn Building's
main entrance. But all that stopped when our mobs blocked access to their
building."

"I'm fully aware of the situation."

"Including the extent of property damage?"

"Of course, and vandalism to the Arionn Building is quite minor, despite
a firebomb some idiot threw. The structure is impregnable."

"I'm getting a message off to the aliens now, suggesting the construction
of underground delivery tunnels between the bakeries and the Arionn Building. With their fantastic engineering abilities, it's my guess they can produce those tunnels in a matter of hours."

"I know about that proposal," she lied.

"You do?"

"I have my sources, as I said."

"I see." Oso bowed deferentially and showed no emotion about Granmère's statement, although he must have harbored something.

"I wonder if your forces or mine have been dealing with the protesters effectively," Granmère said. "That tunnel concept sidesteps the issue. Maybe police action and curfews are the answer."

"You would incarcerate thousands?"

"If necessary."

"Without bond?"

"I hadn't thought about that."

"With all respect, Madame Mayor, it's time you did. The minute they're back on the streets they'll resume their activities. The movement is growing exponentially, and even if you arrest everyone in sight there's more coming out of the woodwork. I served on the moons of Uranus during the resource allocation riots there, so I understand something of the mentality of agitators. Even when they're in prison they have ways of stirring affairs up on the outside."

"We can utilize stockades to back up city and county jails. Kindly coordinate that among the branches of the service, General."

"I will, but even that will provide insufficient space."

"Then the Arionnese can construct more jails for us."

"They already have. We're in their jumbo model at this moment."

Granmère smiled ruefully, then her face hardened. "Cells or no cells, I'm ordering my police into action today. It would be foolhardy to aggravate our hosts. We must at least make an effort to maintain order. We can set up prison compounds with tents, fences, and troops if necessary."

"As you wish," General Oso said. His fingers tapped across the noiseless sicom keyboard: "A SECRET MILITARY MISSION IS BEING PREPARED, ONE I DON'T THINK YOU KNOW ABOUT. A PARTICULAR BODY TYPE OF VOLUNTEER IS REQUIRED, AND WE CAN'T ADVERTISE."

Granmère touched a button on her desk-top control panel. The door closed softly.

"I NEED STRENGTH AND LIGHT BODY WEIGHT," Oso keyed. "LESS THAN 150 POUNDS. OF ALL THOSE IN OUR FILES, A MEMBER OF YOUR FAMILY SEEMS BEST SUITED. FOR THIS REASON AND TO BRIEF YOU ON THE MISSION, I THOUGHT IT PROPER TO CONTACT YOU FIRST."

Granmère felt her lips part, but no sounds issued. Her extended family tallied in the hundreds, and she drew a blank. *Brief* her? He was talking down to her, proceeding no matter what she thought!

"JOSEPH, YOUR GRANDSON."

Granmère reached across the desk, responded: "HIM? HE'S JUST A BOY, AND BESIDES HOW DID YOU GET A FILE ON HIM?"

"HE ATTENDED MARINE SUMMER CAMP WHEN HE WAS 16 AND 17 YEARS OLD. THAT 'DEVIL PUPS' PROGRAM AT CAMP PENDLETON. THEY RAN THE HELL OUT OF HIM, MADE HIM AND THE OTHER BOYS RUN UP OLD SMOKY HILL IN FULL GEAR, HAD THEM DUCK-WALK WITH FULL GEAR BOXES OVERHEAD . . . STUFF LIKE THAT."

"SADISM," Granmère keyed.

"NOT AS MUCH AS MANY PEOPLE BELIEVE. NO TIME TO GO INTO THAT HERE. ONLY A FEW OF THOSE DEVIL PUPS COULD CUT IT, AND YOUR JOSEPH WAS ONE. HE WAS THE BEST, MADAME MAYOR, AND NOT JUST THE BEST AMONG KIDS. NO MARINE COULD KEEP UP WITH HIM."

"THIS SECRET MISSION . . . IT'S DANGEROUS?"

"IT IS."

"GOOD GOD, MY OWN GRANDSON. I CAN'T APPROVE THAT."

"JOSEPH MAY NOT EVEN CUT IT IN TRAINING. THERE ARE OTHER CANDI-DATES. JUST LET HIM GO TO TRAINING, AND THEN WE'LL TALK SOME MORE IF IT LOOKS LIKE HE'S THE BEST FOR THE JOB."

"WOULD YOU GIVE ME DETAILS OF THE MISSION IF I DEMANDED THEM?"

"I WOULD. DO YOU . . ."

She nudged his hand aside. "NEVER MIND THAT FOR NOW. GO AHEAD AND INVITE HIM IN FOR TRAINING. I'LL RESERVE JUDGMENT ON THIS."

"YOU'RE MY COMMANDER IN CHIEF, TITLE OR NOT, AND TECHNICALLY I SHOULD HAVE CLEARED THE MISSION WITH YOU BEFORE ASSEMBLING PERSONNEL. I PRESUMED YOU WOULD APPROVE, AND WON'T BE SO BOLD IN THE FUTURE."

She caught his gaze, nodded. Then: "I DON'T THINK I CARE TO BE COM-MANDER IN CHIEF, AS I INFORMED YOU BEFORE."

"I'M RECEIVING MIXED SIGNALS FROM YOU, MADAME FOUQUET. AREN'T YOU DECLARING THE HABITAT A SPACE VEHICLE AND TAKING CHARGE UN-DER GALACTIC LAW?"

"HOW DID YOU KNOW THAT?"

"YOUR OFFICES ARE MONITORED FOR YOUR PROTECTION. YOU'VE GOT BIG JACK PRETTY EXCITED. HE'S TALKING WITH SIX LAWYERS RIGHT NOW."

"OKAY, I TOLD BRITTANY I WAS DECLARING MYSELF CAPTAIN, BUT BE-

TWEEN YOU AND ME IT'S A MOCK CAPTAINCY, WHAT WITH THE ARION-NESE PRESENCE. THAT COMMANDER IN CHIEF SPOT YOU OFFERED ME IS A FARCE, TOO, AND YOU KNOW WHY." She stared at him.

"YOU MEAN ME? OH NO, MADAME FOUQUET. I REPORT TO YOU."

"YOU'VE BUGGED MY OFFICES WITHOUT MY PERMISSION, STATIONED GUARDS AROUND THE BUILDING, AND SET UP A SECRET MILITARY MIS-SION, AND I DON'T THINK THIS BUTTON PACK WORKS AT ALL."

"THE BUGGING AND GUARDS ARE FOR YOUR PROTECTION. EVEN THE PRESIDENT OF THE UNITED STATES CANNOT SHAKE THE SECRET SERVICE."

"HE'S NOT BUGGED."

"YOUR OFFICE IS A HORNET'S NEST OF ENEMIES. I FEEL VERY STRONGLY THAT . . . He shrugged. "YOU WISH TO HAVE THE DEVICES REMOVED?"

"I DO."

"YOUR INSTRUCTION WILL BE CARRIED OUT THIS AFTERNOON. AS FOR THE BUTTON PACK, I CANNOT PROVE ITS OPERATION TO YOU, BUT IT IS QUITE OPERATIONAL. I MUST EMPHASIZE THAT."

"I CAN HANDLE BRITTANY AND THE OTHER HORNETS AROUND HERE."

Oso smiled. "I KNOW ABOUT THE COMPROMISING SURVEILLANCE FILES YOU MAINTAIN ON ONE ANOTHER. IT'S LIKE THAT IN THE NATIONAL AIR SERVICE TOO."

"JUST TO MAKE MYSELF CLEAR, GENERAL, I AM ASSUMING MORE RE-SPONSIBILITY THAN BEFORE, BUT I STILL REFUSE THE MANTLE OF COM-MANDER IN CHIEF. AS CAPTAIN OF THE HABITAT, I WOULD BE YOUR SUPERIOR, BUT NOT AS SUPERIOR AS I WOULD HAVE BEEN AS COMMANDER IN CHIEF. IS THAT CLEAR?"

"AS MUD, BUT NO MATTER. I AM AT YOUR DISPOSAL."

"TELL ME ABOUT THE MILITARY MISSION."

"ITS GOAL IS TO GAIN COMPLETE CONTROL OF THE HABITAT."

Granmère felt her heart palpitate.

"WHEN?"

"ELEVEN DAYS. THERE'S THE CREW SELECTION PROCESS, TRAINING, AND THE SPECIALIZED EQUIPMENT HAS TO BE FULLY TESTED."

"WOULD YOU HAVE TOLD ME ABOUT THIS IF NOT FOR MY GRANDSON?"

"MAYBE NOT." General Oso looked uneasy, shuffled his feet.

They exchanged stiff smiles.

"YOU AREN'T EXPERIENCED IN MILITARY DECISION MAKING," Oso keyed, "AND YOU'VE BEEN WAFFLING ALL OVER THE PLACE ON ASSUMING RE-SPONSIBILITY. I'M GLAD TO SEE THAT YOU'RE MAKING A MOVE NOW, BUT IT COMES A LITTLE LATE. WE NEED TO STRIKE THE ARIONNESE NOW

WHILE THEIR NUMBERS ARE FEW, BEFORE ZILLIONS OF THEM INUNDATE US ON THEIR OWN PLANET."

Granmère rubbed a mole on the back of her neck. Then: "IT DOES SEEM PATENTLY ODD THAT YOU NEED PHYSICAL STRENGTH IN OUR DAY AND AGE—ESPECIALLY IN ATTACKING AN ADVERSARY WHO POSSESSES INCREDI-BLE TECHNOLOGY."

"THEIR ENGINEERING AND MILITARY ABILITIES MAY NOT BE COMMEN-SURABLE. THE MISSION INVOLVES GOING OUTSIDE THE HABITAT IN A TINY CRAFT, AND THERE IS A KEY MANEUVER REQUIRING STRENGTH TO PROPEL THE . . ."

Granmère pushed his hand from the keyboard and interjected: "OK, OK. WE'LL GO INTO THAT LATER."

As General Oso took his sicom and left, Granmère worried about Joseph, but only briefly. The boy would accept the challenge, placing duty above concern for personal safety. He was a good boy, and she sincerely hoped no harm would befall him. Perhaps Rachel had done something worthwhile with her life after all, for she bore one of the children of salvation.

A frightening thought occurred to Granmère. What if Rachel, by virtue of her position, became a revered and honored figure? Those on the mission team could become like gods if they succeeded, especially if the free human colony couldn't figure out how to get back to Earth. Rachel, the mother of a god?

Granmère almost laughed at the irony of the situation.

Then she began formulating plans to avoid blame if the mission failed and to accept credit, for Joseph and for the mission, if it succeeded. The roles of the other mission volunteers would have to be minimized if success smiled, and she knew that history could be molded that way. Perhaps this was her big opportunity, and General Oso would help her distort the facts.

Or would he? In certain respects he seemed to be a man of conscience, even a brave man, willing to plan and execute a bold mission. But during that first visit to the council chamber he had seemed tentative and almost cowardly, quite unwilling to keep the Button Pack. He seemed genuinely afraid of it then, and she added this to the puzzle of his personality. He was as mysterious as his infernal Button Pack, and she longed for a sure-fire method of testing both.

Should I trust him? she wondered.

Alone in the house, Stu leaned over the big bed in the parental bedroom. Two books were spread open on a pastel blue blanket: Rachel's Bible (removed from its Biblecorder mechanism), and a novel describing the inter-planetary exploits of a female sex surrogate employed by the World Medical Authority. The pages of the novel were slightly smaller than those of the Bible, ideal for what Stu had in mind.

He thumbed through the novel, paused at a passage that looked promising: "She lay on the bed and took the front waistband of his swimsuit in her hands. With a herculean tug she ripped them away, bursting fabric and exposing the not-so-private area mentioned in his medical file. He had become a perverted rake, and it was her job to turn him around, to shape him into the decent human being he once had been. She would work on that the next day. For the moment, her passion . . ."

Perfect, Stu thought.

Using a razor blade, he sliced the page away and glued it over one of the pages in Rachel's Bible, taking care not to cover the coded Biblecorder scanner track along the outside margin. He followed the same procedure for a dozen more pages, interspersing them throughout the Holy Book, then replaced the Bible in its electronic holder.

Of the many pranks Stu had devised during his lifetime, the ones he enjoyed most were those in which he witnessed the victim's discomfort firsthand. It was with this in mind that he crouched inside the kitchen by the doorway to the living room, watching Rachel on the couch with her Biblecorder.

She had the book open, her eyes were closed, and the scanner was traversing each page, casting light upon the pages and transmitting words to Rachel through the headset she wore. At intervals she spoke commands into the headset microphone, sending the scanner searching through the volume for passages she wanted to hear.

It was only a matter of time. Stu could hardly control his glee.

As required in his line of endeavor, Stu had laid out his escape route in advance—through the back porch, into the backyard, and around the side of the house to the street.

He watched the scanner nudge pages, following the scanner tracks along the margins. Was that one of his prurient pages now? He craned his neck, tried to see. Yes, the print was different, not divided into narrow columns. The fiber optic arm danced from side to side, in a wider-swinging pattern than it had followed for the Bible passages.

Rachel's eyes popped open in surprise.

Stu pulled back quickly, then peeked around the corner, carefully.

Rachel had her eyes closed again, and with her face in a wide smile she listened.

Stu couldn't believe she was smiling. This wasn't the reaction he wanted, the one he had toiled to produce.

Reaching the bottom of the page, the scanner flipped to the next sheet and continued, this time in short swings.

Rachel's smile faded. She glared at the page, pushed the scanner arm aside and flipped back to the previous page. Her fingers moved along the edges of the pornographic novel sheet where Stu had glued it down. Then she worked at the edge of the bogus page with a fingernail, trying to pull it free.

Stu prepared to escape.

But Rachel smoothed the page back down.

"Thank you, Lord!" she exclaimed. "That's the best reading yet! But you ended it in the middle. How am I to know what happened next?"

Stu was on his feet, tiptoeing across the kitchen where she couldn't see him.

"Tell me more, Lord!" Rachel bellowed. "Is there more good stuff you haven't shown me before?"

Something in Rachel's tone frightened Stu, and as he let the back door close silently and crept down the stairs his heart threatened to pound through his chest. Reaching the yard he broke into a full run and rounded the corner to the side of the house.

Rachel stood in his path, holding the Biblecorder.

Stu broke stride and darted to one side of her.

But she surprised him with her nimbleness, caught him and grabbed hold of his jacket. Stu tried to pull away, but she was too strong. Her grip sank painfully into one of his arms.

"Don't hit me, Mrs. Fouquet! I'm sorry! I won't do it again!" Stu ran through his arsenal of street fighting techniques, wondering if he would have to utilize any of them. She didn't look particularly angry . . . maybe a little displeased. What was she planning to do, paddle him?

"I just have one question for you, Stu. Do you know what that question is?"

"Why did I do it?"

"I know why you did it, you little bastard. You thought I was a helpless, doddering fool, didn't you? Isn't that the best sort of victim for a coward like you . . . one you think can't strike back?"

"I never thought such things about you, Mrs. Fouquet."

"Where's the rest of the book?"

"I didn't rip any pages out of your Bible, Mrs. Fouquet. Honest to God. The sheets'll peel right off. I didn't use permanent glue. I'd never do anything like that in a holy book."

Rachel's eyelids narrowed. "The *novel* you tore the pages out of, dunderhead. *Where is it?*" Rachel smiled pleasantly. "I want to finish the story."

Stu's mouth fell agape, and he felt the rush of air across his tonsils. "Oh!" he exclaimed, nodding nervously. "I'll get it for you."

Rachel's grip relaxed, and Stu led her back inside, where he retrieved the volume from the midst of a trash sack.

"There's ten or eleven more pages in your Biblecorder," Stu said. "Would you like me to remove them?"

"Yes. Why don't you do that for me?"

In Stu's wildest imaginings, he couldn't have envisioned his practical joke turning out this way. Virtually every prank he had attempted on the Fouquets had failed, this one worse than the others. He couldn't read the rhythms of the family, felt constantly out of place, on the defensive. He'd been on the defensive before, with his stepfather, but that didn't compare. At least that man, despite his brutality, had been predictable. He was what he appeared to be, an asshole. But with each of the Fouquets there were layers upon layers of family history, interwoven in ways none of them could ever explain to an outsider.

When Stu left the house, Rachel had the erotic novel open on her lap, reading the book aloud to herself.

SIXTEEN

The rioting humans were like a single overfed organism with malleable flesh, overhanging the plaza and filling all streets leading to the Arionn Building. Then police helicopters swooped low, announcing martial law and ordering dispersement. Those who refused to leave were marked from the air with purple dye, and targeted crowd sectors became angry purple swarms, hurling barrages of objects against the encroaching fuselages. It wasn't a very efficient police operation, when compared with Arionnese methods.

—Robotic observations, alien
viewing station

The recorded telephone message had been terse, urgent, and intriguing: "Joseph Fouquet, don't forget your appointment with Sergeant Strogh of the National Air Service at two o'clock this afternoon. Room seventeen-oh-nine, NAS Administration Building, corner Military Road and Tweed Way, Oakland."

The call included no telephone number or department, and since it came shortly after lunchtime, Joseph had no time to do any research whatsoever. On impulse he caught the subterranean bus and appeared as specified.

The sergeant at the big desk in room 1709 was a bulky, dark-skinned man, maybe Spanish from the name on his desk plate (Sergeant Terrera), with eyes that studied Joseph's every movement. The man went to his lips with a forefinger and pointed at a sicom screen on his desk that said, "I REPLACED STROGH. TOP SECURITY. WE ARE UNDER ENEMY SURVEILLANCE. PROVIDE NAME ONLY."

Joseph hesitated, then with an awkward salute said, "I'm Joseph Fouquet."

Sergeant Terrera shuffled through a pile of computer print-out sheets. "Ah, yes. Age nineteen?"

"Yes." Joseph felt foolish for having saluted. He wasn't in the military!

"Fill out these enlistment forms, Fouquet."

Joseph accepted the papers hesitantly, watched the noncom's fingers move noiselessly across a keyboard attached to the electronic screen.

"YOU'VE BEEN RECOMMENDED FOR AN IMPORTANT MISSION, AND WE'VE CHECKED YOU OUT," the screen read. "YOUR QUALIFICATIONS MATCH OUR REQUIREMENTS PRECISELY."

Joseph almost smiled. He felt like commenting on his utter lack of qualifications. Could they have the wrong person? Not likely, since they knew his name, where to reach him, and had papers ready. The sergeant's eyes burned with urgency, reminding Joseph of the tone of the telephone message he had received.

Joseph keyed a message: "SPECIFICALLY, WHAT ARE WE TALKING ABOUT HERE?"

"I CAN'T GO INTO THAT. COUNCILWOMAN FOUQUET PROVIDED YOUR NAME, PROMISED YOUR COOPERATION."

"Granmère?" Joseph whispered, barely audibly.

Again the sergeant brought a forefinger to his lips, then returned to the keyboard: "DON'T TELL ANYONE SHE WAS INVOLVED. DON'T DISCUSS OUR CONVERSATION WITH ANYONE, NOT EVEN WITH COUNCILWOMAN FOUQUET OR ANY OTHER MEMBER OF YOUR FAMILY. THIS IS IMPORTANT, YOUNG FOUQUET, CRITICAL TO EVERY HUMAN ABOARD THIS HABITAT. ARE YOU WITH US?"

A chill coursed down Joseph's spine, and he stood a little straighter, with his back arched. "Yes, sir," he said. "I'll complete these forms."

"EXCELLENT. SIT AT THAT DESK BY THE WALL. TELL YOUR FAMILY YOU DECIDED TO ENLIST TO GET YOUR LIFE STRAIGHTENED OUT. A LOT OF FELLOWS JOIN IMPULSIVELY, SO THAT WON'T APPEAR UNUSUAL."

"WHAT ABOUT THE TELEPHONE CALL? YOU DON'T DO THAT FOR ALL RECRUITS?"

"YOU'RE RIGHT, BUT NO PROBLEM THERE. IT'S AN ESTABLISHED RECRUITMENT PROGRAM WITH COMPUTERS MAKING ALL THE CALLS. IT'S BEEN AROUND FOR NEARLY FIVE YEARS NOW."

"BUT I HEARD URGENCY IN THE TONE."

"SURE. MILITARY PREPAREDNESS HAS ALWAYS BEEN IMPORTANT. YOU RECEIVED A STANDARD SALES CALL, FOUQUET, WORD FOR WORD. WE CALL PEOPLE WHO'VE BEEN TO MILITARY CAMP AS YOU WERE, THOSE IN SCHOOL ROTC PROGRAMS, EVEN PEOPLE ON UNEMPLOYMENT. YOU'D BE AMAZED HOW MANY ANSWER THOSE CALLS. THEY DROP EVERYTHING, HURRY ON DOWN HERE, AND ENLIST WITH VERY LITTLE COACHING."

Joseph broke into a broad grin and trudged to the designated desk. A plethora of questions inundated his brain. What did Granmère have to do with this? Was she in this building somewhere, working on the plan or watching him through one-way glass? The enemy? Did Sergeant Terrera mean the Arionnese? Every other enemy of the United States had been left on Earth. Or had they? What about the foreigners who came along with their consulate buildings? Maybe a group of them organized something seditious, sowing discontent among the people who had taken to the streets in recent days. An action against the protesters to prevent dangerous Arionnese intervention. He settled on this, and didn't think again that the sergeant might have been referring to the Arionnese as the target. With their tremendous power, they seemed unopposable.

Joseph skipped dinner that evening and talked Kenny March into driving him to Thyla's house without calling ahead. She emerged into the cool evening air of the porch in a long white cotton dress.

"You want to wear my jacket?" Joseph asked, starting to take it off. Wind was whipping around the pillars of the porch, leaving little shelter. Joseph was cold, even with the coat on.

She shook her head briskly and stood with her arms folded across her chest. "I can't talk with you long. We're in the middle of dinner."

"I just joined the National Air Service . . . report for training at eight A.M. tomorrow."

Her eyes flashed. "What? We're cut off from Earth. I didn't know the NAS still existed."

"It does."

"Why do we even need a military any more, with all that's happened?"

"You heard what the Arionnese told us to do. They want life in the habitat to go on normally, much as it did before. That includes military enlistments."

"But you're leaving so suddenly. I've never heard you talk about wanting to do this."

"I've mentioned it a few times, and you know I've had trouble finding a steady job. I need to do this, to get my life straightened out. It'll be good for me."

Thyla was moving her feet to keep warm. She stared at him angrily.

"I won't be far away," Joseph said. "Can't be, on this setup."

"I've gotta go back inside."

"Try to understand, will ya? I had to get out of the house. My mother's weird."

"Maybe she's not so weird. I feel sorry for her. Somehow you provoke her, Joseph."

"Aw, get off it. You heard about the hatpin. She scared the hell out of me with that thing."

"Did she actually come after you with it?"

"Not exactly. She kinda waved it in the air and spoke in a menacing tone, saying she wanted me to help her with her hair, that I never did things for her."

"Maybe she didn't intend to be menacing. Maybe you took it wrong."

"What about the match she lit next to me while I was asleep? I don't see how that could be misinterpreted."

"Has she done that again?"

"No, but once was more than enough. It took five years off my life, really ticked me off. She doesn't go after the other kids like that. She has it in for me."

"I've thought about that incident. Maybe she was merely trying to be funny, to get your attention. I'm not suggesting she went about it properly, but that match incident *is* kind of hilarious, if you look at it right."

"No way. I can't laugh at that stuff. She's one scary lady."

Thyla shrugged. "How long will you be in?"

Joseph laughed without smiling. "I forgot to ask! Guess I'll find out tomorrow when I report."

Her eyes became emotionless, and her mouth tightened. "I see," she said.

Joseph saw her mental machinery churning. "You wanna see if you can go out for a cola now?" he asked.

"I can't."

"But I report tomorrow."

She didn't respond, and barely kissed Joseph back when he said goodbye.

"We can still see each other," Joseph said. He gulped. "If you want to." It hadn't occurred to him that Thyla would act this way.

"Sure," she said, but it didn't ring true.

As Joseph scuffled to the car, he recalled his expressions of love for Thyla during the year they had dated, and the fact that she hadn't really reciprocated. They had *made* love, held one another, even cried together at Granpère's funeral. But "I like you a lot" was the most endearing comment she had ever made to him.

Now he was off on a dangerous mission, involving secrecy and intrigue. In every movie he'd ever seen, the girl was supposed to tell him to be careful. He sighed, paused, and looked back at her house. Every curtain was drawn.

He recalled the urgency in the sergeant's keypunched message, the expression of concern in his eyes. There had been nothing hokey or even patriotic about the encounter. It seemed more like a survival situation, with people doing things they had to do, because they were pressed into a corner. Granmère was involved somehow and Joseph couldn't talk with her about it.

He turned away, saw Kenny March waiting in the car, peering up the walkway at him. Joseph told himself that this was for the best, that his relationship with Thyla had to come to a head anyway, sending it in one direction or another.

Joseph swung into the car and plopped down on the seat. "Let's go," he said, staring straight ahead. "I need a drink."

Michelle was half-dozing on the carpet in front of the television, thinking about how pleasant a warm bath would be, when Stu brought in the big gift-wrapped box.

Renney sat up next to her and exclaimed, "Wow! What's that?"

From Renney's tone, it seemed that he had forgiven Stu for hanging Dad's caricature on the door. Michelle wondered what sort of trick Stu had in mind now, or if he was groveling for forgiveness.

"Good evening, Mrs. Fouquet," Stu said abjectly.

Michelle saw her mother lying on the couch, working alternately at a cigarette and a glass of clear liquid, probably Snowfly Extract.

"I brought a gift for the family," Stu said.

"How nice," Rachel replied, without enthusiasm.

"Who gets to open it?" Renney asked. He was on his feet, by Stu.

Michelle noticed that the box was wrapped in green Christmas paper, with fanciful red and gold holly twigs on it. Christmas was but a month and a half away, and decorations had appeared on only a few businesses around the city. Christmas on Arionn? What would it be like? She did a quick mental calculation. It had been ten days since the media-covered Arionnese broadcast, leaving fourteen days to destination. They would arrive the day before Thanksgiving, as Dad pointed out.

"You open it, Renney," Rachel said. She took a long draw on her cigarette, causing the tip to glow bright orange.

On the carpet, Renney tore the package open with great ferocity. This revealed a white box inside, which read "Mega-Popper" in Gothic letters on the side toward Michelle.

"These are neat," Renney said. "One of the guys at school has one."

"Where'd you get the money for this, Stu?" Michelle asked, sitting up. "Mega-Poppers are expensive."

"I got it on layaway," Stu said. "No use waiting for Christmas to open it, what with everything up in the air and all." He smiled proudly, perceiving a witticism.

"Deep space isn't air," Rachel said. "If you spent more time in school, you'd know that."

"I thought you didn't care if I went to school or not."

"That was before you started getting into trouble around here."

"Yes, Mrs. Fouquet."

"And that layaway stuff. You mean takeaway, don't you?"

"No, ma'am! I didn't steal this."

"You can't pick up a layaway until it's paid for," Michelle said.

"Maybe I used the wrong term," Stu said, looking flustered. "I made a special deal. One of my friends works in a store that sells these, and he arranged it for me."

"I'll bet he did," Rachel said.

"Honest," Stu said. He glanced around. "Where's Mr. Fouquet?"

"Blasters match," Michelle said. "He wrist-wrestles tonight."

"Oh, yeah," Stu said. He took a deep breath, said to Renney, "Come on. Bring it in the kitchen and let's try it out!"

The three children went into the kitchen. Coley came downstairs as they were setting up the appliance, and she watched silently from a distance, holding a one-armed doll.

The Mega-Popper was nearly a meter high when assembled. Its burnished aluminum bowl sat squatly on four legs on the floor, with a hinged Plexiglas lid that snapped shut tightly. The unit had a large red on-off switch on the side next to a warning label emblazoned in orange: "Danger. Keep out of the reach of children."

Renney checked the lid latch. "This has to be snug," he said.

Michelle didn't worry about the label. Lots of kids used Mega-Poppers.

Stu removed a small bag of megacorn from the box, tore the bag open, and poured one kernel into his hand. The kernel, reddish-yellow, was bigger than a large marble and not quite round. He lifted the popper lid, dropped the kernel into the bowl. It rattled around, came to rest.

"The switch is off," Stu said. "Plug it in, Renney."

Renney located an outlet on the range, connected the popper cord to it.

"Okay," Stu said, taking a flat parcel out of the Mega-Popper box. "Now we seal the room."

Michelle understood why. Mega-Poppers leaked a little by design, absorbing particles of organic matter from the air, from the floor, from the walls, from tables, stovetops, and countertops, purifying everything and removing carcinogens. If you left a piece of bread nearby when the unit was on, the bread would disappear, sucked into the machine. After flipping the switch, they would have fifteen seconds to escape the room.

Stu handed out folded sheets of microthin, clear myplas that were moderately sticky on one side and would go over doors, windows, food cupboards, and the refrigerator. They closed every window, cupboard, and door (including the door on the other side of the kitchen that led to the upstairs children's bedrooms), then covered them with ample pieces of myplas. Michelle had heard that the popper, when on, caused myplas to expand and adhere tightly to surfaces, sealing everything against air leaks and preventing doors and windows from being opened from the outside.

When all was ready, Stu flipped the switch. He, Michelle, and Renney slid past a sheet of myplas and hurried into the living room, closing the door behind them.

"We oughta set it up in a closet next time," Michelle said, leaning against the fireplace mantel.

"No good," Stu said. He glanced impishly at Michelle. "That might suck up your little household friend, Beauregard."

Michelle saw Renney's eyes fill with fear at the mere mention of Beauregard. He slid next to his mother on the couch.

A low machine hum came from the kitchen.

Rachel crossed one leg over the other, tugged at her skirt to cover her knees.

"I shouldn't have used the word 'little,'" Stu said, apparently unaware of Renney's discomfort. "You said it was seven feet tall, didn't you, Michelle?"

She nodded.

"The Mega-Popper is a nifty cleaning unit," Stu said. "Those kitchen walls will be scrubbed when it's done. You could even dispose of a plate full of stinking garbage by leaving it next to the unit, and your megacorn would still come out tasting good."

"What about a plate full of Bumper's turds?" Rachel asked.

Caught off guard, Stu blinked. Then, with a short laugh, he responded, "I guess that would be okay, but I'm not sure I wanna try that. I'm sure Bumper would eat it, though."

"That would save money on dog food," Renney said.

"Maybe," Michelle said, "depending on the power consumption."

Rachel started to say something, but Michelle had a sudden, terrifying thought that blocked everything else out.

"Where's Coley?" Michelle shrilled. She ran to the mini-stairway leading to the kitchen door, jumped to the top step and stood helplessly before the barrier. "She was in the kitchen with us when we were setting up the popper!"

In a panic, Rachel, Renney, and Stu gathered at the base of the stairs.

"She must have left when you weren't looking," Stu suggested, but he sounded uncertain.

"You saw her go?" Rachel asked.

"No, but . . ."

"Mama, what'll we do?" Michelle wailed.

"Renney, go shut off the power," Rachel said. "Run! These poppers take a couple of minutes to warm up."

Renney ran through the basement, out the front door, and around the side of the house.

A loud, unmistakable "pop" issued from the kitchen just before the lights went out.

Michelle pushed the door, but it wouldn't move.

"In fifteen seconds the seal releases," Stu said.

Michelle leaned hard on the door and after what seemed like much longer it squealed open. She pushed the myplas out of the way.

The room was half illuminated in light from a neighbor's high-pressure sodium yard lamp, passing through the myplas-covered windows.

Rachel formed circles with her thumb and fingertips and held one hand over each eye, peering through the openings as if they were binocular lenses. She stalked around the kitchen, looking in corners, under the table, behind the refrigerator.

Oh God, she's flipped, Michelle thought. Michelle didn't see Coley or a sign of her anywhere, watched in horror as Stu removed a huge golden megacorn ball from the popper. Stu turned the ball over and over, and it appeared normal.

"Why are you doing that, Mama?" Renney asked.

"I'm Sherlock Holmes looking for turds," Rachel said.

Michelle tore myplas away from the door to her parents' bedroom and raced inside. Frantically she searched, looking everywhere—in the bathroom, the closet, under the bed. When she ran back into the kitchen she saw that the door leading upstairs had been cleared.

She encountered Rachel on the stairs, ascending slowly, still with her makeshift binoculars in place.

Voices upstairs. Michelle pushed past her mother, reached the second level landing. The voices were louder now, from the next level up. Did she hear Coley?

Stu and Renney met Michelle in the hallway outside Coley's bedroom. Their faces were beaming.

"She's in her room," Renney said, "playing with dolls."

Michelle let out the deepest, most relieved sigh of her life. She took Coley in her arms and lifted her high, whirling around with her.

Coley squealed with delight. "Tickle me!" she said.

Michelle accommodated, wrestling with her little sister on the floor and poking her under the armpits and ribcage.

"More!" Coley urged, when Michelle withdrew.

"That's enough," Michelle said. She saw Stu by the doorway, smiling.

"We should have checked on everybody before turning it on," she said. "There's a remote switch, too, isn't there?"

"This model didn't come with one."

"We'd better keep it locked in the trunk of Mom's car. It's not safe in the house where Coley might get into it."

"Good idea."

Michelle felt Coley's tiny fingers probing her midsection.

"Tickle, tickle," Coley said.

Michelle grabbed the little hand. It pulled free.

Coley dashed around Michelle and into the hallway. "Mega-pop!" Coley squeaked. "Mega-pop! . . . Mega-pop! . . . Pop-pop-pop!"

"She sounds just like a TV commercial," Michelle said, hurrying after her sister. "Come on, Stu. We may as well have some megacorn."

The ball of megacorn was heavy and large enough for all to share. A rich hue of gold, it had petals on it like regular popcorn, but these petals were as thick as a man's fingers.

While Stu broke it apart, put the pieces on a platter and sprinkled salt over them, Michelle thought about her mother, whom she could see from the kitchen, on the living room couch. Rachel had a leftover piece of myplas, which she stuck alternately to her arms, her forehead, her nose, and other areas of exposed skin. She seemed childlike, living in a realm of juvenile fantasy. But for a moment, a potentially critical moment, she had been lucid and had sent Renney running for the master power switch.

Now she seemed as helpless and dependent as toddler Coley.

Michelle saw Renney plop next to his mother and heard him talk to her, in apparent unawareness of her condition. "I'm the best, huh Mom, huh? I'm the only good one."

Rachel didn't respond, kept playing.

The next half hour was spent pleasantly in the living room, sharing the platter of megacorn. Rachel even enjoyed some, and what she didn't consume she stuck to the sheet of myplas, asserting that she was making a wall hanging for her bedroom.

Stu seemed unusually quiet as he sat cross-legged on the floor munching megacorn. Occasionally he flicked impish glances at Renney or Rachel, as if, despite all, he hadn't quite had his fill of mischief. Considering Stu's brief history in the Fouquet fold, this demeanor made Michelle uneasy, and she meant to talk with him privately about it. But in the torrent of other, more pressing thoughts, the girl pushed this one aside, failing to return to it until it was too late.

Drawn by an urge, Stu peeked past the open bedroom door. Renney was alone in the room and lying on his bed, engrossed in a hologram-on-celluloid comic. In stocking feet, Stu made little sound as he slid away from the doorway, carrying a folded white sheet and a glass test tube of water that was supported by a metal laboratory frame. The sheet had a small hole in it, strategically placed, with a section of black plastic mesh stitched across the hole.

These were the necessary props, and as he opened the hall closet door Stu could hardly suppress his glee. Placing the items on the floor he had already cleared for the occasion, he slipped inside the closet and closed the door behind him. Working with the stealth and efficiency of a burglar, he removed both secret wall panels and placed the sheet and test tube inside the adjacent closet. This was the closet he had seen Michelle in during her strange seance, the closet inside the bedroom she shared with her brothers.

From the hall closet Stu listened for noises in the hallway outside. Hearing nothing, he slipped back into the corridor, shutting the door behind him.

Every nerve in Stu's body wanted to leap ahead into the jape, so it was with supreme effort that he sauntered into the bedroom and said, in his most casual tone, "Hey, Renney. How's it going?"

Renney grunted something, half-glanced in Stu's direction, and returned to his comic book.

"I must speak with you about Beau-re-gard," Stu said, drawing the name out ominously.

Renney gaped at Stu, and from the expression in the lamb's eyes Stu knew that the boy carried a foreboding born of his one Great Terror: Beauregard, the ferocious seven-foot monster! It was Renney's greatest fear, the one he couldn't discuss. In nightmares he died in the pincers of the flea. If it so much as touched Renney with its deathly clamminess, he would have a heart attack on the spot.

"Leave me alone," Renney said.

"I'm here to warn you, because Beauregard is angry with you. He's been seen in the hallway outside your bedroom, where he calls your name. I risked my life coming here."

"Leave my room!"

"Get under the covers, Renney," Stu said, lowering his voice and moving close to the lamb. "That way maybe the creature won't see you."

Renney began to whimper. The comic fell from his grasp in a sputter of holo-light, and, turning away from Stu, he rolled into a fetal ball with his bedspread.

"Fleas carry the bubonic plague," Stu said. "Do you know what that is? Your groin and armpits swell up in huge balloons called buboes." He leaned close, shouted: "Then bang, everything explodes! Your arms and your dick are torn off!"

"My dad says there's no such thing as Beauregard," Renney said, sniffing. Ominously: "Has anyone else in this house told you that?"

No response.

"I didn't think so." Stu assumed his most foreboding tone. "Michelle believes in Bo. So does Joseph, and *so does your mother.* Your dad's not home enough to know what happens around here, and I'll tell you something else: Bo doesn't like to be doubted. I think that's why he's looking for you, why he wants to seize you and silence you. When Bo's especially angry, he silences people with acid. Do you know what acid does to the skin? It burns right through, to the bone."

Renney was bawling, trying not to scream out. He pulled his pillow over his head.

"You'll dissolve in a puddle on the floor," Stu said. "That's how Beau-re-gard does things." Stu had deepened his voice and drawn it out deliciously for the name, and this gave him great pleasure. "Beau-re-gard," he said. Then, like a wolf howling at the moon: "Beau-re-gard!"

The name was like a mystical wind breath, parting the branches of moon-lit pines, swaying curtains and seeking out its prey in shadowy hiding places. Stu shuddered, and such a chill coursed down his spine that he looked around, nervously.

Renney turned over and peeked out from under his pillow. His eyes and cheeks glistened.

"I must leave now," Stu said. "I've done all I can for you."

"Don't leave!"

Stu tiptoed to the doorway, peeked around the jamb in both directions. With a cautioning gesture toward Renney, Stu slipped into the hallway and shut the bedroom door.

Within seconds he was inside Renney's closet, entering from the other side. Stu had the sheet over himself and the test tube of water grasped tightly. Through the black mesh-covered hole in the sheet, he saw a sliver of light under the door to Renney's room.

He turned the handle, slowly and quietly, then burst into the room, screeching in a distorted, macabre voice: "You're alone, Renney Fouquet! I've got you now!"

Stu saw Renney's terrified eyes, just before Renney covered himself up and cried out, "Mama, Mama! Help me, Mama!"

"That bedding won't protect you from Beauregard!" Stu roared. He tore the bedspread and pillow away, ripping the bedspread down the middle.

Still clutching part of the bedspread, Renney tumbled off the bed trying to escape.

Stu dumped water on Renney's face, shouting, "Acid feels cold at first, but it's really *hot*! This will fix you!"

Renney ran screaming from the room, trying to wipe away what he thought was acid with the bedding remnant. "Mama! Help me! Aaaaaah!"

Stu acted quickly. Into the bedroom closet he went, where he concealed the sheet, test tube, and tube frame in the airspace. From the hall closet side, he replaced both wall panels, and was about to open the door into the hallway when he heard voices—those of Rachel and a whimpering Renney.

It sounded as if they were coming up the stairs, so he wouldn't have time to hide in Coley's room.

"I don't wanna go back, Mama!" Renney protested.

"You don't have any acid on you, silly child. Just water. Did you make all this up?"

Good, Stu thought. *She doesn't believe him. I was loud, but that TV and Biblecorder are always going . . .*

Stu heard them conversing inside the bedroom, and their voices grew heart-palpitatingly louder as the closet door was opened from the bedroom. A strand of light entered Stu's enclosure.

Impulsively, he opened the door to the hallway, slipped outside and crept toward the open bedroom door, ready to dart past it toward the staircase.

But Michelle stepped out of the bedroom into his path, freezing his motion.

"You!" she exclaimed. "I suspected it was you. Why do you keep doing this to us?" Her eyelids narrowed, and it seemed to Stu that she must be wondering if he had discovered the removable wall panels and if he had been the one to loosen the piece from her hidden metal box.

Rachel became a towering, larger-than-life form in the doorway to his right, and as Stu glanced up at her he experienced some of Renney's terror. The form went out of focus for a moment, then shapeshifted into a ferocious red-eyed flea in an antiquated blue and gray military uniform. The hideous face, set against a very small antennae-equipped head, was covered with ciliated yellow thorns and hooks.

"You facetious little shit!" the flea said, in a shrill, alien-sounding voice. Using a pincer-fitted leg as if it were a hand, the apparition slid a glistening steel sword from its scabbard.

Horrified, Stu tried to get around Michelle. But she pushed him back, with surprising strength.

"You've angered General Beauregard!" the flea said. "*Games.* Always playing *games*, aren't you? Well, I don't like games!"

With a sword tip near his chest, Stu backed across the hallway. The wall pressed against his back. "Don't stab me," he pleaded. "Please!"

"What are you talking about?" Michelle asked.

"The sword!" Stu squealed.

"What sword?"

"General Beauregard's sword!" Taking care to avoid the glistening blade, Stu pointed at the giant form standing over him, glancing sidelong at Michelle as he did so.

"General Beauregard?" Michelle parroted, half-laughing. "You're the one who's playing Beauregard, not Mama."

Stu felt dizzy and slid down the wall onto his buttocks. The image above him metamorphosed again. The sword and uniformed monster disappeared, and Stu saw Rachel glaring at him, her eyes the same angry red as those of the flea. She had no weapon.

"You need a good whipping," Rachel said, reaching for Stu.

He clambered away past Michelle and jumped to his feet. The staircase was ahead, and he broke into a run. He heard heavy steps behind him, felt steely fingers against his shirt that lost their grip as he scurried into a higher, more frantic gear. Stu leaped half a dozen steps at a time, slipped at the bottom and regained his footing just before the hulking, angry form could reach him.

He was two blocks away before he realized he'd left his shoes and coat behind.

SEVENTEEN

When Rachel Fouquet was small, her father said to her, "You're Irish, and you should learn how to plant potatoes." A short while later, knowing that her father was constantly in need of a handkerchief to blow his nose, she "planted" a handkerchief in the backyard.

—Notes on microfiche that were not included in the final Department of Social Welfare report

With a crashing hangover and only three hours of sleep to sustain him, Joseph hurried across the street. It was shortly past dawn, and he heard both nearby and distant police sirens, carried to him on a chill wind. From the middle of the street he saw flashing blue and platinum squad car lights two blocks to his right, with unintelligible bullhorn sounds coming from that direction.

Normally Joseph might have gone to investigate, but not today, when he was due to report for NAS training. He reached the opposite sidewalk and put a corner building and the structures adjacent to it between himself and the commotion. His whole head throbbed, and he rolled his eyes shut, longing for sleep. As bad as he felt, it might have been worse, considering the pace at which he and Kenny March began drinking cognac. Then Joseph remembered the embarrassment and outlandish behavior of his last night out with March, and stopped drinking the rest of the evening. Joseph felt good doing that, as it proved to himself that he could handle the stuff, that he wasn't like his mother. But they'd stayed up late, and this headache! It must have been the brand of cognac that didn't agree with him, he decided.

Joseph hoped he had ample adrenaline to carry him through the day.

As the bullhorn and siren noises faded, he sighted a small marquee for the subterranean railway terminal. This public transportation system was known throughout the Bay Area as the "Sub-T."

He ducked through a scratched and chipped duraplas door into the dank mustiness of the terminal. New sounds took over. A clanking conveyor lift platform dropped to his level, pausing so that he could step aboard. It carried him on a jerky, hangover-pulsing trip down to track level, where he caught a Sub-T car to Oakland. It took him beneath the floor of the bay.

At street level on the other side, the police were just as active as they had been in San Francisco. Joseph watched them herd eight protesters into a paddy van, and Joseph himself was interrogated merely for walking by. They didn't detain him long, accepting his story that he was on his way to catch a bus for his first day of National Air Service training.

"We need more men like you," one of the cops told him.

The learning module at which Joseph sat was similar to units in the public school system, except this one had mirrors to the left and right beneath rectangular windows. If Joseph used his peripheral vision he could see himself: starched tan shirt with blue NAS rocket emblems on the collar and lapel; plain tan baseball-style cap set squarely over a fresh butch cut. Joseph was part of the program now and was supposed to look like everyone else.

A Sergeant Ivanovich had explained the ranking system to all recruits before distributing clothing: each noncom carried rank on his cap, and there would be promotions if warranted before the conclusion of the eight-day session.

"Desk camp," the sergeant called it, derisively. "If I had charge of you pansies, I'd make you carry those desks on a fifty-mile hike."

Fighting temptation, Joseph hadn't commented on the special nature of his mission. Maybe the man didn't know about it. He did look the dunderhead, with an insipid smile and eyes that glared vacantly at each recruit.

The class monitor, yet another sergeant, was a woman who didn't reveal her name at first. She wasn't the sort of female a man would look at twice. She had minuscule breasts, no hips, and a head so large and puffy of face that it seemed to have been transplanted onto her emaciated body. A person who seemed to have nothing positive to say about anything, she scowled constantly.

And her voice! That was the worst part. Even if Joseph hadn't been in the throes of a hangover, he didn't think he could have tolerated her emissions. They were high frequency, undoubtedly resonating from somewhere in that Churchillian head, and came at him through the speakers of his module like amplified chalk screeches, sundering his sanity.

He wished someone would put a catalytic converter over her mouth.

Once, through the front window of Joseph's learning module, she saw him put his fingers into his ears. Then she was all over him. She sprang from behind her lectern and bounded down toward Joseph with her great jowls quivering and her vocal cords emitting the most discordant raspings and scrapings Joseph could imagine. When she reached him she filled his module with such a sonic cacophony that Joseph feared his brain and eardrums would explode all over the place in a monstrous final puke.

Other recruits had been caught looking in their mirrors and had suffered for it. A black man near the front of the class had been the first. She spun him around so that he faced the back of the classroom and began in her most soothing tones, which weren't all that dulcet. Joseph could tell from the pained expression on the man's face that he expected an imminent explosion. He got it, and the command that went with it was so piercing that it must have penetrated every wall of the NAS Building:

"Eyes front you son of a bitch! Whattaya think this is? The washroom at a prom?"

Every muscle in Joseph's body had pointed forward when she said that, and remained thus until she finally identified herself and relinquished her lectern to a robot:

"I'm Sergeant Culbertson," she said, as she stormed from the room. "If any of you fuckers move, that robot will kill you."

The robot didn't move for a full five minutes after Culbertson slammed the door, and gradually a wave of nervous laughter broke out among the recruits.

"You thought I was kidding, didn't you?" the painful voice shrilled, through every speaker in the room.

A compartment in the torso of the robot slid open, and the robot let out a burst of automatic weapon fire that came before anyone could duck for cover.

Joseph heard the shots, which all went overhead, shatter something behind him, probably the wall.

"Warning shots," Culbertson said, from her unseen position.

The robot's compartment closed, and for interminable minutes no recruit so much as blinked. Then the robot began reading from a lesson, and it was then that Joseph dared a peripheral glance in one of his mirrors. The robot hadn't hesitated when he did this, hadn't seemed to notice, and Joseph did it again several times, feeling his pulse quicken with each transgression.

But the image in the right mirror fogged, and when it cleared Joseph was horrified to see the puffy, angry face of Sergeant Culbertson staring directly at him. His eyes darted forward. Then drawn irresistibly, they looked to the side again.

"Eyes front, prick!" Culbertson howled. "You think you can get away with anything at all here?"

Joseph's eyes swiveled forward so abruptly that he felt sharp pains in them.

"Answer me, Fouquet!"

"No, sir!"

"You refuse to answer me?"

"No, sir. I meant I can't get away with anything ever again!"

"You've got that right, air boy. There's only one way to do things, and that's our way. Do all of you understand that?"

"Yes, sir!" the class thundered, in synchronization.

"I'll begin again," the robot said, in its comparatively calm, synthetic tone. "And we'll continue to begin again until we receive everyone's attention."

It ran through the prefatory remarks Joseph had already heard, then said, "Each of you has an electronic manual in the liquid crystal screen before you. Acquaint yourselves with it and memorize the answers to the questions on page nine. There will be an examination tomorrow. Touch the button marked "Page" along with the number designating the proper page."

Joseph activated page one.

Apparently the others did the same, and this seemed to be the proper course of action. Where else to start, except at the beginning?

Intently, Joseph studied the black-on-amber words on his screen: "THIS IS A PRIVATE, TAMPER-RESISTANT LINE, FROM HQ TO FOUQUET. YOUR SCREEN HAS BEEN SHIELDED AND TILTED AT AN ANGLE PERMITTING ONLY YOU TO READ IT. YOUR MANUAL IS DIFFERENT FROM THAT OF MOST PERSONS IN THIS CLASS. YOU AND THREE OTHERS SHOWN ON THE CONFIDENTIAL CLASS DIAGRAM ARE MEMBERS OF AN ELITE COMMANDO TEAM. SINCE WE ARE UNDER ASSUMED AUDIO-VISUAL SURVEILLANCE BY THE ENEMY, THE SECRET MATERIAL IS NOT TO BE DISCUSSED IN ANY

FASHION WITH ANYONE AT ANY TIME—NOT EVEN WITH YOUR INSTRUC-
TORS OR FELLOW TEAM MEMBERS."

Joseph wondered why the screen didn't have a deep frame around it that
came up to his face, activated only when his face touched the frame. He
didn't see any shielding, and the screen's tilt didn't appear unusual. Was
Sergeant Culbertson in on this? If not, was she really prevented from seeing
his screen through the two-way mirror?

Who was the enemy? Would it be revealed, or would Joseph's team be
sent blindly on a mission? Questions would not be tolerated. That went
without saying in this environment.

Do as you're told, Joseph thought. *Eyes front at all times.*

Joseph turned to page two, which turned out to be the confidential class
diagram. There he located asterisks by four names, including his own.
While he didn't dare look back, one was directly behind him, a dark-
skinned Oriental youth he'd noticed when the class was forming. Name:
RUSSELL UCHIYAMA. Assignment: REMOTE-CONTROLLED SAMURAI.

As far as Joseph could guess, this meant that Uchiyama was either an
android samurai warrior or that he operated some kind of a remote-controlled samurai sword. Either way, the guy sounded dangerous.

Joseph's own job description was even more cryptic: SPECIAL TASKS.

The other asterisked team members were ANTHONY BISHOP (PILOT), and
VITALDO MORGANSTERN (GUNNER).

Joseph let the job descriptions sink in. Pilot. That suggested flight of some
sort. This was, after all, the National Air Service. Why a samurai whatever-
that-was and a gunner? Was the samurai supposed to protect against being
boarded?

Page three didn't answer these questions. In narrative form, it outlined
Joseph's training, day by day, for eight days, culminating on the ninth day
with "MISSION."

They looked to be the most important nine days of his life.

He wondered what anyone around him, including Sergeant Culbertson,
knew. Were those people with asterisks really on Joseph's commando team,
or was this misinformation designed to test him or to throw off enemy surveillance? He couldn't so much as wink at anyone.

Asterisks? he thought. *Asses to risk.* He smiled ruefully.

Joseph shivered with excitement. He had been thrust into the midst of a
dangerous, potentially violent struggle. But involving what? He wanted to
know everything, to be entrusted with the most critical, sensitive information. As he was risking his life, he felt he had the right to know.

A sinking feeling swept over him. *I have no rights*, he realized. *I gave them up when I enlisted.*

On to page four: "DAY ONE. 1000-1130: GENERAL ORIENTATION AND MANUAL STUDY."

Nothing about the haircuts at 0800, the bunk assignments after that, and the drawing of uniforms. Standard stuff, Joseph surmised. No need to clutter the screen with things like that.

The next entry was: "1215-1330: WEAPONS ORIENTATION."

Nothing between 1130 and 1230, so that had to be lunch.

Under "WEAPONS ORIENTATION," it said, "THESE ARE STANDARD AIR SERVICE WEAPONS, FOUQUET, AND ARE NOT THE ONLY HARDWARE YOU WILL EMPLOY DURING YOUR MISSION. THAT MATERIAL IS COVERED IN CONFIDENTIAL BULLETINS AND DIAGRAMS THAT WILL BE SLIPPED INTO YOUR CLASSROOM MATERIAL. NO 'HANDS ON' PRACTICE WILL BE POSSIBLE, EXCEPT TO A LIMITED EXTENT WITH MACHINES IN THE WEIGHT TRAINING ROOM THAT SIMULATE SOME OF THE MISSION FUNCTIONS YOU WILL PERFORM. COMPUTER GRAPHIC SUPPLEMENTS WILL AID YOU, TO A DEGREE."

Joseph didn't care for the sound of that, but his concerns were alleviated somewhat by what followed:

"A SPECIAL CRAFT AWAITS YOUR INDOCTRINATION. EACH MISSION MEMBER HAS A PRIMARY ASSIGNMENT COMMENSURATE WITH HIS BACKGROUND AND SKILLS. YOU WILL MEMORIZE THIS P.A., AND SOME INFORMATION WILL BE PROVIDED YOU CONCERNING THE TASKS OF YOUR FELLOWS. TO THE EXTENT POSSIBLE, EACH OF YOU IS TO BACK UP THE OTHERS."

Something irritated the back of Joseph's throat, and he had to hack several times to clear it. Nerves, he decided.

"DURING BREAKS YOU ARE TO DISCUSS ONLY THE STANDARD CLASS TEXT BEGINNING ON PAGE 6. YOUR STANDARD TEXT HAS BEEN CONDENSED AND ORGANIZED ACCORDING TO THE TOMJANOVICH ABSORPTION METHOD TO COMPENSATE FOR YOUR SPECIAL ASSIGNMENT, AND YOU ARE TO TAKE ONE SYNAPTIC MEMORY PILL DAILY FOR LEARNING ENHANCEMENT. THE FIRST HAS BEEN SLIPPED INTO YOUR SHIRT POCKET. DON'T REACH FOR IT!"

He was about to, and his hand, which received two rapid-fire and opposing commands from the brain, twitched.

"COUGH AGAIN, GENTLY. THEN LOOK DOWN AND TAKE TWO SHORT BREATHS, *with your mouth open.*"

Joseph did so, and without seeing anything unusual felt a sudden melting of sugar on his tongue and a faint butterscotch taste. He swallowed, coughed for effect.

"AVOID FRATERNIZING WITH TEAM MEMBERS, TO REDUCE THE RISK OF BLOWING COVER."

He wondered who had slipped the pill to him. It might have been anyone passing near, maybe Culbertson or even a classmate. He felt slightly more lucid than normal, with a tingling at the temples.

"1345-1600: WEIGHT AND DEXTERITY TRAINING. FOUQUET, YOU SPEND AT LEAST HALF OF YOUR FIRST DAY IN SECTION D. IN PARTICULAR, PRACTICE QUICK DOWNWARD THRUSTS OF THE BLUE-AND-WHITE-STRIPED ROTARY BAR, FROM OVERHEAD FRONTALLY TO YOUR KNEES. NO SETTINGS ARE NECESSARY, AS THE EQUIPMENT GAUGES THE USER AND SETS ITSELF AUTOMATICALLY FOR OPTIMUM MUSCULAR DEVELOPMENT. DETAILS ON THE MERITS OF THIS ESSENTIAL EXERCISE WILL BE PROVIDED LATER.

"1615-1730: MILITARY HISTORY. A 45-MINUTE ORAL LECTURE, FOLLOWED BY A 30-MINUTE STUDY PERIOD. DURING STUDY PERIODS, YOUR SCREEN WILL DISPLAY COMPUTER-GRAPHIC MISSION SIMULATIONS. GOOD LUCK, MR. FOUQUET, AND GODSPEED."

Joseph detected sirens in the distance, and bursts of what sounded like small-arms fire. His thoughts turned to Thyla, to her well-being on this dangerous, displaced world. And it *was* a world, albeit an artificial one. "We need more men like you," the cop had said. Why couldn't Thyla appreciate that? She hadn't taken the enlistment news well, but with luck she'd feel differently now that she'd had the opportunity to consider it. His announcement had been abrupt, yanking her away from dinner. He would call her at the first opportunity.

Did they permit calls from this place?

When Michelle ascended the front stairs of her home after school that afternoon, she was surprised to hear her father's booming, angry voice. Rachel was shouting back at him, almost as loudly.

Michelle found them in the living room with the television on, he in his recliner and Rachel on the couch. They weren't watching the set.

Henry lowered his voice when he saw Michelle, said, "We were just having a little political discussion."

"A little discussion?" Rachel said. "Ha! We were getting ready to run for our weapons."

Henry maintained his composure. "We were discussing this police crackdown thing, with cops running around like Nazis, beating down doors and stuff. Your mother is trying to say that Granmère is responsible for all that. That's ridiculous, isn't it, Michelle?"

"Don't put me in the middle of this," Michelle said.

"Liliane is mayor," Rachel said, "so she's in charge. Call her and ask her, and while you're at it tell her you disagree with the repressive measures being taken. Be a man for once, Henry, and stand up to *Maman*."

"She's only a temporary mayor," Henry said. "They have other departments in charge of the cops when temporary mayors are in. I heard that somewhere."

Rachel laughed. "How absurd. If my guess is right, your dear mommy has probably poisoned Mayor Wilde. Nothing opposes Granmère. She's been the iron-fisted matriarch of this family for years, but that wasn't enough for the power-hungry bitch. She's one of the leeches that emerge to full ugliness during crises, when people are suffering. They take advantage of situations, like war profiteers, lawyers, and the quacks who wear white coats."

"You're way off, Raich, so far off there isn't even a chart for you."

"*Maman*'s been cloning her iron fists, dispatching thousands of them across the city to thrash people. Go outside and speak against her police, Henry. Just see what happens to you."

"You're nuts."

Rachel turned to Michelle, who was attempting to slide past the scene, on the way to the back of the house.

"Your father's home sick today," Rachel said. "He's sick in the head."

"I ain't got the credentials you got," Henry said.

"I'm taking that in a way you wouldn't understand," Rachel said, with an unconcerned smile.

"Let's get back to what started this whole thing," Henry said, "and you didn't answer my question. Where the hell is Stu? What did you do with him?"

Michelle was on the top step of the mini-stairway, on the kitchen level.

"Wait a minute, Michelle," Rachel said. "I told your father what Stu did yesterday, and now I'd like you to tell him."

Michelle related the incident, said she hadn't seen Stu since he fled the house after babbling crazily about Beauregard.

"Beau-re-gard chased that kid out of the house," Rachel said. "I had nothing to do with it, you see."

"Oh, shit!" Henry exclaimed, throwing his hands up. "Not that again. It's always Beauregard this and Beauregard that. I'm sick of it!"

"Bo lives in this house, Henry," Rachel said. "One day you'll claim him as an exemption on your income taxes."

"Aw, get off it, Raich. You hit Stu on the head or somethin', made him babble."

"Sure, Henry. Sure."

"Stu was right, anyway, going after Renney," Henry asserted. "It's about time Renney learned to be a man."

"Teasing him with a sheet and fake acid is supposed to accomplish that?" Rachel asked, rhetorically.

"You bet. It's like the Tooth Fairy, the Easter Bunny, and Santa Claus all wrapped up in one. The kid's nine years old and still believes in Beauregard. That ain't normal, Raich, and he needs to be shocked out of it. Obviously Stu had the good sense to see that."

"Preposterous."

Michelle slid into the kitchen.

"Stay here," Rachel commanded. "I want you to help me stuff some sense into your father."

Rachel had never needed help in handling Henry before, and Michelle wondered if she was feeling uneasy for having initiated the Beauregard story, at least the part about the tormented spirit of a Civil War general. Mom wasn't to blame for scaring Renney. It was Joseph who embellished the tale and turned Beauregard into Bo, the giant flea inhabiting the dirtiest regions of the dirtiest home on Earth. Was Rachel afraid that Henry would blame her for that, and did she want Michelle to defend her if he did?

"You had to send poor Stu tearing out of the house, didn't you?" Henry said. "We'll probably never see him again."

"So what?" Rachel said. "We didn't invite him here, and he certainly didn't behave with decorum."

Henry sulked, and Michelle thought she understood something of the pain he felt for his son. Stu wasn't a boarder from Louisiana! It was apparent that Henry had not confided in Rachel about his marital indiscretion.

"You're always ready with the smart remarks, ain't ya?" Henry said. "All the time talkin' circles around me. Well, I got news for ya. Big words don't mean ya got a big brain."

"Big words?" Rachel said. "Oh, you mean 'decorum.' I can see where that would seem big to you, from the abyssal depths of your puny brain. Shall I provide a definition for you of each word in excess of one syllable?"

"You shall not!"

"Excellent syntax." She peered at him superciliously.

"Let's get out of your territory," Henry said, "into reality." He jutted his chin out. "Joseph joined up because he can't stand being around you anymore. And now you drove Stu out. That's two. The house is a goddam mess too, like some kinda indoor junkyard. The joint stinks to high heaven and I don't mean heaven. You ain't a wife, you ain't a mother, you ain't even hardly alive the way you vegetate around here. You probably had something to do with my dad dyin' too. He was quiet mostly, but I know he wasn't happy about you. You added stress to his life."

"You've overlooked one of your best arguments, On-ree. What about your precious career, the way I ruined it, forcing you to work three jobs to pay my medical bills?"

"You did all that, too."

One of her father's oft-repeated quotes floated in Michelle's memory, and she smiled to herself: *"I'm in debt up to my earballs!"*

"Poor Henry the Martyr," Rachel said. "Shall we erect a cross for you behind your recliner? The brutal truth is, you couldn't have held down a good job if you were married to a young Granmère. You're a loser, and an even more deplorable one for not reconciling yourself to your central role in your own failures."

"Oh yeah? Well I coulda got special dishpenshation from da Pope ta get done wid dis marriage! He'da gibben it ta me too!" He glared at her, his eyes bulging.

She had him where she wanted him, and smiled. "Dishpen-shation?" she parroted. "You make the Holy Office sound like a dishpan association."

Henry jerked himself to his feet, stalked past Michelle, and went in his bedroom.

Michelle remained at the doorway, trying to think of something to say to her mother. With a glassy expression, Rachel stared at the fireplace.

"Why don't deez kids ebber hab any food aroun' here?" Henry shouted. "I gib ya money, ya lush, an' ya can't handle it! Ya t'ink I'm a fool. Dat's been made clear. But I ain't sech a big one as ya t'ink!"

So he knew about the food, Michelle thought, and about the diversions of money into booze and cigarettes. Why hadn't he done anything to rectify the situation? Michelle felt a surge of anger toward him, but it softened. Perhaps he felt helpless to change anything about his life. He was swept away by it, inundated.

Henry filled the bedroom doorway, his face purple. He extended a Bible before him, shouted toward the living room: "I went lookin' fer some consulaitchin an' look what I found!" He flung open the volume, revealing to

Michelle a flask of Snowfly Extract hidden between carved-out pages. He hurled the bottle into the living room and it clunked without breaking.

"One a yer hidin' places eh, Raich? Inside my mother's Bible!"

"Don't play holy with me, Henry Fouquet!" Rachel said, and they were shouting without seeing one another, "I've kept bottles in there for more than four years, and you haven't noticed until now."

"In my mother's Bible? Ain't nuttin' sacred?"

"Certainly nothing to do with Liliane."

"How da holy hell didja get on dis planet, anyway? Dere ain't nuttin' like you anyplace else. How lucky I am!"

Michelle was worried about her father. With his eyes bulging and his cheeks puffed full and purple, he looked ready to have a heart attack.

Rachel didn't let up. "We ain't . . . to use your quaint verbiage . . . on a planet, On-ree. Haven't you looked outside lately?"

Henry sputtered, and the Bible shook in his powerful grasp. He squeezed the pages so tightly along the edges that when he moved his fingers, indentations were left. His eyes went to full inferno and he made a motion as if to hurl the Bible. But he didn't let it fly.

"I suppose you're going to pester me for the cutout pages now," Rachel said.

This reminded Michelle of the poems that Joseph had torn apart.

Henry's rage metamorphosed to a sadness so profound that he appeared ready to cry. He stared at the floor.

"There are Bibles and there are Bibles," Rachel said, "depending upon how people use them. The book itself loses its holiness if it is abused by the owner, and Christianity is replete with hypocrites who lean on the religion to further their own ends." She looked at the ceiling, brought her eyes back to his level and added, "You know this one, don't you? 'Please God, give me everything I want.'" And her voice burned with oratorical passion: "How about praying for the benefit of others? Does that ever occur to these people? And what about this one? 'God told me to do that. Too bad what it did to you.'"

Henry stomped into the middle of the living room and roared at Rachel: "Blasphemer! Shet yer witch's mout'!"

"Let's be more specific, shall we?" Rachel said, oblivious to his epithets. "Liliane, the old b-i-. . . and I don't mean biddy . . . never followed the Lord's word a day in her life. She's been too busy grubbing for dimes and quarters . . . all the time trying to manipulate everyone's life. Well, she never has controlled me, and that sticks in her crooked craw. You saw the way I sliced open her defiled book, On-ree. Do you know how that's done?"

Henry closed the volume and let his arms fall to his sides. He heaved a great sigh, shaking his head from side to side.

"It's done with razor blades, On-ree. I've got them hidden around here, so tell *Maman* she'd better not come around."

Was she bluffing? Michelle couldn't tell, but the fear in her father's face was unmistakable.

Rachel averted her face from Henry and began humming gently. Her gaze touched Michelle for an instant, then flicked away.

"People think they can tear up my poems," Rachel said, her tone controlled and hostile. "Well, I have news for *people*. I've memorized all of them, and my mind can't be torn apart."

For the first time, Michelle listened while her mother recited:

> *I travel in moon shadow,*
> *Howling soundlessly.*
> *While others rise and play*
> *I slide apart,*
> *Not in their spheres.*
> *I wake as they sleep.*
>
> *I move behind walls*
> *With demons beyond.*
> *They call to one another,*
> *Pursue me to silence.*
> *Hear me howl.*
>
> *My howl is like the cry*
> *Of a wounded, long ago fawn*
> *Lilting on the High Wind.*
> *It is all that remains of me,*
> *All that I can think to do.*
> *Breathe for me, Shadow Caster;*
> *And hear me howl.*

"Aawoo!" Henry said, rolling his eyes. "Woof, woof! Yer a prize, Raich!" He crossed the living room toward the basement. "My wife writes poems ta Bumper. Ain't dat cute? Hardy har har!"

"It's a sensitive poem, Daddy!" Michelle said.

But he was kicking things out of the way in the displaced basement, cutting a wide swath to the front door. "Hear me howl, Rachel! Woof, woof!"

"I wake as they sleep," Michelle remembered. She thought of the knives and scissors that Joseph had hidden, and of her mother's razor-blade threat. Was she really dangerous, as she seemed to relish making people believe? Or was it a front, a method of fending people away from her because of the cruel onslaughts she so often suffered?

"'I travel in moon shadow,'" Michelle murmured.

She heard her father's car start, and the angry surges of its engine as it left.

EIGHTEEN

The mission ship ST88 is of an experimental, untested design, built before the Bay Area was lifted. Using sicoms to communicate we tabled all testing plans, thinking such activity might arouse the interest of the Criminals. I dare call them that here in my private pages, and one day I will shout it at their faces! Has there ever been a more monstrous, more catastrophic theft? I think not. There are secrets concerning another ship—the one I call *Hope*—secrets I have revealed cathartically in these pages and nowhere else. It is said that a person with a diary gets to know himself better, and it troubles my conscience that I think more and more of *Hope* each day.

—From the journal of
General Toshio Oso

In her bedroom that evening, Michelle studied a scratched and creased snapshot of her family, taken in happier times on one of their trips to Lake Mendocino. A fixed shot, this one had no frame button in the corner to make the subjects move. For several years, Henry, Rachel, and the children had taken regular vacations to the lake, and Rachel had been better then. She looked alert and cheerful in the photo, standing between Michelle and Joseph in front of a cabin. An outsider looking at this picture might not suspect problems, but even then they were evident. Michelle remembered them and saw the signs of pain in her own eyes.

According to Joseph their mother had always retreated into herself, but never with the intensity and frequency she did after bearing Coley. The pressures of carrying and delivering this last child were too much for Rachel when added to "everything else she had to bear," and she became much worse as a result. These words, unelaborated by Joseph, were the closest he ever came to sympathizing with his mother. With Coley's emergence, the trips to Lake Mendocino ceased.

Two thuds, the second louder than the first, brought Michelle out of her ruminations. Leaving the photograph behind, she hurried downstairs.

Her father was prone on the kitchen floor, bleeding from the head and either unconscious or dead! Rachel stood over him, holding the heavy metal bowl of the Mega-Popper.

"What have you done?" Michelle howled. She bent over him, used the bottom of her dress to wipe blood from his forehead. His eyelids fluttered.

"I waited for him behind the door and let him have it when he came in," Rachel said. "Now I'm gonna turn on the Mega-Popper and suck him up."

"You'll do no such thing!" Michelle snapped. She grabbed for the bowl but could not wrench it from her mother's grip. "Are you going to hit me with it, too?" Michelle asked at last, withdrawing her hand. "Are you going to kill us with it?"

"Isn't that what's expected of me?" Rachel said. She placed the bowl on the floor and left the room.

Henry struggled to raise himself but couldn't; he rolled to one side, looking around, dazed.

Michelle retrieved a dish towel, pressed it against his head. He was gashed across the front of his crown, but the blood flow was slow.

He sat up, took the towel and held it in place. "Dat goddam bitch," he said. "She tried to murdalize me!"

"Into the Mega-Popper with you!" Rachel howled, from her bedroom. "A pop for Pop!"

"Are you okay, Daddy?"

"Yeah, but I ain't used ta gettin' knocked off my feet. She blind-sided me."

Michelle heard her mother humming in the other room, saw pills in there scattered across the dressing table stool.

"She threw her pills around, that's all," Michelle said. "I'll make sure she takes them."

"It ain't yer fault, little angel. It ain't eben Rachel's, I guess. But I can't take no more o' dis." He withdrew the towel from his head, looked at the blood it had soaked up, then put the towel back against the wound.

With Michelle's assistance, he rose to his feet.

"I may not go ta church ebbery Sunny," he said, leaning on a counter, "but I'm still Catlick t'rough an' t'rough. I'be stood wid dat woman t'rough ebb-erry goddam t'ing she's done. An' at's a lot! What t'anks do I get? Nut-tin' but a smack inna head, dat's what."

"Someone bring in Henry's cross!" Rachel bellowed from the other room. "He's become a saint!"

"I ain't a saint, an' nebber claimed ta be!"

Holding fast to her father's beefy arm, Michelle felt him quiver as he shouted. Then he let the bloody towel drop and stormed out of the house, paying no heed to Michelle's pleadings.

"Where are you going, Daddy? Don't leave! I'll make sure she takes her medicine!"

"I'm giving out medicine, not taking it!" Rachel shouted. "Tell him to go live with *Maman*!"

During the ensuing days when Henry didn't return, Rachel refused to take her pills. Whenever she scattered them about, Michelle did her best to clean them up so that Coley wouldn't get into them.

A food check arrived with each day's mail, from Henry. But Rachel wouldn't look at the checks, wouldn't even admit they existed. Instead she insisted that they had to hawk everything now that the children's father had moved out and they had no income.

Every morning Rachel dressed in her best clothes and left the house as if she were going to work, carrying valuables to be pawned. The gold and diamond wedding ring disappeared from her finger, and Michelle saw her take Joseph's I-wave radio set and Henry's accordion, on successive days. Henry hadn't played the instrument in years, since happier times, but Michelle had maintained hope. With the instrument her hopes went too. Michelle tried to prevent such rash behavior, even told her mother she had a check from Granpère that they could use to pay the bills.

"Check?" Rachel had said. "What do you mean check? I want real money, money that *I've* earned!" And off she would go, her arms laden with memories.

There was the problem of Coley, too, who wasn't old enough for public school. She couldn't be left alone, so Michelle stayed with her each day, despite the knowledge that truant officers soon would be in pursuit. Michelle gave this eventuality only momentary attention, and didn't discuss the problem with her mother.

Strangely, Rachel appeared to get better in some ways, possibly from the responsibility she undertook of providing for her family (albeit in minimal fashion) for the first time in many years. Each evening she came home sober with a bag of groceries and cooked dinner. The fare was simple but edible—hot dogs, macaroni and cheese, soup and sandwiches.

Michelle didn't like the hot dogs. They had a strange cast to them and were the new synthetic variety placed on retailers' shelves by the Arionnese, from unknown sources. People said the Arionnese did things like that "at night," and Roley Peterson at school postulated the hot dogs were "one hundred percent preservatives and additives," with no real meat or food value in them.

Under her mother's watchful eye, Michelle chewed her hot dogs laboriously and tried to maintain a pleasant expression. The girl thought back on the events of that day, the fifth since her father's departure.

That morning before leaving the house, Rachel had ordered Michelle and Renney to "get rid of some things after school." Rachel wanted the children to approach the neighbors with articles (mostly from the basement, Rachel's bedroom, and the kitchen) and sell them for whatever they could obtain. "We need to pitch in on this thing," Rachel had said. "I don't want anybody going hungry."

Michelle knew it would be a mistake to go to Mrs. Meley because that woman was the nosiest person for fifty blocks. "A curtain twitcher," Rachel called her. But somehow after visiting other houses, with a shopping bag of clattering items in one hand and Coley in tow by the other, Michelle found herself trudging up the brick walkway of Mrs. Meley's house. Now at dinner Michelle had to tell her mother about it.

"One of the neighbors asked me a lot of questions today," Michelle said. "I was over there with Coley and . . ."

"Coley? Who takes care of Coley when you're at school?" From the expression on Rachel's face it was apparent she hadn't thought about this. She looked at Coley, who was picking at her food.

Michelle answered the question truthfully, and her mother grew silent.

Then Michelle continued with the other matter. "It was that awful Mrs. Meley, Mama. I had a bag of kitchen utensils to sell her, and she asked, 'Is something wrong over at your house?' I said no, that these were my things and I was raising extra candy money. She didn't believe me, said she knew Daddy wasn't around and asked about him. I ran away from her."

"Don't worry about that woman," Rachel said. "I can handle her."

"Okay, Mama."

"Tomorrow you attend school, Michelle," Rachel said. "I'll care for Coley."

"Yes, Mama."

Michelle was hesitant to mention her grandfather's check again. Rachel hadn't been very attentive the first time the subject came up, and Michelle hadn't worked to get her attention. Crucially, Michelle hadn't mentioned the amount of the check, and now she was feeling guilty for not having pushed harder to prevent the pawning of so much. But she had been and remained afraid that Rachel would resent the source of the money and destroy the check. Tomorrow Michelle would appear at the bank—any bank, Granpère had said—and present it for payment. With cash in hand she could back up her mother discreetly, providing food without Rachel's knowledge when Rachel's limited source of income went dry.

In some respects, Michelle noticed, the house was looking better with some of the clutter cleared away. This was small consolation. She wished her father would return, and Joseph, too, and that the whole family (even Granmère) might take a trip together to Lake Mendocino. In a serene place such as that they might all get along, enjoying and appreciating one another's company.

But Lake Mendocino is on Earth, Michelle realized, with a sinking sensation that wrenched her midsection. *It's gone.*

She was struck by the permanency of change, and it frightened her to the core. If only she had access to that perfect, harmonious combination of events that eluded her family so effectively. She wanted to lock relationships into position in a fashion that she had only heretofore imagined, in a place that had become only a dim fragment on an old photograph. She tried to visualize the photograph in her room expanding and becoming a world that for all time would encompass the Fouquets. Lake Mendocino became a different, unnamed body of water in her vision, on a planet that resembled Earth but wasn't Earth. Cottages dotted the shoreline between tall cedars, and billowing, multicolored sails glided along the water. Was Granpère Gilbert there at that very moment, readying the place, preparing to call Michelle and the others to join him? Together she and her grandfather had longed for family harmony, but never like this.

Foolish thoughts!

The image lost actuality, became a flat, enlarged photograph of the unnamed place. Then it metamorphosed to Lake Mendocino again, seen from a new but recognizable vantage point, where a little boy was said to have drowned many years before. The photograph began to grow even more than before, but only in one dimension. Dots appeared across it and became monstrous and hideous, like disease markings. Soon the image lost actuality and washed to gray.

The smooth, youthful faces of her parents and paternal grandparents appeared as from a void, approached rapidly, and vanished in an explosion of dots.

Granpère is dead, Michelle thought. *He's not coming back, and I'm not going to see him again, anywhere.*

She fought tears and couldn't swallow any more food.

"What's wrong, dear?" Rachel asked, in the tenderest of tones.

"Nothing, Mama," Michelle said, tugging at an eyelash on her upper lid. The lash resisted, then popped free of its root into her hand.

Rachel was back at her own food, not looking at Michelle.

Michelle held the sundered lash momentarily, between her thumb and forefinger, then let the lash flutter to the tabletop. Making certain her mother didn't notice, the girl returned impulsively to the same eye and lid, and began ripping away two and three lashes at a time, dropping them to the floor beside her. The physical pain was minimal, and after a while she rubbed a finger across the lid, feeling some short hairs she hadn't been able to grab hold of.

In the privacy of her bathroom, Michelle used her fingers and tweezers to pluck all of the lashes on both eyes, from the upper and lower lids.

NINETEEN

There's not a normal one in the bunch. Take that Michelle, for example. She was frolicking in my yard one day, neighing and pretending to be a horse. She even has a ponytail, you know. When I told her to leave, she bared her teeth ferociously at me and whinnied.

—Report by Mrs. Flora Meley to an investigating social worker

"What are you doing in there?" Rachel rasped, banging the closet door open. "Secrets?"

Having sat with her back to the doorway, Michelle spun her neck abruptly and looked up at her mother, who dominated the opening. With the wall panel uncovered and her puzzle box in mid-sequence on her lap, Michelle stammered for words.

"Give me that!" Rachel said, leaning way over and grabbing the box.

Michelle resisted, but lost her hold and watched her treasure rise into the shadow of her mother's body.

"It's mine," Michelle said. "Granpère gave it to me."

"Something valuable, eh?" Rachel said, turning the box over in her hands. "Wonder how much we could get for it."

"Don't sell it! Just this one thing, I don't care about anything else!"

"Methinks you protest too fiercely. It's valuable, isn't it?"

"No. It's just sentimental."

"How does it open?"

"It . . . doesn't. It's just pretty, that's all."

Rachel shook it. "I don't believe you. There's something bumping around inside." She turned, and with the frayed thread edges of her robe trailing behind her she glided to Michelle's bed and plopped down on it, staring all the while at the box.

Michelle followed, wondering if her mother had been the one who removed the puzzle box piece that she found in the airspace. Or had it merely
worked itself free? The piece was back in place, next to one of Rachel's
thumbs.

She slid a different piece a short ways, then tried to slide another. This
second would not budge.

"There's a way into this thing, isn't there?" Rachel asked. She fixed a
hard gaze on Michelle, making the girl feel uncomfortable for having
plucked her eyelashes. Michelle's barren lids had looked strange in the
bathroom mirror that morning, with an almost alien cast to them.

Michelle took a step backward, lowered her head. "No. I told you . . ."

"Liar. How would you like me to smash it open?"

"Don't!"

"Then it does open?"

Michelle hesitated. Then, in a whisper: "Yes."

"Come closer child, and show me how." Rachel extended the box.
"What have you done to your eyes? Come here!"

Michelle inched forward, head down. Her mother's long bony hand took
hold of Michelle's chin, lifting the girl's face. Michelle looked to one side as
her mother stared.

"You have no eyelashes! Why did you do that?"

Michelle freed her chin, shrugged, and stared at the floor.

"Never mind. They'll grow back."

Rachel forced the box into Michelle's hands, and when she had it,
Michelle felt like running. But her mother, apparently with the identical
thought, held Michelle's arm in a viselike grip.

"Open it," Rachel commanded.

"All right, but let go of my arm." Michelle tried to sound firm.

Rachel compelled her to sit on the bed beside her and then released her
grip.

Michelle averted her body and leaned over, holding the box in front of
her midsection. She adjusted the pieces Rachel had moved and resumed the
sequence she had been in when interrupted.

"Hold it over here where I can watch what you're doing."

"No. Granpère made it for me, and I'm the only one who can open it."

Michelle saw the shadow of her mother's hand above her.

"You little brat!" Rachel snapped.

Michelle stared at her defiantly, said, "If you touch me, I won't open
it. And you'll never get inside, because Granpère used military secrets to
make it."

Rachel glowered. "Then why are you opening it for me?"

"Because there's nothing inside to hide from you, and because I don't want you to dent the box. It's beautiful and I love it."

"As you wish."

Michelle resumed the sequence.

"What if it weren't beautiful?" her mother asked. "What if it were ugly, like me?"

"You're not ugly at all."

"Liar. I've just proven that you're a liar. You said the box wouldn't open, and that was a lie, wasn't it?"

"You're not ugly, Mom."

"People used to like me when I was pretty. People don't like you when you're ugly. Your eyelids are ugly."

Michelle sighed in exasperation and completed her grandfather's procedure. Then, in her mother's view, she slid away the lid.

"I like to look at it each day before school," Michelle said. A *lie*, she thought. *I was taking the check to the bank to cash it. For Mom's benefit, but I hope she doesn't see it!*

"Is that a book inside?" Rachel asked.

Michelle nodded. "Granpère wrote a book in French about the old country and his early days in America."

Rachel's eyes narrowed. "In French, eh? Well this is American soil and people speak English here. We don't speak French, even in space, and that's for sure! Give it to me!"

But Michelle said, "I never take the book out, Mom. I can't read it, so what's the use? You can't read it, either, and I don't want it damaged."

"Place the volume in my hand."

Michelle did as she was told, saw an edge of the check-bearing envelope sticking out between pages near the end of the book. She hoped her mother wouldn't notice it.

Rachel leafed through the opening pages. "Granpère despised me, didn't he?" she said.

"No, Mom. He didn't despise you."

"Tell me the truth!"

"He didn't say bad things about you. Honest."

"Liar. Everyone says bad things about me. There are bad things written about me in this book, aren't there?"

A page bent under Rachel's fingers.

"Be careful with it! Please! There's nothing bad about you in there. It's about his life before he ever met you."

"How do we know that for sure? I don't see any dates here, and those would be readable."

"There must be dates in there somewhere. Granpère told me that this is all long-ago stuff. He's not . . . He wasn't like Granmère."

"All these foreign words," Rachel said, her long face bent intently over the volume. "I don't like them. There must be a lot about Granmère in here. Everything about her should be crossed out, ripped away." She made a violent scribbling motion in the air above one page, and the book nearly slipped from her lap.

Michelle saved it from falling and from damage, but the envelope fluttered to the floor.

Oh no, Michelle thought, with a sinking feeling.

"What's this?" Rachel asked, getting to the envelope first.

"A check from Granpère for fifty thousand dollars. I told you about it."

Rachel arched one eyebrow suspiciously, fixed her gaze on Michelle. "And so you did. But you didn't mention the amount." Her face split into a crafty smile, and she ripped open the envelope, withdrawing the check.

"You can have the money, Mom. I wasn't going to keep it."

"How nice," Rachel said, studying the check. "We won't have to hawk the children. What else have you got stashed away?"

"N-nothing."

"So many lies and half-lies, Michelle. How do we separate the wheat from the chaff of your words?"

Michelle felt moisture brimming her lower lids. "I wasn't going to let Coley and everyone else in this house starve," she said.

"Payable to the bearer," Rachel said, reading from the check. "That's me. I'm the bearer." She glared down at Michelle. "Unless you think you can take it away from me."

Michelle looked away.

"Survival of the fittest," Rachel said, lunging to her feet with the book and the check.

The bed jiggled.

"I'm going out now, Michelle, to buy fifty thousand dollars worth of matches to burn up this book."

Michelle buried her face in her hands, and the tears gushed. She heard her mother padding across the floor.

"Please don't burn Granpère's book," Michelle whimpered. "I promise there's nothing bad about you in it." She looked at her mother's backside, added, "Think of your poems, Mama. You wouldn't want anyone to burn up your poems. Please don't."

Rachel whirled, and Michelle saw an instant of confusion cross her mother's features. Then her expression became childlike, with a wan smile. "I have lots of money now," she said, dropping the book to the floor.

Rachel skipped from the room and down the hallway.

Michelle retrieved the book, noting with dismay a small dent in one corner of the binding. She straightened it as much as she could, replaced the volume in the puzzle box and sealed it inside. She would have to locate a new hiding place for her treasure.

As Granmère studied a stack of documents, a piece of blank paper appeared suddenly on the top right corner of her desk top and began fluttering toward her. Startled, Granmère watched the sheet come to rest directly in front of her, atop the documents.

She emitted a squeal of irritation and was about to slide the sheet away when words appeared on it in lavender ink:

"U.S. Military Code Paper," were the first she could read, along the bottom. Then in the center of the sheet, this: "Training complete, and Joseph the best choice. If you approve, do nothing. If you disapprove, ball this paper up and hurl it across the room. Response required within sixty seconds."

Granmère had been considering what to do on this matter for several days, and now, despite her great fear for Joseph's safety, she stared transfixed at the words. Out of focus just to her left, she was aware of the seconds on her watch, as they slid away digitally.

The words on the page began to fade.

She wanted to move but couldn't.

More seconds slid away.

Presently the words were gone altogether, and the paper disappeared. Once again she stared at the documents before her.

Joseph flipped on the video screen and tapped keys to resume at the place he had left off the day before. He rubbed his eyes and thought about a call he received from Michelle the evening before. He hadn't slept well because of it; he needed to find his father and inform him that Mom was giving everything away. Not that they owned many things anyway, and what they had wasn't of much importance, but he thought of Dad's accordion and the wedding ring. He wondered why the loss of the ring bothered him in particular, for he had wished and prayed countless times that his parents would divorce. But now with the ring gone, pawned and never to be redeemed, it seemed too final.

"No leave can be granted," the sergeant had said, after listening to a modicum of detail. "We're sorry, Fouquet."

Joseph focused on the screen and read: "THE MISSION SHIP ST88 IS A HIGH-THRUST-LEVERAGE CRAFT, HUMAN-PROPELLED. AS OUTLANDISH AS THAT MAY SOUND TO THE UNINITIATED, IT IS THE PROPER CRAFT FOR THE JOB. IT IS ALMOST ENTIRELY NOISELESS, WITH ALL COMPONENTS QUIETER THAN THE JOINTS OF A HEALTHY HUMAN BODY. WE HAVE LISTENED TO YOUR JOINTS, FOUQUET, AND YOU ARE ACCEPTABLE."

They're repeating this, Joseph thought. *This was covered on the second day. Or was it the third? Big deal. I don't squeak.*

"YOUR ATTITUDE, FOUQUET!" the screen flashed, in orange letters. "CORRECT IT!"

Joseph glared at the screen, but quickly modified this demeanor. He tried to look intent and interested.

"THAT'S BETTER. REMEMBER THAT THIS IS A PROVEN TRAINING METHOD, GAUGED TO YOUR FATIGUE FACTOR AND OTHER INDIVIDUAL LEARNING FEATURES THAT YOU DISPLAY."

They've decided I'm dopey this morning, Joseph thought.

"EVEN HEALTHY JOINTS AND PERFECTLY FITTED BIOMACHINE COMPO-NENTS MAKE SOME SOUNDS, REGRETTABLY. THESE ARE DETECTABLE BY SOPHISTICATED LISTENING DEVICES. FOR THIS REASON THE SHIP IS FITTED WITH LH3 NOISE ABSORBERS. THE CRAFT IS RATED STEALTH PLUS AAA, UNDETECTABLE BY J-RADAR, CAMERAS, OR THE HUMAN EYE. THIS LIST DOES NOT ENCOMPASS ALL POSSIBILITIES, AND YOU SHOULD BE COG-NIZANT OF THE RISKS INVOLVED."

In three-dimensional computer graphics the ensuing text repeated familiar descriptions of levers, pulleys, bars, gears, dials, toggles, and pedals that Joseph had to operate or understand. Weight training room machines were described that simulated the operation of ship's functions, and in five full days of training Joseph had traveled somewhat surreptitiously between these machines and the explanations in his learning module. The synaptic mem-ory pills worked exceedingly well, and from the second day on he found one in an envelope under his pillow each morning.

He roomed by himself, as did all the other recruits, so there wasn't much opportunity for fraternizing. This was a relief to him, considering the re-strictions that had been imposed concerning what he could say and to whom he could speak. So Joseph went about his tasks each day in some-thing of a void, steeling himself for the mission on the ninth day.

His eyes felt gritty and sore this morning, and he fought an urge to rub them. He was experiencing trouble reading the text and closed his eyelids briefly.

Recalling the comment "THIS LIST DOES NOT ENCOMPASS ALL POS-SIBILITIES," he couldn't keep his eyes closed. He keyed back two pages, reread that section. It was more than he had been told before, but left a great deal to the imagination.

Undetectable by the human eye . . . human eye . . . human eye . . .

Was that a tip concerning the identity of the enemy? It had to be, and had to mean he wasn't assigned to thwart any dangerous human elements. The Arionnese! He caught his breath, went through his reasoning once more, and could come to no alternative conclusion.

The hint had not been all that subtle, and whoever was in charge of this program must have known that he would figure it out. What should he do now?

Impulsively, he keyed, to the unseen controller: "I'M NOT TOO TIRED TO SEE WHO THE ENEMY IS, AND IT IS NOT HUMAN."

The screen flickered. New words replaced Joseph's message: "YOU HAVE WON THE COMPETITION. AND WE HAVE APPROVAL FROM YOUR . . . SUPE-RIORS. OTHER ENTRANTS ARE BEING NOTIFIED THAT THEY HAVE LOST."

What the hell is going on? Joseph wondered.

Joseph scratched his head. He had already been selected for the mission, along with three others. Those names on the class diagram. Or were there other candidates, persons in this classroom and elsewhere?

More words flitted onto the screen: "TAKE A FIFTEEN-MINUTE BREAK, FOUQUET. REMAIN IN YOUR MODULE. YOU ARE FATIGUED, AND A PILL WILL BE MADE AVAILABLE TO YOU FOR THIS. BE DISCREET. DO NOT LOOK AROUND."

Joseph switched off the screen and stared into its mindless blackness. Were they spying on him everywhere, gauging everything he did, possibly even everything he thought? It was an important mission. It was beyond important, so it stood to reason that they were. They eavesdropped on Michelle's telephone call too, knew he hadn't told them all the details of his family predicament. Who were *they*? He began to feel duped, manipulated. They had entered him in a game without identifying it as such, against faceless, nameless opponents.

There were secrets within secrets.

He closed his eyes, and for an instant he drifted into light sleep, leaving a gap in his immediate memory when he snapped to awareness.

Simultaneously, like a wake-up call at the termination of his allotted minutes, the screen beeped and went on by itself, now in red letters on a white background: "THE ALERTNESS PILL IS IN YOUR POCKET, FOUQUET. LOOK DOWN AS BEFORE AND TAKE TWO QUICK BREATHS."

Joseph did so, leaving his mouth open, and tasted milk chocolate melting on his tongue. He swallowed until his saliva bore no taste.

"THE PILL WILL NOT CONQUER ALL OF YOUR WEARINESS, FOUQUET, AS YOUR CONDITION IS BEING FUELED BY CONTINUED STRESS. THINK OF YOUR DUTY TO THIS HABITAT FIRST, AND CONCENTRATE! TO MAINTAIN YOUR ATTENTION, WE ARE GOING TO ALTERNATE TYPE STYLE AND SCREEN COLORS THE REST OF THE DAY. YOU NEED NOT KEYPUNCH PAGES. EVERYTHING WILL BE DONE FOR YOU, AS IN A VEHICLE ON FULL AUTO-MATIC. SIMPLY WATCH THE ROAD AHEAD. THE MATERIAL WILL BE GAUGED TO YOUR COMPREHENSION, AS CALIBRATED BY YOUR PHYSICAL RESPONSE PATTERNS. IN ANSWER TO YOUR UNSPOKEN QUESTION, THERE WILL BE NO FURTHER TESTS."

Joseph hadn't formulated that question, but believed that they couldn't actually read his thoughts. They could make educated guesses based upon his responses, but probably little more. Unless they had selected that phraseology to throw him off track. He didn't put it past them.

The system was outrunning him but assuring him at the same time that it would wait for him as necessary. Waving anger and frustration aside, he let the screen carry him along.

"MAINTAIN A RELAXED COMPOSURE, AND YOU WILL ABSORB NEARLY AS MUCH MATERIAL AS A FULLY ALERT, RESTED INDIVIDUAL."

As if under hypnosis, Joseph felt himself entering deep relaxation, similar to that of approaching sleep. But he wasn't going to sleep. He traveled a parallel course, one that separated him from the infirmities of his body and permitted him to observe his states of consciousness as he moved through them. In its final stage, he experienced what he thought was nearly perfect, pure concentration.

"BACK UP, FOUQUET," the screen commanded. "FROM YOUR EYES WE SEE YOU HAVE GONE TOO DEEP. WE DETECT THE CHEMO-OPTIC DIS-CHARGE OF HUBRIS, MEANING YOU HAVE DECEIVED YOURSELF. YOU'RE IN A RELIGIOUS STATE, IMPRACTICAL FOR OUR PURPOSES."

Joseph felt himself rewinding, locking into place at one of the levels through which he had passed.

"EXCELLENT. WE CONTINUE. YOUR MISSION IS OUR BEST HOPE, NOT OUR ONLY HOPE, BUT YOU MUST TREAT IT AS IF IT WERE. ELEVEN MIL-LION LIVES MAY DEPEND UPON YOUR SUCCESS. AS YOU HAVE LEARNED IN

PRIOR LESSONS, THE BLUE AND WHITE STRIPED BAR IN THE WEIGHT ROOM
IS NEARLY IDENTICAL IN FEEL AND WORK EFFORT TO THE POWER GENERA-
TION BAR OF THE ST88 HUMAN-PROPELLED CRAFT."

I know, I know. I'm a human generator. So let's get on with it!

"YOU MUST RELAX, MR. FOUQUET. YOU ARE WASTING PRECIOUS EN-
ERGY."

Joseph inhaled a deep breath, let it out slowly.

"THAT'S BETTER."

A computer graphic of Joseph's ship appeared on the screen, depicting a
human form in the center where he would be, thrusting and pulling a wide
bar. Three other human forms moved around the craft, which was quite
small, and he identified them as the pilot, gunner, and remote-controlled
samurai. Joseph knew something of the duties and capabilities of these men.
Uchiyama, the remote-controlled samurai, was most intriguing to Joseph,
for supposedly the man would carry a sword that could cut through anything, with energy transmitted from the blade. Remote-controlled: there
hadn't been any explanation of that, so Joseph guessed android. But weren't
androids programmable? Why would one have to sit through training?

The images on the screen changed.

"YOU ARE MORE THAN A HUMAN GENERATOR, FOUQUET. IN THE TRAIN-
ING DAYS REMAINING, WE WILL REVIEW WHAT YOU HAVE LEARNED ABOUT
OTHER TASKS ABOARD SHIP AND GO INTO MORE DETAIL. THE SAME PRO-
CEDURE WILL BE FOLLOWED WITH RESPECT TO YOUR OWN PRIMARY DU-
TIES. AN OVERVIEW: YOU WILL BE REQUIRED TO MAKE TWO EXTREMELY
POWERFUL THRUSTS DURING THE MISSION. YOUR SHIP IS HEAVILY AR-
MORED WITH TITANIUM DOUBLE 17Y, AN ALLOY OF ULTIMATE INTEGRITY.
FROM SPECTRAL AND DENSITY ANALYSES OF THE HABITAT SKIN, WE'VE
DETERMINED THAT THE SUBSTANCE, SHAPE (MULTIPOINTED NOSE), AND
BULK OF YOUR SHIP WILL PENETRATE THE SKIN OF THE HABITAT DOME
WITHOUT ANY PROBLEM. LUCKILY, BATTERING WAS ONE OF YOUR SHIP'S
DESIGN FEATURES. NONE OF THE TRAINS, PLANES, OR WATERBORNE SHIPS
THAT RAN INTO THE BARRIER AND BOUNCED OFF HAD ANYTHING LIKE THE
CAPABILITY OF THIS BABY. IN THE INITIAL BIG THRUST, YOUR CRAFT WILL
BREAK FREE OF THE HABITAT INTO SPACE, COVERING THE HOLE LEFT BE-
HIND WITH AN ATMOSPHERICALLY SEALED HATCH. FOR A SHORT TIME
YOUR SHIP CAN MAINTAIN SPEED WITH THE HABITAT, BUT YOU'LL HAVE TO
PUMP THAT GENERATOR BAR AT MAXIMUM."

Joseph chewed at his lower lip. This was new.

"IS SOMETHING TROUBLING YOU, FOUQUET?"

Joseph took a deep breath, keyed: "WAIT A MINUTE. I'M SUPPOSED TO MANUALLY AND PHYSICALLY KEEP UP WITH A SPACE HABITAT TRAVELING THOUSANDS OF KILOMETERS A SECOND?"

"WE EXPLAINED THE EXPONENTIAL SPEED TOGGLES TO YOU. WEREN'T YOU PAYING ATTENTION?"

"I WAS, BUT . . ."

"WE'LL GO BACK TO THAT, THEN, AND GO OVER IT AGAIN AND AGAIN UNTIL YOU UNDERSTAND."

"YOU'RE BEING VERY PATIENT WITH ME."

The controller didn't respond to this, continued: "WHEN IN SPACE WITH THE EXPONENTIAL SPEED TOGGLE SET AT 1000, YOU ARE TO PULL THE GENERATING BAR BACK AND FORTH TO THE STOPS, REACHING THE STOPS WITHIN THE TIME ALLOTTED BY THE TINY EYE-LEVEL COMPUTER GRAPHIC THAT WILL BE IN FRONT OF YOU. YOU ARE TO OPERATE THE POWER BAR IN THIS FASHION FOR 39 CYCLES WHILE THE PILOT MANEUVERS YOU INTO A SECOND THRUST POSITION, OUTSIDE THE CORE OF THE ARIONN BUILDING. AT GREAT PERIL WE SCANNED THE BUILDING, AND THIS IS THE WEAKEST POINT OF ENTRY. DURING THESE TWO MAXIMUM THRUSTS THE STOPS ARE ADJUSTED AND YOU MUST RAISE THE POWER BAR OVER YOUR HEAD AND SLAM IT ALL THE WAY TO THE DECK (IN ARTIFICIAL GRAVITY CONDITIONS), AS HARD AND AS FAST AS YOU CAN. OUR TESTS SHOW YOU ARE ABLE TO DO SO. SIMULTANEOUSLY, THE PILOT WILL MAINTAIN THE PROPER CRAFT ATTITUDE."

Joseph felt perspiration on his forehead, and beneath his thighs where they touched the chair.

"IF ALL WORKS WELL, PENETRATION WILL BE ACCOMPLISHED, STARTLING THE ARIONNESE SO THAT YOUR CREW CAN BEGIN TO TAKE CONTROL OF THE HABITAT'S PROPULSION MECHANISM. ACCORDING TO READINGS WE HAVE TAKEN, THAT MECHANISM IS INSIDE THE CORE. A ROBOT EXPERT IN SPACECRAFT PROPULSION WILL BE ABOARD. IT WILL MAKE AN INSTANT ANALYSIS AND WILL INSTRUCT THE TEAM. ONCE PENETRATION HAS BEEN ACCOMPLISHED, THE ROBOT IS IN CHARGE OF YOUR TEAM. PRIOR TO THAT, YOU ARE TO FOLLOW ALL COMMANDS OF THE PILOT.

"IF PENETRATION IS SUCCESSFUL, A FLEET OF CONVENTIONAL NAS SHIPS WILL CONNECT A FLEXIBLE 'SPACE TUBE' BETWEEN THE ATMOSPHERIC HATCHES AND WILL FOLLOW, DELIVERING MORE MEN AND MATERIAL TO THE TARGET. YOUR MISSION SHIP, DUBBED 'HAMMER,' IS THE ONLY ONE OF ITS KIND, EXPERIMENTAL AND ENTIRELY UNTESTED, BUILT

BEFORE ALIEN TAKEOVER. WE DARE NOT CONSTRUCT MORE, FOR FEAR WE'LL BLOW WHAT CHANCES WE HAVE BY BEING DISCOVERED. ERGO, YOU CAN'T SEE THE SHIP YET. IT DOZES INNOCENTLY WITH A DUST COVER OVER IT IN ONE OF OUR HANGARS."

There was a pause in the presentation, and Joseph felt as if he should respond in some manner. He started to inquire about the integrity of this message line against eavesdroppers. Ambivalence caused him to hesitate. While he wanted to know everything necessary about the mission, it seemed to him that they were revealing too much, going into areas that a mere crew member didn't need to know. How was he supposed to react to such material?

The screen beat him to the punch: "DON'T WASTE YOUR ENERGY KEYING QUESTIONS. WE STOPPED THE FLOW OF INFORMATION TO YOU WHEN IT BECAME APPARENT THAT YOUR BRAIN WAS FILLING WITH MUD. WE DO NOT READ YOUR MIND, EXACTLY. PROBABLE THOUGHTS ARE DEVELOPED BY THE MAIN COMPUTER BASED UPON NEUROLOGICAL SCANNERS THAT TAKE CONSTANT EXTERIOR READINGS ON YOUR BODY, NOTING IN PARTICULAR SKIN CONDITIONS, MUSCULAR SETTINGS AND TWITCHINGS, AND THE MYRIAD REVELATIONS OF THE EYE. YOU WERE WONDERING ABOUT LINE INTEGRITY AND WHY YOU WERE BEING TOLD SO MUCH?"

Uneasily, Joseph nodded his head.

"THE LINE IS SECURE, AS SECURE AS ANYTHING WE'RE DOING. WE COULD BE POUNCED UPON AT ANY MOMENT, BUT SUCH IS THE NATURE OF OUR AFFAIRS. AT THIS POINT, AFTER ALL WE'VE LEARNED ABOUT YOU, IT DOESN'T COMPROMISE OUR MISSION TO LET YOU IN ON THINGS. IF THE ARIONNESE ARE ONTO US, THEY'RE ONTO US, AND THESE ADDITIONAL BITS OF INFORMATION MUST ALREADY BE KNOWN TO THEM. WE WANT YOU TO KNOW THAT YOU'RE IMPORTANT TO US, ESSENTIAL. THE MORE WE TELL YOU (WITHIN REASONABLE GUIDELINES) THE BETTER YOUR ATTITUDE WILL BE. WE TELL YOU CERTAIN THINGS TO IMPROVE THE ODDS THAT THIS MISSION WILL BE SUCCESSFUL. YOU ARE RISKING YOUR LIFE FOR THIS HABITAT AND HAVE PASSED OUR TESTS. WE ARE CONFIDENT THAT YOU WILL COMMIT YOURSELF TOTALLY."

Another pause, and Joseph knew he was supposed to respond. "I WILL," he keyed.

The screen flickered, and Joseph wondered if his response had been adequate. A new thought surfaced, and he compared the ship's assignment to that of a kamikaze. There was, after all, a "remote-controlled samurai" onboard, whatever that was. He felt himself swept by a sense of the importance of the event. Crucial moments lay ahead, moments when every human on the habitat would be relying upon him. And it went beyond, to a message from all humans that they were not easy prey. The event itself was a living entity, with a voice.

The screen flickered again, and once more a full page of text awaited his perusal. But Joseph had slipped from the absorption mode, and oblivious to the scanners was feeling very good about himself. They needed him. He was crucial to their mission.

The text vanished, replaced by admonition: "BE CAREFUL, FOUQUET! HUBRIS, REMEMBER. IT CAN BE DANGEROUS!"

But Joseph felt strong enough to assert himself. "I DEMAND LEAVE TO SEE MY FATHER," he keyed. "I CANNOT, DESPITE ALL EFFORTS, PERFORM AT MY OPTIMUM FOR THE MISSION UNTIL I HAVE SPOKEN WITH HIM. GIVE ME A FEW HOURS, AND I WILL RETURN."

The response was immediate: "WE DO NOT CODDLE RECRUITS, FOU-QUET. DADDY CAN'T HELP YOU WHEN YOU'RE IN HERE."

"YOU LISTENED IN ON THE TELEPHONE CALL DIDN'T YOU? YOU KNOW WHAT'S HAPPENING IN MY FAMILY, THAT MY MOTHER'S ON THE RAMPAGE AND MY FATHER DOESN'T KNOW ABOUT IT."

"WAIT A MOMENT. I WILL ACCESS YOUR FILE." A quarter of a minute later: "I SEE THAT HERE. I WILL GRANT YOUR REQUEST, CONSIDERING ALL THE TIME WE'VE WASTED THIS MORNING. YOU HAVE THREE HOURS LEAVE, INCLUDING SACRIFICE OF YOUR LUNCH BREAK."

How compassionate, Joseph thought. *Mission first, everything else second. At least they're letting me out.*

"REPORT IMMEDIATELY TO THE STAFF CAR WAITING IN FRONT OF THIS BUILDING. A DRIVER WILL TRANSPORT YOU TO YOUR FATHER." The screen became dark.

Swiftly Joseph departed the module, the room, and the building. A tan and blue sedan was outside, and a stocky woman standing by it motioned for him to hurry. The car's readiness told Joseph that they either knew or thought it likely that he would make the demand. The delay for file access struck him as phony, and he wondered at the veracity of the information they had given him.

The driver, a tight-lipped woman in NAS garb, told Joseph to buckle his shoulder harness. When he had done so, she left the controls on manual and pressed the accelerator to the floor, sending the car lurching away from the curb.

Joseph asked why they didn't provide a helicopter, and as the words departed his lips he wished he could have them back. This driver wouldn't know about the mission.

She looked at him with obvious surprise, arching one narrow eyebrow, then resumed her focus on the roadway. Joseph decided his comment hadn't done harm. She probably thought he was engaged in message delivery.

"You know where Henry Fouquet is?" Joseph asked.

"I know where your father is." She smiled.

So she knew the relationship. How much did she know and who was she, really? Was she the mission commandant in disguise? She had a hardness to her features, fitting Joseph's stereotype of a woman in charge. But she didn't seem old enough, twenty-six or twenty-seven at most.

She took a turn like a pilot banking and accelerated up an inclined expressway access road.

Joseph chastised himself again for the helicopter query. Of course he couldn't have one, for it might call Arionnese attention to him. Granting him leave and a staff car was risky enough.

Joseph thought of Thyla and of the unsuccessful calls he had made to her from the base. According to her mother, who seemed to hover over the telephone in recent days, Thyla wasn't home. She promised to leave messages. But either Thyla wasn't receiving them or she didn't want to talk with him. Joseph wished they would be candid, at least. If Thyla was dropping him, this was an unkind, torturous manner of handling it. He felt a deadening of his affection, and it gave him an ill, empty feeling.

"What's your name?" Joseph asked, when he had composed himself.

"Driver," the woman said.

Joseph grimaced, shook his head. "I get it," he said. "No more questions, right?"

She chuckled. "No. I'm Nancy Driver, airman fifth class."

"Honest?"

"Unfortunately, yes. I don't plan to make *this* my career, and I'd prefer it weren't even a stepping stone. I'm a driver now because one of the officers saw a list and jumped at my name, thinking he could have a little fun with it."

"The military attracts its share of sadists," Joseph said.

"Next week I'm transferring to a wing division at Hamilton for officer candidate school."

"Great."

After crossing the Bay Bridge, they took an expressway to the Sunset district, exiting on Geary Boulevard. A few of the stores had Christmas decorations in their windows—wreathes, ribbons, and the like—but it wasn't like previous years. Most people weren't in the holiday spirit. It didn't help that the habitat was scheduled to arrive on Arionn the day before Thanksgiving, either. People couldn't make normal holiday plans, not knowing what lay in store for them on an alien, potentially hostile world.

"What is today?" Joseph asked.

"Tuesday," she said. "November seventeenth."

"Eight days to Arionn," Joseph said.

Ms. Driver grunted, as if it didn't matter to her. She flicked on a Compu-Map at the center of the console, spoke into it: "Target, ParSell Company truck number one-oh one-oh."

Joseph knew something about Compu-Map, since it was available to the public. But he was amazed that Driver could target something as small as a vehicle. Buildings, parks, and monuments were the norm, so this had to be a special military hookup.

The map was a computer screen, on which the major arterials, structures, and parks of San Francisco were displayed. A green blip representing the NAS car moved along Geary Boulevard, and off to the right several blocks, in a residential neighborhood, another blip moved, this one blue. The vehicle it represented stopped frequently.

Dad on his route, Joseph thought.

They passed a tow crane as it jerked illegally parked vehicles into the air and deposited them on a five-high rack. At the next corner they made a right and meandered into a maze of poorly laid out streets, taking care not to be trapped in dead ends.

When Joseph observed the pale yellow ParSell van plying the street ahead, it occurred to him that his father wasn't necessarily inside. Maybe he had called in sick or quit. Joseph wouldn't blame him if he had resigned, not with the wife he had.

The van jerked to a stop in the middle of the street, and as Joseph's car neared he heard bells ringing and saw the octagonal rooftop readerboard light up, listing the addresses of nearby persons who had packages inside. The driver's door slid open, and a chunky man in a powder blue uniform and cap stepped onto the running board. It was Henry.

The conveyor-connected running board carried Henry around to the rear cargo doors, which opened as Henry came around, revealing packages and a robot arm inside.

The NAS car stopped just behind the van, just as a cluster of housewives appeared there to claim packages. Joseph stepped from the car, caught a glance of recognition from his father, and waited until the customers had been served.

When the women were gone and the doors slid closed, Henry said to Joseph, "You look good in that uniform. The way I used to look in mine."

"I've seen the pictures," Joseph said, approaching. "Still the same old tan and blue. Of course you had Strato Guard stripes. How are you, Dad?"

They hugged awkwardly.

"You some kinda general now?" Henry asked, looking at the driver, who remained in her seat.

Joseph strained to smile. "Naw. They gave me three hours leave. I had to see you."

"I can't just leave work. I got customers wanting stuff."

"I'll make it quick. I heard about you leaving Mom, but did you hear that she's gone berserk?"

"Sure. She creamed me good."

"I mean since then. Michelle says she's pawning everything."

"Let her. I don't give a shit."

"You don't mean that."

"Sure I do. I send 'em a food check every day. And I'm gonna work sumpthin' out on the other bills, too."

"She's not cashing your checks."

"She ain't? Well, I'll look into it."

"Where are you living, Dad? I called Cartucci, and he didn't know."

"Room in a flophouse."

"Are you gonna divorce her this time? It's high time you did. No man should endure what you have."

Henry arched an eyebrow. "You some kinda marriage adviser? What are your credentials? Maybe you're an emissary from the Pope with my dispensation?" He leaned toward Joseph, making the younger man uncomfortable, added: "I've been married twenty-six years. You think you know more than me about what to do?"

"No, I didn't mean it that way."

"Twenty-six years with one woman. That's almost half my friggin' life. You think that's easy to just throw away, to admit it was all wasted?"

"I didn't mean it was all wasted. I was trying to help. You've been struggling too hard and I'm worried about you."

"If I want help, I'll ask for it. You got that? Right now you can help by stayin' outa the way. I don't need pressure."

"Dad, I . . ."

"Beat it. I've got work to do."

"I'm on your side, damn it! Doesn't that mean anything to you?"

"I didn't ask nobody to be on my side! I don't even know what side I'm on myself!"

"Don't wall me out, for crissakes, hiding in a flophouse!"

But Joseph saw disdain in the sardonic way his father shaped his mouth. There had been something too plaintive in Joseph's tone.

I'm revealing weakness, Joseph thought. *He doesn't like that, thinks it's not manly. So simplistic the way he looks at things!*

"Yer startin' to sound like a girl," Henry said. "Is that what they teach you in the Air Service nowadays, to be a girl?"

"You're a bastard," Joseph said. He turned on his heel toward the waiting car, saw it as a blur in front of him. He stumbled on a broken section of pavement but managed to maintain his footing.

He heard the delivery van start, an electric whir. Its engine revved tinnily, tires squealed. When Joseph slumped into the seat beside Driver, he saw the van disappear around a corner.

"I have another stop to make," Joseph said, "Okay?" For the first time he noticed a gray and black electronic device sticking from her purse, on the seat between them.

"Sure. You have more than two hours left."

Joseph nudged the device, left it. "You had that thing trained on me, didn't you, transmitting to HQ?"

"You got it, buster."

TWENTY

According to data left by the students, they planned to produce the habitat's atmosphere by preserving, sealing, and recycling components taken from the air of Earth. Once the facility is on Arionn, with our people coming and going, there will be leakage, and eventually the atmosphere inside will be our atmosphere. Our air, high in nipretomino compounds, is compatible with the human breathing mechanism, although there may be cases of minor lung irritation. The student project team analyzed this correctly.

There is a problem, however, which they failed to consider. Their plan involves utilizing an artificial moon and a working type 81 synthetic sun to simulate Earth conditions. With that sun, photosynthesis and the other solar-dependent processes will continue. Trees and other plants will grow, even thrive for the most part, until they are cut. Then a rapid process of disintegration begins caused by alor, a byproduct of their sun type and our atmosphere that attacks unrooted plant forms. This happened at our frontier bubble city of Globka Haroon, as outlined in confidential reports not available to the students. In the alternative, if we remove the habitat bubble, their plants will not grow in our sunlight.

Wood and wood byproducts are major construction and product components among the Earther race. Every such item we wish to preserve must be treated annually with a phrelite-based substance. Their paper books present a special challenge, in that they preserve cultural information. It isn't practical to treat every page, and it is too costly to provide separate sealed enclosures for every collection. It appears necessary to collect and maintain all desired volumes in a central, government-sealed facility. If you concur, we will engineer and construct it now in modular form, for immediate insertion into the habitat.

—Research team report, ordered by the Triumvirate of Arionn

From her bedroom where she was reading one of Renney's hologram comics, Michelle heard the thud of the front door and footsteps downstairs. They stopped before she could identify them. It was early afternoon, too soon for Renney to be home from school, and Mom had gone out with the $50,000 check.

Michelle scurried downstairs and found her mother's bedroom door closed. She rapped on it.

"Just a minute," Rachel said. "I'm getting ready."

She sounded sober, but Michelle hadn't forgotten the burning threat. Her treasures were secreted in a new place. While Rachel was away and before Coley rose, Michelle had wrapped her puzzle box (containing the book) in old clothes, placing the items in the junk-infested garage amid and beneath unpawnable items. They would be safe there a while.

When Rachel emerged from the bedroom her face was covered in white cream, and she wore a plastic haircap. In one of her superannuated robes, this one a decolorized saffron, she looked like a hideous insane asylum escapee, and Michelle couldn't avoid looking at her mother's hands to see if they bore matches or a weapon.

They didn't.

"Will you brush my hair in a while?" Rachel asked, sweetly. "I want to look nice for your father when he gets off work."

"You went out and saw him?"

Rachel looked bewildered at the query, and this provided Michelle with her answer.

"Mom, Dad hasn't been home in more than five days. You had a fight with him."

"Liar! I won't tolerate any more of your lies!" Rachel whirled and returned to her bedroom, slamming the door behind her.

Moments later, Rachel emerged nude. Her face had been cleared of cream, and she wore heavy, artlessly applied makeup and an old brunette wig. She carried a bath towel over one arm and strode forth almost regally.

"I thought your father might like this outfit best," she said. "I'm going outside now to get a tan. He'll be along soon."

"You can't go outside like that, Mom!"

"I certainly can, and I will." She placed a steel key in Michelle's hand, saying, "This is to the safety deposit box I opened today. The money, less three hundred and twenty-two dollars I collected as a service fee available to adults, is in it. There are two keys, one for you and one for me. It's our little secret."

A portion of Granpère's secret with Michelle had become Michelle's secret with her mother.

"Okay," Michelle said, meekly. She placed the key in a pocket of her dress, wondering about the signature card and whether she, as a minor, could gain access to the box by herself. The matter of interest entered her mind as well, for now the money wasn't earning any.

"Why aren't you in school?" Rachel asked.

"I had to watch Coley again."

"See that you go tomorrow." No mention as to how this was to be accomplished, if Coley were left again.

"I will," Michelle said, shuffling uncomfortably on her feet and trying to look away from her mother. Even if Rachel didn't go out the following morning, Michelle couldn't leave Coley alone, not with this occurring.

Without further ado, Rachel strode through the living room and out of the house, into the front yard.

Stunned, Michelle hurried to the side-turned hallway that comprised their front porch, and peered through the small window by the door.

Rachel kicked a rock away on the grass, spread her towel there, and sat upon it in the sunlight.

Michelle ran to her. "You've got to come inside, Mom! Neighbors will call the police."

"We have such a nice thick hedge," Rachel said, fluttering her eyelids. "Most of them can't see me."

"Mrs. Meley can, and she's the worst." Michelle pointed through the hedge opening created by the driveway, through which Mrs. Meley's house could be seen quite clearly. "She'll cause trouble."

"If she does, I'll knock her on her curtain-twitching ass." Rachel laid back supine, stared at the sky, which was a cool pastel shade of November blue.

Michelle heard Coley whining, and presently saw the tot at the front door, sans clothes. "Mommy! I want my mommy!" Coley rubbed her eyes and pouted.

"Mommy's right here, dear," Rachel said. "Come outside and we'll play in the sun."

"It's not even fifty degrees today," Michelle said, feeling the need to press reality upon her mother.

"That's warm enough for me. I'm from Ireland, you know."

"You've never been to Ireland," Michelle said, watching the still whimpering Coley descend the steps.

"I haven't? Are you certain? I *am* Irish."

"In part, but you were born in St. Louis. You've been to Canada, but never to any other country."

"St. Louis isn't a country, foolish child."

"I didn't mean that."

"I've been to deep space. And that is *cold*. I've been outside the habitat, you know. I walked around out there in a spacesuit and checked everything out."

Nervously, Michelle looked through gaps that existed in even the thickest portions of the hedge, through which she could see portions of the sidewalk and street. The face of a man appeared behind one of the holes, his eyes open wide. He muttered something but continued on his way.

"He's seen you, Mom!" Michelle husked. "You've got to get inside and we'll say this never happened!"

Calmly, as if in halcyon days, Rachel patted the underside of her chin.

Coley brought over a toy plastic bucket that had been left in the yard, and stood on the corner of her mother's towel, peering inquisitively at her.

"Where are your clothes, Mommy?"

"Inside the house, where clothes belong."

"What are those things on your chest?"

Michelle rolled her eyes, awaited the answer. Their mother had never been one to shy away from topics of sex. Joseph used to go before her with his friends, asking the most outlandish questions. And every one was answered, in an earthy fashion.

"Breasts," Rachel said.

"Will I get some, too, when I'm bigger?"

"Sure you will, and yours will be fifty times as big."

This was too much for Michelle. "That can't be, Mom," she objected. "Your breasts are average-sized. Fifty times as big would be unbelievable."

Rachel glared at her, petulantly. "You don't know anything about breasts, Michelle. You don't have any."

"I've seen other people, and I know that what you're saying isn't possible." Maybe an argument would bring her out of it, Michelle hoped.

Rachel rose to her feet and gripped Coley's hand. "Come along, Coley," she said. "Let's go find your play pool and fill it with water. We'll have lots of fun without fuddy-duddy old Michelle. She doesn't know anything, huh?"

Coley brightened. "Yeah! Michelle don't know anything!"

And off they went hand in hand around the side of the house, their buttocks glistening in the prewinter sunlight.

Bumper yelped, and Michelle heard him pulling at his chain.

Embarrassed and frustrated, Michelle climbed the steps to return inside. On the landing, she heard a car clunk onto the driveway and turned to look. It was a government vehicle, tan with a blue rocket emblem on the door. It revved its engine to pull up the short incline of the driveway.

The door on the passenger side opened, and she recognized Joseph as he stepped out.

Apparently Rachel was out of his view, because he trudged toward Michelle without looking toward the side of the house. "Hi," he said.

Michelle didn't respond. She slipped into the house, leaving the door open for him.

When Joseph came inside, she saw anxiety and redness in his eyes. Shadows underscored them, as if smudged in with a makeup pencil.

"Mom's going crazy out there," Michelle said, "and a man saw her. She's running around the yard with Coley, and neither one of them has any clothes on."

"Holy shit!" Joseph said. He removed his cap and fidgeted with it.

Michelle saw her mother returning to the front yard, dragging a plastic children's pool and a length of garden hose with water running from it. Rachel placed the pool near her towel and began to fill the pool.

Coley ran to join her, squealed with excitement. She tossed floating toys into the water.

Michelle glanced up at her brother's face. His jaw sagged, mouth agape, and in his powerful hands he twisted the cap.

"Holy shit," he repeated. "Is this what she's been like since Dad left?"

"No. She wasn't nearly as bad before this, except for pawning and selling our things."

"I talked to Dad, on his route. He's living in a flophouse, I guess with a bunch of bums."

"You saw him today?"

Joseph nodded. "He seemed . . . okay."

"Is he coming home?"

"I don't know. I, uh, made the mistake of mentioning divorce, and he about bit my head off. He'll never go through with it, even now."

Michelle rubbed one of her eyelids, felt a section with stubble near one corner. He hadn't noticed yet.

Joseph slammed his cap to the floor. "I'm gonna drag her back inside," he said.

Michelle didn't want to look. While her brother ventured into the fray, she retreated to the living room, slumping on the couch by her mother's usual place, where the Biblecorder had been left.

Angry voices raged from the yard, including Coley's. Apparently Joseph was having to fight both of them, and Coley was probably beating on him. Neighbors would be gathering around or hanging out their windows. Someone would call the police.

Michelle donned the Biblecorder headset, set the already open book on her lap, and turned on the machine. A soothing male voice drowned out the angry cacophony, and Michelle tried to immure herself within the realm of the Great Events written on these pages. But she recalled hearing that every word in the Bible could be correlated with modern events, on any scale that a person wanted to consider. Michelle found herself trying to tie the words from the headset to the circumstances of her life. She wished she hadn't daydreamed in church on those occasional Sundays she'd gone, and that she had listened more attentively as well to her mother's intermittent Bible teachings. Then she might understand situations better, might deal with them more intelligently. That wasn't her real mother outside screaming at Joseph. That was the sick one, the one who wouldn't take her medication, the one who hit her father over the head and made him leave.

The words she heard now rolled and flowed, like sweet spring water traversing stones and smoothing them. But they didn't make sense to her, and she couldn't make any connection.

The screaming discord intruded. People banged into the house. Michelle turned up the volume, to the point where it made her ears throb.

A tremendous clatter caused her to look toward the doorway.

Joseph was pulling his squirming, angry mother through the basement, and she was pummeling him with her fists. With one hand, he attempted unsuccessfully to keep the towel over her, but she knocked it to the floor, kicked at him, and screeched, like a mother bird disturbed from her nest. And baby bird was getting her licks in, too, as Coley ran alongside Joseph, kicking him, pounding him, and saying that she hated him.

Joseph glared in Michelle's direction as he dragged his mother across the room, and he grimaced at one of Rachel's blows to his groin. He bellowed at Michelle, and despite the earphones she understood every word: "Get off your ass and help me, damn it!"

Michelle felt as though concrete had set in around her. The odd trio fought their way into the kitchen, and Michelle reflected that Joseph undoubtedly thought she was becoming like their mother, sitting on the couch with the Biblecorder.

Maybe I am going to be like her someday, Michelle thought. *Retreating so often to fantasy, just as she does. But I'm only eleven. It's okay for me! What if I go into one, though, and can't get out?*

Michelle felt like a person teetering on the edge of a deep hole, unable to prevent herself from toppling in. People stood by laughing cruelly, lending neither a hand nor an encouraging word. They wanted her to fail, to meet the fate they had predicted for her, to be like her mother. The din of their voices echoed in her headset, and she ripped the gear off, shoving the Biblecorder away to where it had been on the couch.

The soothing words continued from the headset, and Michelle saw the scanner moving across the page. She switched the unit off.

Joseph filled the kitchen doorway, a shouting, angry form. "What the hell are you doing in there? Get off your ass and help me with *your* mother!"

But Michelle was saturated, didn't care what he said to her or thought of her. "She's your mother too!" Michelle snapped. "And what's wrong with her is more your fault than mine! You've never understood her, never even tried!"

The gulf between her and Joseph was wider than ever. Even if she leaped to her feet and helped him now, the gap wouldn't close, and Michelle was too drained to care.

She saw her mother sidling clumsily behind Joseph, on the other side of the kitchen. She was nude beneath her unsecured saffron robe and seemed to be attempting an escape.

Joseph noticed her and cursed. He told her to return to her room and not to come out until she was properly dressed.

Rachel altered course to her bedroom, but not without expostulation. "Babies are always nude," she said. "They have all the fun. I want some fun, too." She slid out of Michelle's line of sight, into the bedroom.

"Aren't you afraid she'll go out the window?" Michelle asked.

"What do you care?"

"I'm sorry, but all this arguing makes me sick," Michelle said, by way of explanation. "I can't stand any more of it."

"You don't think I'm sick of it, too? Where the hell is Stu? When Mom was beating on me she said she was going to do to me what she did to Stu. What did she mean by that?"

"Nothing. She chased him off, that's all. She wanted to thrash him, I guess, but couldn't catch him. It was over a lousy joke Stu pulled on Renney. I guess she meant she was going to do to you what she wanted to do to Stu, if she could have caught him."

"You guess? This isn't a situation where we can guess. The woman is dangerous, maybe psychotic."

Michelle shook her head in protest. "No, she isn't. I can't believe that about her. She has a lot of problems, sure, but she loves us. She loves *you*, Joseph."

"I don't wanna hear that drivel. I saw Bumper from the kitchen, poking around by a fresh mound of dirt in the backyard. Maybe Stu's buried out there."

"Don't be ridiculous."

"You say Mom chased Stu out of the house. Exactly what did you see and hear?"

"Well, Renney was crying because of the mean joke Stu pulled on him, and Stu was trying to sneak down the hallway. Mom saw him and went after him. Stu saw some kind of hallucination, thought Mom was Beauregard, and I saw her chase him down the stairs, that's all. She was real mad, but had every right to be."

"Did you follow?"

"No. I remained with Renney in the bedroom and consoled him. He was terrified."

"Then Stu could have tripped and been caught."

Michelle shook her head, causing her ponytail to bounce in front of her eyes. "I heard the front door slam. He got out."

"You're sure it was the front door?"

"Well, yeah. It was heavy, like, and I've heard it slam enough times around here."

"Someone running away, someone who was really scared . . . I don't think someone like that would waste time slamming a door. He would go through it and leave it open."

"I think he'd slam it, as a barrier to her. It would cost her more time to open than it took for him to close it."

"Maybe. And maybe she nabbed him in the doorway, just as he was pulling the door. She slammed it and then killed him. Broke his neck, probably, with her strength. I'm gonna check in the backyard."

"You're way off," Michelle said, following Joseph down the rear porch steps. She shivered, from the temperature and from the moment. "You don't know her. You just don't understand. She didn't try to kill Daddy when she hit him. She just bopped him out of frustration, that's all. It happens in a lot of families."

"You told me she was going to turn the Mega-Popper on next to him."

"That was just talk. She didn't mean it. She gets attention by saying bizarre things."

"She's totally insane," Joseph said.

Near Bumper's latest digging area, Joseph patted the dog's defoliated backside and nudged him out of the way so that he could examine the mound of dirt. "What have you got here?" Joseph asked, kneeling and scraping dirt with his hands.

Michelle's lips quivered, and in the pastel blue sky she saw the sun barely peeking above a distant housetop. Her knees began to shake.

Joseph made a small hole, with nothing showing yet.

Bumper wagged his tail and licked the side of Joseph's face.

Joseph removed a large soup bone from the hole, then another. He dug faster, and Michelle recalled the hole in which her grandfather had been buried. She struggled to suppress yet another fantasy.

Finally Joseph looked up and announced, "Nothing here. I've reached rock and can't go any farther."

"I told you!"

"Maybe she's got the body somewhere else." He stood and scanned the yard, then trudged back toward the house. "She's brilliant, you know. It could be anywhere. Maybe she uses the garbage chute."

"It's partially blocked."

"Yeah, it's been that way for quite a while." He reached the base of the steps, took another look around the yard. "She probably stuffed some other kid's corpse in there."

"Why do you insist upon believing the worst about her? In your eyes she's guilty until proven innocent."

"That's only because of the way she acts, you dumb little twerp."

"Why don't you get out of here?" Michelle snarled. "We can get along fine without you around. It's you that causes trouble, not her." Michelle heard the rashness of her words, but was not inclined to retract it.

"You're saying she's normal? Running around naked is normal? And what she did to Dad, there's no way I'll accept what you said about that happening in lots of families."

"I'm not saying she's entirely normal. She's been off her medication, and we just need to get her back on it. Even without it, she's not as bad as people believe."

"She's always had a cruel streak, especially with me. I can quote you chapter and verse. Now Stu's probably murdered, Dad got the shit crowned out of him, and you've lost whatever sense and objectivity you ever had. It's like you're blinded or something when it comes to her. You've gotten worse and worse in the last year. I've seen it happening to you."

"How can you mention my objectivity? You're always against her."

"I just explained that to you. Didn't you hear me?" He turned away from her and thumped rapidly up the stairs.

Michelle heard car doors slamming and loud voices from the front yard. She ran around the side of the house. Police cars flashing blue and platinum lights were on the street and in the driveway, behind the car in which Joseph came. A woman in a uniform like Joseph's had emerged from the driver's side of Joseph's car and stood leaning on the door, watching as half a dozen police officers marched past her, going toward the house.

Michelle raced into the front yard, and watched helplessly as the officers climbed the stairs of her house. She saw people gathering on the sidewalk, their tongues wagging excitedly. Mrs. Meley was one of them, in a dark brown coat with a black fur collar. She was talking to a man beside her, undoubtedly making derogatory remarks about the Fouquets. Michelle knew who had telephoned the authorities.

"You bitch!" Michelle shouted. "You're a nosy old bitch, Mrs. Meley!"

One of the police officers, a tall burly man, went to Michelle, asked her if she lived in this house.

Michelle refused to answer and stared up at him defiantly. He was very tall, but not nearly so tall as her Uncle Paul.

"That kid's one of 'em!" Mrs. Meley yelled. "Don't let her get away!"

The officer flashed a disapproving look at Mrs. Meley, then took Michelle firmly by the arm. "Come with me, please," he said.

As she was being escorted to one of the cars, Michelle looked back. Joseph was at the front door, talking with the officers.

"Don't let them in!" Michelle screamed.

When the officers filed into her house, she broke into sobs.

TWENTY-ONE

—Excerpts from the table of contents
of the 612-page class action lawsuit filed
against the Arionnese by the ACLU and
various other organizations

"You did what?" Granmère Liliane roared, nearly toppling her chair as she jerked to her feet.

Big Jack Brittany didn't flinch. With his immense belly hanging over the outer edge of Granmère's mayoral desk, he smirked at her. "This afternoon we filed a lawsuit against the Arionnese," he said. "Would you care to see a copy?"

"I think I would! Why wasn't I consulted?"

Calmly, Brittany leaned across her desk and depressed the intercom button on her telephone. "They can come in now," he said. "With the papers."

"*Who* can come in now? I'm talking with *you*. I haven't invited anyone into my office. What's going on here?" She considered reaching for the intercom to countermand.

"You look a little peaked," Brittany observed. "I think the pressure's getting to you. So many people accusing you of collaborating with the aliens! I guess you're getting your share of death threats?"

Granmère made a spitting sound between her teeth. She had received threats, but they'd gone through General Oso's security staff, and she'd told them to keep a lid on it. She decided that Brittany was guessing.

"Aren't you going to answer my question?" Brittany asked.

"A *la gare*, you corpulent queer!"

"Let me see," he said, smiling derisively. "That phrase means 'buzz off,' doesn't it?"

She glared at him, didn't respond.

"As for the characterization, dear lady, you'll need proof—beyond the obvious. I am fat and admit to that, but only that."

The rhythm and rhyme of his words brought visions of "Jack Sprat who could eat no fat" to Granmère. She heard footsteps and looked toward the open doorway, where no one had as yet appeared. A halting step, she thought, and a second person, both with hard heels.

Peninnah Wilde appeared, wearing a glass helmet that completely enclosed her head. She moved slowly and unsteadily into the office, followed by a young woman in a brown tweed business suit. The young woman toted a legal-size file folder under one arm.

Granmère stared at Wilde, who appeared pale and weak inside her enclosure. Every few seconds Wilde's chest convulsed, as if in a hiccup. But Granmère heard no sounds.

Wilde stumbled into one of the visitors' chairs and glared fiercely at Granmère. Wilde held a forefinger against a gray panel on one side of her helmet and spoke: "What are you doing in my office?" She released the panel.

"This is the mayor's office," Granmère said, superciliously. "You're in no condition to hold office, so I thought it proper . . ."

With an angry jerk, Wilde depressed the gray panel. "You thought it proper?" She withdrew her finger from the panel, convulsed silently, then darted back to the mechanism. "It wasn't proper in the least! You just strolled in and took over!"

"You didn't follow proper procedures in taking charge of this office," Brittany said. "A plethora of irregularities."

"Can the *merde*," Granmère snarled. "It was an emergency and still is. I'm doing what's necessary, no more." Noticing that her own pulse was rapid and that her breathing was labored, she let herself down onto the chair behind her and drew a deep breath.

"It wasn't necessary to occupy this office," Brittany said. "You had her effects boxed and placed in storage, as if she were never coming back. We've examined those boxes, and a number of items are missing, including her Philological Fellows plaque."

"A pack of queers and lesbians," Granmère said.

"As usual, spoken without proof," Brittany said. "And even if it were true, that wouldn't be justification to steal the mayor's personal property. A glass statuette was packed improperly and broken, too."

"Red herrings! I didn't pack her things, and I didn't steal a stupid award plaque. Change the subject."

"Did you give instructions to the persons who packed?"

Seething: "What do you mean?"

"The query is phrased clearly, assuming you are competent to understand."

"Don't try to create the appearance that I can't handle this job," Granmère said. She riveted her gaze on the young woman, who stood motionless just behind Peninnah Wilde. "Who's she? Your witness?"

"I'm Beatrice Pepys," came the response, "with the ACLU."

An emotionless face, Granmère decided. *Without character.*

Granmère looked back at Brittany, who hovered over the desk and Granmère in a great fleshy mass. This was a man who cracked chairs when he sat upon them.

"Why don't you sit on one of the chairs, Brittany?" Granmère suggested. "Or better yet, since you'll break through to the floor anyway, why don't you just sit on the floor to begin with and save the taxpayers some money? I find your point-blank largeness offensive."

Brittany frowned but didn't move. "The question. If you can recollect that far back."

"I transmitted no instructions to packers. Why should I have?"

"To make certain that care was taken, of course. You did employ professional packers?"

"A couple of secretaries did it. You know that."

"A couple of secretaries?" Wilde gasped. "You permitted secretaries to pack my priceless possessions, the accumulation of a lifetime?"

"You don't own anything priceless, Peninnah," Granmère said. "It's clear to me why you and Big Jack are so ineffectual in government, with this typical tangent you're on."

"This is but one of the irregularities that you committed, Fouquet," Brittany said.

Granmère sat back, waved the back of her hand in Pepys's direction. "So sue me. Have Pepys file a class-action lawsuit, in the name of each of Wilde's possessions."

"We have other lawyers to handle you," Brittany said.

"And it's all a waste of energy," Granmère said. "Eleven million people in the crisis of a millennium and you're going to tie up leadership over a petty office occupancy matter? It's utterly preposterous."

"You're acting mayor," Brittany said, "not mayor and not captain of a spacecraft."

"You heard General Oso," Granmère said. "He referred to me as commander in chief." She looked at Pepys, added, "Put the papers on my desk and leave us."

Pepys did so, and Granmère closed the door electronically behind her.

"Let's move to a relevant topic, shall we?" Granmère said, shifting her gaze between Brittany and Wilde. "The matter of the protesters, for example. I've ordered a police crackdown, as you know, Peninnah."

Wilde nodded stiffly.

"Do you disagree with that decision? You'd rather let the protesters agitate the Arionnese, as you've agitated them with your lawsuit?"

"I think we should . . . exert pressure on the aliens," Wilde answered, pausing in mid-sentence to hiccup silently.

"There are irregularities in your involvement with the lawsuit," Granmère said. "You're on medical leave, and technically you have no authority in any governmental matter."

Granmère began examining the papers.

"I'm still a citizen," Wilde said, "and as a citizen I initiated the action. It didn't require your approval."

"Every such action aboard this spacecraft, where I am captain, requires my approval."

"We don't accept your assertions," Wilde said.

"No flight plan filed with the IPAA?" Granmère said, looking up from the papers at Wilde. "That's a federal agency. You got them in on it, too?"

"I did, through their Western regional bureau chief. They have an office in Sausalito."

Granmère shook her head briskly. "Unwise," she said.

"We feel we should do something now," Brittany said, "while the aliens number only a few. It'll be too late once we're on their planet, surrounded by millions or billions of them."

Granmère thought of the secret mission involving Joseph and wondered how the preparations were progressing.

"The Arionnese are people of tremendous technology," Granmère said. "We can't even think of opposing them, no matter how few they number now. Look what they've achieved! I think we should cooperate with them, get on friendly terms with them. If we're not so feisty, maybe they'll arrange for some of our people to return to Earth."

But Granmère knew she was committed to a version of Brittany's position, for that was the rationale for a military attack before the habitat reached Arionn. She was riding the fence, with contingency plans for going in either direction, depending upon the success or failure of the mission. Publicly and in every non-sicom private conversation, her position was the one she had just presented, unalterably opposed to any action against the Arionnese. On the other side, if the mission succeeded, she would have to move deftly and assume responsibility for her grandson's involvement while shunting Rachel out of the limelight.

"You speak absurdly," Brittany said. "After what those creeps did? The coastline of California must be in ruins back there, with who knows how many thousands killed by mudslides and inundations of water. You can't expect to reason with people who've done something like that."

"Maybe they took precautions to spare human life. Have you bothered to ask them?"

"Have you? Isn't that something you should investigate?"

"I'll look into it."

"You speak of cooperation. What's the worst case scenario? Death, right? But aren't we as good as dead anyway?"

"You have no right to imperil the lives of eleven million people," Granmère said.

"They're already imperiled. Besides, they support my position, as you'd realize if you didn't have such an ostrich mentality. They're in the streets, overflowing every jail and prison."

"A minority. Most citizens aren't protesting."

"Let's call a special election and ask them what they want to do."

"I'll think about that," Granmère said. She studied Wilde, who was in some discomfort, hiccuping silently within her helmet.

"Well, think fast," Brittany said. "We're only four days from Arionn, and I'm already feeling island fever. I sent a message to the buggers, asked them what they wanted us for. They didn't respond. You can bet it'll be some kind of a prison, maybe a zoo or a horrible medical research facility. We won't be able to leave, and those of us that aren't dissected will go insane."

"They said we were in no direct danger from them," Granmère said, "so let's try to take them at their word. Insane? San Francisco has always been a haven for the insane anyway. Maybe Earth had us shipped out, to get rid of the weirdos."

"I can't even comprehend your thought patterns," Brittany said, in disgust. He leaned against a wall. Granmère saw the wallboard flex.

"Look," she said. "You don't know for certain that they won't let us travel around their planet. Maybe we'll be able to get out regularly, and maybe it's a beautiful place, prettier than Earth."

"What did they do?" Brittany asked. "Pay you off?"

"I hear emotion in your tone," Granmère countered. "Let's keep this rational, overlooking how we feel about one another."

In return Granmère received a murderous look, and Brittany vowed, "I'll get you one of these days."

"Sure you will," Granmère said, showing no fear. But inwardly she admitted that he had gotten to her. This man had always disliked her, but never before, it seemed, with such intensity.

She discarded these thoughts and turned to Wilde, who had stopped convulsing. "Peninnah," Granmère said, "you and I used to be friends. Perhaps I was presumptuous in taking over your office. If you'd like me to move back to my old office, I'll do so."

"Don't let her sweet-talk you," Brittany growled.

"Remain in the office for the present," Wilde said, her voice weak.

"How does that helmet work?" Granmère asked. "I notice that your voice sounds normal."

"The helmet suppresses hiccup sounds," Wilde said. "I don't hear them and neither do you. Trouble is, it's experimental and no one can hear me unless I constantly work this little gizmo on the side. They say future helmets will let words out automatically."

"Your condition is common?"

"Hardly. But it's not unheard of, either." She grimaced. "We all have our roles, Liliane. At the moment, I'm a guinea pig for medical research."

"Enough!" Brittany said. "The suicide rate is going bonkers, Fouquet. I know about the plainclothesmen you stationed on the Golden Gate Bridge, on Coit Tower, and at the other popular end-it-all spots. Well, you haven't covered everything. You need more men, on every structure. This city's out of control!"

"Nonsense," Granmère said. "The mental health task force that I suggested is already starting to show results."

"He knows about that," Wilde said. "And I heard him praise you for the idea."

Brittany fired an angry glance at Wilde and shifted heavily on his feet.

"Progress!" Granmère exclaimed, looking at Brittany. "Big Jack and I agree on something! We're confined on this bubble and don't know what lies ahead. Suppose it's to be a prison, some kind of a zoo as you suggested? I hope to God it isn't that, but if it is, we can do hard time or easy time. It'll be worse if we torment ourselves and stir things up, so we'd be better off accepting it. San Francisco is a beautiful place. With ingenuity and patience, we may yet be happy."

Brittany clapped, unenthusiastically. "How idyllic," he said.

"What do you say, Big Jack?" Granmère asked. "Can we cooperate with one another?"

"Never," Brittany said, with a ferocious, hateful expression. He stalked from the office, causing the floor to shudder.

Peninnah Wilde studied Granmère. Wilde's chest convulsed several times in rapid succession. "I'll talk with him," she said, working the gray side panel. "But don't expect much."

Granmère formed an appreciative smile. But the fear of Brittany came back, for a few seconds longer than before.

Wilde struggled to her feet. "Have you spoken with your son recently?" she asked.

Granmère's head jerked involuntarily from surprise.

The women locked gazes.

"I maintain daily contact with him," Granmère said, lying. "Why do you ask?"

"According to reports, you spend almost all your waking time here, planning action on the various crises. Admirable, but I wondered if you knew that your Henry moved out of his house last Thursday. After that his wife went on a wacko binge and finally the cops took her away a couple of hours ago. Took your grandchildren, too." She studied Granmère intently for a reaction.

Granmère felt herself losing control of her facial muscles, for she hadn't heard. Her jaw was leaden. "Where did you hear these things?"

"A reporter stopped me as I was leaving the hospital. Asked me to comment, but I didn't."

"Thanks for that."

Wilde departed without another word.

*   *   *

Alone, Michelle sat on a bed in a tiny room, recalling with horror that terrible moment earlier in the day when police officers filed into her house. For a time the officer who had taken Michelle by the arm had left her alone in a police cruiser, locked in the caged rear compartment.

"I hate you, I hate you, I hate you!" Michelle had screamed, when that officer and another entered the front of the car. With both fists, she pounded on the wire screen divider.

"We're taking you to dinner," one of them said.

"I don't want anything to eat!"

The car had backed out of the driveway, which Michelle saw in her recollection from outside, as if she were one of the neighbors standing on the sidewalk. A girl in the back seat had pounded on the side windows and hurled herself against them. Her mouth formed angry words, which were unable to escape the vehicle.

Now it was evening and she was in another cage.

She had not seen the members of her family or heard of their whereabouts. No one would answer her questions, not even the matronly nurse who handed her clean clothes and escorted her to her room. She provided Michelle with drawing pencils, crayons, and paper, and these materials sat unused upon the little desk by her bed.

There were two narrow beds in the room, each neatly tucked, with faded chartreuse blankets and lumpy foam pillows. The white plasterboard walls framed a tiny, barred window above the desk, a mirror to one side of that, and, alone on one wall surface, a picture of a swan. After the nurse left and closed the door there had been an extra click, undoubtedly a lock. Michelle didn't need to try the door.

But she padded the short distance across the enclosure in her stocking feet anyway and tried to press down on the bar handle. It rattled, but no more. She shook it violently and thumped on the door.

A man yelled for her to stop.

Defiantly, Michelle continued her demonstration until she was short of breath, then delivered a final, resounding whack. At the desk she swept the art supplies away with her forearm, climbed on the desk top, and knelt there to look out the window.

It was barred on the inside, with glass or Plexiglas outside. The bars were spaced so tightly that she couldn't reach through to touch the surface beyond. She saw a dark city street, with headlighted vehicles moving back and forth, and past that an illuminated institutional structure. She counted eighteen stories, wondered if her mother, Coley, and Renney were there. What about Joseph? Had they taken him into custody, too?

Tumblers in the door slid and clicked.

Michelle turned as the door opened and felt tightness in her throat as she recognized the matronly nurse. In a spotless white jumpsuit the nurse asked, "Is everything all right, dear?"

The woman left the door ajar as she approached, and Michelle considered darting around her. But there were other doors and other locks beyond, and more people to intercept her. The building was a fortress.

The nurse was close now, with hands on hips, surveying the crayons, pencils, and paper scattered on the floor. A black and gold plastic tag on her lapel read "D. Wilson."

"What is this awful place?" Michelle asked. She climbed down from the desk, almost lost her footing on a crayon.

"Child Welfare, dear. A state agency." She studied Michelle closely, seemed to be looking at her eyelids. Michelle didn't care.

"Where's my mother?"

"I don't know. She'd be in a different department."

"How about my brothers and my little sister?"

"What are their names?"

Michelle listed them, including Joseph and Stu.

Nurse Wilson scribbled on a pad, which she tucked into a big hip pocket. "I'll see what I can find out," she said. "But before I do, I want you to clean up this mess. Those aren't ordinary crayons I brought you, young lady. They create glow-in-the-dark drawings."

"I don't want your stuff! Get everything out of here!"

Nurse Wilson grew exceedingly stern. She removed the notepad from her pocket, tore away the sheet upon which she had written, and let it flutter to the floor. "When this room is clean, we'll talk," she said.

"I hate you!" Michelle shrilled, rage consuming her face.

"You'll have three days in this room to think about what a rude little girl you are," Nurse Wilson said. She went to the door and placed a hand on the handle. "You are quarantined to see if you have any diseases."

Michelle held back tears. She kicked a pencil away, and a wave of sadness enveloped her. It seemed to her that every living creature was imprisoned, not merely herself in this circumstance. To avoid Granmère's web, Rachel shuttled between worlds that were in actuality cells of confinement. The harder she worked to avoid Granmère, the more trapped and dependent upon these worlds she became.

Granmère too, with all of her maneuverings, was ensnared by Rachel, by the webs of every person Granmère contacted and even by the webs of persons she never saw or heard of, in a great societal tangle that choked individuality. From birth, people proceeded through life as if they were primitive two-wheeled wooden cart wheels, men one disc, women the other—and in the high mud ruts of the wheels, deviants struggled to crawl free.

It was a struggle for identity and for expression—to break free of the gray, gluey amalgam of humanity. But ruts provided tremendous security, and they beckoned sirenlike, luring the free spirits to confusion, to regression, to the breeding ground of the primordial cell.

The Arionnese had torn life from that cell and enclosed it in a bubble. Michelle saw cells within cells within cells. She loathed the Arionnese and every other force that confined her.

The door clicked shut, locked.

"I'm not a little girl!" Michelle shouted.

Michelle lay in a death dream, soaked in perspiration, while a specter of herself sat on the edge of the bed. She saw Joseph on one side of the cell and their mother on the other, with Renney and Coley clinging to their mother's legs. Granmère and Henry were lined up behind Joseph, urging him on, and Joseph held a deadly energy rifle, one of the weapons that left no forensic traces. He beckoned for Michelle to come and take it, to use it against Mom.

Rachel stood boldly without a weapon, her head thrown back and her eyes a raging, burning red. She lifted a hand, fingers pointing, and the rifle flew from Joseph's grasp into hers. Would she use it, perhaps on everyone?

The images vanished.

Michelle rejoined her physical form on the bed, and as she lay supine she found herself unable to move anything except her eyes. The white textured ceiling began to ripple, and crimson light patterns danced on its surface. It became alive, a creature that moved in synchronization with Michelle's breathing. It dropped toward her and flashed color as she inhaled, dimmed and receded as she exhaled. When she held her breath, the thing stopped and darkened.

When Michelle resumed breathing, fearfully and shallowly, she noticed that the texture had melted into the surface, a surface that glistened from light deep within. Michelle felt her pulse increase. She was clammy from her neck down beneath the covers and wanted to throw them off. But she couldn't so much as twitch, as if a paralytic toxin had been administered to her.

The plastic ceiling altered to one of texture again, but now with jagged, iciclelike projections all over it. The projections dropped with heart-stopping suddenness, crashing and shattering all around without hitting her, in a riot of sound.

With her heart jackhammering against her chest, Michelle detected a film of smooth, clear plastic just beneath the ceiling, with the original ceiling texture visible through the film. The transparency dropped slowly, and peripherally Michelle saw it encase the top of an open closet door. Then it encased a floor lamp, the next tallest object in the room, and through the plastic Michelle saw the lamp enclosed in a ghostly afterbirth.

She panicked.

The film was only centimeters from her face, about to enclose and smother her. She held her breath but the thing continued its dreadful descent, and slime caressed her face. It slid from her nose, forehead, and cheeks down the sides and front to her neck. Her heart raced and pounded with a frenzy and power that seemed capable of bursting through all confinement, including the plastic. Then her body engine decelerated, sputtered, and stopped. A scream began to build, from the most primitive region of her soul.

She had been offered a choice by Joseph and his cohorts. She had hesitated and now she was gone. But something remained. An embryo, a germ, a speck, a spark of her thoughts. It was a submicroscopic, glowing ember.

The ember suddenly became large, as if inhaled upon from the other end of a cigarette, and the spark of an electrical impulse coursed through Michelle's cells, regenerating them.

In a burst of energy, Michelle sat up and stumbled from the bed, flailing her arms, her legs rubbery. She tripped over the bedding and fell to her knees. The suppressed scream sounded, into a razor's edge of primal sound that cut the remaining threat away and ricocheted from the walls.

She expected someone to order her to be quiet, and for a time knelt shivering in her sweat in the center of the room, awaiting a hostile voice. None came, and she became permeated with the most acute, desolate stillness she had ever known. She was simultaneously at the heart of the habitat, and outside it in the frozen vastness of space.

TWENTY-TWO

The idea of suicide, once germinated in a person's mind, tends to eat through other thoughts. Even worse, it's contagious.

—From a report by Granmère's mental health task force

When Michelle awoke from the tangle of blankets on the floor, she lay a while staring at the ceiling, watching reflected sunlight patterns as the sun and its court of clouds altered position outside her barred window.

"Good morning, Miss Fouquet," a sonorous voice said, from her right.

Michelle sat up with a start, looked in that direction.

It sat on the extra bed in the room, in a gray uniform with battle ribbons and a soiled officer's cap. With four legs arranged neatly out of the way and bent from front to sides, it utilized two shorter pincer-fitted legs that emanated from just beneath the neck as if they were arms and hands, and doffed its cap. The face was hideous, with ciliated yellow thorns and hooks, a pair of antennae and tiny red eyes, all set against an exceedingly small head.

Michelle scuttled to the farthest corner of the room and hid behind her blanket, which she took with her.

"I'm General Pierre Gustave Toutant Beauregard," the creature announced. "You've no reason to fear me. I've lived in your house for two years more than your eleven. We're family, you and I."

Michelle peeked around the edge of her blanket.

"I'm here to help you, Miss, but before your hopes rise too high I must emphasize my limitations. I can do little more than console you and make myself available as your friend. That's infinitely important in the scheme of things, of course, be they physical or spiritual. Might we be friends?"

Michelle didn't reply.

"Would it help if I said 'please'?"

Michelle shook her head, but she lowered the blanket, just a little.

"That hurts my feelings. Do you want to see a grown flea cry?"

Michelle shook her head again.

"Then we *can* be friends?"

"Yes." Michelle's voice, already tiny with trepidation, was further muffled by the blanket held in front of her mouth.

"Good," General Beauregard said.

"Why haven't you ever spoken with me before?" Michelle queried.

"I saw no need to, until Stu set in motion a chain of events that forced my hand." He held a claw up, smiled at having misspoken. "I am a rather curious apparition, even by the liberal standards of the Spiricosm, that dimension I call home."

"Have you spoken with my mother?"

"Not recently. She's precarious now, and my presence could make her worse. She's undergoing surgery, having a medicinal injector installed in her abdomen. If the device functions as it should, you won't have to worry about her taking pills anymore."

Michelle thought for a few seconds, said, "You're a flea, *and* an American Civil War general?"

"Permit my explanation. I'm a Wandering Spirit, and one day while I was between positions I became careless and let my hazy self become visible to your mother, who happened to be nearby listening to a cassette history of the Civil War. It takes energy to maintain invisibility and matterlessness, you realize. One thing led to another in her mind, and before I could vanish she pointed at me and exclaimed that I was the tormented spirit of a Confederate general who had experienced a number of battlefield difficulties. Later your brother Joseph heard the tale from his mother and he embellished it, just as he told you. I became a seven-foot flea among my other purported attributes, inhabiting the filthiest region on Earth."

"You weren't any of those things, really?"

"Spirits aren't the remnants of people, fleas, or any other life forms and never were. That's a serious misconception among your kind. We are separate beings, not leftovers at all, and we inhabit a fold in space that is mostly separate from your own. There are overlappings which I've learned to utilize, and that is why you are able to observe and converse with me now."

"Why do you look like you do?"

Beauregard laughed, a cavernous sound. "You're jumping ahead! Chil-

dren must learn patience. I know you think you're not a child, but you are.
I must tell you that."

Michelle sighed.

"Your General Beauregard has no spirit whatsoever. When he died he
ceased to exist, and that was all there was of him." The flea gesticulated
with a pincer "arm," as if discarding something over his shoulder.

"I have always been and I always will be," Beauregard continued. "I am
but one of jillions all over the universe. Spirits have individual personalities
and quirks, just as humans do. Most spirits don't want anything to do with
humans, and I'm sure the reverse is true as well. I, on the other hand, have
always associated myself with people, particularly human people. I am fond
of watching your kind and participating in their lives. After your mother
noticed my haze and personified it, I hung around your household in invisibility, as an observer."

Michelle felt a chill in her back. She straightened and rolled her shoulders to relax, letting the blanket settle to her lap.

"Your birth was a particularly happy moment, Michelle. During your
first hours of life outside the womb your mother swaddled you in a blanket
and held you on her belly. She didn't do that with any of the other children, not even Renney, I believe because of tension and unhappiness. By
chance you were born at a comparatively serene time in her life, when she
and your father were getting along and your paternal grandmother was off
on an extended holiday, before Liliane decided to re-enter public life."

"That fits," Michelle said, feeling suddenly at ease conversing with a flea.
"I heard Granmère retired at the age of sixty-five, took an interplanetary
vacation, and then found she was bored stiff. My mother holding me like
that. Do you suppose it's why I feel so close to her?"

"Partly. But human relationships are curious and infinitely tangled. No
one thing can be traced as the source of any sense of relationship. Your
mother and Renney are close for an entirely unique set of reasons, some of
which overlap to your life."

"Mom loves Renney more than me."

"On the surface it may seem that way to you. I don't think so, though.
Not deep inside, where she ticks. She's terribly troubled and doesn't always
display her love skillfully. Sharing love is a skill, you realize. It must be
worked at, perfected."

"I'd never thought of it that way, but I can see where you're probably
right."

"Oh, I'm right, without doubt. I've also made a study of human legends, from abominable snowmen to ghosts to leprechauns. These are the stuff of the human imagination, a source of limitless amusement for me and for a small group of my associates. We enjoy becoming the materializations of legends that we hear about. It keeps our lives interesting, which is a considerable challenge when you're condemned to live forever, as we are."

"You're a prisoner, too."

He smiled with his little flea mouth, a mouth as small as Coley's, which was remarkable on a creature so tall. "I suppose I am," he said.

He gave no inkling of understanding the layers of meaning she saw, and she didn't elaborate. There would be opportunity for that later, if they were to be friends.

She asked him if he was as tall as her Uncle Paul. He said he wasn't in his present state but that he could make himself a thousand times as tall if he wished to do so.

"Your legend specified seven feet," Beauregard said. "And your Uncle Paul is a bit taller than that."

"No problem," Michelle said, and she smiled.

"The famous legends don't attract me," Beauregard said. "I travel the back roads, so to speak. I used to listen in at scout campfires to the stories they told. If I took a liking to a tale, I became the monstrous apparition described in it, and scared the bajoobies out of the kids. They loved it and returned for more, because you see that's why they went to the campfire in the first place—to be frightened."

"This is all pretty amazing," Michelle said. "I'm beginning to wonder if you're just another fantasy of mine."

"I just explained that. I'm your mother's fantasy, and Joseph's."

"No, I mean like if I were nuts or something and none of this were real."

"Oh it's real," Beauregard assured her. "As real as anything." He didn't explain to her what he meant by that last phrase.

Michelle heard voices outside, hoped no one would come to her door. They passed, and the voices diminished.

Beauregard scratched his thorax, said, "The legend of a Civil War general intertwined with that of a giant flea was too much to resist. I compliment your family on its creativity."

"Do you really inhabit closets at our place?" Michelle asked, her eyes wide. "I mean, I didn't used to believe in you, and I've got this secret place in a closet where I like to spend a lot of time."

"I've spent a goodly amount of time in that very closet."

"If I'd known that, I'd never have opened the door! You're nice now that I'm getting to know you, but I'd have been afraid!"

"Come over and touch me, child. I'm not going to harm you."

Timidly, with her knees and hands shaking, Michelle crossed the room, to the flea that towered high over her when she stood next to it, even though it was sitting down. She reached out, and with the faintest, most flitting touch, felt the cilia on the side of his horrible face. It was fuzzy.

"Shouldn't my hand have gone right through you?" she asked.

He smiled gently, patiently, and Michelle wasn't afraid at all anymore. "Oh, the misconceptions under which you labor! I feel real to you, but on the other hand, or should I say the other pincer, watch this." He reached out and passed a pincer through Michelle's arm, then withdrew the pincer. "You see? You have no substance to us!"

"How can that be?"

Bo shrugged. "You expect me to know everything? It's why I can only scare people for you, unless I place dangerous objects in their path, which I wouldn't want to do. It wouldn't be sporting. If I'm fair, and my nagging creed requires it, I can't get physical with humans, although your kind can knock me silly."

"I could knock you silly?"

"Woefully, you could. You'd have to mind my thorns and hooks, of course, and the best way to do that is to smack me with something. I shouldn't tell you this, but a baseball bat can send me flying. Rocks are nasty, too."

"It doesn't make sense."

"Nevertheless that's the way of it. I've been pounded more than once by humans, either accidentally or because they didn't fear me enough. It's no picnic sometimes, let me tell you. Fortunately, or unfortunately, as I suggested before, I can't be killed, even by the most vicious human attack. I always heal."

"And that's how you got into this room? You can pass right through manmade objects, too?"

He nodded. "As long as it's not in motion attacking me, I can move into and out of anything in your universe. Even people, so long as the impetus is mine and I remain invisible. Once they see me and become upset, it becomes pretty involved."

Michelle frowned, and was about to ask about something when he produced the very answer she wanted.

"After Stu frightened Renney with fake acid," Bo said, "I entered your mother's form and made myself seen only by Stu. It's a neat trick we have, and made him think your mother was General Beauregard. It worked effectively, as the prankish little twit hasn't been seen around your place since."

"Then he's alive? She didn't murder him?"

"He's fine. Rather cold some nights living in the streets, but he's surviving. I look in on him from time to time, considering his blood relationship with your family."

"Stu wasn't so bad," she said. "There were good things about him."

"Kind, kind Michelle, always searching for the good in everyone."

Michelle recalled Stu's screams about General Beauregard and a sword. "Your sword couldn't have cut Stu, then?" she asked.

"That's a very complex subject. Generally speaking, I could not have cut him with the weapon *at my impetus*. But what is the definition of impetus? Isn't the very creation of an object an act of impetus? As I told you, I could create dangerous objects and leave them in the way of humans, to cause harm. My kind can do this. But I can't employ the weapon. For example, I could swing the sword but it would do no harm. I could pull the trigger of a gun, but the bullet would fly harmlessly into another dimension."

"Strange."

"There's kind of a loophole there, you see. The sword held in front of Stu where he might cut himself . . . a bomb placed but not activated, leaving that task to others."

"If you activated the bomb, it would blow off in another dimension?"

"Precisely. But if you activated it, kaboom and goodbye! With the sword I was extremely careful, for Stu's sake."

Michelle thought this over. Then: "I understand why you dealt with Stu, but what you did was instrumental in the breakup of my mother and father. They got in a terrible argument."

"Your mother would have chased Stu off anyway, and the boy with his pride wouldn't have returned. I merely gave in to an urging of mine and instilled a little extra fear in him. He's a hardy kid and can take care of himself."

"He did say he's lived in the streets before. At times when I talked with him, it seemed he preferred that life."

"Your mother and father were overdue for a rumble themselves, even without the emergence of Stu. Your father's a tired man from all he's had to bear, and your mother's had her fill of medicines and doctors. She feels violated."

"And now they're cutting her open. How will she feel about that?"

"Not happy in her most private thoughts, if she can achieve them when drugged."

"What will she do?"

Bo shrugged.

"I have something to confess to you," he said. "Something important."

She looked at him inquisitively.

"Several days before your grandfather died you were in a closet . . . with his book and the puzzle box. Words came to you on a green mist . . . words that foretold his apparent death."

"You know about that? Yes, of course, you can see things like that happening."

"I . . . I didn't just *see* that event. I participated in it. Your grandfather didn't say those things to you . . . I did."

Michelle went to her mouth, exclaimed, "My God!"

She felt as if the floor had opened beneath her. Beauregard's words rang terribly and horribly true, reinforcing what she had known in her heart for some time.

Granpère was dead.

"I saw that he was dying," Bo said, "and I tried to soften the blow. I was afraid you couldn't handle the added stress and wanted to provide you with something you could hold onto. I had planned to speak to you from time to time in your grandfather's voice, but hadn't worked out how I would tell you the truth, or if I ever would. Then when I saw you in this cell in such a miserable state, I had to reveal myself to you and become your friend. As a friend, I couldn't maintain that lie."

In her blind, crying rage she struck Beauregard on the face before he could elude her for her own protection, and she cut the side of her hand on one of the insect thorns embedded there.

Bo settled her down with consoling words, and with a bandage that he produced magically he covered her cut, utilizing his clawlike pincers with remarkable dexterity.

"I'm sorry I hit you," Michelle said. "I understand."

They hugged one another, very carefully.

Michelle felt a strange sensation of relief that at last she knew the fate of her grandfather.

Beauregard spoke in the background of her awareness, promising that he would try to frighten away anyone who bothered her.

It was nice to have a new friend, Michelle thought. He might be handy against the nurse if she came back yelling, or against Granmère.

Michelle made him promise not to appear unless she called for him, and they developed a whistle signal he said he could always hear.

"After all I'm not a baby," Michelle told him, "and it's better that I work some matters out for myself."

"As you wish," Beauregard said. And with that he vanished.

A sign on the door said to press a button by the light switch if she had to use the bathroom, and when Michelle pressed the button, the area by the wall mirror became a little curtained-off lavatory, with a toilet and a sink.

She washed her face in warm water, and in illumination from three bright yellow globes above the mirror she looked at her face. She saw a dozen stubble hairs along one upper eyelid, half that number on the other upper lid, and a number of fine blond hairs she hadn't noticed still in place along both lower lids. Bo hadn't said anything about her eyes. She touched one of the fine blond hairs with her forefinger but didn't pluck the hair.

I don't want to be ugly, she thought.

From the mayoral office Granmère gazed through the golden Italian balusters of Peninnah Wilde's balcony, past the financial district towers to the suspension section of the Bay Bridge, where sailboats plied nearby waters. Puffy dark clouds skittered over the bay and the cities to the east, like bombers in search of targets for their loads of moisture.

Rain death, rain life. She caught a tangential thought, flung it aside. A person in her position had no time for daydreams.

General Oso's military helicopter had just flown within her field of view, and like a fly landing on her head had set down on the City Office Tower helipad three floors above her. He had called her at home to set up the appointment and had not explained his unavailability during the two days she'd tried to reach him.

There was a tap at the door, and Granmère said, "Enter."

Oso carried a thick folder of papers into the office, placed them in front of her, and said he needed Granmère to sign them. She saw his gaze flicker in the direction of the windows along the outside wall.

Granmère touched a desk button to draw the drapes.

Quickly, he set up his sicom on her desk and keyed: "ACT LIKE YOU'RE READING AND SIGNING."

Granmère opened the folder and fanned the edge of the stack with her thumb. With the exception of the top sheet, designated *Military-Civilian Agencies*, all the pages were blank.

"I'll have to study these," she said, playing along.

"As you wish."

"WHERE HAVE YOU BEEN?" Granmère keyed. "I'VE BEEN TRYING TO

REACH YOU FOR TWO DAYS AND YOUR STAFF WOULDN'T TELL ME ANY-
THING. DON'T YOU KNOW THERE HAVE BEEN DEATH THREATS AGAINST
ME?"

"I KNOW ALL ABOUT IT, AND MY PEOPLE HAVE TIGHTENED SECURITY
AROUND YOU. WE'VE MADE PRESS RELEASES ON YOUR BEHALF TOO, IN-
FORMING THE PUBLIC THAT YOU AREN'T COLLABORATING WITH THE AL-
IENS, THAT THOSE ARE VICIOUS RUMORS. WE PHRASED THEM IN SUCH A
WAY AS NOT TO IRRITATE THE ARIONNESE, OF COURSE."

"I'VE SEEN THE RELEASES, AND THEY'RE FINE."

"I'VE BEEN IN SELF-IMPOSED CONFINEMENT THE LAST TWO DAYS," Oso
keyed, "SPEAKING WITH MY JAPANESE ANCESTORS. THEY'VE BEEN COUN-
SELING ME."

"DON'T GIVE ME A BUNCH OF MALARKEY, OSO. I HAVEN'T GOT THE
TIME.."

"MY ANCESTORS TOLD ME TO COME HERE, TO YOU. I HAD PLANNED TO
BETRAY YOU."

Granmère's eyes widened. From his expression, he seemed to be near
tears.

He continued: "I HAVE AN ESCAPE CRAFT, CAPABLE OF TRAVERSING VAST
DISTANCES. IT'S AN UNPUBLICIZED *IPASA DESIGN, WITH A TOP SPEED OF
APPROXIMATELY 1/5 THAT OF THIS HABITAT. THE CRAFT'S NAME HAS AL-
WAYS BEEN *HOPE*, AND IT SEEMS APPROPRIATE. IF IT CAN REACH EARTH,
AND *HOPE*'S ONBOARD COMPUTER SYSTEM INDICATES IT MAY BARELY
MAKE IT, THE RETURN TRIP WOULD TAKE APPROXIMATELY 117 EARTH
DAYS."

"I DIDN'T KNOW WE HAD TECHNOLOGY LIKE THAT."

"YES. WE'VE HAD MONKEYS AND EVEN PEOPLE ON JOURNEYS BEYOND
THE MILKY WAY. SEVENTEEN DAYS WAS THE LONGEST HUMAN TRIP SO
FAR, AND FINDING NO LIFE ON THE PLANETS VISITED, IT SEEMED POINT-
LESS TO GO FURTHER."

"POINTLESS? THERE IS LIFE ON DISTANT WORLDS, AS THESE ARIONNESE
PROVE."

"THEY'RE THE FIRST PROOF I KNOW OF. *HOPE* IS ONE OF 14 SHIPS,
ISSUED TO THE COMMANDER IN CHIEF AND TO KEY MILITARY AND CIVIL-
IAN PERSONNEL. IT'S THE ONLY ONE ON THIS HABITAT."

"WHY THE HELL DIDN'T YOU GIVE IT TO ME SOONER? OR AT LEAST

* IPASA: Interplanetary Aeronautics & Space Association

INFORM ME? WE MIGHT HAVE DISPATCHED SOMEONE WITH WORD OF WHAT HAPPENED."

General Oso keyed: "I CONSIDERED THAT, AND DECIDED WE WERE BETTER OFF NOT EMPLOYING THE CRAFT UNTIL WE GOT TO WHEREVER THEY'RE TAKING US. IF I'D MADE AN ATTEMPT FOR EARTH TOO EARLY— OR SENT SOMEONE—NO ONE ON EARTH COULD HAVE TRACKED THE HABITAT. THESE ARIONNESE ARE TRICKY. THEY'VE CHANGED COURSE 18 TIMES TO MY KNOWLEDGE. ARIONN IS IN VIEW NOW, AND *HOPE* HAS THE COORDINATES LOCKED INTO ITS COMPUTER. NOW'S THE TIME TO LAUNCH *HOPE* FOR HELP. WITH A LITTLE LUCK, A RESCUE FORCE CAN BE SENT FROM EARTH, WITH ARMIES IN LARGER SHIPS OF SIMILAR DESIGN."

"YOU WERE GOING TO TAKE THE SHIP YOURSELF, AT THE OPPORTUNE MOMENT?"

"I WAS, AND I FEEL GREAT SHAME."

"YOU'RE TURNING THE KEYS OVER TO ME?"

"IN A SENSE. THE SHIP IS VOICE-ACTIVATED, WITH RESPECT TO ITS ALTER EGO, THAT IS. IT'S CAMOUFLAGED TO LOOK AND FUNCTION LIKE AN ORDINARY MILITARY HELICOPTER. I FLEW IT HERE TODAY, IN FACT, AND IT'S ON THE ROOF BESIDE YOUR HELICOPTERS. TO ACTIVATE *HOPE'S* ALTER EGO, SIMPLY SIT IN THE COMMAND CHAIR AND UTTER THE WORDS, 'HOPE. DESTINATION EARTH.' PARTS UNNECESSARY TO SPACE TRAVEL WILL METAMORPHOSE, FALL AWAY, OR SLIDE OFF ALONG INTERNAL CHUTES THAT DUMP OUTSIDE, AND IT WILL BECOME AN ENTIRELY DIFFERENT SORT OF CRAFT. EVERYTHING IS AUTOMATIC ONCE YOU'VE SPOKEN THOSE WORDS."

"CAN *HOPE* BE LAUNCHED WITHOUT ANYONE ABOARD?"

"UNFORTUNATELY, NO. PERHAPS MODIFICATIONS COULD BE MADE, BUT WE DARE NOT ATTEMPT THEM. SECRECY IS PARAMOUNT."

"YOU'RE LEAVING IT WITH ME NOW?"

"YES. MILITARY EQUIPMENT AND PERSONNEL HAVE BEEN AT YOUR DISPOSAL FOR SOME TIME NOW, SO NOTHING WILL APPEAR AMISS IF I RETURN BY ANOTHER ROUTE, ACTING AS IF I HAD BUSINESS ELSEWHERE IN SAN FRANCISCO. YOU SHOULD ARRANGE FOR *HOPE'S* IMMEDIATE USE."

Granmère nodded.

General Oso continued: "HOPE'S COMPUTER TELLS ME THE HEAVILY ARMORED SHIP CAN RAM THROUGH THE HABITAT DOME, AND THAT THE HOLE WILL BE SEALED BY CHEMICALS THAT *HOPE* WILL SPRAY. THE SHIP IS MARVELOUSLY ADAPTABLE."

He paused and decided against comparing this for her with the ST88 leverage craft that Joseph would employ on his mission. Granmère had said she didn't want to know about that.

"WOULDN'T THE ARIONNESE HAVE THEIR OWN SEALING SYSTEM?" Granmère asked.

"HOPE THINKS SO, BUT ISN'T CERTAIN. FROM A SPECTRAL ANALYSIS OF THE DOME, HOPE KNOWS WHAT IT'S MADE OF. THE HOLE WON'T BE VERY LARGE, YOU KNOW."

"OKAY."

"ONCE FREE OF THE HABITAT, HOPE WILL HEAD OFF IN THE WRONG DIRECTION FOR THREE EARTH HOURS, MAKING ANY ALIENS IN PURSUIT THINK THE SHIP IS EITHER CONFUSED OR POSES NO THREAT. MAYBE THEY'LL LET IT GO, NOT TAKING THE TROUBLE TO REEL IT IN. OR MAYBE WE'LL CATCH THEM BY SURPRISE AND GET OUT OF SIGHT BEFORE THEY CAN PURSUE. IN ALL OUR SCANS, WE'VE LOCATED ONLY ONE ARIONNESE SHIP, AND IT'S MOUNTED IN THE APEX OF THE HABITAT BUBBLE AS A WEATHER CONTROL STATION. HOPE HAS ENOUGH WATER AND FOOD ABOARD FOR AN ETERNITY, WITH THE RECYCLING SYSTEM EMPLOYED. THERE ARE SEATS AND BUNKS FOR A CREW OF FIVE. THE FUEL PELLETS ARE CRIMIDUX JEWELS. YOU'VE HEARD OF THEM?"

Granmère shook her head.

"A HIGHLY COMPRESSED NATURAL SUBSTANCE, MINED IN A SECRET U.S.-HELD ASTEROID BELT. WHEN SPRINKLED WITH AMMONIUM CHLO-RATE AND INSERTED IN A SPINNING FUEL CHAMBER, THE STUFF BURNS INTENSELY AND LOSES ONLY MICROSCOPIC AMOUNTS OF MASS IN THE PROCESS."

Granmère considered asking him for the names of three hardy individuals for the Earth attempt, then surprised herself with a feeling that she'd like to go too.

Don't be a fool, she thought. *You're seventy-eight years old!*

"I ALMOST FAILED IN MY DUTY," Oso keyed. "TO YOU, TO THE PEOPLE OF THIS HABITAT, TO MY ANCESTORS. SUCH SHAME I FEEL! THIS MESSAGE CONSTITUTES MY RESIGNATION."

"I REFUSE TO ACCEPT IT."

General Oso didn't comment on this, and he didn't meet her gaze. He bowed curtly, gathered up the folder of papers, and left, leaving his sicom behind.

Granmère wondered how many other surprises this enigmatic little man had for her. She wanted to bring him back and interrogate him. Maybe she would do that, on another day.

*   *   *

The intercom made a crackling sound, followed by the appointment secretary's erudite voice.

"Your son is here to see you, Madame Mayor. Shall I send him in?"

"Tell him to make an appointment!" Granmère snapped into her desk microphone.

"He says it's extremely urgent."

"Just what I don't need, another problem." She sighed. "Very well. But it'll have to be fast."

Henry entered unshaven, in a rumpled ParSell uniform, and stood before her with his cap in his hands. She detected anguish in his expression, especially around the eyes and mouth.

"What is it, Henri?" she queried.

"Rachel's undergoing surgery. An implant to give her medicine automatically. We don't have to worry about her spells anymore, but still the Child Welfare Society says there may be problems with us getting the kids back. They say that even when Rachel took her medication she never cared for the kids."

"And that's news to you?"

"Kind of, yeah. I thought . . . Well, I don't know what I thought." He struggled to keep his enunciation crisp.

"You had blinders on, Henri. Are you finally getting rid of that woman?"

Henry scowled.

"If you do, I have a trust fund that would pay for a housekeeper and a nanny. The children could even attend private schools, where they'd learn their French and proper manners."

"I don't want your trust fund! I'm here to ask for your help, and I don't mean help wrecking my marriage. I love the woman!"

"You don't love her. You're just stubborn, against whatever I want for you."

"What do you know about love, anyway?"

"Don't speak to your mother like that!"

"I need your help, *Maman*. If you'll sign a custody form with me, they say they'll release the kids to us. If you don't do it, the kids will be split up and placed with foster parents. We'll hardly ever see them."

Granmère shook her head. "This too? Why me, Lord?"

"You've gotta come with me right now down to Child Welfare. They say you have to show up in person."

"I have enough problems without getting involved in this."

"You're already involved."

"You're blaming me for Rachel's being loony? That woman's been off key since the day she was born. You've never listened to me, especially when it comes to her."

Henry smiled winsomely, but with sadness in the eyes. "Love does that to a fella, I guess," he said. "Look, I'm not blaming you. I'm just saying that you're involved because you're part of this family. I'm asking for your help."

"All right, but let's leave Renney with Child Welfare. He isn't your son anyway, so you have no responsibility for him. One less child will make the whole thing easier to handle."

Granmère saw shock in Henry's expression, and he thought for a moment before saying, "Rachel would never tolerate that. No, I can't go along with that."

"Have them dope her up so that she doesn't know the difference."

"What a thing to say! You don't think she'd notice her own kid missing, her favorite? I could never do that to her. Besides, all that talk about Rachel running around while I was in the service is . . . well . . . I think . . . I think she was faithful to me. Renney looks a lot like Granpère, if you look at him from the right angle."

"Gilbert and Rachel? How preposterous!"

"That's not what I meant. Features sometimes skip a generation. Renney could be mine and not look like me at all."

"Preposterous!" But secretly Granmère admitted to herself that she had noticed the resemblance between Renney and Gilbert.

"All right," she said. "I'll sign with you for all the children."

"Whoopee!" Henry said.

Granmère heard distant gunfire, and the chop of helicopters. She wanted to throw open the drapes and look outside, but suppressed the urge. In the presence of others she would behave will all decorum and tranquility.

"What's goin' on out there?" Henry asked.

"Let me worry about that," Granmère said. "Wait in the outer office, and I'll rearrange my schedule. It may be several hours before I can get away."

In the child welfare facility, Michelle had undergone nearly three days of quarantine, during which she was screened for disease. Finally she was let out of her room and could mix with the other girls, aged eight and up. They were overall a tough lot, and it was in the caged outdoor play yard that she began to encounter them. In a walk around the perimeter of the cage, she saw the girls playing kickball, basketball, and four-square, with no shortage of arguments. A fight broke out, and two nurses rushed over to break it up. Here and there Michelle saw girls who didn't participate in games and who looked more worn than hardened.

Michelle counted herself among this minority, and for a time she studied the outsiders, considering which of them she might approach. It might help to converse with someone after those days in virtual solitude. But it struck her that she didn't want to discuss her problems, and that others like her were likely to feel the same way.

So she stood holding fast to the wire fence with both hands, peering into an adjacent unoccupied playground like hers. This second area adjoined a flat-roofed four-story building nearly identical to hers, and from somewhere she heard the din of childrens' voices, growing louder. Then she saw them, streaming out onto the separate playground, all boys. Frantically she searched faces, much as a person might do at a spaceport when relatives were arriving from a journey.

She located Renney before he saw her, and she waved. It became obvious that he was looking for her too, and when she yelled his name he saw her and ran to the fence separating them. They smiled bravely at one another and locked fingers through the openings.

"Do you know where Mom is?" Renney asked. Then fear crossed his face, as he looked at something behind Michelle.

Before Michelle could reply or turn around, a stinging slap hit her on the tops of her hands. Her face contorted into a hateful mask, Michelle looked back and up at her attacker.

It was Nurse Wilson, squinting and scowling. "Get away from there!" she rasped. "No reaching or talking through the wire."

Michelle gripped her brother's fingers harder, forcing Wilson to pry their fingers apart.

Another nurse, equally crusty, led Renney away from his side of the fence and compelled him to remain by the boys' building, where he sat on the asphalt in dejection.

After Nurse Wilson withdrew to continue her wicked duties elsewhere, Michelle saw for a split second the specter of Beauregard.

"I'm here," he whispered. "And I'm going to scare that woman for you."

"Don't do that!" Michelle whispered.

"Why not? She deserves that as a minimum, the crunkledotty. That's a Spiricosm insult, handy when I'm enraged."

"Remember our agreement. I'll call you if I need you."

"Well, I think you're being foolish, and I'm going to make her scream.

Incidentally, your eyelashes are growing back, and they're starting to look very nice."

"You scare that nurse and I won't talk to you ever again! I want my family back together, not a lot of frightened people running in all directions. Can't you see what's important to me?"

"I'm helpless to do much for you."

"All right, if you must frighten someone make it Granmère."

"But I rather like your grandmother."

"What? After all she's done to Mom?"

"Liliane might have been more sensitive, but she had her reasons."

"She's a cruel, heartless old . . ."

"She loves you very much, Michelle."

"I don't want to discuss this! Go scare the nurse if you must, but stay away from me! I'm still mad at you for lying to me about Granpère."

"Very well."

There was a powerful rush of wind, and girls between Michelle and Nurse Wilson had their hair and dresses blown wildly. Then Nurse Wilson emitted a chilling scream and ran into the building, followed by a hazy, swirling mist.

It was nearly dinner time, and Michelle had been confined to her room for an enforced nap by the attendant who replaced Nurse Wilson, a younger woman by the name of Nurse Danielle. Unfortunately for Michelle, this one was nearly as stiff as the other. Danielle seemed to be the new nurse's last name, for that was the way they did things here on nametags. But to Michelle it sounded like a first name, and as the girl grasped for positive things to think about she decided that the name had a casual, friendly ring to it. Maybe this one wouldn't be so bad after all.

Nothing had been said to Michelle about what happened to Wilson, so Michelle seemed to be in the clear on that incident. She felt that she should feel pleasure about what her new friend Beauregard had done for her, but even with all her struggle to think positive thoughts she felt emotionally deadened, too depressed even to enjoy the derailment of a tormenter.

Michelle didn't want a nap, and resented the regimentation of this place. She sat in the desk chair, having spun the chair around so that she faced the door. She would scream at anyone daring to enter.

Unseen by Michelle, two girls were fighting in the corridor outside her room, and a male attendant exclaimed, "Grab her! She's got a knife!"

A scuffle ensued, apparently without serious injury, and after a good deal of cursing and thrashing the corridor grew quiet. This left only vehicle noises from the street between her and the building where she guessed they had her mother, and soon even those sounds faded. She retreated inwardly.

Michelle had long blamed her grandmother for Rachel's mental infirmities, but now a fragment of information from Michelle's memory flashed in front of her, something Joseph told her when she was five or six. Michelle hadn't considered it since she had heard it, and now it seemed to explain in part why Joseph didn't blame Granmère for Rachel's condition. Rachel had been mentally bruised before she ever met Granmère, so any pressure might have sent Rachel careening into her private worlds.

Beauregard rather liked Granmère.

Rachel's mother, Eileen Sullivan, had been an alcoholic who died in Michelle's infancy without leaving even the imprint of a face in Michelle's memory. Grandma Sullivan had borne a child, a boy, five years before Rachel. He had died at seven of an incurable virus, but Rachel's mother blamed the doctors and vowed after her son's death that she would never visit one again. During this emotional upheaval, the unfortunate woman entered the fold of one of the offshoots of Christianity that castigated and boycotted the medical profession.

Fearful that misfortune would strike her only remaining child, Eileen Sullivan doted on Rachel. She called Rachel "Babe," and so dominated every facet of the girl's life that Rachel wasn't permitted to make even the slightest decision on her own. The rules were endless and overwhelming, with rigorous penalties for disobedience.

Rachel had the misfortune of being a sickly, rather awkward and clumsy child, and this resulted in a number of traumatic incidents where she didn't receive competent medical care. One of the worst occurred when Rachel broke her arm and her mother set it. Believing the arm wasn't healing properly a month later, Eileen Sullivan broke it again and reset it. She repeated this the following month. According to Joseph, Rachel screamed in agony during these procedures, carried out without anesthesia, and as a result Rachel had nightmares about them.

Joseph knew these things but still took sides against Mom. Maybe with all the events that had occurred in recent years he had suppressed the memories, like Michelle.

Michelle realized now that, despite all Rachel had been through, both her arms appeared normal, and Michelle wondered if she had some of the facts wrong. Might Rachel have broken a hand, a finger, or even a leg? She did walk with a sort of indolent shuffle that might not be the result of indolence at all.

This story surfaced with such force that Michelle wondered how much more lay deep within her memory. What, if anything, would emerge next, and would she be able to rely on the information? Should she relate it to her mother's psychologists, or would they lose it in a data bank somewhere, deciding it was easier to medicate her?

Invariably people did the easy thing, damn them.

And if she mentioned this to Joseph would he laugh at her, saying she had the story all wrong?

Had Michelle originated it in a dream or fantasy of her own, and if so what did that bode for her? This question disturbed Michelle and made her want to keep her mouth shut.

The door opened abruptly, scattering Michelle's concentration and throwing harsh corridor light on her.

"Your mother and father are here to pick you up," Nurse Danielle said. "Come with me. Why weren't you lying down? It's naptime."

"I'm leaving this place?" Michelle asked.

"You are."

"Then I don't have to follow your stupid rules or answer your stupid questions!" Michelle brought forth her most vicious smile, a smile of Great Revenge against everyone who had ever done hurtful things to her family.

"Such an insolent puppy!" the nurse exclaimed. She gathered Michelle's clothes that had been brought in by a social worker and placed them in a black plastic Child Welfare Society suitcase from the closet.

Nurse Danielle led Michelle through two narrow corridors into a long, wide hallway and thence to a nurse's station at one end where Michelle had to stand before an identity scanning machine.

Michelle wanted to skip the remaining procedures, so she could forget the entire episode as quickly as possible. Her mother and father were picking her up!

Reaching the lobby, Michelle saw her father and darted away from Nurse Danielle into his arms.

"Hi, Angel," he said, and the familiar voice, while strained, warmed Michelle.

The nurse placed the suitcase on the floor and departed.

Michelle took inventory of the people gathered around her: Renney, Coley, and Granmère. From a distance, three armed men in tan and blue NAS uniforms watched intently.

Noticing the focus of Michelle's attention, Granmère said, "They insist on going everywhere with me now. It's all the social unrest. What a nuisance!"

Michelle hugged her sister and brother, then looked imploringly up at her father and asked, "Where's Mom? They said Mom was here too."

"She's recovering from surgery," Henry said. "Everything's going to be all right after this."

"You're staying with me tonight," Granmère said. "I'll take care of you."

"You're not my mother!" Michelle howled. "They said my mother was here! You killed my mother!"

"She's not dead, child," Granmère said in a kindly tone that rang false to Michelle. Granmère placed a hand on Michelle's shoulder.

Michelle pulled away. "Yes, she is! You're lying to me! Everyone's lying to me!"

"Your mother will be home soon," Henry said. "She just needs a little time to recover."

Michelle's eyes lit up. "Honest?"

"Honest," Henry assured her.

Granmère again placed her hand on Michelle's shoulder, and this time Michelle let it remain. Aside from everything else in a complex maze of interrelationships and conflicts, Granmère was, in her limited way, a mother figure to Michelle. The girl disliked admitting this, but it was true nonetheless.

"Whatever can I do to cheer you up?" Granmère asked, in a gentle tone that didn't irritate Michelle.

"Get me back my mommy," Michelle said.

"Your mother is not well, dear."

With these words Michelle knew that her grandmother hadn't changed. She was merely glossing over the unpleasantness, packaging it like a skillful, deceiving politician.

Michelle slid away to her father's side. He reeked of perspiration, cigars, and unwashed clothes, but these were welcome odors, far removed from the lifeless, institutionalized sterility into which she had been shunted.

Accompanied by Granmère's guards, who traveled in a separate helicopter, the family ate dinner at a French restaurant and then went to Granmère's house, where she gave the children baths and settled them snugly under comforters in Henry's old bedroom. The children shared their father's big old mahogany French provincial bed, with Coley in the middle between Renney and Michelle.

Granmère said something about hiring a housekeeper to help Henry. Then, saying her work couldn't wait, she rushed off to her office.

*   *   *

Michelle heard her father talking on the telephone, and with Renney and Coley snoring she slid out of bed, taking care not to disturb them. Knowing that Henry couldn't see her from where the telephone was, Michelle turned the door handle and pulled the door open, just a little.

His voice traveled clearly down the hallway. He was telling Joseph about Mom's surgery, that she had been implanted with an abdominal injector that automatically dispensed her medicine. She had a two-year supply and didn't need to worry about taking pills anymore. She'd be "just fine now," Henry said.

Only seconds after Henry hung up, the phone rang.

"How'd you get this number?" Henry asked.

There was an extended pause.

Then: "You busted into my house and looked in my address book when nobody was around? Jesus! . . . All right, I understand. Listen, Stu, it's time you came in off the streets. You can come home the day after tomorrow. There'll be a housekeeper now, and we're all gonna live happily ever after."

Henry chuckled, then started to tell Stu about Rachel's implant.

But Stu must have interrupted with something objectionable, because after pausing in mid-sentence Henry said, in a loud tone, "Listen, I'm your father! Do what I tell you and get your ass back home."

Another long pause.

"Rachel *and* Beauregard?" Henry said, finally. "You say they both chased you, and they were in *one* body? There ain't no secha thing as Beauregard, boy. And Rachel ain't gonna getcha, neither. I told ya, she's gonna be doped up . . . How the hell could you say you're happy livin' inna damn streets? How could that be?"

Henry listened for a while, and Michelle heard him bump into a piece of furniture.

"Waidaminumte, waidaminute," Henry said. "Listen to me. My mom told me that the cops is beginnin' to wonder if Rachel did somethin' awful to you, and that could hold up her bein' released. They just found out about you, and may be gettin' ready to toss in a gorilla wrench. I need you to at least call the investigating officer, okay? . . . Good . . . What'd I do with that number . . . Here it is . . . Call 'em right away . . . Huh? . . . Yeah, okay, hurry it up."

Henry waited, apparently while Stu searched for a means of jotting down the message. Then Henry read off the number and name, adding, "Make it quick, you hear? . . . Yeah, I love you too."

Henry slammed the receiver into the cradle. "Damn that kid!" he said. "Out inna streets. Shit!"

Michelle slipped back into bed, and when Henry poked his head in it must have appeared to him that all the children were asleep. He gave each a kiss, and again Michelle detected his body odors.

Moments later, as Henry prepared a bath for himself in the adjacent bathroom, Michelle heard him cursing Stu's defiance.

Stu's call confirmed the information provided to Michelle by Beauregard, and lent credence to every remarkable thing the ghostly specter had told her, including what he'd said about Granpère's really being dead.

Michelle cried softly for her grandfather.

TWENTY-THREE

On the drive to vacation at Lake Mendocino, the kids used to make Henry crazy asking him when we were going to get there. No matter where we were, he'd always respond, "It's just around the corner." It was like asking him when we were going to be happy, sort of a microcosm of our lives.

**—One of Rachel's reflections,
written on lined school paper**

The initial thrust had been relatively easy, and to the rear Joseph saw a grommetlike atmospherically sealed hatch across the hole that his craft had just made in the habitat base. They were in space, and Joseph felt a stimulating surge of adrenaline.

With the exponential speed toggles set on 1,000, he pumped smoothly with the power generation bar, reaching the programmed stops at the same pace as the computer graphic of him that was in a tiny eye-level screen. Waist to chest, waist to chest, waist to chest . . .

The tiny leverage craft darted silently around the habitat's outer skin, discharging all sounds into the craft's LH3 noise absorbers. Joseph couldn't hear his own heavy breathing or any other sound. He felt perspiration between his hands and the rubberized surface of the bar.

In front of Joseph, pilot Tony Bishop operated the highly sensitive maneuvering levers, barely moving his arms. On Bishop's right and left respectively, Vitaldo Morganstern (gunner) and Russell Uchiyama (remote-controlled samurai) crouched at the ready with their weapons. These two were motionless.

After positioning the craft where he wanted it, Bishop held one hand high and tucked his fingers one by one, signaling the seconds remaining to Thrust Two.

It seemed an eternity to Joseph, and he envisioned the second atmospheric hatch they would leave in their wake. They would be inside the habitat again, "beneath" the Arionn Building, and within moments a team of NAS specialists would be at work (unseen by Joseph and his crew), connecting a space tube outside the habitat between the hatches, through which a fleet of NAS attack ships would pass.

Three fingers had been tucked, then four, then five, and Bishop's hand was a fist.

Now! Joseph thought.

Joseph rammed the bar down the entire length of his body to the deck, felt an impact with the deck, but heard nothing. A jarring impact heavier than that of Thrust One shook the craft and made a sound like rubber teeth chattering. Joseph resumed his pumping action.

Debris from the penetrated skin fell away across their windshield, and to the rear Joseph saw another grommetlike hatch expanding to fit the opening.

"Penetration has been accomplished, the onboard robot announced, through an aft speaker. "I am now in command."

Joseph found the voice startling, but his training had told him to expect it. On Thrust One they had penetrated thin but tough habitat skin only, after LH3-protected crews cleared away dirt and rocks in the area and built them a tunnel in which to make a run. All noise associated with that penetration had been absorbed by equipment. They couldn't set up anything like that at the point of Thrust Two, and the leverage craft's noise absorbers alone couldn't do the job.

Hence the robot voice and an end to the noise blackout. Systems devoted to noise absorption were now suppressed, and every bit of mechanical energy went toward speed.

Joseph was still pumping to generate forward motion, and he saw Bishop remove his hands from the controls, letting the robot guide the ship. The maneuvering levers continued to move without him, and the ship sped into a cavernous entranceway walled in a molded gray substance.

"Pause," the robot ordered.

Joseph stopped the bar at waist level, and quickly the ship slowed. Caverns in the gray walls came into view. Some of these were dark, while others were illuminated in an icy blue glow.

"Pump!" the robot said. "Pace ten!" That was the maximum work effort, but Joseph saw that the exponential speed toggles were on a low setting.

The craft banked left, entered an illuminated cavern.

"Three more, Fouquet," the robot said. "Then cease."

Joseph did as instructed each time, and as the unseen robot guided the ship toward a dock, Bishop and the two men beside him stood up. Bishop looped the strap of an energy rifle over his shoulder.

At the dock, which seemed to be constructed of a glossy black metal, the robot found a place off to one side near a wall and set down on top of the dock well away from the dock edge. Along that edge Joseph could see heavy metal loops for tether lines. The dock stretched for at least a thousand meters aft of the tiny ship, and Joseph felt dwarfed. He saw a number of cranelike mechanisms stretching into the distance and judged that these were for cargo handling.

"Gravity normal here," the robot reported, "and leave your oxygen packs aboard. Near Earth normal atmosphere here."

The front of the ship folded open into a ramp that rested on the dock surface, and Joseph picked up an unfamiliar chemical smell, like glue.

The robot no one onboard had seen yet (except in computer representations) surged from its compartment belowdecks and onto the ramp. It was shiny white plastic, and its head swiveled right and left, without looking back.

Follow the robot, Joseph thought, visualizing red on white words from his learning module. Joseph grabbed an explosives pack, popped a grenade launcher out of its floor brackets, and ran behind the others. As he ran, he put on the pack and connected the grenade launcher to it, via a snap-on Plexiglas tube.

At a burst of yellow light from the robot's head, a hatch splintered away and they were within a huge chamber that was at least as high as the dock had been wide. The white robot darted right, along a black walkway that skirted a row of massive gray pods whose bases rested far below, on the floor of the chamber.

The robot began to outdistance the others, and Joseph felt like passing the other crew members, who seemed to be lagging ahead of him. But he held back, awaiting orders.

On the walkway ahead, the robot's head swiveled all the way around, revealing a horizontal bank of four yellow lights. Before it could look forward again, a section of walkway beneath it dropped away. The robot tumbled to the floor below, where it crunched to lifelessness in a tangle of walkway.

Then a section of walkway behind Joseph dropped off and crashed to the floor, leaving the crew stranded.

They spread out along the length of the walkway, weapons at the ready. Joseph wanted to fire grenades at something but saw no target, only amorphous grayness along the curving surfaces of the pods. Bishop and Morganstern, each with energy rifles, made jerky, threatening motions with their weapons, and they kept looking in all directions. Uchiyama carried a glinting samurai sword in one hand and a white ceremonial cloth in the other. From the learning module, Joseph knew that this was no ordinary sword. It could cut virtually anything, even a titasteel wall ten meters thick, from energy transmitted by the blade. It required only a touch and an indication of the desired angle.

Joseph became conscious of a faint whir of machinery, which seemed to emanate from the pod beside him. He barely thought of this, and looking down saw that the walkway on which he stood was mounted on the sides of two adjacent pods, with no understructure that the crew could climb to escape.

Bishop withdrew a climbing kit from his small waistpack, and was about to rivet its folding ladder to the pod nearest him. Suddenly the walkway beneath him thundered away, and he went with it.

"Don't fire unless you can see the target." These words materialized as red on white from Joseph's training. But his instincts told him otherwise, that if he was going to die anyway he should do it with an empty explosives pack. He cocked the grenade launcher and let fly six capsules across a 180-degree field. They exploded harmlessly against the walls and pods.

"You three!" an authoritative voice shrieked, from all around. "Drop your weapons to the cavern floor. Five seconds!"

Uchiyama spun expertly, and with his sword glowing orange made a slice in one of the pods. Black goo shot over him from the pod and he fell to the walkway, gasping for breath. He and his glowing sword were covered completely, and the stuff dulled and hardened around him, leaving his outline in chilling, enforced rigor mortis.

The flow from the pod ceased, leaving a connection of solidified goo from the slice to the walkway that was like frozen-in-motion faucet water.

"Foolish humans!" the omnipresent voice said, mockingly. "Surrender and you will be treated with dignity. We will bring you before your own public, where you will attest to the folly of opposition. If you refuse, those helpless men in ships behind you will perish. Already we've sealed both the primitive hatches you formed, and your ships are trapped in the space tube."

The pod surface across from Joseph became a white projection screen, showing the space tube seen from space. The tube was clearplex and curved, and he saw the NAS attack fleet inside, ships resting atop one another in a jumble of gravitationalized stillness.

"When your underpinnings fall away, gentlemen, the space tube and all those men and women break away too, into the void. What will it be?"

Joseph caught Morganstern's gaze. They nodded, and let their weapons clatter to the cavern floor.

In a media monitoring room down the hall from her office, Granmère pointed a remote transmitter at the television screen, and the screen became dark. She had just seen Joseph and his crewmate Morganstern paraded before the public by the alien students.

An Arionnese spokesman assured all humans aboard the habitat that they wanted only "peace and the good life" for them, but said that they commanded weapons that no humans could imagine, even in their most frightening nightmares.

Joseph and Morganstern had been ordered forth after these remarks, and with apparent depth of feeling they testified to the undefeatable might of the Arionnese.

Then Joseph and his comrade were led away, and a dispassionate, chilling voice said, "If another attempt is made, we'll jettison one hundred thousand civilian women and children."

TWENTY-FOUR

Beyond the mutter and murk of outrageous civilization lie untapped regions of distillate truth, regions
where light, dark, the holy ways, and all that we've
experienced are uninvited. In my present form I know
no more than this, so I await The Sway, if it is to
come.

—From a scrap of paper found
beside Rachel's surgical platform

In a pew, Michelle knelt with Renney and Coley between their parents on a soft leather ledge. It was Sunday, but so early that the Catholic church was empty aside from them. It was cold here, and as Michelle thought of this she heard the muffled sound of a motor as it went on, somewhere behind the walls. It may have been a furnace.

The Fouquets wore their nicest clothes, although no one dared call them "Sunday best." Today, inexplicably, the raiment didn't look so wrinkled to Michelle, despite many wearings and no ironing. Even wrinkles seemed cooperative on happy days.

On the way to church, Henry had told Michelle that he picked up Rachel at the hospital in the wee hours and then took her home for a change of clothes and a light predawn breakfast. The surgical process that Rachel underwent, according to Henry, was so clean and so discreet that it required very little recovery time. Michelle had noticed only a little more than the normal lethargy in her mother's movements, and from the slight glazing of her eyes and general air of serenity it appeared that the implanted medicinal injector was performing its job. Rachel hadn't complained of pain.

Now Rachel knelt stoically in a yellow suit on one end of the family row, with Henry, in a highly emotional state, kneeling on the other end. In husky, whispered prayer he thanked God Almighty, Jesus, Mary, and the

Holy Ghost for returning his wife to him, and he was so sorrowful about everything that had taken place that Renney and Michelle held one another's hands and exchanged tearful, hope-filled glances.

Henry prayed for Joseph's safe return as well, for he knew of Joseph's capture and of the unsuccessful National Air Service mission. There had been no word of Joseph's fate since the broadcast the day before, and all attempts that Henry made to use Granmère as a go-between had been thwarted. By ignoring his entreaties and not returning his calls Granmère was in effect telling Henry to stay out of the affair, that she would handle the situation in her own way.

During Henry's prayer, an emaciated man and his rather stout wife slid into a pew in the row ahead, off to one side. A boy of six or seven was with them, and soon he had his head goosenecked around to watch Henry.

Presently the boy scuttled around his parents in the narrow confines of the pew, and without so much as an admonitory glare from his parents he took a position directly in front of Henry, kneeling backwards on the seat so that his and Henry's visages faced one another, only centimeters apart.

Henry toned down his dialogue, began mumbling to himself.

"What are those things on your face?" the boy asked. He tried to touch one of the pock craters on Henry's face.

Henry slapped his hand away and glared at him.

But the urchin's eyes narrowed and he remained in place, staring impudently at Henry. "You're an ugly man," the boy said, presently. "You're fat, too."

Henry's face became purple, and his ears radiated heat. "Dis fat'll knock ya fer a loop, ya little smart-mouthed bastard," Henry retorted. He raised a hand as if to cuff the boy.

"Mommy!" the boy said. "This bad man said a dirty word in church!" And the boy remained before Henry, like an indomitable antagonist.

With bulging eyes, Henry glared at the mother. He pressed his jaw forward so that it moved stiffly and comically as he said, "Get yer fuckin' kid outa my face, or he's gonna need a new one!"

"This is a holy place," the woman said, her face livid. "Lower your voice, you stupid asshole."

Henry's mouth moved, but soundlessly, as if his larynx had been shot away. He lowered his hand.

And from Rachel's end of the row came harsh laughter, which sounded peculiar to Michelle. She heard not only her mother's caustic chortle but also the howling, shrieking guffaw of someone else, someone unseen. For the briefest of moments Michelle thought she saw the silhouette of Beauregard's Confederate officer's cap high in the air just beyond Rachel. But the image faded (if it was ever there at all) in less than an eye's blink, and gradually it was only Rachel's laughter that Michelle heard. No one gave any indication that they had heard or seen this. Troubled, Michelle turned her attention to her father.

Henry's face seemed about to burst its capillaries.

Fearfully, the boy slid down the pew toward his parents.

Henry closed his eyes and whispered a short prayer to Jesus, asking for forgiveness. Then without another word to anyone or so much as a glance at the boy or his parents, Henry led his family from the church.

"Look at the sky!" Michelle exclaimed, outside the church at the top of the steps.

Almost directly overhead, in a glowing canary firmament, it was as if an incredible television the size of the sky had been suspended over San Francisco. Portions of the screen couldn't be seen for the skyscraper tops, which stood in the way like tall people in a movie theater.

Craning her neck and looking up along the church spire, Michelle saw the image of her brother Joseph in the foreground of the picture, which was very clear. Joseph stood beside another man, both of them in the tan and blue of the National Air Service. Behind them were bulbous, unfocused alien shapes.

Then the image of Joseph swelled at the expense of every image surrounding it, and the sky became Joseph, in his tan and blue.

In a flash of orange and red, something penetrated the image from the other side . . . a golden flying craft. And as this craft approached and grew larger the image behind it grew smaller, consumed by the hole until once again the sky was a sky in appearance.

The flying craft was a remarkable conglomeration of golden bubbles, four surrounding one, and after it landed in the street in front of the church a long ramp extended from the center bubble to the pavement. This bubble had no windows, but each of the other four did—long curving windshields that wrapped separately around the bubbles and revealed a wide alien face behind each, with what Michelle called "those weird atom-eyes." But only the one in the center opened, and presently Joseph appeared at the top of the ramp, looking bewildered. He began descending, walking unsteadily.

"Joseph!" Michelle squealed. Before anyone could stop her, she bounded down the church steps and hugged him in the street at the base of the ramp.

The ramp swung shut.

Noiselessly and without any thrust of air, the craft pulled away vertically. Soon it was above the building tops and out of sight.

"Now we really have something to be thankful for," Henry said, reaching Joseph and Michelle with a lumbering step. He placed a big hand on Joseph's shoulder, massaged it and added, "I'm proud of you, son."

Michelle pulled back from her big brother and saw that his cheeks were tear-streaked. She felt wetness from her own eyes as well, and this was of joy. Supreme, mounting joy, to the heavens beyond the artificial sky.

"When you were captured," Michelle said, "we thought we'd never see you again."

They gathered around Joseph, holding him, and Joseph lifted Coley high in the air, making her cry out happily.

Henry and Rachel exchanged warm glances that Michelle could not recall ever having seen between them.

Still dressed for church, Henry and Rachel snuggled together on the gut-split living room couch, staring at the banks of family pictures lining the fireplace mantel. Henry's gaze scanned the carpet, which while matted, stained, and bare in spots, had been vacuumed within the hour by Granmère's housekeeper, Percy.

Percy was in the "basement" now, segregating the salvagable from the unthinkable, and Henry heard the rattle and rustle of items being tossed into boxes and sacks.

The housekeeper was gay in Henry's estimation, for no real man would hold such a position. Besides that he wore his trousers too tightly, a sure sign, and Henry felt like ordering the fellow from the house. Under normal circumstances Henry would have done exactly that. But with a kind of mushy sentimentality toward his family and all humanity permeating Henry's senses at the moment, he didn't feel up to the task. He might even try Percy's beef stew, which was emitting savory odors from the kitchen.

Tomorrow Henry would talk with Liliane, asking her whether another sort of person couldn't be sent. Even an androbot would be satisfactory, so long as it wasn't of the sexually active variety. Such devices had been known to malfunction and go on licentious rampages, and Henry didn't need anything like that in his life just then.

"Stu's better off in the streets," Rachel said, and her voice was so peaceful that Henry knew she was on her medication. "He isn't comfortable in a home environment," she added. "He's tough and shrewd. Don't worry about him."

"All right."

It seemed to Henry that she suspected or knew that Stu was more to him than the son of friends, and beyond that Henry saw that it didn't matter to her. In those aging, tormented blue eyes he thought he saw the Rachel of old, the beauteous Irish colleen he had married at the brink of Moon War V. Her eyes were fresh and sparkling again, a reflection of youth's glory. But in an instant they became dull and glazed over, full of sadness for her misspent life.

Rachel began humming and rubbing the bridge of her nose with a thumb and forefinger, signifying that despite her new flow of medication she would not be denied the comfort of her inner worlds.

This was one of the rare moments when Henry wished that he could visit those places with his wife, so that he might better understand her. Such a sensitive, fragile woman! But her sensitivity was also her strongest feature, and he was sure it sustained her through countless trials. In his sentimentality, Henry could even appreciate Rachel's efforts at poetry. He didn't understand them, and couldn't abide reading or listening to them, but he respected their existence and all that went with them.

Some of the hard times he and Rachel had endured swept across Henry's mind, followed by the sweet times, the rare but enduring moments that they had shared.

This was one.

They had been through so much together, and Henry knew that he could never stop loving this woman. He squeezed Rachel's hand and turned his face away from her, so that she wouldn't see the tears.

TWENTY-FIVE

Sometimes a seemingly minor event constitutes the "straw too many." After a reporter's flippant remark, General Toshio Oso flew into a violent rage, nearly killing the man before they could be separated. Had Oso lived, a fitness hearing would have followed, and he would have been forced into early retirement.

—From the police report on General Oso's suicide

Henry took a day off from work to recuperate, and from his big recliner before the LCD TV wallscreen didn't see Joseph poking his head into the living room, from the kitchen.

"I can't stand the TV being on all the time!" Joseph said.

Peripherally, Henry perceived Rachel on the couch in her own vegetable emulation act, with her Biblecorder headset in place on her head. She stirred, lifting the earphones away from her ears.

Henry's gaze slid impassively to Joseph, then to the gray midday sky seen through a portion of the rear porch glass beyond. Henry looked back at the set.

"Mom, why didn't you pawn the damn TV?" Joseph asked, in an increased state of agitation. "It's done more harm to our family than anything else."

"No, your grandmother has done the most harm," Rachel said, her tone nasal and sluggish.

Joseph glared at her.

"Why did you block your bedroom door last night, Joseph?" Rachel asked.

"Why did you check it?" he countered.

"To kiss you good night, of course." Her expression became dreamy, and she said, "I wonder what our new Zip code will be on Arionn?" She replaced the headset over her ears and adjusted the volume.

"She's off the wall," Joseph said.

"She's mellower," Henry said. "I can tell the medicine's working."

Henry turned his attention to a news feature in which a computer-enhanced theoretical projection of Arionn was shown. It included drawings of what Arionnese cities might look like, based upon the building, clothing, and aircraft they had seen.

Joseph forgot his anger and criticism momentarily and watched too.

An artist was talking about the computer enhancement, pointing out how much guesswork was involved. "Sadly," he said, at the conclusion of these remarks, "we may never know how close these drawings are to reality. A rumor is afoot that the Arionnese intend to prevent us from visiting their cities. Are we to be confined? In a few days, we should begin receiving answers."

Henry had seen Arionn as a bright blue star in the habitat's eastern night sky. News accounts told people where it was, and the previous evening when everyone else was asleep Henry had stared at the blue orb for hours. He'd felt the strangeness of great change in his life, and it brought back childhood memories . . . times when his family moved to a new house or his first day at a new school, when everything was waiting to be discovered. Despite nagging fears, this Arionnese adventure had imparted to him a sense of wonder and excitement. He thought he saw the bright planet grow infinitesimally larger.

Now Rachel lifted an earphone away from one ear, and she said, "Nice to see you home, Joseph."

"Yeah," Joseph said. He struggled to be considerate, added, "It's g-good that you're home too."

"Did those nasty monsters torture you, darling?" she inquired.

"None of that, but they threatened awful things. 'One hundred thousand and two,' they kept saying, meaning me, Morganstern, and one hundred thousand women and children were going to be fed to the cosmos if things didn't go right. The room they gave me didn't look like a cell, and I could move freely over half a floor. No fleas, either. That was the best part."

Rachel let her earphone pop back against her ear.

Angered at the implication of Joseph's last remarks, Henry slammed a beefy fist on an arm of the recliner, shaking the old chair as if it were held together by rivets and bolts of Jell-o.

"I'm tired o' hearin' about fleas aroun' here!" Henry raged. "I nebber hardly see any, an' I nebber been bit!"

"They probably bite the hell out of you," Joseph said, "and you don't even notice. Do you notice anything at all around here?"

"I notice dat you take nine showers a day when yer here, so dat Thyla dame won't pick a flea offa ya. Joseph Nine Showers! I'm callin' ya dat from now on 'cause ya strip and spray all day long."

"I never took nine showers in a day! That's a bald-assed lie!"

The eyes of father and son met, like those of opposing army commanders.

"I'be counted 'em, fella," said the elder. "An' I'be paid da friggin' power bills. Ya t'ink hot water's free?"

"You let Mom destroy this house, and that's where the fleas and the dirt and the rats came from! Look at her there, wallowing on her couch like she always does. The persistence of inanimate objects. She's like a rock."

Rachel showed no indication that she heard, and her eyes were closed.

"Yer speakin' too loud," Henry said. "She's gonna hear ya an' den all hell will break loose, eben wid her medication. She don't deserb dat kinda stuff."

Henry shook his head, as he did sometimes when he became conscious of his anger and mispronunciations.

Joseph muttered something and moved close to his father, where he knelt on the floor beside the recliner. "She's a dangerous lady," Joseph said, in a lowered voice. He kept an arm up to fend off a blow, should Henry throw one. "I've gotta tell you some things, Dad."

But Henry was subdued, breathing slowly, and he responded, "Rachel didn't hurt Stu. Is that what you were gonna talk about?"

"Yeah, among other things."

"Stu's alive. She only chased him out of the house over a mean prank he pulled. I talked to him myself a couple of nights ago, and he called the police to tell them he was okay. Rachel doesn't do half the things people say she does."

Joseph's mouth was agape. "She didn't hit him or anything?"

"Not a lick."

"She threatened to throw acid on him. Doesn't that bother you at all?"

"She didn't mean it. She never would have done it. Besides, that was when she was off her medicine. She's got no choice now; it's pumped into her."

"And God help everyone around her if the injector fails," Joseph said.

Henry shook his head in exasperation, levered himself to his feet, and switched off the television set. As he clumped past Rachel (who still had her eyes closed) he saw her adjust the volume control of her Biblecorder. Had it been off, enabling her to hear even hushed voices, despite the earphones?

He saw no indication of alertness in her movements, but in the ashtray beside her a cigarette he hadn't noticed before burned unattended, almost its entire length turned into ash.

It was late evening, long past visiting hours, but Big Jack Brittany had a file on the head nurse, and after a few words that he whispered in her ear she scowled and waved him past.

He slipped into Peninnah Wilde's private room without knocking, closed the door behind him, and shook her awake. She had been hiccuping in her sleep.

Wilde pulled on the hiccup helmet that had been on the bedstand, and grumpily listened to him. While he spoke, she touched a button to raise one end of the adjustable bed so that she could sit up, with her back supported. Showing increased agitation, she arranged a sheet across her lap. In the green patient's gown and helmet she looked to Brittany like a thin bird with a disproportionately large head.

"No!" she protested at last. "I don't want that!"

She fell into a fit of soundless convulsions that reverberated from her chest to her throat.

"You approved the mini-receiver we put in that Biblecorder," Brittany said. "And I put our conversation on video tape, thinking you might try to back out. You promised I'd be in charge someday, and I'm moving the timetable up a bit."

Brittany tried to envision what the alien planet might be like. Futuristic castles, perhaps, and he a visiting king, treated with great honor. He would counsel the aliens in the ways of the humans, assisting the aliens with whatever mission they had in mind. Brittany would save himself, would do whatever it took to accomplish that.

Calmly, he removed a ballpoint pen from his shirt pocket and held the pen up for Wilde to see.

It was more than a pen, and Wilde's eyes protested. Like a dying person fighting her body for a few more words, she depressed the gray panel on the side of her helmet and said, in a choking burst: "We said last resort! Only use it as a last . . . resort!"

Her concluding word barely made it out, and she bent over her lap, one hand on her heart.

Brittany depressed the plunger on top of the pen. Two tiny lights on the side of the device went on—red indicating that Rachel's Biblecorder was on; pale green identifying Rachel as the user.

Looking away from Wilde, he spoke into a transceiver microphone in the pen, overriding Rachel's program and deactivating the machine, so that only his voice came through her earphones, in resonant, hypnotic tones:

"This is God speaking, Rachel. How are you today?"

No vocal response issued, but from the noises that Brittany was picking up he surmised that she must be fumbling with the controls of her machine.

"You can't shut God off," Brittany said. "Is that what you're trying to do, or were you just trying to turn me up a little bit?"

He heard a muffled squeal, as if Rachel made a sound without opening her mouth. She must have been wild-eyed.

"I want you to terminate Granmère Liliane, Rachel. Do it as quickly as you can. She's an instrument of Satan, as you must have suspected. Do you understand what you must do?"

"Y-y-yes," Rachel said.

Then Brittany heard a scream and the sound of glass shattering. The line went dead, and both lights on Brittany's pen went off.

He depressed the plunger several times, got nothing, and this presented him with a problem.

He had just made a hypnotic imprint in Rachel's brain, radio-transmitted by a powerful neurowarp mechanism. The imprint would last from twenty-six to forty-six hours, during which the subject's every waking hour would be consumed by hatred for Granmère and plans for the old woman's demise. At least the brochure that came with the equipment promised that this would be the case. It was a black market weapon, manufactured in the Middle East.

The message needed reinforcement after this initial period, but it seemed to Brittany that Rachel had thrown her Biblecorder at something, disabling it. With luck she would conceive a quick method of slaking her thirst for Granmère's blood.

With the rest of her family asleep, Rachel prowled the darkened hallways and unoccupied rooms in a robe and slippers, brooding. She worked at a cigarette as she went, and when it was nearly spent she found herself back in the living room, standing over the framed photograph of Granmère that she had knocked from the fireplace mantel with a well-aimed cast of her Biblecorder.

The picture had landed on the hearth face up, with Granmère's stern visage covered in pieces of broken glass.

Rachel dropped her cigarette on Granmère's picture, and it landed between the eyes, where she ground the butt out with her foot.

"That wasn't nice," a familiar sonorous voice said. "It's too bad you two women can't get along."

"Stay out of this, Bo!" Rachel said. Enraged, she glanced around, but saw no one. The voice seemed to come from everywhere in the room, even from Rachel's own flesh, and she felt a tingling on the surface of her skin.

"Don't try to merge with me, you son of a bitch!" Rachel snapped. She wriggled and jumped around, as if trying to elude someone or something.

"I had no thought of that," Beauregard replied. "You're misinterpreting sensations. There are so many. We'll have to sit down and go over them one of these days."

"I'll never get along with Granmère," Rachel said. "Never!"

"I'll admit she's been crotchety, demanding, and unfriendly, but I think you could be a little less defiant. That time you . . ."

"If I want your opinion, I'll ask for it! Now get out of here!"

Rachel lifted a knifelike shard of glass and swung it wildly in all directions.

"I can cut you!" Rachel shrilled. "I can do you in!"

"Did I happen to leave my physical self within your dimension?" The voice came from the ceiling, beyond Rachel's reach. "I wasn't so careless, was I? Let me see now. Where *did* I leave myself?"

"You have irritating personality traits! Now away with you!"

The room grew quiet, except for Rachel's heavy breathing. She heard a mouse or a rat scamper in one of the walls, and a creaking somewhere, as houses do at night. There were no indications that she had awakened Henry or the children.

Rachel bared her abdomen, and with the glass shard began digging at the side skin where she had had surgery, staring all the while at Granmère's picture. Anger, hatred, and the "message from God" dulled Rachel's pain and drove her to this task. She dug deeper, spilling blood on the carpet and on the picture.

The injector wasn't deep, and her fingers got hold of it, ripping the device away. This sent a shock wave of pain to her brain, and the resultant defensive-reactive message from the brain nearly caused her to black out. She fell to one knee, cutting it on broken glass, and felt stinging in the palm of the hand that held the shard.

All her senses came awake, although she knew that injected drugs must remain in her system, going about their evil duties, following Granmère's bidding. Granmère was responsible for everything, and now even God could tolerate no more!

Rachel jammed a wad of her robe against the wound in her abdomen, and with her mind focused on survival she made straight for the medicine cabinet in her bathroom, passing Henry without waking him.

Holding the robe in place with one hand, she rummaged beneath the sink with the other, locating a large restorative bandage, the kind that when secured acted as a suction that drew impurities from a wound, depositing those impurities in porous receptacles of the bandage. They had one bandage left, and after tearing away the wrapper she placed the bandage over the torn skin of her abdomen.

Warm medicinal foam surged into the affected area, and she felt its purifying work.

Her other wounds were far less serious, and by compressing toilet paper against them she was able to stop the bleeding.

It took her half an hour to clean up the blood and glass in the living room, and even though she didn't succeed in removing all the stains from the carpet with water and soap they didn't show appreciably, owing to the already sorry condition of the carpet. The day before she'd seen the housekeeper, Percy, working at spots without luck and shaking his head.

Granmère's picture went into a sack of garbage on the back porch.

TWENTY-SIX

Liliane says I ran around on "Sonny Boy" while he was in the service. The old bitch's "proof" is that I wouldn't live with her while he was away. Well, I was smart enough even then to see that I didn't want to stay with her, that's all. She and I have unfinished business.

—A note scrawled inside the binding of Rachel's broken Biblecorder

Rachel hadn't been in bed when Henry arose for work the next morning, and when he located her at the kitchen counter preparing toast she seemed agitated. She wore a rumpled silver and black dress that he hadn't seen in years, and her hair, while brushed across the top and sides, had tufts of resistance in the back.

"Sit down," she said. "I'm the perfect little homemaker preparing breakfast for my man."

In his boxer shorts and T-shirt Henry found a place at the table where he could watch her. She had a lump on one side of her stomach beneath her dress, and he asked her about it, saying he hadn't noticed it before.

"Oh, it's been there since surgery," she said, lying. "It'll be swollen for a few days, but the doctors told me not to worry about it."

Henry detected something disturbing in Rachel's voice. It sounded as it did in her most vitriolic moments, when she was off her medication. And she wasn't looking him in the eye.

He shrugged it off and didn't ask about the cuts that he saw on her hand when she placed buttered toast and coffee in front of him. Rachel's words themselves weren't particularly irksome, and here she was preparing food for him, albeit a simple repast. He decided that she must be on a new form of medication.

"I'll take care of things around here from now on," Rachel said. "And when that housekeeper shows his face I'm sending him packing."

Henry tried to envision Rachel as she might have appeared a quarter of a century earlier, a lithe form bustling about the kitchen. Had she ever done that? He thought she had. Her hair was auburn in those days, tending to red, and there had been no lumps except those that God had given her to entice Henry.

She smiled at him from the other side of the kitchen, the way she used to do when she was thinking about how dignified he looked in his NAS uniform, and her face became one of perfect, sensitive beauty, lineless and no longer sallow.

Henry returned to reality, glanced down at his underclothes and then at Rachel. She stood leaning against the counter, staring dispassionately at him. Had she smiled a moment ago?

"You look ridiculous in your shorts," she said. "Is that any way to come to breakfast? Why don't you put on something more presentable?"

"I think I will. Think I'll call in sick again today, too."

Granmère paced the length of her office lethargically, making scuffle sounds on the carpet. General Oso dead! She'd known about his suicide for nearly a day, but now with the habitat closing on its destination the full significance of his loss was crashing around her.

She didn't know yet who the military hierarchy would move into his place, and she had no intention of interfering in that process. Granmère didn't know any of them very well, and even Oso, whom she'd dealt with most, had remained an enigma. Left open was the matter of the escape craft *Hope*, left to her by Oso. She'd thought about who should pilot it and understood the urgency of its mission, but it troubled her. Using it could enrage the Arionnese, causing them to take terrible steps. Granmère had given the ship only a cursory look and nothing more, not even by emissary, fearing too much interest might arouse suspicion. It looked ordinary enough as military helicopters went, and when inside she had been sorely tempted to say the key words that would set in motion the metamorphosis of the craft.

She had resisted the urge.

Granmère had experienced her share of distractions since her last meeting with Oso, and these had diverted her attention from *Hope*. Of paramount concern to her were the constant complaints her office was receiving over misbehaving humans, despite the extraordinary efforts of the police and the military at controlling them. There were incarceration compounds all over the habitat, and thousands of people were being held without bail. But like the tail of a lizard that when cut off regenerates itself, the demonstrators were irrepressible, and converts kept appearing from the populace.

What if the new general demanded the return of *Hope*, and applied the craft to his own purposes, whatever those might be? With Arionn Primary's coordinates established in *Hope*'s computer bank, the ship should be discharged for Earth. And Joseph, young and strong as he was, should make the journey. She could trust him.

She stopped pacing, rang Henry, and told him that she was bringing a mayoral helicopter to pick Joseph up, if he was home. Henry said that he was in bed, and asked what she wanted with him.

Granmère hadn't thought this part out very well. "I . . . haven't seen him in a while," she said. "I wanted to . . ." Quickly she realized that this might sound suspicious to an eavesdropper, and she said, with all haste, "Why don't you come along too, Henri? We'll have brunch at Le Marseilles."

"I don't want to leave Rachel. She hasn't been out of the hospital long."

Granmère had an out, and she leaped to consolidate it. "That's too bad," she said. "Oh well, please tell Joseph that I'll be by for him within the hour."

"I *would* like to get out for a while," Henry said. "How about if I bring Rachel? She's acting real good now, even made breakfast for me. I think she's ironing right now."

Granmère hesitated, reminded herself of the urgency of the situation, and said, "Okay. She can come along, but have her ready by the time I arrive. You know I don't like to wait."

"Michelle's home too," Henry said. "So's Coley and Renney. They all wanted to be with their mother for a while, and I said they could skip school."

"Bring all of them! I'll use Chopper Six, our big one."

As Granmère said this, she had in mind a private dining room at the restaurant. She would use her influence to obtain its use, even if it had already been set aside for someone else. She also had in mind the sicom that General Oso had left with her after his last visit. Out of curiosity she'd already checked, and when the Button Pack instrument panel was removed from its carrying case the sicom briefcase could be inserted in its place. It seemed to have been designed that way, and now she made the switch. If the Arionnese knew about the Button Pack and its capabilities, they'd think she still carried it with her, when in fact she could carry the sicom in its stead whenever she pleased.

But Granmère realized that to an eavesdropper, if one existed, she had been clumsy in the call to Henry, asking first about Joseph, who had been a member of the squad that attempted to overthrow the aliens. Still, he was family, and he and Granmère had been close. Would the aliens really hurl humans into deep space if another plot was uncovered? One hundred thousand of them? That seemed an excessive threat, born of a position that wasn't as strong as it appeared to be.

A bluff, she tried to tell herself. They probably didn't even eavesdrop. But trying to analyze the actions of aliens was impossible. They didn't necessarily think the way humans did.

Le Taste Marseilles, a sprawling one-story structure, was on a steep terraced hillside overlooking the Pacific Ocean. From her window in the one-table private dining room, Michelle also looked out on a miniature Monet's garden, with paths that skirted rose trellises, irises, and wisteria. All was awash in green, saffron, red, plum, pink, and white, and a brisk Pacific wind ran up the hillside and found its way around the high protective walls of brick into the garden, blowing plants rather harshly. A small lily pond stood to one side of the little enclosure, with a vine and flower-draped Japanese bridge over the water.

To Michelle's right and across the big table her family sat in widely spaced chairs, munching sourdough rolls.

Renney asked for the butter, and turning slowly, Michelle saw him across the table to her right, receiving it from his mother.

Three of Granmère's guards were on the other side of the door, waiting outside.

A waitress in a black-and-white French country girl uniform entered, and from the head of the table by a mirror wall Granmère motioned her over and whispered something in her ear. The waitress nodded demurely and left, closing the door behind her.

Granmère placed her dark blue backpack on the table, and from the pack removed a small brown briefcase, which she opened.

"Come sit by your grandmother, Joseph," Granmère said. "You're of age now, and there are some trust fund matters I want to show you."

Joseph was already seated near her, but she gestured to indicate that she wanted him to bring his chair around to the end, so that he could look over her shoulder.

He did as she commanded.

Two seats down from Granmère, separated from the matriarch by Henry,

Rachel toyed with a shiny steak knife, turning it beneath the prismatic chandelier above table center so that the blade caught flashes of orange, purple, and yellow.

"Secrets aren't nice," Rachel said. She placed the knife back beside her plate and stared blankly at Granmère.

"Just trust stuff," Granmère said. "A little money set aside for the college education of each child."

In the mirror wall behind Granmère, Michelle saw the reflection of an oval computer screen that was inside the briefcase cover, and Granmère keypunched a message to Joseph. From Michelle's distance at this very large table, the words on the screen were small, and this, when combined with mirror reversal, made reading it a task that the girl soon abandoned.

Granmère seemed unmindful of the mirror, and after glancing around the table to assure herself that the others weren't snooping she became engrossed in the data she was imparting to Joseph.

Henry didn't seem interested in the goings-on, and seemed instead to be preoccupied with Coley, who was fidgeting in her chair next to him and asking him to slice her roll into little bite-sized pieces.

Rachel alternately partook of coffee, rolls, and goose liver *pâté*, but Michelle soon noticed that her mother was feigning lack of interest about Granmère's end of the table while peripherally studying the reflection in the mirror when she felt that no one was looking. There were so many words, and all reversed, that it must have been difficult for Rachel to interpret them. She was nearly as far away as Michelle, but the girl remembered that her mother was farsighted.

Rachel's expression did not betray the thoughts going on inside her brain, except that she seemed unusually alert, with an intelligent glistening in her eyes that had been absent so much of the time due to her illness. The muscles of her face, especially around the eyes and mouth, seemed rejuvenated, not sagging as often they did.

Then Rachel grimaced in pain and held her side for a few seconds. She lowered her eyelids, then opened them, and seemed all right.

Something's still wrong with Mom, Michelle decided. And a torrent of fear washed through the girl.

Nearly oblivious to the others, Granmère was carrying on a conversation with Joseph via the keyboard. She told him to sit in *Hope's* command chair, to pronounce the name of the ship and its attempted destination, Earth, and then to sit back for the ride. She informed him that this particular ship would not operate without at least one human aboard. She told him as well that it might not quite reach Earth, that it would be very close.

Like a loyal soldier, Joseph didn't indicate any trepidation about going. After absorbing much of the information, he keyed this: "IF I MAKE IT, I'LL BE IN THAT EARTH RESCUE FORCE. YOU CAN COUNT ON ME, GRANMÈRE."

"THIS TIME YOU PENETRATE THE SKIN BEYOND THE SKY INSTEAD OF THE SKIN BEYOND THE SURFACE," Granmère keyed. "AND HOPE WILL SEAL THE HOLE. WITH LUCK, YOU'LL SUCCEED. WE'LL MAKE EVERY EFFORT TO SEE THAT IT'S INTERPRETED AS A SOLITARY ESCAPE EFFORT ON YOUR PART, NOT AN OVERTHROW ATTEMPT THAT WOULD TRIGGER RETALIATION. I'M TOLD THAT THE ARIONNESE DON'T HAVE SPACESHIPS ABOARD, EXCEPT FOR THE ONE THAT'S MELDED INTO THE APEX OF THE DOME AND USED AS A WEATHER CONTROL STATION. SINCE THE ARIONNESE UNDOUBTEDLY HAVE EFFICIENT METHODS OF ELICITING TRUTH FROM PEOPLE, YOU MUST KILL YOURSELF IF CAPTURE SEEMS IMMINENT. A RESCUE MISSION WOULD IN EFFECT BE AN OVERTHROW ATTEMPT."

She handed him a black and silver man's watch, told him aloud to put it on in place of his old one. "A little gift for you," she said. "I forgot your last birthday, old fool that I am."

Then on the sicom she explained that there were four silver buttons on the sides of the new watch, ostensibly for setting the time and activating the watch's various features. But the button on the upper right side wasn't for any of that, she keyed. When depressed, that button injected lethal cytox into the bloodstream, from a needle beneath the backplate. It meant instantaneous death.

She informed him that she had her own similar watch, and that she was wearing it henceforth.

Coley was crawling under the table, and Henry retrieved her. He administered a gentle swat on her diapered behind and plopped her on her booster seat.

Granmère reached under the table discreetly and passed a yellow plastic card to Joseph.

He flicked a downward glance at it. The thing looked like a credit card, but Granmère keyed that it was a VIP City Office Tower pass, top secret until he had to use it.

"I'LL GO TO WORK AS USUAL TOMORROW," she keyed. "BE IN MY OFFICE BY TEN A.M., AND VIA THE PRIVATE STAIRCASE FIND YOUR WAY TO THE ROOFTOP, WHERE HOPE IS. YOU REMEMBER THE WAY?"

He nodded, having been on a tour of the building with his grandparents.

"THAT PASS WILL GET YOU BY ALL CHECKPOINTS, WITH NO QUESTIONS, EVEN ON THE ROOF. *HOPE* LOOKS LIKE A NATIONAL AIR SERVICE 'COPTER. IT'S TAN AND BLUE, WITH WHITE MARKINGS ON THE NOSE AND TAIL."

Joseph slipped the card into his pocket and put on the new watch.

"Enough of this," Granmère said, with a wide smile. She closed the briefcase and replaced it inside its blue pack. "Henri," she said, "tell the waitress to bring in what I ordered."

A few minutes later the Fouquets were tearing voraciously into their food, as if it were the last meal of their lives.

Agilely, Rachel slid between shadow and quarter light, hugging the corridor walls where the floor did not squeak. For nearly an hour she had lain in bed waiting, listening for the hibernation sounds of her husband. When at last the rhythm of his breathing signified deepest sleep, she had slipped out of the room.

The door to Joseph's bedroom refused to budge, although the handle moved freely. He had set up a barricade again.

"Sleeping babies beyond the door," Rachel whispered. "Safe and sound." She chuckled, glided to the nearest hall closet, and opened the door. On her knees she worked carefully and silently, loosening the two removable wall panels and setting them aside.

She thought of Beauregard, who inhabited closets it was said, and felt renewed anger at him for his intrusions. But she also felt fear, just enough to give her pause.

"Are you here, Bo?" she husked.

No response came.

"If you are somewhere listening, and I think you are, you nosy creature, stay away from me. I can harm you, and I will!"

Rachel didn't actually intend to injure Beauregard, for he had been good to her, and always had her welfare in mind. But he had an increasing propensity to irritate her with his comments, especially those in which he asserted that Granmère wasn't such an ogre. How could he say such incredible things?

She poked her head over the air space between closets, and during a moment's hesitation there she heard a violent creaking of the house, as if some great force were pressing against the outside walls, testing the fastenings.

The house grew quiet again, and she slipped through. Within seconds she was inside the bedroom, standing over Joseph's bed.

By the amber street light passing through the window she saw Joseph asleep on his side, turned away from her. He wore his new watch, and his wrist was positioned on the pillow so that she could press the poison injection button, had she wanted to do so. But while she knew this from the mirror image words on Granmère's computer screen and she considered Joseph an enemy, he was before all else her son. Through all the hurtful years, the medication, and even the sudden compulsion to destroy Granmère, Rachel loved her firstborn.

Tenderly, she touched his temple and kissed him there. Then she slipped a hand into a pocket of the trousers that he had left draped over a chair and withdrew Granmère's yellow plastic card, the City Office Tower pass.

TWENTY-SEVEN

The process of granting trip and project permits includes, as a matter of statute, the guarantee that this government will mount a rescue effort should the permit-holder encounter trouble. As it is, we aren't monitoring their passage and (by statute) couldn't rescue them if we wanted to. We have here, should they meet disaster, the makings of an example that will virtually ensure compliance with our permit process for all time. Of course the opposite holds true as well, *should they arrive safely.*

— From a classified report
prepared for the Triumvirate
of Arionn

It was the day slated for arrival on Arionn, and all across the habitat humans demonstrated and carried weapons. Where they had been passive before they now took to the streets in droves, and those involved in previous demonstrations who had eluded capture were more fervent and frantically importunate than ever. Shots rang out in the air from human weapons, and many people said they expected hordes of alien warriors to attack at any moment.

But the aliens held back and betrayed little concern, even when foolhardy individuals took pot shots at the Arionn Building itself and hurled firebombs at it, without apparent damage. The massive structure stood impregnable, and the space-drive mechanism deep within its bowels continued to propel eleven million humans across the final leg of their journey.

Stu Kroemer hadn't protested before and wasn't protesting now, but he found himself nonetheless in the streets of downtown San Francisco where much of the action was, observing the chaos as it unfolded around him. His only weapon, if it could be called that, was a small pocket knife in his jacket pocket.

A big, loud-voiced man with a rifle strapped to his shoulder stood atop an abandoned car, caving the roof in, and he shouted to the crowd, stirring them to fear and hatred against the aliens. As Stu moved from street to street he found other agitators (women and men) on vehicles, on landings, and on balconies, and many of these people had amplification systems. The majority were armed, and the most ardent called upon their followers to come out bearing their own weapons.

These burgeoning cells of resistance threatened to coalesce into one angry, roaring creature, and if this happened Stu didn't see how the habitat could keep from splitting into space. No longer were these people reasonable, and circumstances were fast reaching the point where only force could stop them.

A section of Howard Street by the Mission of Angels was different. Here the people who were gathered stood in an orderly line awaiting breakfast. They were the tattered, the stained, and the homeless, and like Stu Kroemer they lived in the streets foraging for the leavings of society. Stu fell in behind Mikey Prendo, a young black man with whom Stu had shared a sleeping space one icy night, on cardboard spread beneath a viaduct. That was before the cops came in and threw the bums and hoboes out of there, sending folks scurrying for new quarters like ants from a doomed mound.

Stu and Prendo exchanged greetings, and as other unfortunates gathered behind them Prendo began to talk. First he spoke of innocuous matters, such as the places in which he had lived during his life, the foods he had eaten, and the women he had known. In all categories he had seen both ends of the spectrum, and in his present circumstance he had taken a great tumble, having failed to meet the expectations of his urban professional father.

Then Prendo let fly the bomb.

"I hear they're sending a squad out to your old house," he remarked.

"Huh? What are you talking about?"

"A bunch o' rabble-rousers, that's what. They've got addresses on all the family members of public officials. It's part of keeping the pressure on."

Stu didn't wait for breakfast but caught the Market Street trolley, from which he transferred to buses at Van Ness Avenue and again at Geary Boulevard, with only short waits. At the bus stop nearest Henry's house he bolted from the vehicle and began running along side streets where city transit vehicles didn't go. But as he neared his destination the way became clogged with demonstrators, and he had to push his way through. They were thickest in front of Henry's house, where they milled angrily and shouted epithets, slogans, and threats.

Some didn't remain on the street or sidewalk. A small group of red-jacketed toughs were on the weedy grass inside the hedge, and one, a little crewcut hoodlum that Stu recognized, scratched paint from Rachel's car door with a switchblade.

This was Ace-O, and Stu knew him only by sight and reputation as a mindless agitator, one who acted just to see how much trouble he could generate. He did this without apparent pattern or cause (other than fighting for the sake of fighting), and he had even been written about in the press, where they dubbed him "The Battling Chameleon." He was an urban mercenary, it was said, and beyond that a scavenger without conscience who raked his remuneration from the shambles that he created.

Stu stood back, watching.

Inside the house, all was not serenity.

Joseph hadn't slept well, from the excitement of what he had to do that day. He'd arisen before dawn, at the familiar thump of the front door as his father left for work. For long moments afterward Joseph sat with his back against the headboard and his pillow, watching the sharpening of roof silhouettes through the window as the sky paled and filled with color.

He would perform this task much as he had the other, for God, for country, for family, and for himself. It was personal only to the extent that he had to live with himself and his conscience, for either the short time remaining in his life between then and discovery by the Arionnese or for the longer period if he succeeded. He didn't want to spend any time, brief or enduring, chastising himself for what he should have done.

It was to a large extent an emotional decision. He'd known that the instant he said yes to Granmère in the restaurant.

In the quiet, Joseph wondered whether he would see the next sunrise, and it struck him as funny that he should feel sadness at the prospect of missing an artificial event. These Arionnese had done a good job of everything—he had to admit that. And it occurred to him that maybe the whole habitat had never left Earth, that it was instead an incredible and elaborate hoax, fooling scientists, military experts, and countless other learned humans alike. Even the "deep space" outside the habitat where his leverage craft had gone might be a skillfully prepared vacuum of immense proportions, with an artificial backdrop of stars, planets, and other celestial bodies.

It was only a few steps beyond Hollywood to imagine such a thing, considering the obvious abilities of the Arionnese.

And here he was about to blast through the habitat's skin! Would he enter an artificial vacuum, and beyond that encounter another skin? Would he erupt onto Earth, and if he did, what would he find—a world overrun by aliens?

If this were the case, why had they bothered with the habitat?

Reasoning told him that the habitat was real, that he was in fact far across the universe from Earth, and that if he broke out in the ship called *Hope* he would find himself in the vastness of space with an epic solo journey ahead.

He had felt no fear at this prospect.

But then, almost absentmindedly, he leaned across his bed to the chair where his pants hung. Plunging a hand into the pockets, he didn't find the City Office Tower pass. He was crawling on the floor in desperation after that, looking under the bed, under the chair, in piles of clothing and other articles. He pulled the bedding apart, then retraced his steps to the hall door, which remained barricaded with a chair precisely the way he had left it the evening before. In a mounting frenzy, he searched the halls and rooms of the house, and even kicked dirt around in the backyard, thinking Bumper might be responsible.

From his chain, Bumper barked incessantly, giving Joseph a headache. The pass was nowhere to be found.

As if in reassurance that he hadn't been dreaming, he looked at the new watch on his wrist and at the silver button that Granmère said would kill him if he depressed it. The watch and the pass went together, and now he had lost one. Should he call Granmère? No. Telephone lines weren't secure for such conversations, even if he only said simply that he had lost his pass. She hadn't spoken aloud to him of such matters.

So he went back to the room and went through everything again. The door had been barred all night, preventing entrance by an intruder, he thought. He hadn't dropped the pass in Granmère's helicopter either, because he recalled feeling the hard plastic card in his pocket as he laid the pants over the chair.

It only remained to roust Michelle and Renney, and he did so. From the expressions on their faces and their words he was certain that they'd had nothing to do with the disappearance.

These children set immediately to aiding Joseph in his search.

It was during this joint search of the bedroom, the house, and the yard that Joseph from his bedroom heard a commotion outside. From the window he saw perhaps a dozen people milling on the sidewalk in front of his house. In ten minutes this number had grown exponentially, and they overflowed into the street, preventing the passage of vehicular traffic.

Joseph's first thought was that his mother had done something bizarre, but what could that be to attract so many?

So Joseph poked his head in the doorway of Rachel's bedroom, and saw her first stirrings of the new day. She sat up in her nightgown, and for a moment appeared groggy. She asked about the noise outside and Joseph replied that he didn't know what was going on.

Then her eyes became hard, and her features tightened. She reached under her pillow, and out came the City Office Tower pass, along with Henry's automatic pistol.

"You thought I didn't know where the gun was, didn't you?" she said. "Ha! I'll bet you're wondering how I got the pass too, aren't you?"

Joseph wondered, but he didn't ask. It was *fait accompli* now.

He didn't jump for cover either, despite the unnerving circumstance of his mother, with all the madness he imagined in her, holding a firearm. At least it wasn't pointed at him. It concerned him as well that his mother had spoken aloud of the pass, where Granmère, perhaps intentionally, had not. Were the aliens listening at this very moment? It was too late to worry about that.

"Give me those things, please," Joseph said. "You know Dad wouldn't want you . . . or anyone . . . waving his gun around."

"I'm not *waving* it around, foolish boy. I'm handling it expertly."

She drew back the bolt, let it fly home sharply, and aimed the gun at the chest of drawers that Granmère Liliane had given to Henry.

"Pow!" she said.

She set the safety catch.

Joseph took a step toward her but paused when he saw the gun barrel swing around in his direction.

He could see the hole in the end and didn't like this view. Her trigger finger remained outside the trigger guard, thumb by the safety catch, and she wasn't shaky. Her eyes simmered, and she seemed in total control. Why did she have the pass and the gun? Joseph didn't like to imagine.

He retreated one step and relaxed somewhat. Always he kept an eye fixed on her thumb and trigger finger.

"We're going on a little trip this morning," Rachel said. "Tell the kids to get dressed, but not for school. Have them pack suitcases, warm clothing, and a few toys. Not too many toys. You're not going, by the way."

"What are you planning?" Joseph asked. He thought of *Hope*, wondered if this mad woman might be planning to take her youngest children on it, with some foolish, romantic idea of escaping into space. Did she know about *Hope*?

"A little trip, as I said. Now hurry, boy. Time's a-wasting."

"Are you taking them on . . ." He locked gazes with her for an instant but gave way under the ferocity of her stare.

"On *what?*" she asked, smiling craftily.

He spoke impulsively, without looking at her: "On *Hope?*"

"*Hope?* Whatever do you mean?"

"I think you know. Somehow you know." He felt uncomfortable speaking aloud of this subject, wanted the conversation to end before too much was said. But he had to find out.

Rachel's smile stiffened and dropped, and the face became as stone. "I'm not so stupid as you and Liliane thought, eh? Who's the smartest now, when it really counts?"

Joseph shook his head in dismay and frustration.

"As far as you're concerned, we're going on a little car trip, that's all. A vacation."

"Where?"

"None of your beeswax! Now do as I say, and don't try sneaking yourself or anyone else out through windows or the back door. It won't go well if you do."

"Give me the yellow card," Joseph said, lowering his voice. "You don't need it on vacation."

"You think I don't know what's going on? You think I don't know where guns and passes are concealed? Liliane wouldn't approve of what I'm going to do, but you know what? I don't care! This is my moment, Firstborn, a time for *my* choices. You will do as I command!" Her thumb twitched by the safety catch.

"All right," Joseph said, his voice small and distant. He swallowed in a dry throat.

Stu did not feel at all endearing toward Rachel, for in his mind she was a crazy old coot with a mean streak. But nonetheless it angered him when he saw Ace-O scraping his switchblade against Rachel's car. This ragtag red-jacketed hoodlum was on Henry Fouquet's property, and after the car what next? Stu was not about to let harm befall his father.

So Stu stepped forward, with nothing but the small pocket knife that he left secreted in his pocket, and told Ace-O to get off the property.

"Who the hell are you?" Ace-O asked, brandishing the long blade so that all could see it as it glistened in morning sunlight.

People moved in close behind Stu, and he heard their excited whisperings and goadings. Some of these were Ace-O's red-jacketed followers, and they urged him into battle.

Ace-O wasn't the sort who needed urging. He was eighteen or nineteen, but only a little taller and heavier than Stu. When Ace-O lunged in a threatening gesture with his knife, Stu didn't flinch.

"I said, who the hell are you?" Ace-O repeated, from only a little more than a meter away. "I like to know who I'm killing."

Stu was not about to admit that he was a son of Henry Fouquet, not in the midst of this throng.

"I'm just a guy," Stu said. "A guy who happens to know that a mentally ill woman lives here, and that she and her family are poor. That's her car that you're ruining, and I suppose it makes you feel like a big man to hurt helpless people."

"The Fookeys live here," Ace-O said, raising his voice for the benefit of the onlookers. "Isn't that right? The family of that collaborationist Mayor Fookey lives here."

A man corrected his pronunciation.

Another man shouted, "Down with Mayor Fouquet! She plots with the aliens against her own kind!"

A woman called out the address of this house, as if from a list, and gave the name of Henry W. Fouquet as the owner.

"Go ahead and hate Mayor Fouquet," Stu said, raising his own voice to be heard above the clamor. "But hate her for this too, what she does to her own family. Look at this house and yard. These people don't have any money. They aren't in the Nob Hill class. Hell, they're just scraping by, and Mayor Fouquet hardly gives them the time of day."

Stu kept both eyes on Ace-O, and from the crowd heard a murmuring of assent that gave Stu strength. They spoke of the pitiful, weed-choked yard, of the odd-looking house that needed maintenance, and of the unfortunate woman that Stu said lived inside. They began urging Ace-O to leave.

But Ace-O held his ground, and from the look of savage defiance in his eyes, Stu saw that this problem wasn't going to dissipate easily.

Stu had his own fighting skills, and he remained just out of range of the knife. He sensed fear in this adversary, beyond hesitation brought on by the crowd. Ace-O's demeanor was bravado, Stu's instincts told him, flashiness that concealed an inner terror.

"Quit fuckin' with me, mawn," Ace-O said, waving the blade. He kept his distance from Stu.

"I'm not fuckin' with you," Stu said. "I just want you to leave."

"Mawn, I'm a spiritual leader. Can you dig that, babee? My words are never questioned."

"God with a switchblade, eh?" Stu quipped, calculating that anger in Ace-O would take the edge from his fighting skills.

Several people in the crowd snickered.

But one of Ace-O's punks became agitated, and screamed, "Don't take that crap! Stick 'im!"

"Ace-O asshole!" Stu shouted. "Ace-O asshole! Ace-O asshole! Ace-O asshole!"

The crowd took up the chant.

Ace-O's face became a crimson mask, contorted in hatred. "Smart aleck, aren't you?" he said. "Maybe I'll cut your tongue out!"

"I call an ace an ace," Stu said, loudly. "Or should I say an ace an ass?"

Ace-O lunged with the knife, toward Stu's face.

Deftly, Stu stepped to one side, grabbed his opponent's wrist, and kicked him hard in the groin.

Ace-O groaned, and an ensuing kick to his midsection knocked the wind out of him. He dropped the weapon and fell to the ground, moaning.

As Stu retrieved the knife, closed it, and pocketed it, two of Ace-O's followers helped their leader to his feet and led him off, into an opening that formed in the throng.

Michelle brought her puzzle box, a couple of worn but serviceable dresses, and a few other articles, all of which she packed into a small pastel blue and pink suitcase that had to be secured with an elastic cord. She preferred this suitcase, despite its condition, to the black plastic one she had been sent home with from Child Welfare. That one had bad memories.

Joseph had behaved strangely, she thought, as if he had something terribly important on his mind. He merely went through the motions of getting the children ready, and seemed dispirited. He wouldn't answer questions either, such as the one that Michelle put to him: "Where's Mom taking us?"

His response to that had been a look of torment, so Michelle asked him what was wrong.

"Just get ready!" he snapped. "And don't waste time!"

Michelle felt like an adult in a child's body, being treated like a child. Elders were making decisions for youngsters as if it were a God-given right or as if they were in the military, where information was on a need-to-know basis. She resented this and wanted to be consulted on matters of importance, especially to the extent that they affected her. But she hurried and helped with Coley and Renney nonetheless, and they met their mother in the living room.

"To the car!" Rachel said with great intensity. She kept one hand in a big pocket of her long gabardine coat, and a wary eye on Joseph, who remained off to one side in the kitchen doorway.

He'd told Michelle that he wasn't going, but again no reason had been provided. "Why isn't Joseph coming?" Michelle asked, looking at her mother.

Rachel herded the children toward the front door. "He isn't one of us," she said.

"What do you mean?" Michelle asked, from the top of the stairs, outside. She heard Bumper barking in the backyard.

Rachel didn't answer, and she rushed the children down the front steps to the car.

In the crowd that was still gathered on the street and sidewalk, Michelle saw Stu, and was about to call out to him. But he ducked out of sight into the throng.

Roughly, Rachel pushed Michelle into the backseat of the car, along with Coley and the suitcases. Renney sat in front, beside his mother.

"Somebody scratched Putt-Putt," Rachel said angrily, as she plopped into the driver's seat. She slammed the door. "If I ever get my hands on that person, look out. Who in the hell are all these people around here?"

Rachel turned the car around on the grass, and from the rough pumping sound of the motor it sounded like a lawn mower. She rolled her window down as the car proceeded forward, down the driveway.

"Who are you people?" she shouted out the window. "What's going on here? Get out of the way!"

No one answered, and this seemed fitting to Michelle, although she would have liked to have known the answer herself. She envisioned a world in which everyone had questions but no one had answers, and this didn't seem that far from the reality of life on the habitat.

The crowd parted easily to let the car through, and Michelle couldn't locate Stu's face again. Through the rear window she saw Joseph outside on the top of the steps, where he had been when he admitted the policemen to the house.

Michelle recalled her confinement in the back of the squad car that day, the sense that she couldn't get out of the car and that she was being taken somewhere against her will, somewhere apart from her mother. Michelle was with her mother now, but felt the same confinement and helplessness. She'd been fearful then and was again now, but now, paradoxically, her fear was even more disquieting.

When his mother's car was out of sight, Joseph ran for the telephone, trying to decide before he got there which of three calls to make first: Granmère, the police, or a taxi.

He settled on that order, then couldn't get a dial tone.

Joseph swore and slammed the receiver down. Every few seconds he tried again with no success, and the frustration of it nearly caused him to rip the instrument from the wall.

TWENTY-EIGHT

I reminded myself rationally that no one had ever before been in this set of circumstances, but innately it seemed to me that the participants were traveling backward in time, reliving events and altering some of them, where opportunity presented itself. It was as if Time had become an immense, turgid thing that could crawl forward no more. It was feeding upon itself.

—One of Beauregard's observations

With her children behind her carrying luggage and toys, Rachel marched into the lobby of the City Office Tower, her head held high. She carried a single brown Naugahyde shoulder bag that was swollen, as if it had just been fed.

In search of the wild nauga, Michelle thought, nervously. This was something from a humorous movie she'd seen, and it struck her as strange that it would pop up now, when everything around her was all seriousness.

With one hand kept in her right coat pocket, Rachel used the other to slip the yellow plastic card into the slot of a machine that was blocking the way. The bag slipped from her shoulder, and she struggled with it.

Michelle noticed a guard seated nearby, a man in a light blue uniform. He eyed Rachel and her brood with curiosity and more than a little amusement.

A light on the machine changed from red to green, and the card plopped into a shiny metal tray. Rachel retrieved the pass and slipped it into a side pocket on her bag, then led the way through a gate that clicked open for them.

Ahead of them was an arched weapons detector tunnel, monitored by two guards, and beyond that a bank of elevators. Michelle had been here before, and normally visitors would have been required to pass through the weapons detector. It was out of order today, however, as a woman in navy blue coveralls had pieces of the machine scattered on the floor, and she was scanning the arch with an electronic device. She wore a belt of tools.

The guards studied Rachel, and then one of them waved her around, to the elevators.

While awaiting an elevator, Michelle noticed that her mother was perspiring and that she seemed a little short of breath. Rachel leaned against a wall.

"Are we going to see Granmère?" Renney asked, when the four of them were on the elevator.

Rachel didn't reply but fumbled with something in her coat pocket. Her eyes had a dull sheen to them.

Michelle repeated her brother's question.

"Ehh?" Rachel let the shoulder bag fall to the floor, wiped her glistening brow with her coat sleeve. She blinked her eyes, and they seemed to clear. "I'm going to see Liliane while you children wait outside," she said. "A little personal matter to take care of."

That didn't make a lot of sense to Michelle, but she made no comment about it. "She's on floor eighty-three," Michelle said. "Shall I press the button?"

"Yes," Rachel said.

As Michelle took care of this, Coley stretched and reached one of the lower buttons, before Renney pulled her hand away.

Coley squealed in protest.

The elevator doors slid shut, and after a wasted stop on the third floor the car shot up.

Michelle thought about the Civic Center tour that her grandparents had given the grandchildren. Granmère had been pleasant that day and had taken everyone to lunch, with specially ordered ice cream desserts.

The elevator filled with the lemon aerosol scent of ear gas, and Michelle recalled her grandfather explaining that it kept a person's ears from stuffing up and popping. It didn't work this time for her, and she noticed the muffling of sounds around her.

She poked around in one ear with her little finger.

On the eighty-third floor Rachel showed the plastic card to a henna-haired receptionist, who held it and called for the guards. When no one appeared, she muttered, rose, and went to a smaller version of the first lobby machine, where she inserted the card.

"This isn't my job," she groused. "Those fool guards know they aren't all supposed to go to coffee together. Who are you here to see, anyway? Are you sure you have the right floor?"

A red light on the machine turned to green, and the card rattled into a tray. There was no gate.

"I'm here to see Mayor Fouquet," Rachel said. "As you can see, I have VIP clearance."

The receptionist, who had a frosty way about her, looked Rachel up and down, and the children as well. "Is she expecting you?" this woman asked, handing the pass back to Rachel.

"Irrelevant," Rachel said.

"I beg your pardon?"

Rachel glanced around and told Michelle and Renney to take Coley to a waiting room that was off to one side and to remain there.

From the doorway of the waiting room Michelle saw her mother's backside, and Rachel seemed to be showing something to the receptionist. There was a startled expression on the receptionist's face.

Rachel's right arm moved, as if she were placing something in her right coat pocket. She gave the receptionist a shove.

Reluctantly, the receptionist led the way down a hallway that Michelle knew led to Granmère's office. All the while Rachel kept her back toward Michelle, and something told Michelle to run after them, calling out a warning for Granmère.

Rachel seemed to have a weapon, maybe Dad's gun, and there could be but one target for it. What had set her off?

But despite ominous signs Michelle refused to believe that her mother was capable of using a deadly weapon against Granmère, or against anyone else. The woman who composed those touching, sensitive poems could not perform such a heinous act.

Rachel was now in the hallway, heading for Granmère's office!

No matter, Michelle convinced herself, with her heart kabumping in her chest. Even if Rachel thought she was going to go through with it she still had a crucial decision point ahead of her, when she would change her mind.

Michelle spoke a silent prayer, then retired to the waiting room with her brother and sister. This was something that her mother had to work out for herself.

But Michelle didn't leave it at that. While Renney and Coley squabbled, Michelle lifted her consciousness to a state of pure faith and love for all sentient life, human and alien. It was an energy-radiating state, and she hoped it would permeate the walls and doors of this place, reaching her mother's ears as a whisper.

Bound for home with his car on manual, Henry drove the crowded streets recklessly, forcing pedestrians out of his way. In retaliation some hurled objects at his car, and on Geary Boulevard his windshield was split in the center, sending radiating cracks across his line of vision. This made driving more difficult, but he refused to put the car on automatic and continued on.

Somehow he didn't mow down any unfortunates, and he made it to his driveway, where he leaped from the car and thumped up the stairs.

Joseph met him at the top.

"The whole habitat's goin' nutso," Henry said. "Everybody's on the streets!"

"Mom left with the kids almost an hour ago," Joseph said. Briefly, he told his father what Rachel had done, mentioning as well the City Office Tower pass and the spaceship *Hope*.

"Holy shit!" Henry said. "She went on vacation, you say? "With a gun? And all that spaceship stuff!"

"Don't yell it, Dad," Joseph cautioned. "I shouldn't even have . . . aw, hang it all, what difference does it make?"

Henry lapsed into solecisms, said, "Ya just sat aroun' da house after dat?"

"I wanted to call Granmère's office, but all the lines are snarled. Can't even get a dial tone. Couldn't call a taxi or the police either."

"We're wastin' time. Get inna car an' let's get downtown!"

As they ran for the car, Stu appeared and asked to accompany them.

"Get inna back," Henry said.

Henry barreled into the driver's seat and was hitting the manual controls just as Joseph and Stu were jumping in through the front and rear doors on the other side. The passengers slammed their doors just in time, before the car lurched into motion, backward. Henry screeched the car around and directed it down the driveway like a missile, sending two old ladies on the sidewalk scurrying for safety.

There were only a few demonstrators in sight through the cracked windshield, and these confined themselves to the sidewalks, carrying out an orderly exodus from Henry's neighborhood.

The radio blared a news broadcast, and Joseph reached to turn it off. He hesitated by the dial when he heard a familiar name:

"Paul St. Germaine of Menlo Park says that he sent a written proposal to the Arionnese, offering them a group life insurance policy. He says he hasn't heard from them yet, but he's an optimistic fellow. The deal he offered them is at a big discount, by special arrangement with the insurance carrier, and St. Germaine says he'd like to get his foot in the door. He talks about selling policies all over the Arionnese planet when we get there."

The news announcer went to another story, and Joseph switched it off.

"Uncle Paul!" he said. "Imagine that!"

"Yeah," Henry said. He sounded unimpressed.

From the back seat off to one side of the driver, Stu saw an instant of fuzziness in Henry's facial profile, like the fuzziness he had seen around Rachel just before she took on the appearance of a giant gray-garbed flea. But this time there was no shapeshift, and soon when Henry came back into focus Stu forgot this latest, ascribing it to eye fatigue.

The car rocketed onto Geary Boulevard and headed east, toward downtown.

"Isn't that a kick about Uncle Paul?" Joseph said. "Well, he's the guy to do it, I guess."

"Shadup," Henry said, and incredibly he made the car go faster. As if in another realm, the car and its occupants roared and careened across San Francisco at great peril, with the driver, a madman, peering through spaces between cracks in his windshield.

In late morning sunlight that slanted from the east, Granmère sat on a simulated leather chair on Peninnah Wilde's balcony, gazing across the city and the bay. Wearing a light overcoat, she felt no wind and only a modicum of warmth from the sun on her face and hands.

The streets in all directions (and especially around the old City Hall rotunda that she could see below) were clogged with people, and they milled like angry bees in a hive, shouting messages to one another that she could not make out. There were speakers and responders below, leaders and followers, and these worked in concert . . . first one and then the other . . . each elevating the emotions of the other.

The situation threatened to explode into full-scale rebellion at any moment, and the military must have known it, for they were trying to get through to her. She didn't feel like talking with them before Joseph was on his way, dispatched to Earth. She didn't want more military men than the guards she already had around the building, for that might make Joseph's task more difficult. She couldn't leave to meet them somewhere else either, not until she saw Joseph.

Where was that boy? Of all times to be late for an appointment!

Such a delicate balance. If crowds overran the building in an angry wave, they were likely to destroy *Hope*.

She wondered what the crowd reaction would be if she suddenly switched on the balcony projection mechanism and had her image projected across the side of the City Office Tower, as Mayor Wilde had once done. Wilde had been ridiculed for it, but circumstances were different in those days. This situation called for a strong leader, and Granmère wished that every building side in the city could project her image.

The mechanism was operable. Granmère had tested it shortly after taking over the Mayor's Office, and the technicians had performed their tests and repairs without illuminating the side of the building.

There were two activating buttons in the floor of the balcony by her right foot, and if she kicked aside the protective control panel housing, they would be exposed.

Within moments she would do this, she decided, and despite her lack of oratorical skill she would rise to the occasion and deliver an emotional speech that would both reach the hearts of the populace and calm them. From that point on a wave of serenity would spread across the habitat. People would return to their homes, awaiting notification of their fates!

Granmère laughed at the thought of herself as a stirring orator. She had gotten by during her political career, mouthing the words her constituency wanted to hear, but it hadn't been memorable stuff. Her rise to power reflected more than anything else the skillful maneuverings of a master in governmental detail.

She knew the intricacies of the hive.

But now she felt a galvanizing within, as if the great orators and statesmen of history were coaching her, arranging her thoughts and words in precisely the proper fashion. She was Cicero; she was Susan B. Anthony and so many others, and she would rally her people. History was speaking to her, helping her to a proper place in its annals.

Granmère was about to kick aside the control panel housing and proceed extemporaneously. Then such a commotion arose behind her in her office that she barely noticed small-arms fire and the bellowing of bullhorns from the streets below.

She turned, and through the open Italian doors saw Rachel inside the

office, holding a gun on the receptionist, Hennie Modahl. Rachel backed
Modahl into a louver-doored closet and shut her in there, cautioning her
not to "budge an inch."

Before Granmère could move or speak clearly, Rachel was approaching
her, ordering her to her feet.

The frightened old woman on the balcony seemed small to Rachel.
Granmère's hands, clasped before her, shook like loose, vibrating parts on
an engine that didn't have long to run.

"You look shriveled," Rachel said, from the balcony doorway. She
pointed the gun at Granmère, safety catch off.

"What are you doing here?" Granmère demanded. But her voice was
weak, and Rachel noticed this.

Granmère backed up, until her thighs were against the low balcony railing. The railing was dangerously low, she realized, and it gave her a peculiar, queasy feeling. She leaned forward a bit, as a precaution.

"I think I'm finally seeing you as you really are," Rachel said. "As a sick,
pathetic old bag of bones. Aren't you wearing heels today?"

"N-no."

"Pity. You're so tiny. You're not in control of this situation, though you'd
desperately like to be, so I guess it's your day to be small. You want to
control everything, bitch. You need to, by your very nature."

Granmère wanted to say that she hadn't wanted to be commander in chief of
the humans on this habitat, that the mantle had been thrust upon her and she'd
only accepted it reluctantly, without the title. She hadn't actually controlled
Granpère, either. There had been an arrangement between the two of them in
later years, resulting in lives that touched daily but also ran along separate
tracks. Granmère admitted to herself that she may have meddled too much in
Henry's life (and as a result, in Rachel's), but all of it had been for Henry's good.
He was her only son. Why couldn't Rachel understand that? But Granmère
saw it was futile to say anything now, with a gun on her and only moments of
life remaining. Granmère's voice would only agitate the woman.

But Granmère hated being misunderstood, and the twisted way that
Rachel viewed her seemed a preview of the perspective that history would
take. Liliane Fouquet would be blamed not only for her family's woes but
for the entire Arionnese debacle. Those epithets against her in the street
would prevail, and word would get back to Earth that she had been a collaborationist who from the beginning aided the Arionnese. Rachel Fouquet,
that "heroic, tormented daughter-in-law," would be the heroine of this story
for all time, for she succeeded in killing the traitor.

"Get it over with," Granmère said. Her hands stopped trembling.

"Since the day I met Henry you've kept us from being happy," Rachel said, her tone a low boil. "You've interfered in everything, made me feel like I was worthless. I hate you!"

Granmère closed her eyes and awaited the report of the weapon. Would she hear it, or would death outrun sound?

"God didn't tell me which weapon to use," Rachel said, her tone suddenly childlike. "Maybe this is the wrong one."

Astounded, Granmère peered at Rachel through half-open lids. Rachel was looking off in the distance and the gun barrel was dropping. Rachel now held the weapon only loosely, and it was pointed at the floor, seemingly ready to fall from her grasp.

Granmère felt a coiling power again in her legs, the resurrection of life there, and she pressed her buttocks hard against the railing, to push off from it. She wouldn't move yet, wouldn't attract attention to herself until the gun clattered to the floor. Then she would spring forward, screaming for help and clawing at Rachel's eyes. Granmère would be strong in that confrontation, albeit against a larger and younger person, for Granmère would be fighting for her proper place in history.

But the gun didn't fall, and Rachel refocused on her adversary. She saw Granmère glance down over the balcony edge, and from the vertiginous look on Granmère's face Rachel decided that the height must have affected her. Rachel felt an unexpected welling of pity for this woman, despite all that had transpired. Granmère seemed too minuscule, too insignificant to kill, and besides that Rachel abhorred the instrument of violence she held in her hand. Rachel knew now that she couldn't kill anyone, not even this maleficent creature before her.

Rachel hadn't known this until this instant, when it came time to pull the trigger.

"You know," Rachel said, nodding her head. "I thought God wanted me to kill you, but I must have imagined it, as a sort of justification. I haven't been well, you know, but I see it all clearly now. You aren't worth killing."

Rachel felt satisfied at this, for at least she had told Granmère off and seen her cower.

But an expression of derision formed on Granmère's face, and Rachel felt the return of anger. She wanted to shake sense into the old woman and took two quick strides toward her, halving the distance between them.

Rachel heard the sharp report of a weapon, and it sounded far off, as from a dream.

Granmère, her hands thrown up to ward off Rachel, jerked back, lost her equilibrium, and tumbled backward over the balcony railing. It was a most undignified spill, revealing the fine laced underclothing beneath her dress. Without a scream or even a cry she was gone, and Rachel stood alone on the balcony.

God did it, Rachel thought, for when she looked at her hand she saw that her trigger finger was around the handle, well away from the lever. *When I faltered, I only thought I heard a gun. It was a blast of wind from Heaven, ricocheting like a shot off the building.*

She smelled the barrel, confirming that it hadn't been fired.

Briefly, Rachel felt despair at having failed in the Lord's assignment. But it seemed cruel to her that God would involve her in one of his executions. It struck her that this had been a loyalty test, and that she'd been given a difficult assignment that had to be completed without question. It was the way every military force did things.

Go forth and kill.

It seemed to Rachel that this God she loved should be above such tactics, that He should provide reasons and justifications for His wishes. If evil old Granmère had to die, so be it, but He shouldn't hypnotize subordinates to do his bidding. But it occurred to Rachel that God would waste considerable time in such efforts, and that his entire system might break down. Yes, she admitted, authority had its place.

But she recalled when as a child she had questioned decisions made by her mother, especially those that affected Rachel directly. There had been arguments, and each time her mother ended them by saying that the thing would be done and that there would be no further discussion. Rachel lost respect for her mother in the process.

And so it was now. Rachel felt disappointed in God for having placed her in this position. Would He answer her if she called out? She thought not, and besides the thing was done.

She backed into the office, turned, and fixed her gaze on the blue pack that Granmère carried with her everywhere. It was on a small side table by the desk. Rachel recalled fiddling with an instrument panel inside when reporters had visited her house, how upset Granmère had been that time, and how Granmère had produced something different from the pack in the restaurant, a brown briefcase.

Rachel crossed the office, set the gun on the desk, and hefted the pack. She opened it, saw that the instrument panel was inside, and reclosed it. The briefcase wasn't in sight around the room, and it occurred to her that there might be two blue packs.

A noise in the closet to her right took her thoughts elsewhere, to Granmère's tumbling from the balcony. Confusion and terror overcame Rachel, and she wanted to be far from this place. With a sweep of her hand she sent the gun flying to the floor, and she ran from the office, with the pack.

Joseph sensed that his father would not be deterred from gaining entrance to the City Office Tower. It would be brawn against bullets if necessary. But to Henry's credit he maintained his composure, even when the guard said that he needed a pass to enter and Henry didn't have one.

"I'm Mayor Fouquet's son," Henry said. "She needs to see me right away on family business." Henry produced identification from his wallet, and a photograph of him with his mother, taken many years earlier.

"What's all that racket outside?" the guard asked, as he accepted the items. He was a young man with black hair, no cap.

"I don't know," Henry said, shrugging. "The whole crowd was running around to the side of the building. We couldn't see anything."

The guard grunted, handed the identification documents back to Henry, and looked toward the other two guards, who stood by the elevators. "Sometimes we make exceptions," the guard said, "but I can't approve it. See Jensen over there."

Jensen was a balding man around Henry's age, and when this man spoke Joseph detected a similarity between him and Henry. There was a coarseness to Jensen's speech that was like Henry at his grammatical worst, and in Joseph's mind it was as if the two men were sitting together on bar stools at the corner beer joint.

Jensen told Henry that the photograph didn't look much like him.

"Sure it does," Henry protested, but he didn't slip into his alternate dialect. "Look at the nose and the ears. Sure I've lost some hair and gained weight, but you can still tell. Take a closer look."

Henry went on like this, and Joseph noticed a twinkle in Jensen's eyes, as if Jensen were enjoying his position of power, but in a good-natured way, without realizing how anxious Henry was.

He'd better not push Dad too far, Joseph thought. *Or this place is comin' apart.*

"What about all those unsightly marks you have on your face?" Jensen asked. "I don't see them in the picture. That's Granmère Fouquet there, I can tell that for sure. But the guy with her . . . Gee, I don't know."

Henry was beginning to boil. "I don't have time for this," he said. "Look, I got one of those pox diseases when I was a kid, and after that the marks went away. When I got in my forties they started comin' back. I'm in a big hurry, mister, so if you could make this quick I won't have to do something you wouldn't like."

Jensen shot a ferocious glare at Henry.

The other elevator guard interjected, just in time. "I've seen this man with Granmère," he said, "and someone said they were related. They went off to lunch I think, a couple of months ago before she was Mayor."

"That's right," Henry said. "Thanks."

"Okay," Jensen said, passing Henry's documents back to him. "Go on up." He held an elevator door open, and Henry marched on, followed by Joseph and Stu.

Henry punched the button for floor eighty-three, and the door closed.

"I think Jensen knew who you were all along," Joseph said, as the car shot upward. "He had that look on his face, and I hear those guys have computer files on all the family members of government officials."

If Henry had arrived only a few seconds later, he wouldn't have been allowed into the elevator without a fight. As he and his sons ascended the building's core, the lobby became pandemonium.

Mayor Fouquet's plummet to street level was reported to the guards by a National Air Service lieutenant, who had been stationed outside as part of the additional squad assigned to the building by General Oso. Flanked by six of his men, the lieutenant ordered Jensen to notify all personnel of the emergency. The City Office Tower was being sealed off.

When Joseph followed his father and Stu into Granmère's outer office, the area was empty of people. But from the receptionist's desk Joseph heard a woman's excited voice in another room. She said "something terrible" had happened, and she was chastising someone about a long coffee break.

Then Joseph heard the gruff, anxious voices of several men from the same area. They were talking about coordinating a search of the floor.

"All personnel!" a speaker in the ceiling blared. "Seal the building and detain all visitors! Bring them to the lobby immediately!"

A man in a tan and blue NAS uniform ran into the reception area, saw the visitors, and continued past them, to the elevators. "Ross and Murphy!" the man shouted. "Come out and handle these people! I've gotta get to Monitoring!"

An elevator arrived, and he scurried onto it, disappearing from view just as two more NAS men appeared from the direction of the voices that Joseph had heard. They were with a red-haired woman.

"Who are you?" one of the men asked. He approached Henry, and looked very intense.

"Who the hell wants to know?" Henry retorted.

This wasn't what the man wanted to hear, because he took Henry by the arm. "Come with me, sir," he said, and Joseph saw that he was a corporal. The other man was a private.

The corporal tried to spin Henry around, which was like tugging on an angry bull elephant.

Henry swatted the fellow to the floor.

This brought on a rush from the private, and he met the same fate. Both NAS men then attacked at once, and ended up in a heap on the floor for their efforts.

Thinking the battle done, Henry turned his back on them and shouted, in a great booming voice, *"Maman!"*

Joseph both heard and felt the sound, from its vibration.

Before Joseph could call out a warning, the corporal leaped to his feet and swung a truncheon at the back of Henry's head, striking a tremendous blow.

Henry wavered on his feet and went down. But he grabbed the fellow by the legs and brought him down too. A wrestling, punching battle ensued, and when the private stirred to life and joined the melee, Stu ran to his father's aide.

"Come on, Joseph!" Stu shouted.

But Joseph held back. He had been in this place before, on the grand-childrens' tour. That small private elevator around the corner to his left led to the roof, where the spaceship that Granmère had spoken of waited. Joseph's instincts told him to run for the roof, that he should put aside whatever was happening on this floor.

What had the woman meant, "something terrible"? She had run off to another area, probably to call for assistance.

Joseph ran for the private elevator, skirted it, and bolted through a fire door that led to a staircase. With the clamor of fighting in his ears, Joseph took the staircase up, leaping half a dozen steps at a time.

He threw open the heavy door at the top, and directly ahead on the roof he saw it, the craft Granmère had described, half in sunlight and half in the shadow thrown by Chopper Six, that big mayoral sky bus that could accommodate the entire city council and staff.

He let the door close behind him and stood transfixed, gazing at *Hope.*

Hope was, in its present state, a tan and blue tri-rotor military helicopter with neat white stripes on the nose and tail. It wasn't the type of craft that had a lot of glass, so Joseph assumed that the pilot's lack of visibility had to be compensated for by instrumentation. The lack of glass undoubtedly made its hull more battle- and space-worthy, and Joseph found himself wondering what it would look like when modified for the journey to Earth. He wondered as well if he would be able to see the ship's exterior while in flight via a television system, and his mind began flitting to the technical problems involved with the transmission of such pictures. He wasn't an expert in these matters, so these thoughts didn't run very deep or take very long—half a minute at most.

When he realized that he was daydreaming he scolded himself and began running across the rooftop.

Movement on the other side of *Hope* brought him to a halt. He saw the lower half of someone standing on the running board—a skinny-legged girl in a brown, checked dress. He recognized that dress without seeing the face: Michelle!

He called her name and ran around to the side where she was.

Michelle didn't respond, except to flick a glance at him with terrified, anxious eyes. She clutched a small blue and pink suitcase, and beyond her was Rachel, kneeling on the deck inside *Hope*'s cabin.

"Get in quickly, Michelle!" Rachel exhorted. "We're going to Earth!" Then Rachel saw Joseph, and her hand went to her coat pocket, where the gun had been.

"Stay back, Joseph!" Michelle said. "I think she has a gun!"

"She showed me the business end of it this morning," Joseph said. He directed a stony gaze at his mother, asked her, "What happened downstairs?"

"The wicked witch is dead," Rachel answered.

To Joseph, Rachel seemed like one immersed in a fairy tale, and for the first time he compared the personality changes of his mother and father. In both the changes came on quickly, and hers were deeper and more troublesome. But his father's changes of dialect—one for normal conversation and the other when he was angry or upset—struck Joseph as similar to his mother's condition. For mother and father there were different gears of the mind, and it seemed to Joseph that the shifts came about involuntarily.

Behind Rachel, Renney and Coley were cowering on the cabin deck by a bulkhead, holding onto one another. Over their heads was an arrangement of round instrument gauges that were above and to the sides of a blue National Air Service rocket emblem. On the floor beside the children were Rachel's shoulder bag and the blue pack that Granmère carried with her everywhere.

Why did Rachel have the pack?

"The controls of this bird are simple," Rachel said. "All I do is speak and the thing goes. But you know that, don't you, Joseph?"

She looked at Michelle, asked, "Are you coming?"

Joseph moved to Michelle's side, so that his head was about level with hers, the difference in their heights equalized by the running board on which Michelle stood.

"Is Granmère dead?" Michelle asked her mother. Michelle felt numbness as these words cut air.

"I would presume so," Rachel replied. "Unless she can fly. Witches fly, you know."

"She's off her rocker," Joseph said. "She killed Granmère!"

"I don't believe that!" Michelle said. "You didn't, did you, Mom?"

Coley began whimpering.

"It's all right, babies," Rachel said, turning to look at her two youngest. "Mama's here." She whirled back to glare at Joseph, lest he dare make a move on her.

"I don't think you should do this, Mom," Michelle said. "It's not safe."

Rachel laughed. "What makes you think it's safe on the habitat? What makes you think it's safe anywhere?"

"Leave the kids here, Mom," Joseph said. "For God's sake if you're gonna do this, do it by yourself. No one's sure if this thing has Earth range capability."

"Beauregard assures me we can make it," Rachel said.

"Oh come on, Mom!" Joseph exclaimed.

"Where's my captain's cap?" Rachel asked. "We can't go off into space without proper attire."

Keeping a wary eye on Joseph, Rachel scooted back to Coley and tickled her, saying, "Cap, cap, did I forget a captain's cap?"

Coley squealed with glee.

Staring at Joseph all the while, Rachel reached into her shoulder bag, which lay on the deck close to Renney. She brought out a drawing pad and a pencil, handed them to the boy.

"I have art supplies," Rachel said, "self-cleaning diapers, and toys. Even a machine that makes clothes from the tiniest pieces of material. I picked up a few things last night at K-Mart. We're all ready to go!"

Rachel's gaze slid to Michelle, and Rachel said, "I want you to come with us, but I won't force you. I changed my mind on the ride over, Joseph, and decided that this mission was for volunteers only."

"You didn't force Coley and Renney aboard?" Joseph asked.

"We wanna be with Mom," Renney said. He looked at his little sister. "Huh, Coley?"

"Yeah!" Coley said. "Make us fly, Mommy!"

Michelle heard angry male voices from somewhere in the building, along with a number of hard thumps. It sounded like a fight in the stairwell that led to the roof.

"I'm afraid," Michelle said.

"Of me?" Rachel snapped. "You think I bumped off the old hag?"

"No, Mom. I didn't mean that. I just think we shouldn't . . . okay, I'll come!"

Michelle placed her suitcase inside the cabin and was about to step aboard when she felt Joseph's powerful grip on her arm. She tried to pull away but couldn't.

"Let go of her, Joseph," Rachel ordered, her tone level and deadly.

But Joseph held tight, and whispered in Michelle's ear: "Mom murdered Granmère. I don't know how exactly, but she did it. That pack in there was Granmère's."

"I don't care what she has or hasn't done," Michelle said, keeping her voice low. "She's my mother and I love her. She needs me. Try looking at her with a little compassion for once. Look at her in there. She's like one of the babies. Sometimes I feel like I'm the mother and she's the child."

"Secrets aren't nice," Rachel said.

"Let go of me!" Michelle screeched, into Joseph's ear.

He jerked his head back and anger filled his face. But he held fast and shouted at his mother, "Get out of that ship, you crazy woman!"

"Crazy," Rachel said. "That's kind of like safety, isn't it? Who's crazy and who isn't? Are you a proper judge?"

"With you I am," Joseph said.

"Are you using your own sister as a shield?" Rachel retorted. "That's pretty low. I can't think of anything lower."

Joseph and Rachel argued back and forth briefly. Michelle tuned out the details. As in a dream, her thoughts accelerated to another plane, compressing tremendous detail into only a few seconds.

She recalled places she had been with her mother in better times, halcyon periods that were like oases in a great desert of hot sand and wind. They'd taken a simple walk in the neighborhood one fall day two years past, and there were red and gold leaves on the ground. They talked that day, laughed, and had a battle with piles of leaves in front of Mrs. Meley's house. Grouchy old Mrs. Meley came roaring out, and she screamed about the mess, saying she'd just had her yard raked.

"That'll teach you to be neat!" Rachel shouted back.

Michelle returned to the present for an instant and peered at Joseph's face as his mouth moved in angry shapes. She tried to envision him the way he used to be, when he and Michelle were close. It hadn't been so long ago. A different person occupied Joseph's body now, a stranger almost, and she didn't like him.

He kicked cats.

She wanted her old Joseph back. Then her thoughts avalanched, and details poured forth. She realized that Joseph had always expressed feelings of hatred and revulsion for their mother. How was he different now? Was he more vociferous than he used to be, more abusive of the life-tired, luckless woman who happened to be their mother?

Happenstance, Michelle thought. *Oh but for happenstance!*

To be honest, Michelle had to admit that Joseph hadn't changed perceptibly over the years. He seemed always to have fought with Mom, and he was ever willing to leap mercilessly on her flaws while ignoring the mountain of good that was in her. The changes were in Michelle. Originally the girl had accepted Joseph's behavior as a lamentable fact of life and looked up to him despite it as her older brother, her protector. But Michelle was less tolerant now, more demanding of loyalty to blood.

Perhaps it was inevitable that Michelle would choose sides, and it seemed to her that she had been in a cloud before, wandering aimlessly in a trance. She remembered her nightmare, when a cloudlike, smothering plastic creature dropped from her ceiling and suffocated her.

The clouds of nightmare and indecision were behind her, and Michelle was an adult at the age of eleven. The avalanche in her mind grew quiet, and she saw that the big and little rocks of thought had tumbled into a pool of blue water. Her thoughts became like gentle, rippling water, lapping from a point that marked her place in the universe.

"I want to go with Mom," Michelle said, facing the hazy form that was Joseph. Her tone was low but even and smooth, like a sound skipping across water.

Joseph heard her, and responded with something angry and harsh. The precise words escaped her but they didn't matter, since his tone was clear. He was a shape only, without detail of appearance.

Then his visage came into clarity, and simultaneously she understood his words. He was talking about their father.

"Michelle, think about Dad. You can't go off and leave him. He needs you, dammit, and so do I."

"There's no stopping Mom," came the response. "She's going. Can't you understand that? You and Dad can get along without me, but Mom isn't as strong."

Michelle heard louder sounds of fighting from the stairwell, and their proximity imparted urgency to her.

"Tell Dad I love him," Michelle said. "I love you too, Joseph. Now let me go!"

Michelle saw him looking past her into the cabin, scanning the interior.

"I can only wait one more minute, Michelle," Rachel said. "Then I'm literally going through the roof." She smiled.

Joseph shook his head in dismay, asked his mother, "How long will the trip take? Did Beauregard tell you that, too?"

Michelle thought he was stalling, hoping the people in the stairwell would burst out and stop the takeoff. She struggled to get free, kicking him in the calf. It was to no avail.

"One-hundred and seventeen days," Rachel said. "He was very precise about that actually, had it figured down to the nanosecond."

Joseph's eyes rolled. "Oh, I see. And how do you know there's enough rations for that length of time?"

"I asked Beauregard that, too. He assures me that there's an endless supply of food and water aboard."

"That doesn't make sense," Joseph said.

"And what does?" Rachel asked. She looked at Michelle, said, "I brought your father's French lesson cassettes. You have Granpère's book in your suitcase, don't you?"

"Y-yes," Michelle said.

"And you can't read all those foreign words he wrote, can you?"

"No, I can't."

"How exotic," Rachel said. "French lessons in deep space! Oh, Bo, would you come here please and knock Joseph for a loop? We must be on our way!"

"Bo can't do that," Michelle said. "He explained it to me. We can pound him if we can find him but he can't do it to us, except he can create dangerous things that we hurt ourselves on."

"I know all about that!" Rachel said. "But Joseph didn't until you told him. Bo doesn't like Joseph and wouldn't tell him special things like that. General Beauregard likes the ladies."

Rachel rose to her feet and looked forward. "I'm sorry, Michelle," she said, "but I don't see any way to work this out. I've got to . . ."

Suddenly Joseph lifted Michelle out of the way, deposited her roughly on the roof below the running board, and sprang into the cabin.

Michelle lost her footing, tumbling over her suitcase. The elastic strap came loose and the suitcase opened, spilling its contents.

"*Hope!*" Joseph shouted when he was inside. "Destination Earth!"

"Get off!" Rachel snarled, and she slid away from him along the bulkhead. "I don't want *you* with me!"

Michelle fumbled with her suitcase, trying to get everything back inside. But the suitcase wouldn't close properly, and in her anxiety it tumbled from her grasp.

Joseph turned from his mother and ran forward. The ship hadn't responded to him. He recalled his grandmother's precise instructions: he had to sit in the command chair.

The stairwell door flew open, and Michelle heard the excited voices of men, running toward them.

Michelle decided to grab her puzzle box and leave everything else, and as she got it she heard Joseph repeating his commands.

"*Hope!* Destination Earth!"

Michelle leaped onto the running board, just as the door shut crisply in her face. Machinery was activated in the ship, and she felt it begin to lift off, even though the rotors were not spinning.

Strong arms grabbed her around her midsection and pulled her free.

"Get away from it!" a man yelled.

Michelle realized that it was her father holding her. He took her a safe distance away and set her down.

The helicopter rotors fell off, tumbled to the roof, and the ship lifted slowly.

Inside, Joseph was seated in the command chair, and before him lay a half circle of instruments that glowed and blinked in amber, mauve, and orange. All around him he heard the whirring and snapping of mysterious electronic and mechanical devices. Through a side window he saw his father below, standing by the big helicopter with Michelle and Stu, and through the stairwell door came a steady flow of men, in a variety of uniforms: NAS, city police, building guards.

"Now you've done it!" Rachel said.

He glanced over his shoulder, saw that she was crouched with the children, and all stared at him.

Joseph turned forward, and from somewhere a computer ditty issued, followed by an asexual, Japanese-sounding voice that came across unseen speakers:

"Humans of the Fouquet family, you are aboard a ship having long-range capability. LH3 noise absorbers prevent outsiders from intercepting my words, so hostile fire is not expected. We are in activation. Get to your seats within forty-five seconds and connect your seat harnesses. Anyone failing to do so will be surrounded in a protective cocoon which will remain in place until stable space flight has been achieved. Do not worry about loose personal articles; they are being dropped belowdecks now, and will be safe, available to you later."

Joseph swung out of his seat to help the others and saw Rachel's shoulder bag and Granmère's blue pack disappear into a floor hatch, which snapped shut afterward.

"Hurry, children," Rachel said. She tugged and pushed them to a pair of seats forward on the bulkhead. She and Joseph snapped weblike safety harnesses over them.

Joseph and his mother ran forward, and with no time to spare they got into their own seats and connected the harnesses. Her chair was to the right of his, and it had only a fold-down table in front of it, with no instrumentation.

Joseph looked outside again, at his family on the roof. They were a bit lower than before, but in the next instant color and shape seen through the window blended together into an unidentifiable streak. He turned forward, and through the small windshield saw streaks of white and sky blue.

He felt a slight jolt, and these colors were replaced by black with streaks of silver. There was an intense emptiness in the pit of his body, as if he had left his stomach behind, and with that came a slight sensation of dizziness, not an unpleasant feeling.

"We've got a lot to talk about," Joseph said, thinking of the questions he had concerning his grandmother's fate and her blue pack.

He glanced back and to the side, assuring himself that Renney and Coley were all right. They sat speechless, looking nervously in all directions, and Joseph was impressed that little Coley wasn't crying.

"That we do," Rachel said. "If I'd known you were going to barge your way in, I'd have brought some things for you. Henry's shaving gear, for example. You're going to look awful by the time we get to Earth."

Already Joseph missed those left behind, and he envisioned terrible fights with his mother over Granmère. Maybe he shouldn't bring up the subject.

"You heard about the French tapes," Rachel said. "I also have some tapes that Uncle Paul left with us. I like his voice, and thought it would be a nice thing to hear on the way. I assume there's a cassette player aboard."

"There is," the Japanese-accented computer voice said.

"Not those insurance tapes, Mom? We have to listen to those for a hundred and seventeen days? We'll go nuts!"

"So what?" Rachel said. "The computer told me it had a therapy function. Of course it's probably a bit wacko, like all the therapists I've ever seen."

"I beg your pardon, Mrs. Fouquet," *Hope* said. "I'll have you know that I've been tested with the finest equipment! Mr. Fouquet, for your information this ship is well-stocked with a variety of diversions. There are audiovisual tapes, standard sound recordings, books on microfilm, computer games, and delights too numerous to list. All in Japanese, of course, since General Toshio Oso, rest his soul, programmed me. Don't panic! I'm capable of translating everything. By the time we arrive, you'll be experts on the history and culture of Japan. It was a special interest of the general's."

"Can this ship drop me off in Ireland?" Rachel asked. "I'd like to see my grandfather Millihan for the first time. He's nearly a hundred years old, you know. It's about time we spent some time with *my* side of the family."

"If your son assents," *Hope* replied. "I follow the wishes of whomever sits in the command chair."

Nervously, Joseph glanced at his mother, and behind her through the side window the blur of silver on black was focusing into a universe filled with pinpoints of light.

"I don't have a weapon with me," Rachel said. "And if I did I wouldn't use it against you. I wouldn't use it against anyone." She told him what happened on Granmère's balcony.

"I love you, Mom," he said when he had heard, nearly choking on his words.

"Silly boy! I know that!"

After watching the ship disappear in the sky, Michelle took her father's hand on one side and Stu's on the other.

"They'll be okay," she said. "And so will we. We'll see them again!" She stared at the rotor parts that had been shed on the roof, thought about the cuts and bruises she had seen on her father and brother from the scuffle.

Nearby, guards and city police conversed in low tones, looking at Henry. They kept their distance from him.

Michelle felt grief setting in, as if she had lost forever the people on the spacecraft. She realized as well that a part of that grief was for her grandmother. Everything had happened too quickly, and she would need to sort out her feelings.

She looked up at her father. His thick face was upturned to the sky, his mouth agape in anguish. Did he know about his mother?

"Have you heard about Granmère?" Michelle asked, forming her words with extreme difficulty.

"I heard," Henry said, not looking down. "And Rachel didn't do it." He paused. "Beauregard told me."

Her father's profile shifted a little out of focus, and his lips moved again, this time producing the voice of another: "You knew she was innocent, didn't you, Michelle?"

It was Beauregard.

"In my heart I did," she said.

"Sometimes, young one, that's the best place to know a thing."

Her father's features became clear, and he brought her close against his side, the way Granpère used to do.